TELEPATHIC DOLPHIN EXPERIMENT

RON S. NOLAN

PLANETROPOLIS PUBLISHING
222 Santa Cruz Avenue, No. 11
Aptos, California 95003
www.planetropolis.com
nolan@planetropolis.com

This book is an original publication of Planetropolis Publishing.

ISBN: 978-0-692-81883-1

DEDICATION

Adele Gerard Tinning
(A Real Psychic)

Michael H.D. Dormer
(An Unreal Artist)

Robert S. Kiwala
(My Good Friend and Dive Buddy)

Robert K. Johnson
(A Great Marine Biologist)

Julie Kay Adams
(My Soul Mate)

I was extremely fortunate to spend many evenings with Adele Gerard Tinning who had a profound connection to the paranormal world and who opened my mind to phenomena way beyond current scientific understanding.

Susan Gomon was an inspirational and supportive force that enabled me to focus on writing this novel.

If you would like to be notified when my new novels are published, send me an e-mail at nolan@planetropolis.com

(Your contact information will not be shared with anyone else.)

My website has book descriptions, interviews and back-stories that reveal some of the amazing adventures that have shaped my career as a science fiction author.

WARNING

My name is Dr. Sandra Grant. My research focuses on mental telepathy and my experimental subjects are dolphins. I have given Ron S. Nolan the exclusive right to publish this book about my findings, which are too important not to be made public. If any one nation, corporation or terrorist group obtained this psychic ability, they could conceivably wipe out every computer in the world!

Although THE TELEPATHIC DOLPHIN EXPERIMENT was classified Top Secret by the government in 1991, I feel enough time has expired that it is my civic duty to reveal what really took place. I personally assure you that this chronicle is based upon fact and that we really did make discoveries that have made a major contribution to the field of parapsychology.

If you have similar paranormal experiences to those described herein, please contact me through Planetropolis Publishing. I would like to you hear your story too!

I appreciate you purchasing this novel and I hope you will take a few minutes to write a review on Amazon and/or Goodreads.

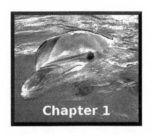

Chapter 1

Key West, Florida 1965

Newcomers to Key West–at least those who came in search of island history, often as not received directions to the order of, "It's near the center of the grounds...just look for the birds. You'll find it." And looking up they would seem to notice for the first time the gaggles of gulls circling and screaming–a kind of parody of nearby Duval street along which shuttled disoriented tourists in a never ending, back and forth, coast to coast rush. Homing in towards the center of attraction, the visitors would find a full-sized, steam-powered locomotive, a relic of Averill Harriman's inter-island railroad, standing rock-solid on a short section of track, baking waves of searing heat from its shiny black plate.

Seagulls gracefully slid and crisscrossed overhead, sometimes landing briefly before lifting off towards the crystalline sand of Baker Beach and the rich fishing grounds of the Gulf. The train served as a social commons for the birds; a strutting ground where newly formed pairs enacted their preprogrammed rituals of courtship–leaving beneath their perches frozen drips, like vanilla frosting melting in the hot sun.

Small well-kept clapboard houses crafted in the classic style of historic Key West bordered MacArthur Park. Like most of the homes in the neighborhood, the Grant residence was washed chalk-white. The front porch was screened as protection against Florida's ravenous mosquitoes and remained cool even in the heat of the afternoon.

Overhead, suspended by brass links, a carved wooden sign in bright paint announced 'GRANT'S PET SHOP'. A green and red enameled parrot grasped the top of the 'O' in the word 'SHOP' hanging tight with yellow talons. A busy jungle of tropical banana, pink and red bougainvillea, and blazing birds of paradise engulfed the small yard separated from the sidewalk by a cedar hedge. Cement birdbaths and low benches were stashed haphazardly in the lush foliage. Looking more like a home than a business, a passerby would have never guessed the extent of the menagerie within–especially in the middle of a very quiet neighborhood in Key West, Florida during the summer of 1965.

Past the porch packed with faded wicker furniture and choked waist-high with neat stacks of yellowed newspapers, a wooden door with a cracked white porcelain knob led into the shop proper. Assorted bamboo birdcages, small and large, jammed side-by-side, harbored chirping and flitting, tropical birds in effulgent plumage. A chorus of demanding mynas, punctuated by piercing monkey screams, blended with whirling hamster wheels and the rhythmic throbbing of electric aquarium pumps. The whistles, chirps, and whisper of fine bubbles bursting free from row upon row of fish tanks laid a matte finish synthesis upon which grew warm earthy smells reminiscent of a moist, tropical rain forest spiced with a tinge of fragrant pipe tobacco.

TELEPATHIC DOLPHIN EXPERIMENT

Grandma Erma Grant sat on her favorite wooden stool, hidden behind a forest of suspended aquarium nets, dog brushes and red and yellow displays of Hartz Mountain parakeet seed. As usual, she was absorbed by the shop's ambiance, daydreaming amidst the collage of sounds, motions and smells and listening to the dialog of the animals as they freely expressed themselves in languages that she seemed to fully comprehend.

As a rule, she favored loose-fitting flowered blouses and long skirts which gave plenty of breathing room to her ample girth, but she never appeared in the shop without her forest green, full-length apron with pockets bulging with thermometers, sunflower seeds, yellow wooden pencils and cellophane-wrapped packets of Kleenex. She wore her thick silver hair braided and wrapped tightly in a bun just barely restrained by sturdy hairpins. She was the kind of person that people liked immediately upon meeting for the first time.

Grandma Grant stooped over gingerly and looked down into the cardboard box lying on the floor behind the counter. Seeing just an empty bowl of water and a few wilted lettuce leaves, she frowned and then called in a deep, rich voice toward the back of the shop, "Grandpa, I just knew it. I knew something was wrong around here. He's got out again, that little rascal. Shut the back screen and help me find him, will you dear?"

Her husband, Roland Grant, was five years older than she. Tall and thin, his bristly jaw was forever clenched to the stem of a briar pipe filled with tobacco. And like most pipe smokers, he enjoyed the ceremony of filling, lighting, tamping and scraping almost as much as the taste of the Wedgeworth tobacco smoke. Grandpa Grant could either be jovial or cantankerous and some-times a little bit of both at the same time. He was set in his ways and accustomed to doing things according to his own well-established routine. So like many people do

RON S. NOLAN

for some reason or other, he pretended not to hear Grandma on the first call even though his hearing was as sharp as ever.

Grandma smiled, knowing his tricks, she repeated her request, but a notch louder this time and then waited patiently.

From the rear of the shop, over the effervescence of aquarium air stones, she heard his deep baritone answer, "Old Gopher Brain is back here, dear."

Grandpa, wearing a blue work shirt and faded overalls, shuffled up the aisle hefting a struggling ten-pound desert terrapin whose stubby legs vainly breast stroked in empty space.

As he lowered the AWOL tortoise back into the box he continued. "He's just getting senile like the rest of us. Didn't get back 'fore you noticed he was gone this time did he?"

Grandpa gave the turtle a gentle rap on the top of its shell. "Here you go old Gopher Brain, you are a tricky fella, aren't ya? 'Bout time for Sandra to be comin' home, ain't it? Bet she stopped off at the park. She sure loves that train, doesn't she Grandma?"

"Grandpa, I love that child. I just wish her parents could have lived to see how she is turning out. She's a real charmer, and sharp too! Some day some young man is going to thank his lucky stars when she says 'yes'."

"You're right, but I don't think that's gonna..."

Grandma's eyes suddenly rolled up into the back of her head and she slumped forward. Her broad elbows landed with a thud on the wooden counter. She cradled her head in her palms and slowly rocked back and forth.

Cut off in mid-sentence, Grandpa snapped his jaw shut and puffed a cloud of blue-gray smoke from the stem of his pipe. It was another one of her 'spells' and he had learned to keep still at moments like this. Not until several years into their marriage had she cautiously

4

revealed her secret–that she often heard voices from another place and time. By now Grandpa was convinced that she often did.

Roland...Grandpa...I just had the most wonderful vision about Sandra. I've known for years that she has my psychic gift. She is already starting to develop a power like mine in some ways, but different in others. I saw her grown into a beautiful young woman and swimming in the sea with dolphins. There was a very handsome man falling in love with her...and so were the dolphins."

"But Grandma, Sandra told me that she was going to wait for me until she grows up," laughed Grandpa. "But since she's only in junior high school, I don't think we have to worry about marrying her off quite yet. She still insists she wants to go to the University of Miami and become a psychologist. She sure has your way with the critters around here, I'll vouch for that."

Grandpa exclaimed "Hey! I just heard the front door slam. I bet that's her. Let's get the milk and the cookies going. This jabbering is making me mighty hungry for some of those wonderful, home-made chocolate chips you just baked."

Chapter 2

Randamount College
Santa Rosa, California 1991

D r. Sandra Grant, Professor of Parapsychology at
Randamount College, had been waiting on pins
and needles for a call from Robert McCord, a long-time
friend that she had known from way back in her grade
schools days in Lawrence, Kansas. If they had chosen
different career paths—he to become a corporate lobbyist
for defense contractors and she to become a researcher
studying the paranormal, they might have hooked up.
But that was water under the bridge. Still, their friend-
ship remained strong.

Two weeks ago when Sandra explained to Robert
that she was having difficulties raising funds for her
research on dolphin behavior, he requested a copy of her
proposal and promised to do what he could to help.

When they spoke a week later, they went over a list
of Robert's questions and he told her, "I don't want to
get your hopes up, but I have a possible lead for you. I
am meeting with General Pratt Houston this evening
and I will call you as soon as I get his answer."

TELEPATHIC DOLPHIN EXPERIMENT

Sandra oscillated between pacing back and forth and staring at the phone. But after waiting until midnight on the East Coast with no call, she figured it was a no go and went to bed. Just as she closed her eyes the phone rang.

She prayed, *let it be Robert with good news.*

It was Robert and he had very good news. His voice boomed, "Sandra, I apologize for the late hour, but I gave your proposal to the source I mentioned. You got it. Full funding...one hundred percent of your proposed budget and two bottlenose dolphins to boot courtesy of the NUC."

"You mean it? Really? That's fantastic! A pair of dolphins and full funding?"

"Yes, the whole package. I'm over at General Houston's house right now and you wouldn't believe the shindig. Every who's who in defense contracting is here. These defense guys really love their fireworks and firewater. Anyway, the General took me to his study, unlocked his private bar and brought out a special fifty-year-old bottle of Glenfelten. I knew that was a good sign, but I was still surprised. Lots of very happy defense contractors here tonight. Congratulations!"

Only a few minutes earlier, General Pratt Houston, a staunch Republican and an unyielding supporter of President George Scott, had announced to Robert in his typical patriotic fashion, "I spoke with Commander Cummings about the dolphin proposal that you provided us. You know I have found that timing is the key to success and this seems to be one of those occasions. It turns out that supporting this project would help us in a very pressing diplomatic matter that has been causing all sorts of problems. Our Military Application of Marine Mammals Program has come under fire by animal rights groups and we need to show that we've cleaned up our act so we will fund this project through my office as an unsolicited proposal. Robert enjoy this fine whiskey and use my private line to give Dr. Grant the good news."

In a lower tone of voice after giving Robert a joyful slap on the back on his way out, the General confided, "And tell your boys at NevTech that they are looking good for the semiconductor contract. Would'a taken it down today, but those lame brains in the General Accounting Office need some other kind'a damn disclosure form or something. It's just a technicality—not to worry."

******

Sandra hugged herself with joy. *Nearly a two million-dollar federal commitment to pursue her studies in dolphin behavior. Plenty of funds for travel and equipment—and to outfit a dolphin research lab including study animals. Fantastic!*

Sandra Grant was young, brilliant, single and much sought after by Randamount College's cadre of bachelors for whom she could spare no time and had little interest. In fact, she had no steady lover or felt that she needed or wanted one—an occasional overnighter was enough. Her work was her life and she was already recognized as one of the pioneers in the new and begrudgingly accepted field of parapsychology. She possessed rare, dual Ph.D.s from the University of Miami. Her first doctorate was in probability mathematics. After completing the requirements for her doctorate in math in a brief three-year period, Sandra had surprised her graduate adviser by continuing on and winning a second degree in theoretical psychology.

Her training in math provided a crucial foundation for her work in parapsychology. By employing the exacting discipline of probability analysis, she was gaining insight into the phenomenon known popularly as 'coincidence'. In fact, Grant called her work the 'quantification of coincidence'.

Not on close personal terms with her adviser, she had only revealed that she wanted to be certain that she could find a job when she graduated. But really, all was unfolding according to a plan laid long before she had moved up the coast from Key West to Miami for her college education and then on to Santa Rosa for her first faculty position. She had always been extremely careful never to mention that she possessed paranormal abilities—or that she had been raised in a pet shop of all places and by a psychic grandmother! She reckoned that there was only so much eccentricity that the university establishment would tolerate as she tried to make her way through the system.

Now in her second year on the faculty at Randamount College, she was venturing for the first time beyond number crunching and the painstaking analysis of mounds of probability data into the study of the causal mechanics of paranormal event. But to avoid the skeptical reaction of her colleagues, she only revealed that her new project would be focused on understanding dolphin behavior—especially the means by which they communicate with one another.

However, Sandra lusted to discover the mechanisms responsible for telepathy and to learn the 'how' and 'why' of ESP. Her telepathy experiments might even break the communication barrier between man and animal—something that her Grandmother seemed to have achieved long ago. With this new major source of research funding, her new experimental subjects would be Pacific bottlenose dolphins. Now she just needed to hire lab assistants and building contractors. At last she would be able to test her theories in a controlled environment without worrying about new project funding.

Sandra moved to the old oak table in her cozy kitchen. She knew every scratch and stain on its surface. The table had been a graduation gift from her grandparents when she had moved to an apartment in Miami. Sitting at the table brought back memories of her college days when then, like now, the table served as her connection to her grandmother.

She made sure that both of her feet were firmly planted on the linoleum floor, and then pressed her palms against the grain. Within moments, she felt pressure as the smooth wood gripped her skin. Her palms tingled electrically.

The table tipped upward at a sharp angle braced on two legs. Then it pulsed slowly up and down, barely touching the floor with the tips of its front legs.

Sandra asked, "It's you, isn't it Grandma? I can feel your presence."

The table slid forward towards Sandra until it nudged softly against her waist. She could feel a sensation of warmth around her navel. The table nuzzled like a loving pet greeting its master.

"Thank you, Grandma, for the healing. You know my project has been funded. I am so happy. Look I'm even crying."

The table lifted and then made a series of fast, light taps that sounded much like laughter. Closing her eyes, she could see her Grandmother's smiling face and bright blue eyes.

"Tell Grandpa that I love him too. Thanks again for all you do. I'll be thinking of you both always."

The table fell lifelessly from her palms and banged to the floor. What only minutes before seemed alive and full of energy was now just an ordinary kitchen table. Her grandmother had gone.

Just sitting at the table brought back memories. Sandra closed her eyes and leaned back in her chair.

Chapter 3

Key West, Florida 1965

I t was a warm winter day in Key West. The palm glistened, still wet from an afternoon shower. Sea gulls flew erratically in the gusty breeze that had accompanied the storm. A dark curtain of rain squalls stationed on the far horizon threatened to bring more rain so Sandra hurried home in her bright yellow rain gear, her books wrapped tightly in a plastic bag.

She paused at the front step to enjoy the special fragrance that erupted from the slightly open door–the aroma of home. The two tiny spider monkeys raced around their cage while the macaw that stood guard in a cage by the door barked, "Pretty Sandy...Pretty Sandy," until she gave him a treat.

Her grandmother was sitting serenely at her station behind the counter with eyes closed and fingers lightly following the motion of the planchette on a much worn Ouija board. Her grandfather, broom and dust pan in hand, smiled and elevated his bushy eyebrows as if to say, *There she is...at it again, jawing with spirits.*

Grandfather Grant patiently accepted his wife's

preoccupation with the paranormal. It was apparent that she knew a lot of things that were beyond his reach—or at least beyond his power of reason. Accordingly he was careful to treat her gift with respect—especially since she always seemed to know exactly what he was thinking. He went with the flow, expecting the unexpected. Most of the time he really didn't think about it at all.

True to form, Grandma opened her eyes, smiled, and shook her head knowingly at him. She pulled a chair over so Sandra could join her. "Grandma, please tell me who you were talking to."

"Well dear, someone that doesn't live on earth anymore...but misses us greatly."

"How does the Ouija board work Grandma?"

"I'll show you, dear. Put your fingers on this side...lightly now and I'll put mine here. Now we'll ask the spirit to answer a question. See if you can think of one that you really don't know the answer to."

Sandra thought for a moment then asked, "Spirit do you know where I left my knit purse—the one that belonged to my mom?"

"Dear one, you need to be more exact in your question. Ask the spirit to tell you where the purse is located."

The planchette moved slowly at first, then accelerated determinedly. It spelled letter by letter, 'N...E...W...S...'

Grandma exclaimed, "Do you mean newspapers?" The planchette quickly drove to the top right of the board and stopped over the word "YES" which was neatly embossed in large yellow lettering.

"Sandy, go take a look around Grandfather's pile of newspapers—the ones on the front porch that he saves to line the cages."

Sandra returned with the missing purse. "Miracle of

miracles, it was right on the shelf hidden by the pile of papers. Oh Grandma, the spirit was right. It really works doesn't it? Thank you so much for helping me."

Grandma laughed, "Of course silly, you don't think I would waste my time on a farce do you?"

"But Grandma, when you were my age, did you know about these things? How did you learn to talk to spirits? I want to do that too."

"You will child...in time. Be patient, it will happen soon enough."

"But how did you know the first time–that it was real I mean? With a board like this?" Grandma's laugh was always a surprise–deep, masculine, and full of joy.

"I'll tell you about my first time. It was pretty funny now that I think about it. My brothers were little troublemakers, always playing tricks on me. My mother and I were outnumbered by the men too, four little brat brothers and dad against only mom and I. Really it was all in fun, but sometimes there was quite a battle of the sexes going on at our house."

Grandma smiled and seemed lost in thought for a few moments then continued. "Well anyway...where was I? This story takes place back in the twenties when we lived on a wheat farm in Sharon Springs, back in a time before electric dishwashers–actually even before electricity had come to the rural areas in western Kansas–if you can imagine that."

Sandra scooted her chair forward, raptly listening to the story. Her grandmother resumed. "We had a regular schedule: one washer, one dryer, one stacker. There were four of us so we rotated–that way one of us always had the night off–at least that's how it was supposed to work. The schedule for the week was posted on the refrigerator and after dinner, father would read off the job assignments. Well, sometimes dad let us trade off. And you guessed it, one of my rat brothers would always figure out a way to fix it so I ended up doing every shift.

"It was on about the sixth or seventh night in a row when I had gotten stuck with kitchen duty that I finally got mad as a hornet about it all. First I was mad, then I started crying but mom and dad had gone to play pinochle and I had no one to turn to. So I toughed it out and did the dishes in record time.

"As I stormed out of the kitchen I took a big spoon and slammed it against the kitchen door. I said to myself 'stay!' and I kept going thinking that it would fall on the hard floor and make a racket. I ran to my room and pulled the blankets over my head and began sobbing about what a rotten deal I was getting and asking God why he hadn't given me a least one more sister and one less brother.

"About an hour later my parents came home. Mom came in my room and held me close. She rocked me gently in the dark. She just held me real tight for a long time. Finally she said, 'Erma, please come with me to the kitchen'. I thought to myself something like, 'Darn, there must be more dishes to do'.

I was surprised to see that all my brothers and my dad were all in the kitchen–I figured that I must be in hot water for talking back to the boys. Mom wiped the tears from my eyes with the dish towel then gently turned me around; I just couldn't believe it. That old spoon was sticking pretty as you please right to the door. You could look close and see that nothing was holding it up–it was just doing what I told it to do. It was *staying*.

"My mom said, 'Go ahead honey, make it come down'. I looked up at her. She was smiling and looking kind of scared at the same time. I just shrugged my shoulders and thought 'down' and it dropped like a shot–clanged just as loud as I thought it would have the first time. All of a sudden you could've heard a pin drop in that kitchen. No one said a thing and Mom took me back to my room and tucked me beneath the covers. Her face was wet with tears when she kissed me goodnight.

"But the next day, it was like I had awakened to a new world. My brothers seemed to notice me for the first time—I was suddenly treated like a real person. From that day on they were my bodyguards at school and wouldn't let me do any heavy work around the house."

"Oh Grandma, really? Is that really a true story?"

Beaming, Grandma took a yellow pencil from the pocket of her apron, stood, and then lightly touched the pencil to the wall. She turned towards Grandpa who was grinning ear to ear. She carefully removed her hand. The pencil stayed put.

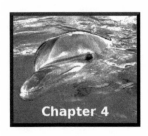

Chapter 4

Washington D.C. 1991

General Pratt Houston, a longtime veteran of the Defense Department, was beginning to show wear around the edges. His once muscular frame had turned to flab and his loose belly slopped over his belt buckle. Once pomaded in a smart crew cut, his gray hair had receded to a fringe above his prominent ears. And in spite of the General's indulgence in expensive hand-tailored uniforms, he still looked more like a retired shopkeeper than a decorated war hero.

But he had been slim and ruggedly handsome when he began his career at the University of Kentucky as an Army ROTC cadet in the fall of 1955. By the end of his first year, Houston had found his calling in the service. A few months into his junior year, he was promoted to the rank of lieutenant of his unit and was shunned by every girl on campus. Even the senior cadets found him to be a queer young man capable of unexpected bouts of intense antisocial behavior and racial bigotry. Ironically, in spite of having few friends and even fewer social invitations, Houston was a natural leader–taking command of the situation whenever the opportunity arose.

Houston, a self-proclaimed (albeit largely unsuccessful) womanizer, did excel in his capacity to consume alcohol. Even though his countless boasts of female conquests were mostly fantasy, Houston did manage to win the heart of a quiet, somewhat plain-looking girl whose father was a senator from the state of Rhode Island.

Upon graduation, Houston was admitted into Fort Knox Armor School. The bustling town of Louisville was a twisted version of paradise for the newly commissioned lieutenant.

The local prostitutes, who performed their service to country on their backside, soon discovered young Houston's enormous appetite for intercourse. His drink of choice shifted from beer to scotch in accordance with the time of day. Most evenings during the week, and Friday and Saturday nights without exception, Houston drove his 1958 Chevy convertible into town on Dead Man's Road—that section of Interstate 84 between Fort Knox and Louisville upon which dozens of overly intoxicated soldiers had smashed their big bore V8s into head-on collisions with bridge abutments and on-coming traffic.

Alcohol and sex were Houston's lifeblood. The fact that he never failed to show for duty, even though oftentimes a little unsteady in the command seat of his tank, attested to the remarkable resiliency of his constitution. His hard-driving escapades on and off the base won him a great deal of respect during an era when young army officers displayed their prowess with booze and broads as proudly as their service ribbons and insignia of rank.

A week into the Korean conflict, Houston volunteered for combat. He was promoted to the rank of captain and sent overseas. Captain Houston was outspoken in his disappointment that his beloved tanks were only playing a minor role during the Korean War. So, he changed venue and shifted to another of his passions, artillery, which found heavy action. Company C, Third Battalion, Fourth Brigade, under Houston's ardent command, devastated enemy installations with furious day and night barrages of high explosive rounds. Under his rule, the ordnance gunners and loaders learned to sleep in four-hour shifts and Houston's Company expended more ammunition than any three other artillery companies combined.

By the cessation of hostilities, Houston proudly claimed credit for the death of hundreds of enemy soldiers and his gung ho performance was recognized in the form of a field promotion to the rank of major–but his aberrant personality had begun to develop hairline cracks deep within the recesses of his subconscious.

Following reassignment to the Pentagon in Washington, Houston married his college sweetheart. Even Annie had thoughts of backing out of the marriage up to the very day of the wedding, but her father was highly impressed with Major Houston's ambition and service record. He privately advised her that she might not find a better catch.

To Houston's bitter disappointment, there were never any children, a circumstance that he blamed on Annie and which ultimately served to kill any passion which he may have once harbored for his wife. Houston buried his domestic frustration by delving deeply into the study of military strategy while developing liaisons with the high-class hookers who worked the expensive restaurants off Pennsylvania Avenue.

By the time that the U.S. involvement in Vietnam had escalated to full-scale combat, Houston had been promoted to the rank of general and given the command of the 14th Armored Division. General Houston was overjoyed that tanks did play a major role in Vietnam and the 14th Division's primary assignment was to lay waste to suspected Vietcong hideouts. General Houston was particularly proud of his contribution to the design of a new kind of tank weapon that disintegrated jungle, hooch, and VC in an intense explosion of jagged steel pellets. The 14th's upper echelon officers were alarmed when Houston insisted on personally participating in firefights. Shocking reports filtered back from the front line describing the General standing erect on the commander's seat of the lead tank, can of warm, foaming Budweiser in hand, urging and coaxing as much death and destruction to the enemy as his detachment could deliver.

An account in the widely acclaimed History of the Vietnam War by James Frost concluded, 'If General Pratt Houston would have had the real support of President Nixon and the American people, Houston would have single handedly wiped every Vietcong off the face of the planet'. When Houston did not get that kind of backing and when he learned that American college students had turned against his country, he became chronically disturbed.

Houston was literally the last American officer to leave Vietnam. Fatigues encrusted with rice paddy mud, face blackened with camouflage grease paint, he continued to fire his M-16 into the jungle as the chopper lifted off to transport him to a waiting carrier. The Navy gunner who finally yanked the weapon out of Houston's hands was startled to see tears running down the General's face making rivulets of mud in the grease paint. Houston had become very much insane.

As a matter of fact, the more unbalanced Houston became, the more he was promoted until after only twenty years in the service, he had advanced to the rank of Four Star General charged with the duties of Army Chief of Staff and had gone totally bonkers. His paranoia and bizarre notions about the communist threat deepened and became even more convoluted with every day of his appointment. The softening of relations with Russia particularly infuriated him. To his thinking, glasnost was nothing more than a premeditated Soviet plot to weaken the U.S. strategic position.

Houston was absolutely convinced that the on-going reciprocal arms and NATO troop reductions had been intentionally contrived to foster global complacency. The Soviet offer of peaceful relations was nothing more than a trick to encourage a false sense of trust–a communist ploy to achieve the Soviet's primary and unwavering goal of world domination.

Whenever circumstances permitted, he reminded the President that the Soviet submarine fleet continued to proliferate with more than enough multiple and retargetable nuclear warheads to forthrightly annihilate the United States with a preemptive attack–especially now that world attention was focused on the Mid-East and President Scott and the vote-hungry members of congress were inanely playing into communist hands To Houston, the stakes were simply too high to take the risk. Something must be done and the time was ripe for action. With President Scott and his cronies playing kiss ass with the Russians, Soviet security would be at an all time low–an opportunity too precious to waste.

Houston's first move was to convince President Scott to authorize a new post in the government to be known as the Office of Defense Technology. In his new role, Houston automatically assumed the authority to direct and oversee the development and integration of all newly developed defense systems within each branch of the military. Houston argued successfully that a coordinating bureau was desperately needed in order to maintain inter-branch system compatibility and interchangeability as a plethora of new high-tech systems came on line that were developed during the War in the Gulf. His point that without a coordinating clearinghouse, each branch of the service would be likely to procure technology from their own favored, independent sources was looked on favorably by the President and the Congress.

Houston's early insistence that the President put an end to the Iraqi war by using tactical nuclear weapons had been such a dangerous idea politically that the top brass in the administration were relieved that Houston's proposal to cut costs (and stay out of the way) were well received. Thus the new Office of Defense Technology was given an unusually prompt birth.

But in reality, Houston had de facto gained an inside position of power that was much superior to that of his fellow Chiefs of Staff. The General's authority now encompassed all forms of technology throughout the military complex–including approval rights for all new weaponry purchased by the Army, Navy, Air Force and Marine Corps. His coup d'é tat had caught the military establishment off guard with no time to prepare a logical counter proposal. Too late they realized the significance of Houston's adept political maneuvering. But since another election year loomed on the horizon, they understood that opposition to any sure fire scheme to cut the budget deficit would be impossible to circumvent. At the same time, the high ranking military officers that had opposed Houston had their hands full with the aftermath of the Gulf War.

Houston immediately seized the opportunity to use his newly acquired power to initiate a tightly guarded secret operation–one that was intended to completely wipe out the USSR!

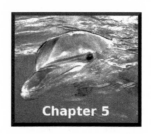

Chapter 5

Usually General Pratt Houston had the ability to imbibe a phenomenal amount of alcohol and show no outward effect. Tonight was an exception. His cheeks and nose were flushed and his forehead glowed with a slick sheen, yet he was in very good spirits. That very afternoon the successful bidders on several billion dollars worth of high tech military systems software and hardware had been announced. Tonight the joyful recipients joined in a time honored ritual–a wild series of concurrent Georgetown parties hosted by the ranking Senators of the Armed Services Committee and General Houston. Defense contractors were notoriously heavy party givers–they were living particularly high thanks to the President's commitment to royally outfit Saudi and Israeli forces.

Plus Houston had his own reasons to celebrate–the messy situation in Hawaii that he had inherited from the Navy would soon be resolved. Dr. Sandra Grant would see to that. She would take the now-famous dolphins off his hands and get the public off his back. Houston reflected about the crazy circumstances that led him to be concerned about the safety of a pair of marine mammals. The dolphin story was really strange—and one he wished would go away.

******

Sally and Tom, Pacific bottlenose dolphins, were the property of the United States Naval Undersea Research Center (NUC) located on the windward side of Oahu. Until recently, they had excelled in their training as underwater saboteurs and had reached the top of the ladder with a rating of Level Five. The dolphins had also demonstrated a very high innate intelligence, which at first surprised, then elated, and finally challenged the trainers. Then they had gone on strike.

Sally and Tom were siblings—if they had been humans they would have been termed identical twins. They were born secretly in captivity at the NUC in 1989. The serial numbers branded on their backs just ahead of their dorsal fins designated them as D109 and D110. Their parents had also been property of the United States Navy (D099 and D078). They had the distinction of serving as the original components of the Military Application of Marine Mammals Program (MAMMP)—that is until they were lost in action during the Gulf War.

MAMMP was a top-secret project loosely designated as 'wet-black technology'—therefore it had recently fallen under Houston's jurisdiction upon the formation of the new Office of Dense Technology. The program consisted of an arsenal of twenty-six painstakingly trained animals housed covertly at Navy bases in Hawaii and Florida. Of this cadre, only D109 and D110 had ever posed a problem, but now they threatened the very survival of the entire MAMMP operation.

Sally and Tom seemed to have extraordinary capabilities. The first indication that something was amiss occurred during a routine training exercise. The handlers were using traditional methods; like those used at Ocean World to make the dolphins perform tricks. But Sally and Tom startled their trainers by performing the designated acts before the hand signal was delivered.

At first the trainers supposed that it was just a game. The dolphins were merely showing off and guessing what the next command would be. So the trainers mixed up the order of commands to throw them off. Still the dolphins performed the correct maneuver **before** the signal was given. The trainers rationalized that somehow they were giving some sort of subtle cue that was being picked up the dolphins.

However, ten days later during the next suite of exercises in which the human trainers were replaced by a bank of underwater signal lights, Sally and Tom continued to provide the correct behavioral response before the lights blinked their message not just once, but on every test. Eventually the trainers became convinced that out of the ordinary events were indeed occurring. Following standard military practice, they carefully drafted reports documenting their observations and filed them with their superior officers who, with only cursory attention, rubber stamped them and routinely advanced the dolphins to the final stage of training.

Level 5 was the most involved and complex stage in MAMMP in which dolphins were trained to conduct strikes against enemy targets. In essence, the dolphins constituted the Navy's biotech version of the stealth bomber. As living tissue, they were invisible to enemy sonar and could closely approach their target. In time of war, the sand bags harnessed to their backs during training would be replaced with pouches containing C-4 high explosive. The dolphins were trained to select the appropriate target and then ram headfirst into the side of the enemy vessel. The impact would activate a plunger strapped to their snout that would not only destroy the ship, but explode the living torpedo as well.

Sally and Tom quit performing during the second day of Level 5 training and stubbornly refused to obey commands delivered in any form. In his report, the lead trainer commented that the pair might be protesting on moral grounds. But after training valued in the hundreds of thousands of dollars, the trainer's conclusion was not viewed lightly by the program administrators and he was assigned duties elsewhere. After ten days of persistent non-compliance, the NUC top brass concluded that Sally and Tom were unfit for duty and should be retired from MAMMP. They were especially concerned that their behavior might spread to other marine mammals in the program; therefore they recommended that Tom and Sally be terminated.

It was a strange coincidence that just a few days after the NUC's decision, a reporter citing a confidential source had exposed the details of MAMMP operations in a series of blistering editorials in the Honolulu News. The public was outraged and animal rights leaders infuriated. Students at the Pacific Islands University campus organized a massive demonstration at the main gate of the Kaneohe Naval Air Station.

Much to the delight of the local newscasters and reporters, who seemed to relish any controversy regarding the military in the Islands because it always boosted viewers and readers, the weekend student demonstration turned into a long-term vigil. Activists from the mainland offices of Greenpeace, PETA, and the Sierra Club became involved. Senator Michael Kahana called for a senate investigation. The Humane Society filed suit and the number of protesters carrying signs and chanting 'Save the Dolphins' swelled into the thousands. In a related incident, two PIU students were jailed for breaking into the World Marine Fisheries Service Lab at Kewalo Basin and freeing a newborn humpback whale being studied by fisheries biologists.

The ensuing highly publicized trial of the students who had been charged with freeing the whale pitted animal rights activists against the United States military establishment. The NUC brass, concerned that they might lose access to their experimental weapons, brought in the Navy's top legal team. The afternoon that the students were sentenced to a year in the state penitentiary, several thousand animal rightists launched an impromptu siege of the courthouse and broke windows in the federal building.

At Governor James Hiroshi's insistence, General Houston had flown to the islands in his private Cessna Citation to meet with concerned officials. Houston took out a series of full-page advertisements in the Waikiki Daily and appeared on local newscasts where he insisted that the Navy dolphin project was a humanely conducted operation that employed dolphins only to rescue trapped submariners.

When questioned by reporters, Houston specifically denied that Navy mammals were trained or ever would be trained for any kind of offensive capability. He cited security protocol as the reason that tours of the NUC were prohibited and even went so far as to categorically deny the very existence of any program called 'MAMMP'. The General always felt that it was a privilege of his rank to never reveal the truth about any sensitive military affairs. "Incompetent civilians should mind their own damn business and leave the defense of the nation to us professionals." Houston had barked to his aide Commander Cummings after one of the heated sessions with the Governor.

TELEPATHIC DOLPHIN EXPERIMENT

Concluding that the situation in Hawaii was out of control, the General made arrangements to relocate MAMMP to the Naval Air Station at Key West, Florida. All records and the entire dolphin arsenal would be airlifted to the east coast by the end of the month. But Tom and Sally remained a problem. Just on principle, Houston was reluctant to set free animals in which such a large investment in training had been made in case they might be useful in the future, but these dolphins were now a liability to the program.

Robert McCord, a well-established consultant to defense contractors, had approached General Houston at one of the gala parties on the DC cocktail circuit with a brilliant and timely solution to the dolphin dilemma. It seemed that a scientist whom Robert knew needed funds to set up a dolphin research station to conduct behavior experiments. He had explained that the proposal had received favorable concept reviews at the World Science Foundation, but appeared to be stuck in the bureaucratic milieu due to concerns about animal rights.

The General would be able to comfortably rid the NUC of the dolphins–Professor Grant would have to take them both–meanwhile score points with the activists and get Kahana and Hiroshi, who demanded to know what the final disposition of the animals would be, off his back. Houston would emphasize the humanitarian aspects of Navy operations and capitalize fully upon the government's supportive collaboration with academia.

What the hell, maybe there is something to this ESP stuff anyway. If there is, I want to own it before the Russians get it for themselves. Yes two million dollars is a cheap price to pay for this neat package–plus if she wants a perfect site for her research project, it is just another weird coincidence, but I have just the right spot

*in mind. It's located 2,400 miles out of Honolulu...due
west. It's called Enewetak Atoll and it is an ideal location for Grant's new lab–and we will be able to keep a
close eye on her and those rebellious, twin dolphins.*

******

Enewetak is a coral atoll in that part of the tropics
once known as the Pacific Proving Ground. Now it
served as a radar tracking station and a home for the
Pacific Islands University Marine Lab. It was also a
perfect place for dolphin studies according to the PIU
chancellor–a bureaucrat savvy to the political process
and a close friend of Senator Kahana.

One extremely trying afternoon the General had
gotten an earful from both the chancellor and the
senator on how important the marine lab at Enewetak
was to the field of marine biology. In the end, making a
contribution to support the PIU Marine Lab had seemed
the only reasonable means of getting the senator off his
back and killing Kahana's investigation of MAMMP.

Houston was not unaccustomed to blackmail
disguised in the form of pork barrel politics and agreed
to a substantial endowment to the University. A telephone call was made and Houston was off the hook.

******

It was just after two in the morning when the
General careened into the bedroom and collapsed next
to his graying, soft, and featureless wife. During their
three decades of marriage, Anne had been a useful
hostess. Her family name and fortune had opened doors
for him that otherwise would have remained impene-
trable. He swallowed down the squirt of bile that flooded
his throat as a blurry vision of his wife's coagulated cold

cream, hair net and rollers swam nauseatingly in front of his eyes. He abruptly cut off her tentative attempt at conversation by snapping off the bedside lamp. Houston drifted away into dreams featuring the cold-blooded execution of Viet Cong insurgents...first one, then another until the barrel of his M-16 glowed a dull red.

Chapter 6

A Year Earlier (1990)
Arizona Institute of Technology DigiLab

Carl Eiger sported a neatly trimmed beard and shoulder length hair tied in a thick ponytail. He typified the Silicon Valley high tech executive look–establishment suit coat and tie above the waist, blue jeans and Nikes below. His exceedingly poor eyesight, a consequence of years spent staring into computer monitors, demanded that he wear heavy horn rim glasses, which rested uncomfortably on his thin angular nose. Eiger constantly sponged at his forehead and wiped his glasses to soak up a never-ending deluge of perspiration, which he emanated in spite of the lab's air conditioning–a new development that his body had played upon him since his conscription by the General.

Eiger's graduate studies had been conducted at the Arizona Institute of Technology DigiLab, a powerhouse for innovation in computer technology. His genius resided in what was then the arcane field of advanced software systems–specifically in creating programs that processed data in parallel fashion. Most computers, even the Cray supercomputers, performed their calculations one at time in series. Parallel processing computers however, were able to perform many functions simultaneously–just like the human brain.

The DigiLab's Connexion Machine was an experimental parallel processing computer endowed with great speed and awesome calculating power. Containing 64,000 processors in a multi-dimensional array, the 'CM' offered the first opportunity to quickly solve enormously complex problems, like assembling and analyzing the vast amount of data needed to accurately make weather predictions.

Eiger's doctoral research had been an attempt to teach the machine a simple, but vitally important attribute of the human brain–the ability to learn through trial and error experimentation. His work plan had consisted of programming a host of parameters into the CM then providing a set of rules, which specified exactly how the CM could manipulate the parameters. He had also designed a performance testing sequence by which the CM could evaluate whether the outcome had merit or should be discarded.

The topic to be learned had been to determine the fastest way to New York City from Cambridge under a wide range of traffic conditions; time of day, day of the week, and weather conditions, etc. CM tried thousands of alternate routes under a given set of circumstances until it found the optimal path. Once the CM had 'learned' the procedure, the task had been changed to Chicago then LA with nearly instantaneous results.

The research had proceeded much faster than anticipated–so fast that Eiger had feared that his work might be considered trivial and inconsequential. Therefore Eiger, following his well-developed instinct for survival, had stalled for time.

For several weeks he had fooled around with the

program, tweaking it to increase its performance. At the end of this period, he began to speculate that there might be an immediate practical application for his program. And nothing could be more practical than to have the CM use his new program to design a faster microprocessor for itself.

In simple terms, Eiger had designed a set of software algorithms that taught the CM how to analyze the layout of circuitry on an existing bank of semiconductor chips and then to experiment with variations in the layout (using a mathematical model) until it improved the original design—at least in theory. Programs like Eiger's would eventually serve as the architect of a future new generation of supercomputers.

Eiger had assembled the massive documentation for the CM's Intel master microprocessor bank and scanned it page by page into the computer. Then he had loaded his designer software and activated the program. By dawn of the next day Eiger had been astonished to discover that the procedure was a success. In addition to thousands of attempted modifications that failed and were rejected, one version had appeared in theory to hold the promise of astronomical improvement—at least in a simulated mock-up design.

Naturally, he had yearned to test the results in the real world to see if they would actually improve the CM's performance—or even function for that matter. But by then he had diverged so far from his original thesis topic that he had been reluctant to reveal his new program to his adviser Eiger had already been warned by his doctoral committee not to get sidetracked. During his five years as a grad student at the DigiLab, he had developed a reputation for not completing a project. However, this time things were different. He had finished his project and now he wanted to go onto the next stage and bring it to life. But there was a problem.

TELEPATHIC DOLPHIN EXPERIMENT

At the time, Eiger had thought, *If I present my findings for these new studies, most likely they'll just say 'Here's your degree, son. You have graduated. You can pursue this at your next faculty position'. The problem is that no one else has a CM and my designer program won't run on anything else. I just have to find out if it works before I leave...maybe there's a way!*

He had found one. The Innovation Branch at the DigiLab was heavily underwritten by RICON of Japan, one of world's foremost manufacturers of semiconductors and one of the few companies that had bothered to invest in the expensive development of one-of-a-kind prototypes.

Every week dozens of chip sets from RICON had been sent via courier to the DigiLab for testing. Diskettes with design modifications had been sent back and new chips had been returned for another round of testing. There had been a lot of coming and going.

But these are simple chips, like those used in PC's. Nothing as complex as a CM microprocessor array. But if I divide my new design into separate but linkable processor bank components, the director and his staff might not notice anything out of the ordinary. I could insert the sub units into a receptacle bank array and substitute it for the existing master array. I'm sure that it would work. Now how do I get them to make the sub units without finding out what I am really up to?

After Eiger had hacked into the security system that protected the DigiLab's inventory management database, it was an easy matter to set up a fictitious account and to enter his design specs into the traffic flow to RICON. Two days later he had picked up the packet from the delivery room without so much as a question asked.

In order to gain more privacy, Eiger had shifted his time slot to access the CM from four to six in the morning in order to minimize the risk of discovery. During the rest of the time, he hid out in his office and poured over the volumes of circuit diagrams that depicted the CM's inner workings until he had the component names and functions indelibly inscribed in his memory. On several occasions he had secretly accessed the CM's central processing compartment and run through a dress rehearsal. It was like looking into a maze of circuit boards interconnected with strands of multi-colored spaghetti. One slip and he would have had a serious problem. He was basically a programmer not a computer engineer, but pulling out the existing processor array and substituting another had seemed fairly straightforward.

Eiger had procrastinated for days on end, debating the potential risks of installing his new processor array. *What if it shorts out the entire compute system?* He had decided time and time again that the procedure was too risky; the reward was not worth the risk. Still, the array with the new chips had remained locked in his office closet enticing him to give it a try. After several days of internal debate and stress, he had realized that walking away from the lab, degree in hand and never knowing if his secret project would have succeeded would have been worse than not having a degree at all. Finally, he had decided to install the new array.

He had waited until three AM and then casually checked the CM lab. A rather pretty girl had been slumped forward in her chair in front of a Macintosh apparently asleep with her head on her folded arms and Jose, the janitor, had just finished mopping the floor around the Coke and candy machines and left the lab. It had been the most deserted he had ever seen the lab—even for the wee hours of the morning.

He had quietly entered the chamber containing the racks that held CM's complex electronics and took a deep breath. In less than twenty minutes he had shut-down the CM, installed the new array and rebooted the system which appeared to have been operating normally. He had left the chamber, returned to the control room and run the accessory program that moni-tored its calculation rate. The CM's capacity to perform, measured in 'floating operations per second', had leaped from its normal five hundred kilo flops to over five thou-sand! His new chip had been an unqualified success!

By four in the morning he had replaced the new array with the original and had returned to his apart-ment where he had lovingly admired his new creation. But the moment of exaltation had been short-lived because he had begun to wonder what would happen if he ran his master designer program with the new array installed. Would it work again; could the CM be driven even faster?

He had decided to take a break and think things over. A week of strenuous hiking and cycling in the brisk air of Laguna Mountains had somewhat restored his body, but not a moment had gone by in which the temptation to try his new system once more failed to consume his every thought. Finally the compulsion to know had once again exceeded his fear of detection. Upon returning to the lab in the early hours, he had immediately installed his new array and run the designer program. In less than an hour he had another improved design and had deposited the diskette in the outgoing mailbox.

Again the new array had exceeded even those incred-ibly fast one that he had tested earlier. In too deep now to quit, Eiger had sent a third generation design to RICON for prototyping and had continued to repeat the design prototyping cycle until the CM could map a new generation chip in only a matter of minutes.

When he tested the CM with the most up to date

array, it had been transformed into a machine rushing to fulfill its own destiny–the CM was evolving. And by now, because of the billions and billions of trial and error iterations, even the CM's vast memory lacked the vaguest recollection of the path that it had taken to create the latest chip complex. Certainly no human could ever replicate the nearly infinite number of experiments that the CM had conducted nor reconstruct the monumental flow of decisions that the machine had made. There had been no trail to follow, no gigantic room-sized flow chart tracking the latest processor's circuitry. It was if the souped up processor array had simply materialized out of a vacuum.

Eiger had been acutely aware that he was treading on very thin ice in tampering with this particular computer because the Connexion Machine development had been the lifeblood of the DigiLab and the lab director took personal pride in its creation. Two weeks after Eiger had begun his escapade his worst fears had come true. He had received a message to meet with the lab director. As soon as he had entered the office and saw the head of lab security, several men wearing black suits, and a military officer, he had known that it was all over. The director had played back surveillance camera footage that showed Eiger's last experiment. At the director's insistence they had retrieved Eiger's latest array, downloaded his research data from the lab system and closed his account.

Since the Connexion Machine was sponsored by the U.S. government, specifically the Office of Defense Technology, Eiger's activities were regarded as a federal offense. The FBI had been brought in and Eiger was arrested and had been taken into custody. But, unlike the investigators who had planned to prosecute Eiger to the fullest, General Pratt Houston had listened to Eiger–very carefully as a matter of fact–and Houston had been more than willing to intervene, have the charges dropped and allow Eiger to continue his research.

He had given Eiger a choice. Either he could join Houston's newly formed Smart Weapons Group at Chalmer Lab and build his own custom Connexion Machine—or he could spend the rest of his life in prison and be publicly branded as a traitor. As a bonus, Houston would make sure that Eiger received his doctoral degree.

So it was not much of a choice at all. Eiger had moved from DigiLab in Arizona to Chalmer in Pasadena where he had assembled a collection of top computer gurus, ordered the required expensive computer hardware and had begun building an improved Connexion Machine that he simply called the 'EXXION'.

Chapter 7

A Year Later (1991)
Chalmer Laboratories
Pasadena, California

Carl Eiger was sweating even more than usual this afternoon because General Pratt Houston was en route from Washington to Pasadena and wanted to meet with him privately and as soon as possible. Luckily, Eiger had outstanding results to report that should make the General very pleased.

The massive olive drab Huey helicopter throbbed to a landing on the concrete pad fronting Lawrence Chalmer Laboratory's main gate. The General was halted by immaculately polished, rifle-bearing MPs at the entrance checkpoint. While the General admired their weapon, they carefully inspected his identification papers. Even though the General was an internationally known figure, the guards checked his ID and cautiously inspected his leather brief case before admitting him into the compound. Houston was impressed.

Eiger stood at the door of the hallway on pins and needles, chain-smoking furiously, sweat drips making dark spots on the gray carpet. Per standard operating procedure, two armed guards waited with Eiger at the EXXION lab's only entrance, which was guarded twenty-four hours a day by very intense soldiers with a rank never less than that of lieutenant.

At last, looking just a little annoyed about having his ID checked once again, the General was cleared into the lab. Impatiently he stormed into the laboratory and was immediately overwhelmed by the thousands of multicolored indicator lights that glowed like a miniature city at night spanning the width of the dark room. A maze of cables and conduits sprouted from a honeycomb of ports forming a web, which silently transmitted a vast stream of data and supplied power to the EXXION. The laboratory was dark except for the radiance of the flickering lights and a green glow that emanated from a large, central monitor. A cloud of frost billowed from a duct overhead and seeped slowly downward forming a gray fog that sank slowly towards the floor.

Eiger explained that the lab must be maintained just above the freezing point in order to keep the behemoth from overheating. Even the EXXION's internal circuitry was flooded with liquid nitrogen. Wispy vapors eerily snaked from dozens of vents at the top of the machine. As the frozen mist sank past the indicator lights, it radiated a rainbow of hues.

A thick metal door braced by stainless steel locking cylinders slid smoothly into place sealing the lab. There was a whoosh of air and their ears popped. Eiger informed the General that the EXXION would now send out radio waves to search his body and brief case for hidden microphones or electronic bugs and that the EXXION would repeat this procedure at random intervals whenever an outsider was present.

The General gratefully accepted a silver-coated down parka and zipped up the front. Eiger, wearing just a white lab coat, offered Houston a steaming cup of hot coffee and the General relaxed into a high-backed red leather chair at the console next to Eiger. It amused the General to see his breath even without smoking.

Blowing steam, the General exaggerated, "Damn Eiger, didn't you pay your heating bill? It's cold enough in here to freeze the butt off an Eskimo! Teach the old gal to talk yet?"

Although the EXXION was perfectly capable of speech communication, Eiger had insisted that it not be equipped with a voice synthesizer. He wanted all inter-actions to be personal and private and he was adamant that others not be allowed access to his baby. But strangely enough, he had never given the beloved computer a nickname.

Eiger moved to a bank of red filing cabinets at the rear of the room and placed his index finger in the fingerprint lock, which acknowledged his ID with a beep and the top drawer opened. The microchip in the lock automatically logged the time that the drawer opened and the code name of the file that was removed. Some files, especially those stored on computer tape or diskette, could not leave the lab unless Eiger manually overrode the system. Otherwise as soon as they were taken past the door, a detector alerted security and the ever-present guards with loaded M16s and no sense of humor took aim right between the eyes of the careless violator.

Not being much for words, Eiger handed a file folder to the General and said, "This where we stand as of this morning."

The file that Eiger handed the General carried a 'Top Secret, Eyes Only' classification in bright red ink. The title stated 'An Improved Version of the SDI Early Warning System Nimbus IV CC454'.

Eiger pointed at the folder and continued, "Disregard

the title. That's just a smokescreen. This is an operating plan and budget for what we have been discussing in confidence—a plan to build the ultimate weapon of threat and destruction code named 'ANX'."

Smiling, the General slipped the file into the rear compartment of his leather briefcase, confident that even though his case would be searched by security upon his departure, the inspectors would be unable to distinguish the design of a modified Nimbus IV satellite system from the design of the ANX virus.

The General boomed, "Great! Give me a SITREP. How long? How much?"

In a low halting voice Eiger replied, "Six to nine months...maybe more...maybe a little less. It is a very difficult process. The first step is to make even more improvements to our new EXXION. I am sure that ANX can succeed, but I'll need more support. The cost...the cost will be high—plus we are going to need to establish extremely high security levels."

"I figured that already Doctor. Let me worry about the money. You figure out the security requirements. Let's get going, we don't wann'a keep the boys next door waiting do we? Just remember, say absolutely nothing about ANX. Right now that's just between you and me."

When fully developed, ANX would possess an awesome potential to create havoc in any computer network not protected with a unique top-secret authentication key. ANX was analogous to a living virus, and like a virus; it was capable of infecting the host and replicating itself. Once ANX was introduced into a network via an e-mail, diskette or Internet connection it would search the operating system for the secret code key. If after 120 seconds no key was found, ANX's internal clock would initiate a propagation sequence causing the original code to replicate into hundreds of millions of identical segments—each a gene containing a program with which to build more propagules that could be programmed to execute specific tasks...including changing or corrupting data files, retrieving classified documents, and issuing military orders. The changes and commands would be immediately distributed throughout the network, and once they had been completed, ANX would delete the operating system and remove all traces of its activity and then shut it down completely.

If the infected computer was linked to another computer, which was the case for nearly every computer in the Soviet Defense Network, ANX would spread quickly and throughout the entire chain. Since the computers in the SDN were dependent upon continuous interactions with one another to perform their assigned duties, disconnecting or shutting down the system was a physical impossibility. Over fifty thousand different SDN computers housed in the offices of Russian government officials and civilian contractors routinely accessed one another in an intricate electronic web. But the real target was more specific; disrupting the guidance systems of Russia's fleet of ICBMS was the General's primary objective.

He realized that the same kind of network was in place in the United States and her allies so they would be just as vulnerable as the SDN, therefore developing a safe method of disseminating the top secret key code that could not be obtained by the enemy was a top priority. The other priority was security in the lab and Houston was convinced that Eiger was crafty enough to keep ANX under control.

The concept of a computer virus was of course nothing new. In November 1988, a computer virus absorbed memory space in a minor epidemic that nearly blazed out of control. Many government agencies, including Chalmer, had been infected by the viral program. A Harvard graduate student had developed the virus as the topic of his doctoral dissertation. He claimed in his later testimony in court that he had been conducting an experiment that had exceeded the control systems that he had relied upon to shut down its dispersal, Luckily this particular strain of virus only haphazardly occupied a few vacant RAM sites–it was more of a nuisance than a catastrophe. But if circumstances had been different, the 'Harvard Virus' could have consumed years of important and irreplaceable data and might even have jeopardized national security.

Still the threat had been real. Defense Department computer engineers and programmers became aware for the first time just how vulnerable their computer systems were to sabotage. The potential consequences of a viral terrorist act had finally struck home. After the 'Big Scare', as it was labeled by the media, experts in the electronic security field began developing safeguard programs and software add-ons in the first attempts to prevent identity theft. But the public furor rapidly died down and computer viruses became regarded as not 'imminently dangerous'–except to General Pratt Houston who viewed them as the new high-tech weapons of the future...and his man Eiger was just the genius to make it happen. Putting Eiger in charge would be the General's next move.

Chapter 8

E iger led General Houston to the meeting he had requested with the Chalmer Lab's Board of Directors and senior technical staff. The Strategic Operations Room at Chalmer was lined by solid concrete block walls covered with a cheap veneer of plastic mahogany. The ceiling bristled with test tube brush shaped electronic bug detectors. The recessed lighting fixtures were plugged with piercing 100-watt bulbs. Although the ten foot long conference table was actually real, rich mahogany—as expensive as money can buy, no one ever felt comfortable in the "ops" room.

In front of every seat a new yellow legal pad and ball point pen waited ready for the participants to take notes. A paper shredder stood by ready for any waste. Behind the legal pads, sipping their sixth or so daily dose of extremely black steaming coffee, the top Chalmer division leaders fidgeted nervously. Many of the head weaponry scientists and defense system strategists incongruously were academicians drawn to Chalmer in order to have access to the center's one-of-a-kind, abhorrently expensive computer system. The group members certainly never looked forward to the periodic status review sessions with General Houston, but they were compelled to play the game because the scramble for high energy research funding could be described only as intense and never ending. Their theoretical work in advanced computation systems was entirely dependent upon how the hawks in the Pentagon viewed the long-term applicability of their research and General Houston was universally regarded as the hawk of hawks. He also held the government's purse strings.

Even though there were several senior staff at Chalmer who held much higher government service ratings than Eiger, the key administrators admitted to one another in private that Eiger had all ready gained a high degree of influence over lab operations and his equipment requests were given top priority. The old timers resented it deeply. The signs were evident, Eiger's section had the largest operating budget and his lab was off limits to the rest of the staff. Although to a member they each respected Eiger's genius in computer science, they would have preferred to be rid of him entirely. They referred to him as 'Doctor Ogre'—though never directly to his face.

As Eiger followed the General into the room, chairs rattled and collided as the scientists hastily rose to their feet. A pen clattered onto the table while a legal pad plopped to the floor. In spite of the prominent displays of NO SMOKING signs, the General lit a pungent smelling cigar and announced to the standing group, "At ease, gentlemen. Please be seated won't you?"

He began, "I love coming here to Chalmer because this is where our nation's freedom and security lie in trust. You scientists have a great heritage. Not only did you invent the first nuclear weapons, then the super bombs—America's benchmark of freedom—but you are now creating sophisticated satellite weapons that will defend the free world against attack. America's future lies in your hands."

Pausing to blow smoke at the ceiling, Houston warmed to his subject. "Most of you are now committed full time to the development and deployment of 'Star Wars' weaponry. The SDI warning system is a noble enterprise that will result in a long sought after, fool-proof system to defend this continent. I'm certain that you and your families will sleep better knowing that a blanket of extremely high-powered lasers will be patrolling the night sky—waiting for incoming warheads. And they'll come someday too! Mark my words, in time they'll come." *Sooner than you think too, you bunch of eggheads.*

With the noted exception of Eiger, the group collec-tively squirmed. Faces flushed red while questioning looks were discretely exchanged. Chalmer Director, Dr. Ernest Bradford, managed a feeble "Hear, hear."

The scientists inwardly assumed that the General was simply insane. They stoically translated Houston's soliloquy into just so much noise, which it was even to Houston. Crazy yes, but a fool, no. The General knew exactly what effect he was having on the men. He needed to rock the boat to cover the new secret project. It was time to start the ANX ball rolling and this group of inquisitive minds must be diverted away from any clues about its development before they gained an inkling of the real plan.

"You all have done a fine job here at Chalmer," Houston continued. "I am very happy to bring you good news from the Department of Defense administration. Your funding for SDI has been increased by twenty-five percent—that gentlemen is another two hundred and fifty million dollars added to your budget."

Houston abruptly sat down and added nonchalantly. "Congratulations. I am certain that the nation's taxpayers will get more than their money's worth. Oh and by the way I am extremely pleased to announce that Doctor Eiger has consented to accept a major assignment in this new expanded program...and will be, ahem...starting tomorrow, initiating a new top secret and extremely sensitive counter offensive project–code named Nimbus IV. If you guessed it is computer-based, you're exactly right. What else is there with Eiger anyway? Ha! Ha!

"Nimbus IV will be a major component of the SDI Smart Weapons System; I want you all to cooperate with Doctor Eiger to the fullest extent possible. Our country needs Nimbus as soon as possible and I thank you in advance for your determined efforts. Any questions, gentlemen?"

The startled audience stared at the General and looked from side to side at one another. An embarrassing silence followed.

Dr. Bradford was stunned. He felt dizzy and cradled his head in his hands. *Why didn't I know about this?"* he raged silently. *What an insult to my position, my career here is definitely at an end. What will I tell my wife? And what will I do now? I'm still young–at my peak!* Bradford slumped forward and said nothing.

Eiger averted his gaze to beneath the table and studied his worn Weejuns. Without thinking, he wiped a flood of perspiration from his forehead.

The General wound up, "Of course this is a surprise to you all and I am sure to Dr. Bradford especially. But please keep in mind that we are all on the same team and everyone has to do his or her part. If we don't do our jobs the best that we know how, those sneaky Russians will try to take us down. Professor Eiger will brief you on an as-need-to-know basis starting tomorrow."

The General unexpectedly stood followed by the sudden raking of chairs as the group, caught off guard, scrambled to achieve a facsimile of military attention.

Houston concluded, "One more thing. You probably are already aware that security clearances base-wide are being reviewed as a precautionary measure. As usual your friends and neighbors will be calling you to report that some man in a dark suit has been asking personal questions about you...wondering if you are a commie—or if you ever come into contact with a commie. You know the procedure. We have all been there many times before."

The room reverberated with Houston's booming laughter as he abruptly turned on his heel and marched out the door.

As the General bustled past the main gate with Eiger in tow, Houston said, "Don't worry Professor. I know that it will take some time to start the new program. I just wanted to make old Bradford squirm. I thought he was going to have a coronary. Ha! Ha! By the way, I want my own personal entrance into your building. I will supply the contractors and security. Commander Cummings will be in touch to make the arrangements. Within moments the Huey lifted off in a roar and the General was gone. But his presence was never felt more strongly at Chalmer Laboratories.

After Eiger returned, Director Bradford asked Eiger to join him in his office and said, "So Eiger, it looks like you're now in charge. I hope you know what you are getting into."

"It's all a surprise to me Director. As far as I am concerned you are still the leader but the General wants my operations to be off limits."

"What are you guys up to?"

"I'm sorry, but I am not at liberty to discuss my work with anyone outside of my staff."

Janet Williams had been Professor Eiger's personal secretary and administrative assistant since his arrival at Chalmer. During that time she had never been reprimanded, taken sick leave, or ever been late for work. On Monday morning at eight thirty she arrived as usual at Chalmer's South Gate to receive the shock of her life; security would not admit her into the complex. The guard matter-of-factly stated that her security clearance was invalid and confiscated her badge. He handed her a box, which contained her personal belongings, a letter of recommendation and a severance check.

Using a pay phone at a nearby Chevron station, Janet furiously rang up Eiger who painfully explained that matters were out of his hands. For some reason unknown to him, she had lost her top secret clearance rating. He kept restating that the situation was beyond his control. He did not know why, but he was sorry. He pleaded with her to understand that it was not his doing. She had never before heard real passion in his voice during their 1 cordial relationship and realized that Eiger must have been telling the truth; there was nothing else to do. This chapter of her life was over. It was time to move on.

Janet's replacement was named Stacy Powers. She was well dressed and seemed friendly. When Eiger asked about her experience, she gave him her résumé, which indicated that she had played the lead role in the development of several computer security related projects, some of which had been blacked out on the page. Upon further questioning, she admitted that she had worked for General Houston for several years and her job now was to serve as a communication bridge between the General and Eiger.

Eiger got the message. She was a spy!

Chapter 9

Aboard Lockheed C-141 Starlifter
En Route to Marshal Islands

After Tom and Sally were delivered by a flatbed truck from the Naval Undersea Center in Kaneohe, Hawaii to Hickam Air Force Base in Honolulu, they were unloaded, strapped into the cargo hold of a C-141 and covered with wet blankets. Sandra rubbed their heads and spoke comforting words. They seemed extraordinarily calm considering the circumstances. The flight would be a long one—over 2,700 miles and she had had only a few days to take advantage of Houston's offer to get started. The twins seemed to be dozing so Sandra went back to her seat and scanned the briefing sheet provided by the PIU marine lab for new arrivals.

Background

Originally Enewetak Atoll (aka Eniwetok Atoll) consisted of forty small islands—one of which was entirely vaporized by 'Operation Mike', which in 1952 was the first ever full-scale detonation of a thermonuclear fusion device.

According to a radiological survey performed in 1978, there was no remaining radiation danger on the atoll–except on the island of Runit, which is absolutely off limits–however, more surveys are planned now that the native islanders are being repatriated. Due to their proficiency in handling small boats, the Enewetakese will eventually repopulate all of the small islands that surround the lagoon (with the exception of Runit which will not be habitable for the next twenty-four thousand years). More radiological surveys are planned. Be advised, under no circumstances land on Runit Island.

Land surface area: three square miles.

Number of coral species: over six hundred (branching acropora corals are notably in abundance).

Number of fish species: over two thousand dominated by chaetodontids (butterfly fishes), labrids (wrasses), scarids (parrot fishes), serranids (sea basses), and carcharhinids (sharks).

Water visibility: 200 feet or more.

Water temperature: 85 degrees Fahrenheit year round.

Number of inhabitants: approximately sixty civilians employed by Centron. Centron's function is to build housing and a utility plant for repatriated Enewetakese. Centron's current Site Manager is Jim Donaldson. Donaldson is also District Marshall. In addition there is a small population of less than one hundred islanders, which are the first vanguard of residents returning to the atoll. Their Chief is popularly known as 'Mr. John'

RON S. NOLAN

(real name John Sturtevant, descendant of a German copra merchant who found a native Marshallese girl very attractive after five years at sea in the early 1880's).

Sandra put the booklet down, lay back, and closed her eyes. *Imagine! What Grandma said was true! I'll be diving in the sea with dolphins. I wonder about the man. Can you hear me, Grandma? I feel you with me. Is there a mate waiting for me too? Please help me succeed with this project. I can't believe that I just got on this plane— short notice, very little time to prepare. But I feel it was the right thing to do. I am so excited and happy. Thank you Grandma for your help and keep Grandpa safe and well too. I wonder about Grandpa. I only hear your voice and never his. I love you Grandma—tell Grandpa I miss him!*

Preparing for the trip on such short notice had involved several stress-packed days with little rest. Lulled by the monotone of the engines, visions of her childhood swept before her closed eyes.

MacArthur Park
Florida Keys, 1965

It was a typically beautiful Key West afternoon. Not too hot or muggy because it was mid-January, but warm enough to feel just right outside in a pair of shorts and a T-shirt. Sandra loved it when the air had cooled a little because then she could climb into the engineer's seat— sometimes in the summer the train was so hot that she couldn't bear to touch the metal ladder on the side of the locomotive. On those days she had to return in the cool of the evening.

Somehow, sitting here always brought her peace. It was funny. She really wasn't into playing engineer or conductor anymore. She just liked to sit and look out at the park—especially on a day like today when no one else was around. She leaned back into the hard metal seat, closed her eyes and let her mind wander. She would never admit to her classmates in school that voices talked to her here. Sometimes they called to her in other places, but they always waited for her here.

Sometimes they were more like feelings, not clear voices like you hear when you talk to someone for real. Sometimes the feeling was like her mom and another like her dad. The sensations were very loving and protective—in harmony with the unassailable solidity of the locomotive.

When a classmate hurt her or a teacher scolded her, she came here and all was healed. Problems didn't matter anymore. Those angry or hateful people were really very childish. She tried hard not to do things that would anger or hurt anyone and hoped someday to understand why people acted so strangely.

It seemed to her that most of the time their behavior didn't really have much to do with her at all. She was just a convenient outlet, a defenseless little girl who happened to be around at the moment they needed to release some sort of pent up hostility or aggression. If she closed her eyes tight and tried very hard, sometimes she could actually make out what other people were doing. Right now she could see that Miss Rundgrens, her English teacher, was working at her desk at school, which was strange because today was Saturday. She seemed to be grading compositions and was laughing in despair at one that was so poorly constructed that it was almost funny.

Miss Rundgrens had a boyfriend named Jack. His father ran a sports fishing boat and on Saturdays when they had a charter, Jack served as crewman. She sensed that Jack was fishing today—that the boat was quite distant from shore—maybe as far as the blue water of the Gulf Stream. No luck either. She would ask Miss Rundgrens on Monday if Jack had caught anything–just to see if her vision was right or playing tricks on her. Sometimes her perception was very right. Other times it got pretty confused by her imagination–or by her wanting too much for something to be true.

Just then she sensed her Grandmother's presence. She could see her plain as day, sitting on her stool looking towards the park. She could even see a little wave of her hand, but her lips didn't seem to be moving. "Sandra dear, start home now my love. Grandpa has lit the grill and the fresh grouper he bought at the seafood market is making his stomach growl. I love you dear."

"Yes Grandma. You really can see me here can't you?"

"Of course dear, who else would I be talking to like this? But, you're the only person I know that it works so well with."

Grandpa was just turning the fish when she came into the backyard. Grandma had set the picnic table with a red and white gingham cloth and was going back for the silverware when she looked up at Sandra and said as she smiled, "See, it was true. If it weren't, you would have missed supper," then she gave her a light whack on the seat of her shorts.

True to his blunt nature, Grandpa grumbled, "Listen you two, let's cut out the jaw flapping. I'm hungry enough to eat this fish...head and all, if it's of any interest to either of you."

Later helping Grandma with the dishes, Sandra asked, "How does it work, Grandma? Why is this connection only between you and me?"

"It was the same way between most of the women in our family–something in our genes I guess."

"Sometimes it scares me, Grandma...sometimes I wish it was gone."

"For land sakes child. It's a precious gift. Just make sure that you don't ever abuse it or it will go away."

"What do you mean abuse...how?"

"Well, the way I figure it, we're all born with psychic powers. As we get older we just learn them away. But some of us either have stronger abilities than others...or we just never figure out how to suppress them."

Grandma continued, "But if you ever use them to hurt anyone, or to inflate your own ego, they'll go just like that." She sharply snapped her fingers.

"But Grandma, Miss Rundgrens says that all psychics are fakes. She says that they are just con artists...like magicians at the Dade County Fair."

"Oh no child...not all of us are fakes. But I have a theory that goes something like this. Take a nice old lady like me that is gifted. Well say I get down on my luck and run out of money—God forbid! So I decide to put my psychic talents to work to solve my problems. Well that's alright until it hurts somebody or until my ego gets in the way...then the gift just slowly goes away. I would lose my connection. But I still know what it used to be like so I can still put on a pretty good show. I think that a lot of the phonies out there are just psychics that once had power, but abused and lost it. Once they lose their connection, they just make things up as they go. And that's why psychics have such a bad reputation."

"Oh, I remember. It's the lesson you once taught me when I was a kid! You know that a few bad apples spoil the barrel. But how can anyone tell if someone is really a psychic or not?"

"Well, I do know one good way. Chances are that if they charge money for their services, they've lost their power. Too bad, poor dears."

Laughing, Grandma reached down and gave Sandra a hug. "Yes young lady you are growing up aren't you? Remember to keep your talents pure. I see you swimming with dolphins and spending your days with a man that will truly love you waiting for you in your destiny. You want to be ready for them don't you?"

Chapter 10

The Air Force flight loadmaster, Sergeant McReynolds known to the crew as 'Mac', emerged from the rear of the plane, his bald head sandwiched in a set of bulbous yellow headphones. Beneath his double chin swung a wire mike, which allowed him to communicate with the cockpit. The headphones were necessary in order to hear over the roar of the whining turbines. Short, with a beer belly, Mac tried hard to manifest a John Wayne *could give-a damn look*. His demeanor was calculated to read, 'this is just another day off the ground...just a little joy ride'. The military machismo manifested on the outside was just a facade; inside he was quaking in his boots. Mac was a weekend warrior out of a Long Beach Air National Guard unit and he had never made this particular flight before in his life. When in his normal civilian mode, Mac dawdled through the days as a life insurance broker and had joined the Guard in a spasm of patriotism following the defeat of the Iraqis. He also needed the extra money since his wife had opted for a career as a housewife. The junkets to Hawaii, which he normally flew, were fine.

But taking this twenty-eight year old bird to a packed coral strip several hundred miles from the nearest flight mechanics made him extremely nervous and Mac was desperately afraid that he would get stuck out in the middle of nowhere waiting for parts to be flown in if the bird broke down. That was not a remote possibility either because it had happened twice before on this particular mission and the timing couldn't be worse. Tomorrow he was taking the family on a long-planned vacation to Yosemite. Mac's marriage was already on shaky ground—too much time on the job was the usual complaint. He wondered if Janie would divorce him if he didn't make it back tonight. Every day of the vacation had been worked out to the nth degree and cutting the trip short, even if by just a day, would have been a heart breaker to the kids.

The rear bay was packed to capacity. Mac sat carefully on a mesh bag bulging with dive gear, captivated by the strange cargo. Sally and Tom lay side-by-side covered with wet army blankets secured by the webbing of a bright orange net. Their liquid black eyes reflected the dull silver aluminum of the aircraft's interior. The dolphins occasionally emitted high-pitched squeaks. It was hard to judge, but they didn't look or sound at all happy.

Sandra studied Mac as he began talking into his mouthpiece. But with the deafening roar inside the plane and ears plugged with a pink, pliable substance that looked like bubble gum, it was impossible for her to discern what he was saying. Even Sally and Tom's ears were protected by foam pads secured with black electrical tape. Sandra wondered if their ears were popping like hers; the plane seemed to be descending.

The FASTEN SEAT BELT sign flickered several times then stayed lit. Mac tapped each passenger and pointed to the sign. Sandra figured it must be some sort of regulation because it was easy to see that she and the other two passengers were snarled in the same complex type of harnesses that bound her so uncomfortably. By twisting around Sandra could catch a glimpse of blue out of a small porthole. Turning further and sliding one shoulder free of the canvas restraint she caught the first sight of her new home, a home at least for the next year. She caught Mac's attention and he shuffled over, slid one of his ears free of the headset, and pressed it close to her face. Using a combination of improvised hand signals and shouting at the top of her lungs, Sandra asked if they could circle around the atoll; she wanted to see the famed necklace of mini-islands and shallow reefs that surrounded the lagoon before landing. Mac raised his eyebrows, gritted his teeth then spoke into his mike. In a moment he gave her a thumbs-up sign. The plane began a gradual bank to the left and the turquoise lagoon filled the horizon. Sandra squirmed until she was plastered fully in front of her oval window.

The narrow the islands stretched out like stepping stones in a long circular arc. In the center of islands a peaceful lagoon lay protected by the outer reef where waves crashed and boiled in a white froth. The lagoon was a greener shade of blue than the open sea, and depending upon the depth, ranged in hue from deep green to light turquoise. The beaches were a pure radiant white. Her heart raced to see lush groves of graceful palms, their fronds dancing wildly in the trade winds. Flocks of delicate fairy terns rose beneath them, their tranquility shattered by the low pass of the plane. The words 'tropical paradise' formed softly on her lips.

The C-141 lined up with the coral gravel strip of the Main Island and dropped to a smooth landing on the hot shimmering runway. Sandra was the first passenger off the plane. Standing on the ramp fishing in her bag for sunglasses, she felt a blast of hot, humid wind, which launched her Raider's ball cap dancing down the runway. Three young Coast Guardsmen, technicians who manned the Loran station, raced to rescue her hat. They were quick to seize an opportunity to meet this knockout gal who had materialized unexpectedly and sent their blood pulsing. Yet even their considerable ardor was abated when the pallet holding Tom and Sally slid down the roller ramp at the rear of the plane and landed in the baking, hot sun. The Coasties were willingly commandeered into service and formed a bucket brigade. Hand over hand, they passed plastic pails of water dipped from the nearby lagoon and sloshed them over the squirming, chattering animals.

Enewetak airport consisted of a single aluminum Quonset hut. A plywood sign bolted to the front of the building sported the yellow caricature of a sun face wearing dark shades and beaming a happy grin.

Someone with a sense of humor had carefully painted in large letters, 'Welcome to Enewetak International Airport'. Passengers waiting to board the return flight stood smoking and talking to their friends. Their bright aloha shirts, recently pressed Bermuda shorts, Samsonite brief cases, and paperback novels clearly delineated them from the rest of the onlookers who would remain on the atoll. Most of the action centered around a big ice chest where every few minutes one of the men sidled in to squash an empty can and fish out a fresh beer. Nearly everyone was keeping a close watch on Sandra and the dolphins as they waited for the lab manager to arrive."

The sky seemed vibrantly close and the pure white clouds overhead were much more striking to the eye than that of northern California where the air and clouds seemed to seep together in a blend auto emissions and coastal haze. Rotating her head, Sandra could see from one horizon to the other where the sky merged into the sea. The brilliant puffs of white clouds streamed by low overhead in orderly processions propelled by the steady push of the trades.

A dilapidated stake bed truck bearing the name 'PIU Marine Lab' in weathered paint on the doors rattled into the compound towing a rusty forklift. A tall, athletic man in cut-offs and a faded work shirt, obviously behind schedule and looking harried, ran up to Sandra and gasped, "Damn battery was dead again...had to get jump started...sorry I'm late...how are the dolphins?"

Barely stopping for a breath, he continued, "Let's get that pallet into the back of the truck...I set up a temporary pool until we can transfer them to the big crater tomorrow." Then he abruptly thrust forward a calloused tan hand for Sandra to shake, which she enthusiastically pumped sweat and all.

He took a step back and said, "Hi, I'm Jim Morrow—all my friends just call me 'Morrow'. I like it better like that. Welcome to the Marshall Islands."

Sandra held on for dear life as the truck bounced and swerved to avoid potholes as Morrow gunned the truck down the Main Island's one and only road. The aging truck coughed and wheezed past a sign posted along the roadway that warned would-be trespassers of the dire consequences awaiting those charged with unauthorized entry.

Morrow parked in front of an aluminum building hidden within a grove of coconut palms. The lab was located at the northernmost tip of the island on a little spit of sand. The air smelled of hot tar from the creosote-impregnated pier, which jutted into the lagoon providing docking space for the lab's small fleet of dive skiffs. At the head of the pier, two students stood by while a clattering compressor filled their SCUBA tanks. The lab building was fronted by a spacious lanai filled with rows of observation tanks packed with a variety of marine specimens. A jumbled assortment of outboard motors, gas cans, anchors, ropes, and dive gear was stashed haphazardly against the walls.

Sandra stood transfixed in front of a large tank full of colorful reef fish, many of which she recognized from her pet shop days back in Key West.

Morrow pointed out a red and white fish with long trailing fins and a blunt head. He said, "Watch out for that one. It's called..."

"A lionfish," interrupted Sandra, "and it has deadly spines."

"I'm impressed, Dr. Grant. You seem to know your fish taxonomy."

"Only the most interesting species," she laughed. *This reminds me so much of the pet shop in Key West. Are you there Grandma? How do you like all these tropical fish?*

Morrow led her to the side of the building where a green shade cloth drooped loosely over a low tank of water suspended at each corner by a cord tied to a nearby palm. The fifty-foot circular pool was filled nearly to the top with clear lagoon water. As they were talking, several pickup trucks crunched to a halt in the gravel driveway by the pool and a crowd of Centron workers gathered around to see the new arrivals. Word traveled fast on the island–especially when it became known that a new female had arrived on the weekly flight–and that she had brought dolphins all the way from Hawaii.

Sandra immediately enlisted the men's help in freeing the dolphins from the pallet and carrying them one by one to the pool. She jumped in with the Twins to keep them company and to make sure that they revived fully. As she got soaked, her revealing T-shirt and shorts caused a minor sensation in the group of onlookers. Realizing too late that she was indeed putting on quite a show, Sandra was forced to endure a few wolf whistles as she patiently walked the dolphins around the pool while talking to them in a soft voice.

She tried to reassure the dolphins that this stopover was only temporary and that she was their friend and guardian. Within half an hour every nonessential island resident had joined the party. The crowd was now several men deep around the pool and an endless stream of beers were being handed forward from somewhere back in the ranks. The whistles died down as the men became mesmerized by the blowing and clicking of the dolphins.

Now standing waist deep in the warm water as the Twins swam around the tank grazing her outstretched palms with their smooth skin, it occurred to Sandra that things were certainly moving in unexpected directions. Only two days ago she had arrived at the Naval Undersea Center at Kaneohe where a nervous civilian who introduced himself as the operations manager had met her. He had immediately escorted Sandra to an off limits area of the base which had once served as an airplane hanger and now held a shallow pool. Sally and Tom rested motionless on the bottom, only rising to the surface to breathe. It was obvious that they were very unhappy creatures.

The operations manager had proven to be uncooperative and refused to discuss any aspect of the Twins participation in the Navy dolphin program.

During a few minutes while the manager left to check on the transportation arrangements, Sandra had managed a brief conversation with one of the NUC mammal trainers. Although reticent to discuss any of the details about the kind of instruction that the Twins had received, the trainer had revealed that they were very clever animals and on several instances had correctly anticipated commands before they were issued.

When the manager returned, he had informed her, "Sorry Ma'am. I just spoke with General Houston. He said that you must move the dolphins out on the next available MAC flight, which leaves at 0600 tomorrow. Sorry for the short notice, Dr. Grant."

Sandra's hastily conceived plan had at least been orderly. First scout out the dolphins and then return to her office in California to plan, organize, and pack for the move. She figured it would take at least three months to put the package together and another six months to build the lab and set up the equipment–and all of this before the Twins would have been transported to Micronesia.

Well so much for that plan. It looks like I have no choice but to go with the flow. The opportunity to work with twin dolphins that may have already demonstrated psychic abilities is just too valuable to risk. If I ask for more time, they might give them to someone else...and I would lose my funding too. Only a day to prepare and when I get there what will I do? At least I'll make sure the dolphins are safe, and then I'll bring the team over and then somehow build a research lab and begin investigations. Quite a challenge!

The chancellor of the Pacific Island University was sympathetic and quite helpful. He assured her that the Enewetak Marine Lab would be placed at her disposal and offered the services of the lab manager until her team was mobilized.

So with just a couple of stops at the Ala Moana Shopping Center to get extra shorts, tops and shampoo, a local dive shop to purchase a new set of dive gear to replace the gear left in California, she had spent as much time at NUC in the tank with the Twins as the operations manager would allow with the goal of establishing a sense of trust in the dolphins. They took to her immediately. After years of military discipline, Sally and Tom warmed to the affection she showered upon them. Still, like it was only yesterday, she remembered thinking, *how do you tell two dolphins they're about to fly to Micronesia?*

Now she suddenly found herself here, standing in this pool in the Marshall Islands surrounded by strangers. It was hard to believe that only less than a week ago she had been innocently sitting in her office wondering what had happened to her research proposal. Now she was the center of attention of a south Pacific all male tribe telling two bottlenose dolphins not to worry, everything is going to work out fine. *Just calm down now you two. I'll try to do the same.*

Jim Morrow was her savior. During her short stay in Hawaii she had learned that he held a master's degree in ichthyology from the University of Hawaii and a doctorate in marine biology from the Pacific Islands University. His graduate research had been performed at Enewetak and since joining the Pacific Island University faculty on Catalina Island, he had returned every year to do fieldwork. Morrow's specialty was the study of coral reef fish communities and Enewetak Lagoon was an ideal research location. Not only did the atoll's lagoon have lush reef ecosystems, it was also serviced by weekly flights to and from Honolulu and a well equipped and staffed marine lab.

The sun edged toward the sea. The trade winds had diminished to just a breath that barely ruffled the surface of the lagoon creating tiny wavelets that reflected the sun's rays sending lightning flashes across the sea surface. A sense of serenity enveloped the island. The residents had retired en masse to the club to do some serious drinking and to exchange comments about the newcomers. The Twins seemed to relax allowing Grant to shift her attention to Morrow. He was tall and muscular with short sandy hair. He looked like the stereotype California surfer, blond and bronze. She had once heard that most Pacific Islands University grads were surfers.

Seated with Morrow in the cafeteria after finishing off one of the Centron's gourmet dinners, Sandra took Morrow's hand. "Thanks for your help today. I simply couldn't have managed without you. Those goatfish you provided made the Twins feel right at home. They seem much happier now."

Morrow suggested that they adjourn to the lab. Producing two bottles of Primo beer from the refrigerator, they moved to the deck and plopped own in lawn chairs. They arrived just in time to witness a spectacular green flash just as the sun dropped into the lagoon.

Sandra said, "Please tell me about your research. Is it true that you conduct your studies underwater? I have dreamed about diving on a coral atoll; it must be wonderful."

"What my team is investigating is the role that shelter plays in the development of a coral patch reef community. Hundreds of species coexist in a very close quarters. One way they accomplish this is by dividing the day-night work shifts. As soon as the sun goes down, the day active species take shelter in the reef's nooks and crannies and the night shift workers, like moray eels, go on attack. Not only is the size of the reef important, but also the diversity of corals and plant life actually shapes the structure of the community. Sorry....I could go on about this for hours."

"No please go ahead. How do you conduct experiments...or do you just rely upon correlation analyses?"

"Wow, you are a sharp lady! Basically we build artificial reefs and monitor recruitment of the larval fishes and invertebrates. In some experiments, we enclose the entire reef in a frame and a net to keep out predators. This is our present study focus."

TELEPATHIC DOLPHIN EXPERIMENT

"Speaking of predators, I hope we can find a safe place for the Twins. Do you have any suggestions?"

"The PIU chancellor told us you would be looking for a home for your dolphins. Tomorrow my assistant and two of our graduate student helpers will rig net barriers across a channel connecting North Island and the lagoon. There are a few sharks, but it should be a safe place for your dolphins—plus we have a small lab and a solar power system for electricity and several grass shacks for the kitchen and sleeping quarters. There is plenty of space to make new additions if needed,"

"I had no idea. I have funds to build a lab, perhaps they should be used to expand the facilities that you already have in place?"

"That would be wonderful!"

"Next week when my assistant arrives, we can all sit down and come up with a budget and a new plan. I didn't realize that everything would have to come by boat. In the interim, I brought my own SCUBA gear... maybe you and the Twins could give me an underwater tour? I got my certificate when I was a teenager and love to dive. But we didn't have shark problems in Key West—not so here according to what I have read. I would appreciate it if you would fill me in on how to cope with the dangerous ones before I get into the water."

Morrow related some of his underwater experiences in the local waters: one dive buddy had been bitten into two pieces. Another buddy, the dive master from PIU, had a big chunk removed from his elbow. "It's the first thing he still talks about in his dive classes," laughed Morrow. "He always wears short sleeve shirts too. It's his badge of courage."

Morrow continued, "There are more. A Centron worker who called himself 'Old Shot Ziller, the Old Shark Killer' had been mouthed head on by a big tiger shark and had required stitches in his head—and he was an expert at self defense. That's what makes it scary!"

When Sandra asked why his buddies seem to get nailed and not he, Morrow warmed to the subject. "The secret is quite simple actually," he explained. "If you see sharks, you must get out of the water as soon as possible or know precisely what you are doing. I do. The others didn't. If your exit is obstructed, maneuver your tank against the reef and wedge yourself in between the branches of the corals. Don't get excited and hold your breath. If you do, you'll float upwards and provide them with an easy target. While you're fending off one attacking from the front, another shark will approach from the rear and attempt to snatch you from behind. Finally, always make sure to fire your power head from a controlled position and get out of water as soon as possible."

"What's a power head?"

"It's a shark defense weapon that consists of a fiberglass shaft tipped with an explosive cartridge. They were invented by a former bullfighter named Rhett McNair who filed a patent for the design in 1977. I helped him test the prototype right here in Enewetak Lagoon. They are quite effective. I still have a spare you can use while you are here."

Sandra was impressed with Morrow's composure while describing in detail such horrifying events. Morrow went on, "Surprisingly the greatest danger here is a small carcharhinid called the gray reef shark. They don't get much larger than six feet, but they are very, very aggressive. You might call them the ocean's version of the pit bull. Grays don't attack you to eat you—only to defend their territory. After all, they were here first. On the other hand, the pelagic white tip and the big tiger sharks are definitely real bad news. They also aggressively defend their territories, but they are different. They seem to like human flesh...very vicious and very dangerous. But even though the whites and tigers are as bad as it gets, they are relatively uncommon and you may never see any while you are here. So remember, it is most critical to keep an eye of the grays. They are exceedingly fast, curious and abundant. That makes for a volatile situation. Sometime I'll tell you about their dance."

"Sharks that dance? That sounds very cool. I read about a radioactive island in the lab guide. What's going on there anyway?"

Morrow took a long hard pull from his bottle of Primo then answered, "Who knows? This place is full of secrets. Runit Island was the site of two nuclear detonations. Cactus in 1958 and Lacrosse in 1956. The U.S. military used the crater formed by Cactus as a dumping ground for radioactive wastes and covered it with thick concrete panels. One thing for sure is that Runit Island is strictly off limits. The rumor goes that it is the most radioactive spot on the earth's surface."

He continued, "It's funny. I was here during one of the first radiological surveys that the AEC conducted in the mid-seventies–before they had allowed any of the natives to come back. They hired me as a consultant to pick up soil samples from Runit since one of my study reefs was just offshore. That's how they found out that Runit was hot. I brought them a baggie full of dirt, which looked like ordinary sand to me, but it pegged their Geiger counter."

As he expertly twisted the cap off a new bottle of Primo, he concluded. "Eventually I learned that they found pieces of pure plutonium in the bottom of the bag."

"Oh great, I'll make certain to avoid that island," exclaimed Sandra as she rose to study a chart of the atoll thumbtacked to the lab wall. Runit was marked with a skull and cross bones and a labels stating

RON S. NOLAN

'DANGER STAY CLEAR. NO ANCHORAGE. NO LANDING PERMITTED. RADIOACTIVE CONTAMINATION'. She noted that they would pass by Runit on the way to North Island–the island on which she planned to establish her new base. *I wonder what happened there that left pure plutonium lying around on the surface. Wow!*

As if reading her mind, Morrow offered, "The story one of the AEC crew members leaked while he was on a brutal bender at the club, was that some of the weapons experts back in the sixties wanted to know what would happen if a bomber carrying an armed nuke crashed on takeoff. You know, would the nuke go off or not? So the AEC took a small nuclear fission device, set it on a big charge of dynamite and lit the fuse. Other than the dynamite detonating, nothing happened except that the fission device's case cracked open spilling plutonium into the sand. They probably figured 'no big deal' and went home. That was long before there was any kind of environmental consciousness. The whole incident was forgotten until I collected my little sample twenty years later.

"Telling you this story now, I realize how outrageous it must sound. But that makes it even more believable to me. Whatever you do, don't waste any energy trying to get a straight answer out of the Centron guys. They are under strict orders not talk about Runit Island at all. You'll see them around; they're the guys in the bright orange suits."

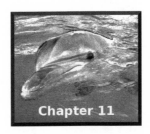

The next morning Sally and Tom were once again strapped to the dreaded pallet, covered with a wet blanket and secured by an orange cargo net. They were aboard a World War II era landing craft en route to their new home. An hour later, they approached the picturesque, palm laden North Island where three young men waved and ran to greet them. The landing craft's transmission clanged into reverse followed by a throaty roar from the diesels as the engines revved in reverse. The heavy boat quickly lost momentum and lightly kissed the rickety dock.

One of Morrow's team tossed a loop of heavy line over a piling and made it fast to a cleat on the deck. Once the landing craft was lined up properly, the front ramp ratcheted downward into position forming a loading ramp. The rust-riddled lab truck, tires squat and bulging with the weight of the dolphins, camp gear and provisions, splashed reluctantly into the shallows and into the soft sand, got stuck then stalled. Amidst a quick flurry of shouted introductions, Sandra and the crew jumped into the knee-deep water and shoved with all their might until the old truck groaned and creaked its way up onto the beach.

The lagoon waters were entrancing–a gem crystalline blue in the deeper reaches melting to a light sapphire green in the shallows. Just offshore, Sandra noticed irregular patches of dark reef separated by lighter corridors of sand. The water was so clear that Sandra could even make out large green fish darting from reef to reef. Morrow identified them as parrotfish–a species that chisels and grinds living coral with its hard beak. According to Morrow, this was one of the richest shallow water reef communities in the world.

The truck edged over a rise in the middle of the island. As Morrow promised the far side was quite picturesque. It reminded Sandra of a tropical grotto near Hana on the Island of Maui. A dense grove of palms descended down to a pristine beach. Thousands of iridescent white fairy terns took to the air as they rumbled onto the sand. Graceful palms with necks like giant, sinuous snakes grew right to the water's edge.

Tom and Sally began squirming against their restraints as soon as the truck backed to a halt next to a narrow channel that led to the lagoon. Within minutes the dolphins had rolled off into the water and were off exploring their new domain. Tom caught a goatfish and proudly displayed it to Sandra before wolfing it down headfirst. It was the first time he had ever captured his own wild game.

Sandra and Morrow stood knee deep in the lagoon cheering on Sally as she too made her first catch. All of a sudden Tom turned, lifted his tail and slammed it down hard on the surface sending a wall of saltwater cascading down upon Sandra and Morrow.

Laughing, Sandra screamed, "Well I guess that's an invitation if I've ever seen one. Shall we? Then she stripped off her shorts and top to reveal a stunning black string bikini and dove headfirst into the water. Morrow jumped in shorts, shirt and all.

As Sandra and Morrow sun dried on the beach, the Twins put on a heartwarming show–swimming and jumping free of the water in perfect synchronicity.

"Yes! Yes! Yes!" Sandra cheered them from the sand, alternating between jumping for joy and sobbing hysterically. Sally and Tom were savoring the first taste of freedom that they had ever experienced. They were also becoming very attached to their new comrades.

Morrow disappeared into the lagoon with his mask and fins. In short order he returned all smiles, his dive bag bristling with an enormous spiny lobster. They roasted the "bug", as Morrow insisted on calling it, over a hot fire fueled with dry coconut husks. Then to Sandra's amazement, Morrow magically produced a chilled California chardonnay to complete the feast. As they sat close together, coals glowing intermittently from little gusts of breeze, the dying sun painted the sky with broad bands of reds and oranges in a horizon-wide blaze of color.

Later they lay next to one another on sleeping bags pulled out from the tent. They held hands awestruck in the darkness, their attention totally consumed by a coal black sky saturated with constellations and galaxies. A shooting comet sliced brightly east to west across the sky then raced beyond the horizon. She looked up just in time to see Sally and Tom jump together in a high, graceful arc. As they plunged back as one into the water, the reef erupted in a shower of blue-white sparks emitted by luminescent plankton.

Sandra reflected that Morrow was definitely a friend in time of need. He was also very handsome. Up close she could see that his hair was actually brown, but bleached by years in the sun. He had a strong chin, which by now was showing a hint of afternoon shadow and golden brown eyes. She could not help notice that his muscles flexed smoothly when he moved, maybe a little like the sharks he knew so much about. And more than once she had caught him studying her carefully. *Is it him, Grandma...is he the one you saw in your vision? The handsome man swimming with dolphins?*

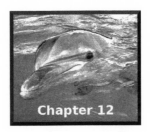

Chapter 12

As soon as it was unexpectedly announced that the General and his aide had arrived without notice at the new 'Houston Gate' at Chalmer, Eiger fought to gain his composure and hurried to greet them.

"Eiger my man. I wholeheartedly approve of your new security precautions. They seem first rate as far as I can tell. This is Commander Richard Cummings. He is my numero uno and has my complete confidence. We're here for a SITREP."

Now that he was actually beginning to program the early sequence of the ANX code, Eiger had insisted on several new safeguards to tighten security. He had installed a unique password system that only permitted access to his building according to a complex set of commands–a formula that only he and his most trusted assistants had committed to memory. All other personnel, computers, telephones, fax and closed circuit television–as well as the cable networks that once supported them, had been pulled from the walls and removed. The hallway, which formerly lead to the main entrance, was now sealed with two layers of concrete block; the only way in or out of the complex was the new 'Houston Gate'. Eiger had even dismantled his administrative office and moved it, along with his very reluctant assistant, Stacy Powers, into a mobile construction office parked just inside the perimeter fence. He had given a great deal of thought to the risks involved in building ANX. If the virus escaped his control, it would be impossible to stop. An incalculable disaster was certain to occur. ANX would assimilate and destroy every bit of data stored in any computer that it had contact with. Any computer net invaded by the virus would grind to an irreparable halt within minutes of exposure. All banks would close; the stock market would disintegrate. Without access to cash or credit, all transactions would cease; the nation would be brought to its knees, and the international economy would be shattered.

After the EXXION performed its standard series of surveillance scans the General queried, "Just how contagious is this ANX at this stage. Is all of this security really necessary? You even got poor little ole Stacy stuck in a trailer out there in the parking lot. "

Eiger cleared his throat and replied, "General this project will fabricate what could be the most dangerous device ever conceived by man. It is also extremely infectious."

"Well Eiger, I guess that sums it up. Are we safe with the work you have done up to now?"

"Frankly General I am not as certain as I would like to be. Just like in biological systems, we are dealing with a case of emergent properties. We won't know how virulent ANX will be until it is finished—just as it is not possible to predict the nature of a cell from its component subunits. If we underestimate, we will have serious difficulties."

Before the General could interrupt, Eiger continued,

TELEPATHIC DOLPHIN EXPERIMENT

"Now sir, so as not to prolong your busy itinerary need-
lessly, I will be specific. We have removed all forms of
telecommunication from this entire building and
Chalmer's security is maintained at peak levels. But
General, the point is that we are situated only sixty
miles from downtown San Francisco. This building is
bombarded day and night by thousands of electronic
signals emanating as radio and television waves and
satellite transmissions. With so many electromagnetic
activities, I am very uneasy...frightened of what we
might unknowingly unleash upon the nation."

"Okay Doctor, do you have a suggestion? I mean you
have already gone to a lot of steps here, it would be too
bad to waste the effort, but..."

"What we need is an isolated place where we can set
up a target computer, call it the 'PIG' and connect it
remotely to the ANX computer which will launch
attacks at the PIG. In essence, we will use the PIG to
test a host of secret key defense codes and the ANX to
develop offensive programming. That way every time
the PIG becomes infected, it can be shutdown, wiped
and a new operating system installed. You can see why
isolating both systems is imperative."

Commander Cummings interjected, "Sir, if I may join
in to the conversation...as you know, I just returned
from the Enewetak Atoll in the Marshall Islands where
you sent me to begin monthly checks to determine if and
how much radiation is leaking from Cactus Dome on
Runit Island."

The General nodded. "Yes, proceed."

"Looking from a worst case viewpoint, locating the
new mainframe EXXION system carrying ANX on
Runit Island would insure its security because the
entire island could be torched and sterilized if it should
get out of control. It is not likely that anyone would
notice another destructive event on that island with its

long history of device testing. It also has a power system and underground living quarters—plus there will be security provided by Centron under contract to Chalmer."

"Okay, what about the target computer; the one Dr. Eiger calls the PIG?"

"South of Runit there is another island on the atoll named 'Parry' that would serve as a perfect location for the PIG. It has extensive underground caverns dug by the Japanese during World War II, as well as a power station and living quarters. There is even a dock for boats and a ramp for seaplanes. It would be fairly easy to connect both computers with a submarine cable which could be activated or inactivated with the flip of a switch."

The General nodded in approval. "Plus this way the members of the staff involved in each system will have zero contact with each other. That should prevent any sort of cross contamination. What do you think Dr. Eiger? Does this satisfy your concerns about safety and security?"

Eiger looked concerned. "I agree that it does seem unlikely that anyone would venture to an island if they think it is dangerously radioactive, but how about me and my staff. Will we get zapped?"

Cummings replied, "That is unlikely. Although we did detect some leakage from the dome, we could set you up at the opposite end of the island and it wouldn't take long to build a complex of lead-lined underground chambers to protect your team and computer equipment. Adding a power station would be straightforward because Centron has the equipment and resources. We could get started as soon as the budget is approved and building plans are in place."

Eiger replied, "In that case, I think this plan makes sense. We can preassemble both systems here, break them down into parts and then ship them to the atoll We are going to need quite a bit of help, but when the EXXION on Runit Island is up and running, I will make a single copy of the most recent ANX version to a tape and hand deliver it myself to the island. Don't worry, I will destroy the rest."

Houston held up his hand halting Eiger in mid-stride. "It sounds good to me Doctor. You're calling the shots, but from now on can we establish a new protocol and simply call the sites 'ANX' Island and 'PIG' Island? Less confusing to me at least. If you want to work up the parts here and put them together out in the boon-docks that's just fine."

"As you wish General, Fine from now on its ANX Island and PIG Island."

You know I just got rid of two pain-in-the-butt dolphins by shipping them out there. What a coincidence don't you think? Sent a lady scientist along with 'em. Her name is Sandra Grant...another scientist like you. *In my sixty plus years I have never head the mention of that set of islands so many times in such a short period of time. It's funny too...I've never even been there. Consolidation of my pawns into a very small remote arena. Makes good battle sense to me, coincidence or not.*

The General slapped Eiger on the back and then he turned and left without saying goodbye. Eiger slumped into his chair, lost deep in thought

Chapter 13

Taking a much welcome break on the Main Island to meet the arrival of her crew coming in on the weekly flight from Honolulu, Sandra waited impatiently while the stairway was rolled up to the door of the aircraft. She remembered how she had felt as an outsider venturing down that ramp for the first time into a world unknown. Now she was enjoying a beer and catching up on the latest island gossip. Not to say that she had been accepted into the island's inner circle; she still remained a disturbingly attractive female to the majority of the male residents, but at least she knew several of the carpenters and plumbers who were helping out with the new lab.

She caught a glimpse of Chet's face as he emerged into the sunlight. He looked lost and out of place with his long black hair barely constrained by a beaded head-band. He wore army shorts layered with pockets bulging with ballpoint pens and mechanical pencils and he was wearing wire frame glasses with Polaroid clip-ons flipped up like a pair of automobile sun visors. *I wonder if Enewetak is ready for an encounter with an archetypal nerd from the Bay Area. Funny I never even noticed that Chet looked a little strange when we were back on campus. Probably because back at home he looks just like everyone else!*

The rest of the technicians, two guys and two girls, paraded down the ramp loaded with plastic shopping bags and backpacks jammed with scientific journals and lab notebooks. Sandra was overjoyed to see them and gave them each a welcome hug. Everyone had a million questions to ask, the subject repeated most was whether it was always this hot. The new arrivals were amazed to see their leader in shorts, zories and a polo shirt. After sixteen weeks in the islands, Sandra had toasted to a golden brown and radiated a sense of peace and composure very much unlike her frenetic nature on campus. One of the girls couldn't resist holding her pale white arm up to Sandra's.

"Dr. Grant You've gone native. Look how tan you are!"

Sandra warned, "I got fried on the first day. It took me a week to recover. Definitely you should go for the sun block. Let's get on with it," she shouted as they piled into the back of their shiny new lab truck. "Oh and welcome to paradise."

Now that her team was on hand, Sandra often spent the night on the Main Island. She was surprised to find out how much she missed the serenity of their base camp on North Island, but she enjoyed the fresh enthusiasm of her comrades and felt that they needed her attention too.

******

Sandra and Morrow made daily trips to North Island to monitor the construction of the new lab and check on the Twins. Sticking to his word, the General had pushed the lab construction to the fullest of his abilities, and most of the Centron's population had been conscripted to the task. They soon learned that Sandra was determined that the construction be done properly as well as quickly. Every morning at seven she met with the foreman to receive a detailed progress report. The rest of the team waited on the Main Island, bivouacked in Centron's concrete block dormitory. By the end of the first week they had transformed the dorm lounge into a makeshift office and set up several workstations. Under Sandra's guidance, Chet organized sessions to plan the detailed experimental procedures that would be conducted as soon as the lab was ready.

Normally meals were taken cafeteria style in the mess hall. The food was first rate, prepared by Filipino chefs and served in all you can eat amounts. But Wednesday nights were much different. As all newcomers learn soon after their arrival, the atoll's activity schedule revolved around the once a week flight from Honolulu. Thursday was popularly referred to as 'Plane Day' and was the most looked forward to day of the week. Mail and supplies arrived along with returning passengers with tales to tell about their vacation adventures. Accordingly, Wednesday night was a cause for celebration and had been branded 'Club Night'—a cook your own New York strip and lobster tail barbecue at the Pau Hana Club during which a large amount of alcohol was consumed by the locals. Steak bones and scraps were automatically tossed over the deck railing to schools of little black tip sharks patrolling the shallows waiting for the handout.

One of the highlights of Enewetak life was the weekly show put on by 'Tricks', a seasoned bulldog missing one ear and with deep scars lining his flanks. Encouraged by the crowd who cheered him on relentlessly, the tough old dog would wade out belly deep and lunge at any fin within reach. This act of bravery would be followed by a small explosion as the shark joined battle with the dog. Invariably the shark attached itself firmly to some convenient part of Tricks' anatomy and in the melee was dragged to the beach. Once the shark began to suffocate out of the water, it released its grip and thrashed in the sand. A beached shark held little interest for Tricks who resolutely would wade out for another victim leaving the ones previously caught to flip and wrench their way back into the water.

By the third week since their arrival, Chet and his flock had Club Night wired. They had even staked out their own special table on the deck and joined in throwing food to the sharks and playing a fierce game of high stakes bingo. The girls had adjusted to their elevated status and tried to democratically share their attention with as many interested parties as possible. Later in the evening, when the party was really rolling under the influence of fifty-cent drinks, they made sure that Chet was close at hand to protect them from too much attention.

During their free time, the technicians snorkeled in the lagoon and combed the beaches for seashells. As neophytes to the tropics are often inclined, they took turns shinnying up some of the more inviting coco palms–the ones that had gently slanting trunks to shake loose the hefty fruits. To their delight, the milk was sweet and the white meat firm and delicious. The group posted a calendar in the lounge and ritualistically tracked the passage of time by crossing out the most recent plane day. Their cache of electronic equipment in their newly built warehouse on the North Island filled with wooden crates and metal cabinets with each weekly arrival.

******

.

After weeks of commuting back and forth to the Main Island and dealing with a wide assortment of logistic delays and problem solving, Sana and her team were aboard the landing craft, finally heading to their new research lab and home on North Island.

Morrow pointed out Runit Island as they passed by the Deep Channel. From a distance they could see a newly constructed concrete wharf running outward from the shore into the lagoon. A sleek cabin cruiser rocked lightly against the pier cushioned by rubber tires fastened to the dock. Through Morrow's binoculars, Sandra could make out the figures of three men walking along the beach wearing orange coveralls. She winced as the glasses magnified a sharp flash of sunlight that reflected like gun steel, but the distance was too great to make out the source. Seeing the luxury yacht tied up to the off limits island made Sandra wonder how dangerous the island really was–or if something weird might be going on over there.

The scene at the beach reminded her of a television newscast about an industrial complex in the central Florida that had been swatted by a tornado. Wrecked landing craft marooned for decades since the Battle of Eniwetok lay helter-skelter–some partly submerged, others high and dry. A crumbling building stood in ruins at the base of the pier, its roof buckled into its interior. In every direction, she found stoic concrete bunkers riddled with serrated iron reinforcing rod that made ugly rust stains as it weathered in the salt air. And there were scores of derelict vehicles: dump trucks, pickup trucks, flat bed trailer rigs, bulldozers–even a crane with its scoop left hanging in mid-air. It was a macabre scene from a junkyard horror movie. Fuel pump stations, a dormitory for a hundred men and a flat concrete pad that might have even been a tennis court were buried in drifting sand and strangled by bird's nest ferns and blooming purple morning glories.

Morrow held up his hands and said, "Don't ask me; I have no idea what's goes on over there. This was one of the support bases for the Atomic Energy Commission during the nineteen fifties. Several hundred homesick technicians and engineers were stationed out here. That explains the buildings, bunkers and towers. The boats on the beach are wrecks left over from World War II. Obviously neither the military nor the government cared much about the environment back in those days. I've read some of the published accounts about the nuclear testing period. The attitude seems to have been to just *use it up*."

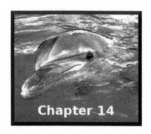

Chapter 14

M orrow found Sandra seated in a deck chair using a packing crate as a temporary desk. He asked, "It's a beautiful afternoon, why is everyone around here so glum? Are the seemingly unending delays placing a damper on the troop's morale?"

One of the carpenters working on the new lab was from Molokai. He had been giving Sandra lessons in pidgin. She tried some out on Morrow; "Eh braddah you know what brah, you right you know. We got nuth'un to be but wait brah."

Reverting to 'normal speak' she continued, "Morrow it seems like we have been waiting forever. The Centron boss says two more weeks to hook up the power plant and water system–then we'll be up and running. All of our equipment has arrived and most of it is unpacked and installed. For six weeks my guys and gals have slaved over the experimental design. The lab's almost ready, but not quite. We have to finish the channel connection to the lab's observation area and install the big operation view port window. That way we will be able to monitor the Twin's body language under water during the testing process. We have what you might call a bad case of channel fever. We are very anxious to get underway."

"I see your point. But in all the years that I have worked out here, no project that I know of has ever come together this rapidly. Every time I go back to the Main Island, it seems like a ghost town. You must have everyone on the atoll over here pounding nails."

Sandra relaxed and leaned back as Morrow massaged her shoulders. "Guess what? As usual, I'm part of the experiment. I will go through the same training program as the Twins."

Morrow bent over and looked into her eyes. "You mean you'll be locked up in isolation for days at a time?"

"In some of the tests...yes, I will."

"Well we better make the most of the situation," replied Morrow with a mischievous wink and a toothy smile. He whispered close to her ear, "Maybe we should take the skiff out for a couple of hours...you know, official business. I know of this little island called 'Ruby' that lies up the lagoon a ways that I have been planning to show you."

"Ah ha! I get your drift, doctor. A consultation does seem in order, doesn't it? I'll change and meet you at the boat in fifteen minutes. Why don't you bring some cold beer? It'll be hot out there—especially this time of day."

The challenge of observing and the joy of playing with the dolphins in a natural three-dimensional arena had been fascinating, but it did seem like Centron was taking forever to finish the work. The building framework had virtually sprung up overnight, but it was the little things that were dragging on and on.

Although the lab was relatively small and simple in design, the demands of the research required that the walls be thick and carefully fabricated. The experimental stage, called the Sensory Deprivation Chamber,

or SDC for short, would need to be entirely stimu-
lus-free in order to control subtle influences that might
bias the results.

Sandra had explained to the foreman that the lab
was like a sophisticated darkroom, except in this case
power surges and all minute sound intrusions must be
controlled in addition to preventing light leaks. Tiny
variations in electrical cycles, illumination levels, or
sonic vibrations could provide cues to the world outside
of the lab. These clues might only be detected by the
subconscious mind of the experimental subject, but
could seriously impact the outcome of the tests.

Extraneous signals could likewise not be tolerated
because they affected circadian rhythms–the endogenous internal cycles inherent in living organisms. Circadian rhythms were revealed when an animal or a plant
was confined in a constant environment. During the
early stages of circadian research, investigators were
amazed to find that regular patterns of behavior were
manifest as alternating bouts of rest and activity–even
when natural cues, like the sunrise or sunset, were
eliminated.

Songbirds, being conveniently small and easily
isolated, had provided a favorite subject in early circadian studies in which a chart recorder wired to a
wooden perch automatically recorded the frequency and
duration of periods of activity and rest. Under natural,
ambient circumstances, the bird behaved normally; it
flew about its cage during the day and slept quietly on
its perch at night. Even when the cage was installed in
a soundproof box and the lights were constantly
dimmed, the bird still maintained a regular pattern of
movement and rest that corresponded to the conditions
outside–even though it had no way of knowing what the
conditions were. The same phenomenon was observed if
the lights were left on continuously.

But over a period of a few days, a noticeable change in the cycle took place. Each day the bird woke up and went to sleep a few minutes later than the day before—its internal clock had drifted off schedule. After several weeks, the bird's activity cycle gradually shifted until it was the exact opposite of the conditions outside. However, scientists found a way to arrest this slippage. A brief flash from a strobe light caused the bird to entrain its rhythm to the new artificial dawn. The technique of using an intense flash of light to reset the internal clock was now an accepted therapeutic technique used to treat chronic insomnia in humans.

The study of circadian rhythms became a popular research endeavor at a number of colleges and universities in the U.S. After five decades of research, circadian cycles had been discovered in every species of plant and animal that had been studied—even microorganisms demonstrated internal rhythms. Entomologists documented the precision by which locusts, which spend seven years in a larval form hidden deep in the forest leaf litter, suddenly emerge on cue to mate. Similarly palolo worms in the Caribbean simultaneously erupt from the sediments after twelve months of feeding in the bottom muck to inundate hundreds of square miles of the ocean surface with copulating adults. The act of mating lasts only for a few hours, and then the spent worms sink into the abyss and die.

Just as hermit crabs use their clocks to gauge the rise and fall of the tide, plants coordinate the blossoming of their flowers with the increasing length of days in the spring. And studies on humans revealed that many individuals wake just before their alarm rings—all processes carefully timed and regulated by circadian rhythms. An accurate internal clock was even discovered to play a key role in the transoceanic crossings of migratory birds. Periods of rest, feeding, digestion, and reproduction were all cued to the mysterious internal rhythms of life and death.

Scientists had yet to uncover the cellular clockworks that time these events, but there was no doubt whatsoever about their paramount importance of circadian rhythms to the healthy conduct of life. Medical researchers discovered that if the endogenous rhythm of a human were disturbed over even short periods of time, altered states of consciousness would develop. Longterm disruption of that phase of sleep characterized by rapid eye movement was particularly devastating to the subjects–an effect long known and utilized by Viet Cong interrogators during the Vietnam War.

At Randamount College, Sandra had conducted experiments in which she had floated motionlessly in a thick solution of saltwater sealed in a sound and light-proof sensory deprivation tank. With the water and atmosphere maintained exactly at body temperature, her nervous system became completely cut off from outside stimulation. She had used sensory deprivation in combination with the potent mind calming method of meditation to achieve a mental state characterized by long period alpha waves. Under these stringently controlled circumstances, she had consistently been able to manifest statistically significant rates of success in the identification of playing cards and the shapes of objects located in another room. But 'statistically significant' was the hitch. Only after thousands of trials would the trend emerge. The numbers indicated that ESP was there all right, but it was only a very slight improvement over random chance.

In hindsight, Sandra's breakthrough was quite obvious. She had hypothesized that the manipulation of a subject's circadian rhythm prior to sensory deprivation might unlock a more powerful form of ESP. After enduring a seven day regimen of constant dusk level illumination, during which her internal rhythm had slowly drifted away from that of the outside world, Sandra had been able to make card and object identifications with a ninety percent confidence score—a dramatic improvement over chance results.

This was an earthshaking discovery in the field of parapsychology and she had been amazed that no one had previously thought to combine the rhythm alteration and sensory deprivation. She had reasoned that the process of convincing her subconscious that day was night had bypassed or short circuited some of kind of neural hardwiring that normally inhibited ESP.

For a brief period of time, Sandra had even displayed signs of precognition—she seemed to know when the phone would ring and had accurately predicted the morning on which Santa Rosa received a wall-rattling thunderstorm—in spite of the on-going California drought. But the experience had been short-lived. For reasons unknown, she had become confused about the input that she was receiving. She soon lost confidence in her abilities and her test scores slid until she was actually performing worse than chance guessing would predict.

In the months that followed, Sandra and her team carefully repeated the entrainment process and duplicated the tests, but they failed to match their previous success. Since the results could not be repeated, the prior achievements became suspect. Sandra concluded that she had overloaded, there had just been too much input to quickly. Her system had shut down. She remembered having similar experiences as a child. Sometimes her visions had been exactly right, but on other occasions they were only artifacts of her subconscious.

Sandra again had come face to face with the basic primal question—how to distinguish her real psychic input from self-generated delusion. The disappointing conclusion was that her objectivity had been compromised–serving as both the principal investigator as well as the experimental subject had led to complications. The group had discussed the situation at length before reaching a consensus. Finally, they agreed to cut back the scope of the project to a more controllable format. Sandra had suggested working with a dolphin–an idea that was immediately embraced and adopted. She was convinced that dolphins had paranormal powers–plus they were easily trained. Unlike Sandra, a dolphin was not likely to become caught up in a spiritual whirlwind and lose its mental focus. The experiments would be conducted over the period of a year and begin with simple tests and finally expand to more complex tasks– if the dolphin cooperated that is. A specially designed computer would be incorporated into the project design to eliminate, or at least minimize, human interference. That only left two major questions: *How do we get a dolphin and "how do we get the money to do the research?*

Within a month the group had drafted a project plan and budget and submitted it to the NSF–where it would have remained for an interminable time without the fortuitous intervention of Robert McCord and the surprisingly generous financial support of General Pratt Houston. And now they had two dolphins instead of one, a new lab nearly ready for action, and a newly developed project plan just itching to be put into place. In the first round of tests, the computer in the control section of the lab would direct a robotic arm to select one of three wooden objects from a box and place it on a small pedestal.

Sandra would remain isolated in the SDC and attempt to use ESP to choose the shape of the object. The Twins would enjoy a ringside seat and be able to view both Sandra directly and the object on a large monitor. In this fashion, the dolphins would learn techniques which they would be subsequently asked to emulate. Then the Twins would be tested. If they demonstrated any vestige of extrasensory perception, a second phase of experimentation would be initiated. In this experiment, Sandra would mentally visualize an object and the dolphins would attempt to make the correct identification. The goal was to determine if, under controlled conditions, information transfer was possible between human and dolphin. If they made it that far, the group hardly dared to speculate what wonders might lay ahead.

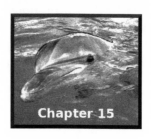

Chapter 15

PIG Island

The Lockheed C-141 jet carrying Eiger and his precious reel of tape containing the ANX virus touched down on the Main Island strip at three in the morning; the late hour chosen because he wanted to arrive as inconspicuously as possible. As soon as the jet rolled to a stop, two Centron personnel under contract to Chalmer loaded his gear into a pickup and drove him to a modern looking cruiser, which was waiting with diesels pounding at the dock. As soon as the crew cast off the mooring lines, the boat edged into deeper water and ran parallel to the Main Island on a heading that would take it to Parry, which according to General Houston's wishes was now referred to as the 'PIG' Island.

Eiger rested in the bow cabin, briefcase on his chest. The rhythm of the surging craft and the drone of the engine lulled him into an uneasy sleep. An hour later, he awoke to the changing pitch of the diesel as the boat slowed and settled deeper into the sea. On deck, sipping steaming coffee from a Styrofoam cup, Eiger could barely see the low shape of the island and the silhouette of palms in the starlight. When they docked, orange-clad Centron security police greeted them as they arrived and escorted them to the PIG lab.

The low vibration of underground air blowers, which resonated in the stairwell, grew in intensity as Eiger descended to the PIG lab entrance. Waiting at the bottom, a man wearing a t-shirt and shorts shook Eiger's hand and introduced himself as Dave Johnson, the facility supervisor.

"Welcome you to our little piece of the rock, Dr Eiger. We are very much honored by your visit. You will find that we enjoy many perks to make up for our life of isolation. First and foremost we have excellent chow. We also have a workout gym, an underground lap pool... and a voluminous library of music, literature, and movies on videotape. All we lack are a social life and suntans." He pulled the neck his shirt and said, "We dress pretty informally here. I hope you don't mind."

"Don't concern yourself Dave; I'll probably do the same. But what about the PIG? Is it up and running? I would like to see the latest performance stats."

"I am sure that you will be pleased. We followed your assembly instructions to the letter. The PIG currently exceeds all target parameters with a whole armada of viral detection systems in place. Follow me and I will introduce you to the new member of your family."

As Eiger stood gazing in appreciation at the EXXION, he held up his briefcase containing the tape holding the ANX virus and said, "Meet your opponent PIG. You are about to go to war!"

Dave said, "Does this mean that we can finally get started on ANX testing–yes I have been cleared by Commander Cummings. When he visited a few months back, he filled me in on your project. Now I understand why you have gone to all of this time and expense to build two of the world's most advanced computers in the middle of nowhere."

Eiger nodded. "That's an affirmative. I will be installing the virus in the ANX computer tomorrow night and then begin the first attack. Commander Cummings thinks it is best for me to travel at night, so since we are near dawn, I guess I'll have a chance to try out your atoll cuisine and guest quarters."

The Next Day
ANX Island

The Centron guards waiting in the darkness to greet Eiger as they docked at ANX Island were wearing the standard orange uniforms, but this time their attire included helmets and heavy, lead-soled boots. As Eiger disembarked, one of the guards handed him a uniform and helmet and then demonstrated how to put on the boots and use the respirator.

They trudged eerily through the darkness; their breathing systems emitted metallic rasping noises, which quickened with their exertion. Three men preceded Eiger and one followed behind as they shuffled along the path that glowed a dull white in the early morning light. The path angled upward from the beach and meandered through the dense jungle in the interior of the island. Eiger laughed out loud when his imagination conjured up an image of the burial procession from 'Twenty Thousand Leagues Under the Sea'.

A rush of chill air greeted Eiger as he pulled off his helmet and respirator and then followed the others into the underground chamber. Dim red lights along the walls provided barely enough illumination to navigate the treacherous steps. The EXXION that would launch the ANX attack commanded center stage behind a long span of glass. It would soon be home to Eiger's brain-

96

child that would instigate a barrage of viral attacks on the PIG.

Stacy Powers was very pleased to see Eiger and gave him a brief kiss on the cheek. "The only way we have to communicate is via our daily boat trip to the Centron post office. I just got the note that you sent alerting me that you would be arriving today. It is good to see you; the four of us on site are starting to drive each other crazy. It's like being in one of those NASA experiments investigating the effects of prolonged confinement on astronauts."

She handed Eiger a passkey and said, "I have one and now you have one; that's it. Just as you ordered."

Eiger told Stacy that he needed some privacy and was only to be disturbed if General Houston should call.
After she left, he took a seat at the computer station and typed in his password. He patted the EXXION's control panel and said, "It's you and me now kiddo. I hope this doesn't backfire and turn into a disaster."

He pulled the tape from its case and inserted it into the digital tape drive which whirred into motion as it loaded the ANX virus assembly algorithms into the EXXION's memory banks. After seeing flashing green lights sprinkled across the control board, he took a deep breath and then punched the launch sequence activator button to initiate assembly of the ANX virus. The lights went out and then flashed red– warning that the ANX virus was alive and dangerous.

Chapter 16

The Boston Whaler canted to one side, its bow resting on dry sand secured by an anchor set high on the beach. The usual trade winds had momentarily subsided, leaving a glassy resin-smooth finish on the placid lagoon. Ruby was a tiny islet of palms completely encircled by beaches the color and consistency of table sugar. The deeply saturated hue of the lagoon waters and the sand soaked in the afternoon sunlight gave the scene a vibrant touch like a slick travel poster touting the color and romance of the South Pacific.

Morrow leaned on one elbow and playfully caressed Sandra's shoulder. "Now you know why I like this place so much. When I'm back in California lecturing and performing all of the rituals demanded of a tenured faculty member I often think of this little beach. It is amazing that one life can encompass two existences so markedly different. And now you're here with me...and I hope that you will be with me back there too...somehow. I know that we have only been together for a few weeks, but I think that I could be falling in love with you Sandra Grant. You've made my life quite interesting!"

TELEPATHIC DOLPHIN EXPERIMENT

"Oh Morrow. I didn't think I'd ever say it, but I feel that way too!" Breaking from a deep kiss, Sandra pleaded, "But let's not rush things. Okay?"

Morrow laughed and released her gently. "All right then. I just can't seem to get enough of you. Tell me, how do dolphins fit into all of this? You told me about John Lily's work...and dolphins do seem to be very intelligent, but do they have paranormal powers...and what makes you think so?"

"When I was a little girl going to school in Key West my grandparents loved to take me to the Dolphin Research Center up on Grass Key. They have an incredible program there in which they allow tourists and local dolphin fans to get into the water with the animals and the dolphins love it. They get caressed and entertained by humans morning and afternoon, day in and day out. They must like it because they can leave whenever they want. They are all wild animals that swim voluntarily into the facility's lagoon. They aren't fed either—unless they are sick."

Morrow replied, "I remember reading about that place. Animal rights activists made a big stink about dolphins being held in captivity and all that. Then they found out that the center is like a zoo in reverse. The animals are free to come and go and the people are restrained...they couldn't complain much about that kind of setup. You know, sometimes people with no background whatsoever in science get all worked up about the stupidest things. As far as I can tell, they crave the limelight more than the cause which they advocate. They could be against the teaching of human evolution in the classroom...or cutting up frogs in biology lab. They are regular pains in the ass if you ask me. Eco-terrorists are obviously the worst."

Sandra sat up and laughed at Morrow. "Wow that's a strong condemnation coming from a person that is so dedicated to saving the ocean. But I see your point. It seems that a lot of uniformed people with too much time on their hands learn a few buzzwords and become an expert overnight. Ask them to define an ecosystem and they'll draw a blank. But they'll raise hell protecting one that they think is threatened.

"I agree with you one hundred percent."

"Anyway, my grandmother had well developed psychic powers. Don't look at me that way. She really did! And like I said, she was able to converse with animals including the dolphins. She claimed that they had highly evolved telepathy. We had been to the dolphin center so many times that the director let us in after hours and was flabbergasted to discover that the dolphins always knew when my grandmother was coming for a visit. They gathered at the end of the lagoon milling around and waiting. When she got out of the car, they raced around in a circle and did flips."

"Sandra, I can honestly say that you are the only person on this planet who could tell me a story like this that I wouldn't think is crazy. Your credentials speak for themselves, but why is this a secret? Why don't the dolphins just send us an ESP message to the press and let the cat out of the bag. A story like this would be certain to top the evening news."

Sandra fished in the ice chest and brought out a pair of frosty bottles of beer and handed one to Morrow. "Now this may sound to you like a lot of religious hocus pocus, but the dolphin's abilities are indeed recognized by many people who believe that their ESP powers exist. I'll explain what I mean. The Dolphin Research Center receives most of its operating budget from foundations that sponsor learning programs for disabled children. There are many well-documented cases in which severely retarded individuals, ones with long histories of unresponsiveness to parent or teacher, were immensely improved in just a single afternoon at the DRC. One reason is that as soon as a handicapped person enters the water, the dolphins go out of the way to compensate–touching a blind girl or allowing a crippled child to cling to their back and experience the joy of swimming.

"Wow, I have never heard about this. Please continue."

"The standard medical explanation is that the dolphins sense the deficiencies with their sonar, but that just reflects the bias and closed mindedness of the scientific community. In my opinion there is a lot more going on than just sonar sounding. The dolphins are able to associate with the human subconscious. But a quote 'normal person' has so many defenses built up that they entirely miss the exchange. Retarded children obviously have special problems. That is true...but they also retain an open mind that is lost later in life. They still believe in magic. The point seems quite obvious to me. Any autistic child is a very different person around a dolphin. For the time being they become tuned in and the life just seems to pour back into them. There are cases in which young people have been permanently healed after only one session at the DRC."

Morrow interjected, "I have been around closed minded scientists all my life. I can easily believe that they would not even consider the possibility that ESP or any kind of spiritual process might be involved."

"Of course not. They are quite threatened by the concept. History is filled with book-burners and bigots. For some reason, the field of parapsychology especially arouses the wrath of non-believers. Hollywood scriptwriters haven't helped either. Astrology, tea leaves and paranormal ghost stories have been lumped in with bonafide psychic research in the minds of most people. Religion is against it too–which is really funny if you

RON S. NOLAN

think about it. The purpose of religion is to control human behavior and only selected leaders are God's official ambassadors to earthlings. Well, talking to God seems right off like pretty substantial evidence for psychic phenomena. But the church refuses to consider the possibility of ESP; they relegate it to the same category as witches and warlocks–definitely not good wholesome Sunday folk. Now there's some real bigotry for you."

"I have so many questions about this subject that I don't know where to start. All I can say is that it's just one more reason to spend the rest of my life with you. I want to find out how all this works. But one last question for now. Your grandmother talked to dolphins. Do you?"

"That's a good one. As a matter of fact that is precisely what we are here to find out. My grandmother had extraordinary abilities. I don't know of any other person alive today who can do what she so easily did back then. At this time, I probably get about the same feelings around the Twins that you do. Sometimes I sense the beginning of what may be thoughts. It's funny. Sometimes I think that they are in charge of this entire experiment. But just like you, I have all sorts of conscious barriers that interrupt communication. My work here is to test some theories that may ultimately break those barriers down."

Morrow grasped Sandra's hand and squeezed it tight. He asked, "Well, were you able to communicate with your grandmother...by telepathy I mean?"

Sandra smiled and kissed him and said in a soft voice, "Yes sometimes I could see and talk to her from a distance. She had a way of making it happen–like a catalyst in a chemical reaction. I'm searching for that missing element. I haven't been able to connect with anyone other than Grandma. But I do have a distinct advantage over other paranormal researchers–I know that it is possible and I believe! What we learn from the Twins may show us the way. And now...Psych 101 class is over for the day. We better head back before my teammates get worried."

"How about a quick snorkel out to one of my study reefs?'"

"Let's do it and then head back to the lab."

Chapter 17

Department of Defense
Washington, D.C.

C ommander William Cummings apologized for his tardiness even though he was right on time.

"Have a seat, Commander."

As Cummings sat on the leather couch, the General rose and paced back and forth. Behind Houston, two American flags stationed on each side of his wide desk gave the impression that the General was marching in a veteran's parade.

Cummings asked, "Is the room secured sir?"

Houston nodded affirmative.

"Then I report mission accomplished. The data tape containing the ANX can be smuggled into Cuba. Once the Havana KGB inserts it into their mainframe, it will flash directly into the USSR command network."

"Give me the details Commander."

"First, as you are well aware, new technology continues to show up in Soviet hands despite our government's most determined efforts to stop the flow. With the new trade agreements, U.S. Customs is only able to inspect a small fraction of the shipments to the USSR. Things get through one way or another and some of those items are software programs. Using your authority at the National Security Agency, I obtained a list of a half-dozen suspected software leaks."

"That sounds about right, scary, but about right."

"I screened the suspects and found our mole. This is a strange case. Our man is Frederick Sampson. He is a research scientist at Kiwala National Laboratories based out of San Diego, California. He was a member of the team that developed sensors for the Brilliant Pebbles component of the Strategic Defense Initiative, which was terminated last year. So far he has not been assigned specifically to a new project; instead he has been on-call to help other researches on an as needed basis—which has given him wide access and carte blanche to learn about a wide variety of secret SDI programs. For the last couple of months he has been working on weekends and taking Mondays and Tuesdays off."

"Well he certainly has the opportunity to sell us out big time. But what's his motive and who does he report to?"

"For a scientist with his experience and background it is very unusual not to be assigned to a project for more than a couple of months. I spoke to his boss at Kiwala Labs and he said that he couldn't explain anything additional about the case because it was personal matter. I have no idea what he was talking about or how it all got started."

"Maybe he caught Samson in bed with his wife. We really don't care, do we? How does he deliver the classified goods and to whom and where?"

"He transports the contraband as files on tape and delivers them to the KGB in Havana—so far he has made two trips this month."

"How does he get to Havana?"

"Since he is based in San Diego it is pretty straight forward. Early on Monday morning he drives his car to Tijuana, parks in the lot at the border, walks over the bridge to the airport, flies to Mexico City on Avolar Airlines, and then continues to Havana on Aeromexico. He returns the same way on Tuesday so he is back to work at Kiwala Labs on Wednesday morning."

"Can we bribe or force Sampson to double on them?"

"No sir, I don't think that it is wise to involve him—at least knowingly that is. He is fairly new at the spy game and might reveal ANX if interrogated KGB style."

"Yes, I see what you mean. Better to stick with the pros when it comes to this operation level. How will you make the switch?"

"First I would like to set up a twenty-four hour surveillance on Sampson to track his every move before his next mission and be ready to move in on short notice. Once we get the details, we will do a dry run. The plan will be to stop several boarding passengers at the Tijuana airport security gate, which will involve taking them to an interrogation room and moving their carry-on and luggage to another room for inspection, and then returning it to the passengers who resume boarding. We will photograph the tape model and label information to make sure the ANX version will be unde-tected by Sampson after we make the switch. Of course we will have to work some sort of arrangement with the Mexican authorities and station our agents nearby."

"That shouldn't be a problem. Make sure you coordi-nate the exchange with Eiger."

"Roger that. As soon as Eiger gives me the ANX tape we will be on alert for the next time Sampson heads for Tijuana and go through the passenger check routine once more. Sampson should not be overly alarmed since he will have been through the procedure before."

TELEPATHIC DOLPHIN EXPERIMENT

The General rose to his feet and raised his fist. "But this time we will switch the tape. Right?"

"That is correct, sir."

"When do you expect Eiger to deliver the ANX?"

"He is currently on the atoll and has begun preliminary testing. I will give you updates as I receive them."

"You have done well Commander, proceed as soon as possible."

Chapter 18

The Sensory Deprivation Chamber held a potent mystery like a stage, quiet and waiting for the players to arrive. The deep pool occupied most of the room—its silken surface cast a diffuse blue glow on the walls, which were lined with acoustical paneling that resembled cardboard egg cartons layered as cushions and painted black. A bank of one-way mirrors in the far wall provided observers in the adjacent control lab an unobtrusive view into the vault. The paneling was so effective at absorbing sound that the experimental subjects experienced a sense of vertigo when they first entered the chamber—a sudden sort sinking feeling that the floor was falling away. A white tile-lined tunnel connected the pool with the channel allowing the dolphins easy access to the chamber. To prevent the transmission of tidal forces, which might serve as clues to cycles and rhythms outside the lab, a metal hatch provided a watertight barrier.

A plexiglass partition spanned the length of the chamber. When lowered guillotine-like from the ceiling, it fused solidly with the pool floor, bisecting the SDC vertically from top to bottom. The vibration-proof wall was designed to provide complete sensory isolation between the compartments of the chamber, but internal louvers could be opened to allow visual communication. A maze of umbilical wires draped like tree snakes from both sides of the partition connecting cameras and sensors in the chamber with monitoring equipment in the control lab. The investigators could either gaze directly at the pool through the panorama of one-way mirrors or consult a wall of monitors that displayed continuous images captured by the surveillance cameras.

The human half of the chamber was endowed with all of the conveniences of a modern efficiency apartment. A system of lightproof tunnels allowed food and supplies to be transferred with ease—perishables were replenished simply by opening a panel in the back of the refrigerator. Sandra had several choices for exercise; tethered laps in the pool, a workout on a compact Nautilus gym, or an exercise bike. The apartment was furnished with an extensive library of popular fiction and a collection of classical and popular CDs. At the last minute, Sandra had lugged into place a VCR with a case of movies she had saved for the occasion. Every effort had been made to make the seven days of isolation as comfortable as possible.

The needs of the dolphins were also attended to. Their favorite toys, a beach ball and a foam life ring, floated in their half of the SDC. They would receive twice daily rations of cut fish supplemented with vitamins—even live fish could be slid down a stainless steel trough to alleviate the boredom of confinement.

The solitude of the SDC contrasted markedly with the commotion and chaos of the control lab where concrete walls and floors reverberated with the hum of sophisticated electronics and the whoosh of cool air conditioning. Conversations were accordingly loud and strained, reflected inward by the bare walls. Finally, the last of the Centron construction workers, an electrician, packed up his box of tools and circuit testers, bowed to the cheering group of onlookers and departed for the relative tranquility of the Main Island.

The grad students and technicians were fast to stake out personal territories in the new facility. Government Issue gray metal desks were stashed wherever space permitted. Cork boards were epoxied to the cement walls in short order sprouting the flow charts, photographs, and cartoon characters that characterize the usual decor of a research laboratory. A hanging mobile fashioned from silver wire in the shape of dolphins gyrated slowly over the water cooler stirred by currents from the air conditioning.

Most of the technicians' activities centered around the Convex supercomputer. The Convex directed the experiments and precisely monitored and regulated the SDC environment. A flatbed console carpeted with switches, meters, and keyboards provided access to the computer. Above and behind the console, a bank of video screens displayed the output of each high-resolution remotely controlled camera in the chamber and presented scrolling banks of color-coded graphs, tables, text and figures.

The Convex also controlled the 'droid', a plastic and steel robot fitted with articulated limbs and delicate carbon fiber fingers. The droid stood firmly bolted to the floor next to the flatbed control station. Fine cables and mini pulleys linked the multi-jointed appendages serving as the robot's muscles and tendons. Two video cameras provided stereovision to the droid. The cameras were directed towards a brightly illuminated stage upon which the robot arm, under control of the Convex, would place objects for the experimental subjects to identify.

TELEPATHIC DOLPHIN EXPERIMENT

Video monitors in the dolphin and human sectors of the chamber were wired to deliver either Convex generated commands or an image of the stage. Either monitor could be switched on or off depending upon the design of the experiment. In the dolphin side, an oversized, waterproof keyboard had been installed next to a video screen located just beneath the pool surface. The electronic gear allowed the dolphins to respond by pressing the appropriate key with their snout. The keyboard had six large keys–four in the shape of the objects to be chosen, a (+) that meant 'yes' and a (-) that meant 'no'. Sandra's input device was more compact, the size of a hand-held calculator, and contained an identical set of symbols and characters.

At five in the afternoon, after a harried last-minute session of equipment testing, Sandra popped the cork on a bottle of champagne and carefully portioned the contents into Dixie cups. Toasts and congratulations abruptly halted the settling in process. Another bottle quickly replaced the first. Caught up in the spirit of celebration, Sandra announced that the rest of the lab setup could wait one more day and ordered a celebration in honor of the occasion. At last the lab was finished! As usual, everyone ended up in the lagoon swimming and playing with the Twins.

Morrow had invited his close friend, John Sturtevant to meet Sandra and her team. Preferred simply to be called 'Mr. John' or 'Chief', he was a descendant of the original German traders that had engaged in a basic copra economy with the Marshallese in the 1880's and was currently the chosen leader of the Marshall Islands His long kinky hair and hibiscus flowered lavalava matched his islander origins, but the colorful illusion collapsed in the wake of his clipped German accent and sharp wit which he had honed at Harvard where he had received a Masters in Business Administration.

RON S. NOLAN

Mr. John certainly didn't look much like a bureaucrat. His hair was wild and thick, and his skin tanned so deeply that he was nearly black. He was solidly put together with broad shoulders, well-defined muscles and smooth, glistening skin. He had an uncanny ability to look formidable in spite of his somewhat frivolous lavalava. But most remarkable were the bright blue eyes from his German ancestral heritage that contrasted with the darkness of his skin—eyes that shifted constantly, seeming to take inventory of everything in the vicinity.

Sitting half submerged in the lagoon while carefully cradling a cup of champagne and enjoying himself to the fullest as was his inherent nature, Mr. John delighted in pointing out the spiritual qualities of water. He laughed at the audacity of 'new age' fads centered on water-based rebirthing and psychic healing.

"Water has been the main source of spiritual enlightenment and inspiration in my people since the beginning of time," he declared to the group of fascinated listeners. "Just think about it. Even Christian baptism is a water ritual. We are after all, composed of mostly water ourselves. Sound carriers faster in water. Likewise, we are weightless when we swim. Getting wet stops our internal dialog. No matter how many problems we have, floating in water makes them unimportant—at least until we hit dry land again. These 'New Agers' advocate water's powers like they had discovered them themselves. They certainly haven't been paying much attention to the obvious, have they?"

"Well, I have observed," laughed Sandra raising her cup of champagne, "that a cold drink thrown into the face of an obnoxious drunk does an excellent job of stopping them in their tracks."

"I'm sure a beautiful young blond like you would know about things like that," interjected Morrow.

TELEPATHIC DOLPHIN EXPERIMENT

"But seriously, researchers at PIU found that immersing a harbor seal's head in seawater instantly lowers its heart rate–they called it the 'diving response.' I watched them conduct some of the experiments. Instead of going to all of the trouble to put sensors on a diving seal at sea, they just trained a cooperative harbor seal to stick its head in a bucket of water. That simulated a dive exactly."

Sandra was especially interested in Mr. John's ideas. His claim that water was a spiritual medium closely paralleled her own beliefs. She maintained that one of the reasons that dolphins might be endowed with paranormal abilities was linked to the extraordinary properties of water–especially water's ability to induce altered states of consciousness. However, there was one indisputable reason why dolphins might be more psychically tuned than humans, marine mammals had evolved consciousness millions of years before the first hominids strolled across the African savanna, dolphins had the advantage of a lot more time to evolve their paranormal powers than had humans.

Around a campfire, which rivaled the fiery display of the tropical sunset, Chet broke out a bottle of his favorite white wine and opened a can of sardines that he had brought with him from California–much to Mr. John's amusement.

Mr. John choked, "Now I know why you American's continue to baffle me. You fly at great expense canned fish netted in Europe to a lagoon twenty thousand miles away that abounds in just such delicacies."

And then he laughed until tears appeared in his eyes and he began to hiccup in uncontrollable spasms. Finally he stood and burped, then retrieved a jointed Hawaiian spear and a dive mask from his pack. He rummaged deeper in the pack and withdrew a mesh bag cinched with a drawstring. After screwing the sections of the shaft together, he waded into the lagoon. The Twins immediately joined him. Seeming to detect his plan, they became agitated and chattered eagerly. He was after fish...never before had a human hunted with them!

The white soles of Mr. John's bare feet and the silhouette of the Twin's dorsal fins were all that those waiting on shore could see in the dusk. As darkness settled, Morrow pointed out green streaks of phosphorescence as the tail thrusts of the dolphins agitated luminescent plankton in the water. Sandra observed that they seemed to be diving together and surfacing very close to one another.

Just as the stars brightened in the blue-black sky, a large "V" shape fast approached the beach. Morrow jumped up, alarmed that it might be one of the lagoon's fierce tiger sharks, but the disturbance began hooting and laughing hysterically. Morrow relaxed, it was Mr. John clutching tightly to each of the Twin's dorsal fins as they ferried him to the beach where he landed with his dive bag full of wriggling goatfish. Covered with sand, he stood and lovingly rubbed Tom and Sally on the tops of their heads. Then he reached into the bag and pulled two goatfish out by their tails. He tossed the fish to the dolphin's open mouths. "One for you...and one for you too my friend. Thank you for showing me your hot spot...and the ride back."

Although the fish broiled over the open fire were magnificent and the evening electric, Sandra sat silently and withdrew into her thoughts. She felt that something of the highest order had taken place.

Could it be that the Twins had really shown Mr. John where to fish...even assisted him in fishing? They certainly gave him a lift home. Has he been able to establish a link with them somehow? In such a short period of time? Maybe he has had a moving experience...perhaps the Twins touched him with their power and Mr. John needs time to think it over before broaching such a bizarre notion to relative strangers. As a matter of fact, probably no one has even told him what we're doing here. Maybe he thinks my group is connected in some way to the military. He might even think we are conducting secret tests for the Navy! No matter, tomorrow we begin. The very first experiment...featuring me, Dr. Sandra Grant, is about to commence.

Morrow was gone when she awoke. The island was still, the trade winds not yet charged to life. After a quick breakfast, she found Chet sitting in front of the Convex. She could see the excitement in his eyes. Without speaking she entered the SDC and closed the door of the mini apartment. She lay on the bed staring at the ceiling, still wondering if Mr. John had somehow already accomplished what she was just now setting out to do.

******

Without a sign that anything was changing, her days became the night of those outside. Sandra adjusted effortlessly. During her daily sensory deprivation sessions, when she floated in the pool in the mask and wetsuit, her grandmother stayed very close at hand— almost as if she was watching over her. Sandra lapsed into dreams of her past so vivid that she gradually lost contact with the experiment. She often had visions that involved the train in Key West. When she could control the dream, she would climb into the engineer's seat. And even though she was only visualizing the experience, the magic of the train was still strong. Her grandmother seemed to be coaching her, revealing her methods. Often the train was moving, speeding so fast that she could only catch flashing glimpses of the surroundings.

Then suddenly her grandmother would appear on the tracks in front of the train, the engine would slow, and then stop. Then the cycle would repeat. Throughout the days, she listened to her grandmother's teachings–lessons unlike those in books or the classroom, but instruction based upon feelings and sensitivity.

Once she even visualized the dolphins swimming along besides the train. She discovered that she could speak to them. The Twins seemed to be warning her that something was wrong, but when she pressed to know more, they became silent.

Later, in reporting the experience to Chet, she lightly explained away the visions as wishful thinking about the outcome of the experiment. Sandra recognized that she was venturing into what might be considered dangerous territory. She risked losing contact with reality permanently.

The effect that she was purposely striving for was indistinguishable from psychosis. She wondered if that was why the words 'psychic' and 'psychosis' were so similar. After all, both terms had their roots in 'psyche', the Greek word for "soul." She used her growing love from Morrow as her emotional strength and her trust in grandmother as her guardian spirit. Ultimately, however, she relied upon Chet to make sure that she did not cross too many boundaries–go down so deep that she couldn't come back.

Chet and Sandra had agreed upon a system, which they called the "reality check." During a deprivation experiment, Chet would casually interject a minor technical question into the conversation. The question was a prearranged signal–a test to see if, despite appearances to the contrary, Sandra retained control of her mind.

If she overlooked the question, or hesitated in responding, Chet would pull the plug and halt the experiment.

TELEPATHIC DOLPHIN EXPERIMENT

Up until now, Sandra had always passed the test. She might be pretty far out there, but she had always known the bottom line. Nevertheless, the lucidness of some of her visions centered on the train frankly scared her. It might be going just too far. It was as if some powerful force seemed to draw her to that old engine.

Chapter 19

At precisely midnight on the eighth day of the experiment, Chet took his position at the console of the Convex and directed the Twins and Sandra to their stations. In the SDC, feeling fine and ready to get on with the experiment, Sandra taped dozens of sensors to different parts of her body. Then careful not to jar any of them loose, she struggled into the tight fitting, neoprene wetsuit and entered the warm water. She attached the snap ends of several elastic tethers to rings on the arms and legs of her suit; they would hold her lightly in place. Then she floated onto her back.

After checking that she could easily see the monitor high on the wall, she placed the keyboard on top of her stomach. Sandra keyed the (+) button in response to the computer prompt 'READY TO ACTIVATE TEST'? The louvers inside the partition slowly opened presenting the Twins with a clear view of Sandra. The dolphins seemed to sense that something new was about to happen. They swam in a circle, alternating between watching Sandra and their underwater monitor, which for the first time displayed a split-screen view of the empty stage in the left half and a close up of Sandra's keyboard in the right.

After a week of isolation–the time it took to completely reverse Sandra's circadian rhythm, she was more than ready to get on with the experiment. But because of her excitement, it took longer than usual for her to sink into an alpha state. She focused on synchronizing her personal mantra with the rhythm of her own breathing.

Whispering softly to herself, she began the ritual.

'L i g h t' (inhale)...
'S e a' (exhale)...
'L i g h t' (inhale)...
'S e a (exhale)...

'L i g h t' (inhale)...
'S e a' (exhale)...
'L i g h t' (inhale)...
'S e a (exhale)...

Slowly she attained a mental state known to parapsychologists as the 'combined effect'. It was the cerebral state for which she had so diligently prepared. The effect only materialized after repeated sessions of complete sensory deprivation–and only then if the subject's internal rhythm had been exactly reversed. Her hypothesis was that the effect would provide a momentary window through which high-level telepathic powers would briefly emerge.

The soft pounding of Sandra's heart was her only sensation. The beat increased in volume until it formed the totality of her existence. Time ceased to have meaning. Her mind floated calmly into a void of nothingness. Then a tiny mono tonal voice drew her back to the pool.

The voice was calling, "Sandra, time to begin...you must come back, Sandra."

Sandra heard the sounds, but they had no meaning. She felt a slight surge of irritation as the phrases intruded again and again into her conscious awareness.

Suddenly she jerked at the knees and elbows. Her mind was beginning to surface.

Chet scanned the wall of readouts. "Okay gang, this is it! She's there now. Keep alert. Give me a full systems check...right now, darn it!"

The technicians reported, "Green on physio...green on EEG...green on vital signs."

"Affirmative on green...here we go. Please watch your readouts carefully and let me know immediately if she begins to red line," ordered Chet.

"Sandra...Sandra can you hear me? It's Chet, Sandra. You may open your eyes now."

Her eyes suddenly snapped open like the dead reawakening. She looked confused and afraid and began to struggle against the harness.

"It's okay Sandra. You're doing just fine...just relax now. I repeat you are doing just fine. We're right on target."

Sandra mumbled incoherently. Then she tried again. "Chet what happened? It didn't work for some reason."

Chet smiled as he glanced at the strong alpha wave signal displayed on the uppermost monitor. "Oh don't worry, girl. You're there all right–right where we want you. Just stay relaxed; all indicators are right on the mark. How do you feel?"

"That's just it...I don't feel anything. I can see around me, but I can't feel anything at all. Now I remember... this is normal, isn't it? I really am there, aren't I?"

"Yes, yes, yes. You're reorienting faster than ever before. Just don't rush it, okay?"

"Easy for you to say," she retorted in a more normal

voice. "You haven't been stuck inside this contraption all week. Let's get on with it. I think I can move now. I feel certain that I have reached center. Let's give it a try."

Sandra remained in the water to maintain a constant body temperature. This helped prolong the period of prime awareness. The experiment must begin immediately. After all of this preparation, she would only have three hours of enhanced telepathy–that is if it worked at all. She would then gradually lose her newly acquired ability as the combined effect dissipated. And so far, the method had only worked on her.

Sandra's monitor displayed 'READY'. After a few moments, a '?' appeared. Sandra then focused her mind on the stage located on the other side of the wall. Somewhere behind her eyes, an image of a sphere appeared. She punched the symbol of a circle on her keypad and was immediately rewarded with a beep from the monitor–her choice had been correct!

A side view of the train suddenly materialized on the screen. Sandra momentarily averted her gaze and a '?' took its place. She sensed a cube, and then responded. Another beep was followed by still another question mark. Her thoughts wandered to Morrow, but she forced her concentration back to the monitor and began the cyclic repetition of her mantra. Automatically her breathing fell in sync with the phrasing. She closed her eyes and saw a cylinder, then keyed the pad followed by another beep. Every time her mind began to drift off course, she forcibly grounded her thoughts by repeating her mantra. She realized that she was now audibly droning the words as the session continued.

"Very good, Sandra." Chat's voice surprised her. "You're really right on...that's two hundred and fifty correct choices. No errors whatsoever. I think your audience on the other side is quite impressed–they have their noses glued to the screen. Let's take a break."

•

RON S. NOLAN

"That's amazing. It seems like I just got started."

"For you information, we've been at this for two hours. Mr. John brought over some fresh ahi sashimi. I'll put a plate in the back of your refer. Let's take a half hour and then finish up."

As Sandra awkwardly used chopsticks to wolf down the raw fish, Chet coached her over the PA. "Now don't start thinking about any goofy stuff. You just gotta stay tuned to the experiment. Remember you are only here to show the Twins how ESP works—you're not to go way out on us." And then he threw in the check phrase.

Sandra responded, "I get the message. I'm fine. I can't believe how right on I feel. There is no doubt about the choice of objects. I just know which one is on the stage. It really must be that I see it somehow, although I hadn't realized that until now—just this second while I was talking."

Chet replied with obvious relief, "That's great to hear. You were never this accurate at Randamount. I mean, how could you do better than perfect? Just one word of caution. Something very different is happening this time. When you were asleep last night, you manifested some form of telekinesis. That's why your notes were spread all over the floor when you woke up this morning. You put on quite a performance. I have it all on videotape too."

"I wondered about that...thought I must have been sleepwalking or something. No kidding...telekinesis. You're right, let's wind this up. I really need to get outdoors and feel the sun on my face. I think I've lost my tan already," she laughed nervously.

Now there was a definite air of concern in Chet's voice. "Look, if you start hearing or seeing things that aren't part of the experiment, we'll stop. Okay? Doc, you are wonderful. Morrow is here watching and—never mind. I don't want you to get off track."

TELEPATHIC DOLPHIN EXPERIMENT

Sandra looked up at the one-way mirror and saw her image in the reflection. She said, "Hi Morrow, pick me up at eight–or in eight hours whatever time it really is out there?"

Then she zipped up her wetsuit and returned to the pool for the final round of testing. The experimental procedure was repeated with the same results–all perfect scores. But ninety minutes into the test, her accuracy dropped off dramatically. Then only rarely did she hear the beep after she made her choice. The effect had evaporated.

Sandra left the pool, her duty as test subject completed. She impatiently stripped of the wetsuit and probes and sprinted into the control lab. Chet embraced her briefly then handed her a cold beer. She surprised the group of onlookers by draining the whole can in one long, continuous guzzle. She laughed and roughly jerked her forearm over her lips in an exaggerated cowboy-like gesture. "One of the Centron construction guys taught me how to do that," she laughed. "Now the fun begins. Let's see if the Twins learned anything."

Chet keyed the Convex to repeat the test protocol in the dolphin sector. The Twins' monitor cut to a single screen and flashed 'READY' as the robot placed a wooden cube on the stage. Then a '?' appeared. Tom immediately keyed the square symbol with his lower jaw. Both dolphins squeaked and chattered when the beep sounded.

Sandra closed her eyes, fingers tightly crossed. "Come on. Do it again...I know you can!"

But this time Sally slid past Tom and made the correct response. Another beep sounded along with more excited chattering. Again and again they politely took turns. Each time they keyed the correct symbol.

Chet counted, "Thirty-eight yes. They've got it. They've got it too!"

"Calm down now Chet, we have to be scientific about this." Sandra smiled as she gave his hand a tight squeeze. "Let's go until we find attenuation."

It was more a sense of relief than surprise that during the balance of the experiment, the Twins each tallied a perfect score. The experiment was an incontrovertible success. The Twins had telepathy! Five hours later, the dolphins were still making the correct decisions. The unknown agent that had degraded Sandra's telepathy was not affecting the Twins. Not only had they learned the rules of this bizarre game—but also they had outdone Sandra with their amazing results.

Chet reminded Sandra, "Look...this is all exciting— actually breathtaking is more like it, but you should take it easy now. You've been through a lot this week. Here comes your mate now."

Sandra leapt to her feet and lifted a surprised, happy Morrow off the ground with a hearty bear hug. She said over her shoulder, "Are you kidding? I've been cooped up in this prison all week and you want me to take it easy? Let's take the Twins and get the hell out of here. Where's the champagne? Get the champagne!"

Sensing the excitement, the Twins nudged at the canal entrance, chattering like a flock of fairy terns until the hatch swiveled open and they blasted into the channel at full speed. Instantly everyone, clothes and all, leaped into the lagoon and engaged in a crazy bout of dunk'em and ring round the rosy. The Twins behaved as if nothing out of the ordinary had just taken place.

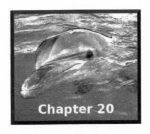

Chapter 20

Even as she slowly relaxed lying next to the Morrow on the beach in the starlight, Sandra could not halt the message running through her mind, *Wow! Now we really have something, don't we?* At last she collapsed into a dream state and drifted back to another place and time.

Lawrence, Kansas
1963

The trees were elms, not palms. Muddy river water boiled and churned as it swept beneath the suspension bridge and sorted its way past the dam through rows of wide metal culverts. A strong bull of a boy named Albert made his home in a grove of aspens next to the dam. The only commercial fisherman in Lawrence, Kansas, he lived in an Army surplus pup tent on the bank of the Kansas River–known locally by the Indian name as the 'Kaw'. Using homemade goggles cut from an inner tube and lenses from an old pair of glasses, Albert 'noodled' for giant catfish by holding his breath and plunging head first into the torrential flow blasting outwards from the massive tubes. Straining with all his might, he would push forward as far as possible—searching for the slippery, wide head of a mud cat that might weigh in at a hundred pounds or more. Noodling for catfish was not only illegal, it was also dangerous. Their fins possessed sharp, finely serrated spines ready to deliver a painful dose of toxin. A jab inflicted by a mud cat spine produced a jaw clenching pain and a severe ache in the groin. Even worse, the cut invariably became infected.

A hundred pound mud cat proved to be a formidable opponent for a young barehanded black man. But Albert was a tough kid and noodling was the only regular work he could find, other than stacking cartons at the cardboard box company—which he did when the river ran high, flooding the spillway.

This morning he could see bits of blue sky through rents in the canvas of the weather beaten tent. The early sun brought little warmth to his stiff, slept-on-the-cold-ground bones. His first thoughts were about the new fish—maybe the biggest one he had ever seen. Last night at dusk, he had spotted its massive head and long, black shiny whiskers protruding from the seventh tube. The sound of the river boiling and hissing lulled him back to sleep. He dreamed that another man was after 'Mistah Big' and awoke with a start. Jumping to his feet and throwing back the flap of the tent, he relaxed when he found no one else around. He shuddered as he gazed at the cold chocolate water surging over the dam and passing into the wide-mouthed tubes where the mud cats lived—wedged tight against the ribbed aluminum with their stout spines erect, sucking down gobs of crawdads washed from the banks of the Kaw.

A semi truck rig wound its diesel engine tight, shifted and then wound up again as it headed for the plant to pick up a load of boxes destined for the textile factories in downtown Kansas City. Albert had a ringside view of bridge traffic from his tent. If the game warden caught him—or even worse if a truant officer called the cops on him, he would either go to jail or back to school. He would prefer jail if he had a choice. School brought back bad memories—except for Brenda. Brenda Lee Brown was easily the fastest person he had ever met. Skinny arms and skinny legs, she could really fly down the track. She was something else, that Brenda. They had made it once in his tent. Then he'd heard over at the plant that she'd dropped out and married Hobart Perry— he had probably knocked her up or something. Hobart was something else too—a real dandy. He rode a red Cushman scooter to school and acted like Mr. Cool—even wore a vest and tie every day to class. Rumor was that Hobart got his dough by selling LSD to KU students.

Enough of this lollygagging around. I gotta get Mr. Big before somebody else beats me to him—or maybe that damn fish is gonna swim down river today. The water sure looks cold, I tell that straight out.

Albert edged along the narrow shelf above the culverts careful to maintain his balance on the slippery algae-covered ledge. If he lost his footing and went over the tumultuous falls, he would be in serious trouble. He carefully lowered himself into the violent flow, hyperventilated several times, sucked his lungs full then plunged his right arm into the conduit while holding tight to the tube with his other hand. He felt the deep-s-carred face of the old mighty fish. The head seemed about two feet wide. Albert stuck his gloved hand into the mud cat's open mouth.

This one's huge! Maybe go hunnerd and fifty pounds. Lot'a bucks for this big guy if I can just get 'im up.

The cat bit down hard. Albert shoved and levered his arm forward past the sharp teeth that lined the back of the fish's throat. He pushed his arm further right into the big cat's gullet. It went in up to his shoulder before his hand finally found and reached through the gill slit.

I got you now Mistah Big!

Once he had plunged his hand past the spiny gill rakers, Albert had always been able to pull the fish from the tube and drag it onto the ledge. But this fish was too big, its stout body wedged too firmly in the culvert. Albert realized that he was trapped. The rakers and teeth caught and held tight; he couldn't free his arm. He was anchored to a fish that would not budge. His lungs were bursting and his vision constricted to amber pinpoints of light. Then there was blackness. The cat held tight until Albert went limp and then bit cleanly through his arm, swallowed and grabbed another bite.

******

Much to the dismay of the Douglas County Sheriff's Office, a single lane dirt road snaked along the bank of the Kaw leading to a lover's parking spot known locally as the 'sand bar'. Small boys came here to set traps for muskrats and otters. Bigger boys came to seduce KU coeds or the loose girls from the motorcycle beer bar in North Lawrence. Middens of trash revealed the games played on the sandbar: discarded condoms, expended shot gun shells and .22 brass cartridges, and rusty cans of Old Milwaukee and Budweiser, along with an occasional red and white Prince Albert tobacco tin.

Sandra was so excited that she leapt from the station wagon, leaving wide open the door of the new El Ranchero and flew down to edge of the river. She plopped down on her bottom, stripped off her sneakers and waded out onto the soft sand. She stared with awe and fascination at the passing eddies which swirled like slow motion maelstroms on their way down the river. She waited impatiently for her father to bring the long cane poles, garden worms, bobbers–and the cooler with the drinks and frozen Snickers bars. Sandra was very happy to be spending the morning with her dad–as a new instructor at Kansas University, he always seemed to be too busy grading papers and making lesson plans to have any time for fun. And besides, today was special. It was her ninth birthday.

She wondered what was taking her father so long. Slowly she waded into the river. She didn't think that going in just up to her knees would be dangerous. She enjoyed the silky feeling of the sand as it slid between her bare toes. Suddenly Albert's fingers wrapped around her ankle. She reached down and grabbed his slimy hand thinking it was just a piece of waterlogged cardboard from the box company. She tugged and Albert's bloated corpse slid upward and forward just as she lost her footing and fell backward into the water. Her small frame was engulfed by the dead boy.

Hysterically she shoved and attempted to yell for help, but Albert's heavy body pinned her to the bottom and the current started to carry them both away. Gritty water ran down her throat and stifled her screams. Albert's one arm wrapped around her slight chest. She couldn't come up for air. Black water and gruesome icy flesh consumed her.

Suddenly her father was holding her and crying for her to be all right. They stood looking down at the purple-black mass lying on the brown sand. She recognized the twisted face. It was the same boy that once helped her climb aboard the ancient locomotive in Central Park. She remembered that afternoon. The step was too high and she was too shy to ask for help. Albert had reached down and hollered, "All aboard–you too, little lady," with a happy smile. Through her tears, she saw that same grin, now lifeless and grotesque.

******

Sandra gasped for air, struggling with the body that smothered her. She pushed and tried to squirm out from beneath, but she could not get free. Morrow awoke and tried to calm her, but she pounded him with her fists. Then her eyes opened and she realized that the form next to her was Morrow...not the boy in the river. She sobbed into his chest, her frame racked with tremors.

"Oh Morrow... a poor boy drowned in the river–a boy I had met on the train engine in Central Park when my parents and I lived in Lawrence, Kansas. It happened at the end of summer. A few weeks later, Mom and Dad died in a car crash on the turnpike and I moved to Key West to live with Grandma and Grandpa. Somehow I had buried the memory of that drowned boy...because of my parents being killed in the accident I guess. So there was another train all along."

Then she gagged and vomited in the sand.

******

Eiger noted the time, a quarter until one in the morning, then lightly pressed the return key. The computer began inoculating the PIG with activated ANX. Twenty minutes later, ANX had eradicated every byte of the PIG's stored data and had replaced it with rampant chaos.

Chapter 21

Sandra delegated Chet to continue the remote object recognition tests with the Twins while, in the solitude of her private quarters; she laid plans for the next round of experimentation. She had mixed feelings about going forward because it meant returning to the SDC for another week of isolation and entrainment. But the next tests were of major importance; she would actually try to establish a direct telepathic connection with one of the dolphins. To do this, she needed the enhanced ability provided by the 'combined effect'...and that meant going back into the SDC. Still, she delayed, not yet ready to commit to another week of isolation and was thankful that they could conduct other experimental tests directly with the Twins in the interim.

On the afternoon of the third day of the new test series, Chet breathlessly burst into Sandra's room. His face was ashen as he stammered, "Sandra come quick...something is terribly wrong."

Within minutes Sandra was seated at the control station next to Chet. She looked carefully at the bank of monitors, everything appeared quite normal. Through the wide mirror, she could see the Twins. They had been separated; now each dolphin was stationed in its own quadrant of the SDC. The chamber partition was secured and the louvers locked shut isolating them from one another. Chet had designed the experimental design to allow each dolphin to identify the same object simultaneously. Tom and Sally floated motionlessly with their heads toward their individual, underwater video screen. Their snouts were within easy range of the wall-mounted keyboards.

Sandra demanded, "What's up? Everything looks fine to me...what's the problem?"

Chet shrugged and pointed to the wall monitors. He whispered, "Just watch."

A tiny green light flashed on the panel, indicating that the Convex's random selection program had just decided which object the robot would display. Both SDC monitors flashed the prompt 'READY' followed by the '?'.

The overhead cameras in each compartment displayed the images of Tom and Sally both moving forward and tapping the keys that symbolized a sphere. The Convex beeped twice signifying that they had both made the correct choice, but the robot arm had just extended and was still reaching for the object. Each dolphin had identified the correct choice **before** the droid had even touched the sphere.

"My God, precognition...could this be precognition?" She mumbled to no one in particular. Then to the group of technicians that had gathered around the console, she asked, "Did you do a systems check? Are they getting an electrical impulse somehow? Are our control systems up and running? What is happening here?"

Chet interrupted Sandra's list of questions. "All systems check out. Everything is on line; this is a real time event."

Chet repeated the experiment with the same results.

Somehow they seem to be determining the computer's selection prior to its physical manifestation.

He asked, "Do you think they are really experiencing precognition?"

"What else could it be then?" exclaimed Sandra.

As if to answer her question, the Twins responded to the next flash of the indicator light. Two more beeps sounded immediately. Then the Convex and the dolphins continued onto the next test; the light blinked and the beeps sounded. The droid's command storage buffer accumulated the backlog of unexecuted instructions and ordered the mechanical arm through its paces, but the robot was falling way behind the dolphin-computer feedback loop. The alternating flashes and beeps quickened in pace until the indicator light stayed on and the tone sounded as a continuous high-pitched squeal.

Sandra looked over at Chet who held up his hands to show that he had no idea of what was going on. He said, "Perhaps they are mentally accessing the Convex?"

Suddenly the tone stopped and a message scrolled up onto the main monitor.

:::::::CAUTION! BUFFER OVERLOAD:::::::

:::::::MALFUNCTION OF DISPLAY ROBOT:::::::

Then the message repeated. A klaxon alarm, like that sounded by a diving submarine, broke the silence.

Chet yelled, "Watch out...get back," just as the robot arm smashed down against the stage upsetting the tray that held the wooden symbol objects, scattering them across the concrete floor. The droid's overloaded servomotors generated a shrill scream and emitted a cloud of smoke that reeked of sizzling circuitry. The arm swung to the left and then slammed down hard on the stage tipping the robot over on its back and ripping the shoulder joint from the steel frame. Free from restraint, the arm convulsed, jellyfish-like, and erratically grappled itself across the floor until the power cord snapped. The severed hand jerked spasmodically, slowly opening and closing as the charge ebbed from the machine.

Sandra stood trembling over the amputated appendage. She jumped at the searing whoosh from a fire extinguisher that Chet used to smother the robot in a sea of foam. Everyone was screaming about what had happened. But Sandra mentally floated inwards, removed from the scene as if someone had punched the mute control and halted a violent scene on television.

Mentally accessing the computer...could this really be happening?

She grabbed Chet by the arm and yelled into his ear, "Come on...we have to talk. Get the tape recording."

To the others standing around in shock, she said, "I'm sure that there is a logical explanation. Let's clean up this mess and call it a day. Somebody let the Twins back into the channel."

As they left, the lab hummed with the animated conversation of the techs, each offering their own explanation of what had just taken place.

Back in the tranquility of her room, Sandra passed Chet a beer then punched the play button of the VCR remote. After, they ran the tape for the third time, Chet said, "It happened alright...somehow the Twins guessed which shape would be chosen before the droid even approached the object."

She opened a second beer and leaned back in the armchair, then replayed the sequence one more time. Living with Grandma Grant and pursuing a career in parapsychology had prepared Sandra to accept nearly anything. And the chance to discover a new phenomenon like this was exactly why she was in research in the first place. But to actually witness the dolphins nonchalantly performing the seemingly impossible was still a tremendous, albeit unexpected, surprise.

There they are...correctly anticipating an action before it happens. Just like there were performing a tail walk or high splash...just like it was a normal day at the office. They **must** *be mentally accessing the computer. There is no other explanation. Precognition seems just too far out to consider at this time. Maybe I'm more of a skeptic than I thought.*

Chet agreed to keep their conversation in confidence and returned to the lab to check on the technicians. Sandra locked the door and sat at her desk. She placed her face in her hands and rested her elbows on its scratched metal surface–a position she remembered that her grandmother sometimes assumed when she became spiritually connected. *The possibilities are endless. Where should I begin?*

Along with the excitement of discovery, Sandra felt a twinge of paranoia. *If General Houston finds out, he will surely take over the project. He already told me that he thought my work had implications for national security. I thought he was nuts at the time. But after all, the Navy did once try to brainwash the Twins. My work could be buried in top secret red tape. I'll never be allowed to publish my findings. And what would happen to Tom and Sally?*

Not only that, but Houston is coming to visit next week. No explanation offered, just a telex from the Main Island saying that he planned to stop in for a tour of the facility–the timing just couldn't be worse. All the way from Washington for a tour. I wonder what his real agenda is."

Sandra whispered, "Yes, now we really do have something here, don't we? But what? I just need time to figure this out. Mentally accessing computers–oh my God!"

Sandra spent a fretful night, tossing and turning in a deluge of nightmares. She dreamed that the Twins were running the experiments and she was the subject. She arose at dawn and collected Morrow and Chet. Together they conspired to hide the supernatural events from Houston. She was steadfast in her determination that the General be kept in the dark. No one must be allowed to interfere in their work—not now that they had just gotten started.

After much heated debate, they decided that the technicians posed the greatest risk of detection. It would be a simple matter for Chet to rig the equipment so that Houston would observe nothing out of the ordinary. However a major deception like that would not be easy to explain to the rest of the team—and they would have to be included if the plan were to work. Sandra would in effect be asking them to lie for her, maybe even putting their lives in danger—or at least jeopardizing their careers if the conspiracy was detected. To safeguard the project, the techs would have to go. They would be sent home.

"But is that a realistic option?" asked Morrow. "How can just the three of us run all of this equipment? Wouldn't sending them back derail the project?"

Chet was fast to reply, "No, not in the least. Everything is now automated." He glanced at Sandra. "And...I'm just guessing, but I would bet that the experiments that we will conduct from now on out will be very different from those that we originally planned."

"He's right," added Sandra. "We will redesign the program from scratch. No more long, drawn out entrainments for me either. I'll be in the lab full-time from now on. I just can't tell you what all this means."

Morrow replied, "Well, I guess it means that those dolphins of yours can read the computer's mind. Hmm...I see what you mean. You're right; the Defense

TELEPATHIC DOLPHIN EXPERIMENT

Department would be very interested in this kind of capability. The feds would certainly put the lid on this right away. It would make the other superpowers mighty uncomfortable knowing that the U.S. knew their secrets, wouldn't it?"

They worked through the night fabricating a plausible story for the techs and designing a show and tell demo for Houston that was certain not to reveal the Twin's powers. If pressed by the General, Sandra would explain that paranormal expressions, if any ever materialized, would be very subtle and would take months of statistical analysis to detect. She would do her best to make it all sound dry and technical.

The meeting ended with the consumption of two six packs of cold Olympia and many irreverent toasts to the General's health.

******

Surrounded by a group of curious technicians, Chet made a big production out of laboriously disassembling and testing several racks of electronic equipment. Since the experiments were temporarily suspended, many of the techs drifted off to the beach. Later that afternoon, Chet informed one of the girls that yesterday's fiasco was most likely just a bug in the Convex's operating system. By evening, the rumor that the sensational events were nothing more than a misfiring circuit board had been widely accepted.

Saturday morning, at an impromptu meeting convened by Sandra in the control lab, the techs looked dramatically out of place in their swimsuits and zories. They gathered in a semicircle around the control station where Sandra and Chet were seated. Chet officially informed the group that a short in the wiring had been the culprit—the dolphins had merely been detecting electrical impulses conducted through their keyboards. He demonstrated exactly how it had happened. The errant signals matching his explanation were easily detected by a voltage meter thanks to an all night effort to fabricate the illusion.

Sandra read easy acceptance in the faces of her young team members. She even overhead a remark about getting back to the volleyball game on the beach. She thought, *such a short attention span–they're not even disappointed.*

Playing the scene lightly, she commented that evidence for precognition or even remotely accessing computers would have certainly been something for the evening news and that she was glad that no reporters had been on hand to perpetuate the unintended hoax. She then casually suggested that, in order to prevent more mistakes, everyone needed a vacation. And she had just the right solution–she had made reservations for everyone to go back to San Francisco on the next weekly flight. She told them to plan a two-week vacation while thinking, *I don't want to alarm them and tell them they are never coming back. I'll just send them a telex next week informing them that we have a budget overrun and we need to cut back. Being in the university system, they're used to bad news like that. I just wish that things were different, but I have to look after their protection as well as the Twins.*

The meeting broke up in high spirits. The tech problem had been solved!

Chapter 22

A Week Later
Pig Island

The General zipped up his parka and rubbed his hands together and offered his standard greeting. "Christ, Eiger. You even got this place freezing cold! What are you half Eskimo or something? What do you think Commander, brisk enough in here for you? Okay, Professor, are we secure? I mean after all we are out here in this godforsaken bunker in the middle of the Pacific Ocean. Let's hear how the project is coming."

In preparation for Houston's visit to the atoll, Eiger had laboriously downloaded into the PIG's memory register a   complete set of AT&T telephone listings for every city, town and suburb in the U.S. With an air of gravity, he unlocked the wall safe containing the ANX program and loaded it onto the one-inch digital tape deck.

Eiger explained, "Right now gentlemen, we have a large capacity computer in normal operating stasis." He pointed to the far wall of the cubicle, which sparkled from floor to ceiling with thousands of minuscule blue lights. "This panel represents the memory banks of the computer. They contain over one hundred billion cells packed with numerical and textual data. The situation is similar to what we might find in a first level strategic defense network. As you can see all the lights are blue in color."

"Now I will introduce ANX into the operating system. This is the latest version developed on ANX Island and which I brought here by hand this morning. After today's demonstration the tape will be returned for safe-keeping."

He punched a code into the computer's keyboard. The aluminum reels of the digital tape deck spooled to a blur then snapped to a precise stop.

Abruptly a shrill alarm blared followed by the computer generated announcement, which was repeated twice.

WARNING...ENTER CLEARANCE KEY CODE
YOU HAVE TWO MINUTES TO COMPLY

A clock symbol appeared on the screen accompanied by the monotone countdown in five-second intervals.

Eiger quickly typed in the secret code and the computer responded:

ANX INSERTION ABORTED
YOUR SYSTEM IS NOT INFECTED

The General asked, "Only two minutes? Wow, is that enough time for our people to find the key and enter it?"

"We could make it longer, but that would increase the risk of someone discovering where the attack is origi-nating from. We can also quickly change the code if unauthorized parties are able to get a hold of it."

"So if someone we trust turns on us and tries to leak your clearance code to one of our enemies, we just change the code and let the rest of our friends know the new version?"

Eiger nodded and said, "Okay that was an example of the manual pass code procedure in operation. We can also program it to function automatically. You can think of it as a vaccination that makes the recipient computer immune to ANX without any notification to the system operator."

The General thought for a few moments and said, "I definitely think the auto vaccine is the way to go. Please make that a standard feature—at least for now. How do we control which computers receive the vaccination treatment?"

"I will have my team at Chalmer Labs put together a database of friendly targets starting with the Department of Defense, then include banks, stock market, medical, emergency services,...and so on. We will need a large bank of supercomputers programmed and ready to launch the vaccine through the Internet, but we will wait until shortly before the ANX release to avoid complications. The group I have working on the database know nothing about ANX."

"This all sounds reasonable. Let's see what happens if we let ANX rip."

"I will now reintroduce ANX and let it run full course like it will in any defenseless system." Eiger initiated the ANX infection a second time. After the initial warning, the clock began the two-minute countdown.

To Eiger and the Commander's dismay, Houston lit a thick cigar, casually put his spit shined loafers up on the edge of the console and leaned back in his chair. The General's eyes shifted back and forth from the digital clock to the memory panel while Eiger mopped his glistening forehead with a soggy handkerchief and watched the seconds count down on the monitor.

This time at zero, the screen went black and there

was a sudden hush in the computer room. Just as Houston was about to comment that nothing seemed to be happening the computer voice stated, "Warning. Viral intrusion has occurred. Internal safeguards have been defeated. Significant data loss is likely."

Eiger exclaimed, "You see...we are already getting results. The present loss of data is already severe...oh I would say about the equivalent of all of the Social Security numbers ever issued by the United States of America. Within twenty minutes, the memory registers will be like a vacuum. That would be like losing the records from the Internal Revenue Service and the holdings of the Library of Congress—all in less than an hour."

Houston tapped the ash from the tip of his cigar. "How will you spread it?"

"If this computer was connected to others in the net—and we obviously know that the PIG here is not—all of the associated computers would soon be infected. And so on and so forth until every computer in the target system was crippled. It is an exponential function. First there is one problem, and then there are two, then four, then sixteen, then two hundred and fifty-six."

Eiger pulled a calculator from a leather pouch attached to his belt and used the eraser end of a pencil to enter a series of numbers. He continued, "And then it takes off like a banshee. Next there would be 65,536 contaminated systems, and then 4,294,967,298 violated computers—all in a matter of a few hours. No useful information would be derived from these infected systems until ANX self-destructs twenty-four hours after inoculation. But by then, the data will be irretrievably lost forever."

The General slapped his thigh and stood looming over Eiger and then grabbed his hand and gave it a fierce pumping. He turned to Cummings. "Commander,

TELEPATHIC DOLPHIN EXPERIMENT

I have seen enough. You and Eiger work out the details on how to get ANX into the USSR without turning the damn thing loose on us. Be ready to move within two weeks. You sent a message to the dolphin doctor to expect me tomorrow, right? Well, I'm ready to go over there now. Let's give her a little surprise why don't we?"

******

Sandra cringed when she saw the cruiser fast approaching the island figuring that it was the General arriving a day ahead of schedule. She explained to him that the tech team was on a much-needed vacation and that the project was going well. To her surprise, the meeting was short and the General even offered his compliments on the layout of the lab, but he was disappointed not to see the dolphins that were apparently fishing in the lagoon. Due to his tight schedule, the General couldn't wait for them to return to the lab so he headed back to the Main Island where his Lear Jet waited to take him back to Washington.

Chapter 23

The Twins' abilities continued to improve with each test session. Sandra and Chet had a standing joke that the progress was merely the result of the humans learning to better communicate with the dolphins–they were not really teaching the animals anything new at all. In fact it might be the other way around; the Twins were actually the teachers and the humans, the students.

An icon-based computer program that used pictures instead of objects replaced the original experimental regime. Once mastered, the next logical step was to teach the dolphins to respond to commands expressed as simple expressions. And that is when it happened.

A train of greetings, statements, and questions scrolled and bounced from monitor to monitor across the video wall–messages from the dolphins. Messages of simple composition, yet with such an awesome portent. In retrospect it was to be expected. If the dolphins had been able to mentally access the computer during the first ESP tests, it was logical that they would use the computer to talk back to the humans. They had only been waiting patiently for the means to do so and the computer language provided the vehicle to share their thoughts. But it still took Sandra and Chet by surprise. They were actually able to carry on an intelligent conversation, at least by keyboard and monitor, with two marine mammals.

Sandra's dream had come true. Fluent, two way communication evolved quickly with the dolphins mentally accessing the Convex and Chet and Sandra feverishly typing a new response to a sometimes off the wall queries from the Twins like, "What is the tide forecast for midnight tonight?" Or, "Has the tuna fleet given up purse seining for yellow fin?" For the scientists it marked the beginning of an odyssey into realms never imagined in the field of parapsychology or animal behavior.

The distinct personalities of the Twins emerged. Sally demonstrated an artistic, nearly poetic enchantment with life and was extremely interested in comparing notes with Sandra about the role of a female in their respective societies. Chet informed Sandra that if analytical Tom had two legs instead of fins, he would have been considered a whiz kid genius. No abstraction was beyond his comprehension. With Chet's enthusiastic assistance, Tom refined his mastery of Turbo C, the Convex's program language. Both dolphins were phenomenally adept at assimilating and storing vast amounts of data and frequently amazed their handlers with their power of retention.

On day ten since first contact, Chet was already hard at work at the console by the time Sandra arrived to begin the morning session.

He leaned back in his chair, took a deep breath and then pointed at the screen. "You will not believe what just happened!"

Sandra read the message on the main monitor; it was

a standard greeting that the dolphin's routinely displayed at the onset of the day.

GOOD MORNING FRIENDS, HOW ARE YOU?

"What's wrong Chet? "They always put up that greeting."

"But Sandra, like we planned, last night I shut down the computer and trashed the BIOS operating system. This morning I was planning to install the latest version just released by Convex. Right now the computer is running without any software—no program whatsoever. Let me rephrase that. The Convex is obviously running a program, but it is not our program. Somehow the Twins have supplied their own operating system. We're talking about a task that would take me years of hard work to handle...and without a ceiling high stack of Convex's proprietary, in-house specifications I could never make it happen.

"See all the applications are in place; even the data files that I purged and dumped to tape for storage have been replaced. No one in computer engineering at Randamount would ever believe me if I told them that this was accomplished overnight without an army of technical support—let alone by two marine mammals. I am truly astounded."

"Well, why don't we just ask Tom what is going on?" Chet typed:

DID YOU PROGRAM COMPUTER?

A reply appeared instantly upon the monitor.

YES...TO HELP YOU CHET.

"Don't just sit there silly. Ask him how he did it."

TELEPATHIC DOLPHIN EXPERIMENT

A reply flashed even before Chet could enter the question.

FIRST: WE REPLAYED THE PROGRAM OPENING
SECOND: ADDED SELECTIONS
THIRD: RESTORED MEMORY DATA

IS SYSTEM OPERATING PROPERLY?

Flustered, Chet spoke directly into the microphone that connected to the SDC, "The opening, is that in characters or numbers?"

NO, ALL PROGRAM IS IN +/- ELECTRICAL CHARGES.
WE PUT CHARGES BACK IN PLACE

Chet rose and paced the lab floor. Sandra took his place at the console and watched him as he walked around in what looked like a daze. Suddenly he blurted, "Do you know what this means?"

Before she could reply that she hadn't even the foggiest idea, with a quavering voice he whispered, "They didn't use program language...they used machine language. Somehow they restored the exact correct sequence of binary coding. There must be a hundred billion, billion bits in the operating system alone. Only another highly advanced supercomputer could do that. I'm sorry I just can't believe any of this anymore. It's way too much for me."

"Chet, you are a computer genius. But how would you compare the complexity of our beloved Convex with a human brain? How many stacks of specs would you need to do that?

"Okay, when you put it that way, I see your point. We are obviously dealing with a game-changing situation. I just don't understand how they could have done this."

Sandra looked through the one-way glass into the

dolphin sector. She bent towards the microphone and asked, "Tom, was this difficult for you...did it take very long?"

Tom didn't move but the monitor flickered a few times then lines of text began scrolling upwards.

YES IT WAS A LOT OF INFORMATION
TOOK FIVE MACHINE CLOCK HOURS
DID WE MAKE A MISTAKE?
IS PROGRAM INCORRECT?
DO YOU NOT ALSO FIX COMPUTER THIS WAY?
WE ASSUME YOU MAKE COMPUTER

Sandra leaned back in the chair and gave Chet a small smile. "How about a swim in the lagoon? Let's take the rest of the day off and think this over."

Just then she thought she heard two voices give a gurgling cheer. "Sure boss!"

She dropped her notebook and flashed a questioning look at Chet. He slowly nodded in the affirmative; he had heard it too. He croaked, "I don't think we'll be needing the monitor anymore," and shook his head in disbelief. Then he raised his arms upwards and outwards. "What next? Now I really have seen and heard everything!"

******

Morrow and Mr. John, back from a reef census, banged along the road with a load of empty SCUBA tanks looking forward to a cold beer and lunch at the lab. They were surprised to see Chet, Sandra and the Twins beached in the shallows of lagoon channel.

Joining the group, Mr. John good-naturedly queried, "Did you get them talking yet? I haven't been back over here since the party and I thought that they might be chattering away like a couple of disk jockeys by now."

TELEPATHIC DOLPHIN EXPERIMENT

His eyes widened and he looked in amazement at the Twins and then at Sandra. "Oh I see. They finally did break through to you didn't they? Congratulations, welcome to the world of talking spirits and talking dolphins." Then he waded into the water and stroked Sally's head until Tom barged in asking for attention.

Sandra laughed, "You knew, didn't you? I thought so. I remember the night they took you spear fishing. I sensed then that something very extraordinary had happened. They spoke to you then, didn't they?"

Morrow, thinking that this was all a put on, searched Sandra's face for the hint of a smile. "What's going on here?" he interrupted. "I must have missed something major." But no one paid him any attention. All eyes were on Mr. John and the dolphins along side.

Mr. John continued, "Well, yes of course. But they only touched me with their joy and excitement...sort of like a fireworks display and a Sunday sermon all at once. They didn't seem to know English then and I didn't know any dolphinese."

Morrow could not contain himself any longer. He gently gripped Sandra by the shoulders and turned her to face him. "Could you please tell me what you two are talking about?"

Tom slapped his tail on the surface and reeled sideways while emitting a high-pitched series of chirps. Morrow heard a light voice, like that of a young boy. But it sounded inside his head, not through his ears. *Greetings Dr. Morrow, how are you feeling today? Hopefully you are well!*

Morrow looked stricken. "What...who said that?" He looked accusingly at Sandra who had plopped onto her bottom into the shallow water in a spasm of laughter.

Here Dr. Morrow. It was I. You know me as Tom. The dolphin gave a vigorous shake of his glistening head.

Sally wiggled forward and placed her snout on

149

Sandra's lap. A new voice, higher than the one before, drifted into Morrow's mind like a phantom. *We want to thank you for saving us from the men on the other island–before we flew in the air. We join you to our pod and want to help you find the answers, which you seek.*

******

Eiger was nearly finished. So far at least, ANX had performed exactly to his specifications as he continued to inject the PIG with the virus again and again. By week's end he was certain that ANX was ready. He figured that one or two more days of testing in which the ANX virus would obliterate the test target phone book files stored on the PIG and then Eiger would go to the Main Island and call Commander Cummings to arrange for his flight back to the mainland. He would gladly turn the project over to the General, destroy all of his notes on the viral structure...'evidence', he thought, and finally deliver his resignation to Chalmer Labs. The long days of isolation and the sheer sinisterness of the project had sucked away his youth and ambition. He could only hope that once Houston finally had the ANX virus that the General would see to it that Eiger had enough funds to live on until he found a new career–anything that did not involve the military. *Maybe I can get a little place in the City and teach computer science in a local junior college. Just a few more days and this fiasco will be over.*

Chapter 24

Chet drained the last of the cold coffee from the Styrofoam cup. The bitter grounds felt like sandpaper on the roof of his mouth. It had been a long day. The new series of experiments on image retention had taken much longer to conduct than he had anticipated—the dolphins didn't seem as willing to concentrate as usual. It seemed to Chet that throughout the day the Twins had been off in their own world—distracted in some way or the other and not paying close attention. *Maybe they're tired too—or maybe getting a little bored with all of this testing.* It was approaching five o'clock and even he was having difficulty maintaining his train of thought. *Just one more experiment, then we're finished for the night! I'm even too tired to eat. It'll be straight to bed for me.*

Just as Chet reached to begin the next set of experiments, large green letters slid one by one across the screen.

FOR WHAT PURPOSE IS OTHER COMPUTER?

Chet typed in a reply.

WHAT OTHER COMPUTER?

Tom switched to direct telepathy, bypassing the computer connection. "Across the ocean pass, on the damaged island called Runit. That computer. Is it a secret, Chet? Am I not supposed to ask about that computer?"

"I don't know about another computer, Tom. That island is radioactive. I doubt if there is a computer over there. Maybe you are thinking about a computer on the Main Island. They probably have several in the administration office."

No Chet...there definitely is a very powerful computer nearby. It has a different kind of system. Its memory is full. I believe that I can read some of it if you would like me to. It is a list of numbers in binary code. They may be digital instructions. Would you like me to translate one for you, Chet?

Not knowing if this was a new manifestation of the Twins' enduring sense of play, Chet humored the request and out of habit typed.

YES GO AHEAD

Then in his mind, he heard,

The list is quite long. The entries consist of three numerals in parenthesis followed by three digits, a hyphen, and then four more numbers.

Chet replied, "It sounds like a phone number, Tom."

Yes I agree. I will give you one to try. This one is the number of James A. Johnson at 409 Hillock Street, Dallas, Texas... (214) 636-8359. Could you please check to see it that is his telephone number?

TELEPATHIC DOLPHIN EXPERIMENT

"Tom that is long distance and who knows what time it is in Texas even if you are right."

Please Chet. I only ask because I sense that this could be important.

Impatient and exasperated about being sidetracked when he was exhausted, Chet used the SATCOM line to dial the mainland. The connection was clear for once. A woman with a Spanish accent answered the phone. "Si esto es la casa de señor y señora Johnson. No estan aqui ahora. Quien llama?"

Chet's single year of freshmen year of Spanish had not been totally forgotten. He said, "Mea culpa, buenas noches, Señora."

"You were right Tom. That is James Johnson's phone number in Texas. It's probably just some sort of weird satellite connection or maybe a boat went by that had a laptop?" *Who knows who or where Tom and Sally connect? Back to work. It'll be midnight before I get out of here at this rate.*

An hour later Chet was about to throw in the towel. Tom and Sally kept sliding in and out of the testing routine. They weren't really making much headway at all.

Tom broke the impasse. *Chet, I think something is seriously wrong with the other computer. It is losing its memory. The phone number for Mr. Johnson is no longer there. I just checked. It has been erased. The entire phone book file is missing now. Some other files nearby are also gone. Can you tell me about the injured computer? Chet I am very concerned that something is seriously wrong with it. I now sense the other computers that you mentioned on the Main Island. They are very small. Are they toys? Some seem to have games on them. But I think they are getting sick too. There is definitely something wrong, Chet.*

"Listen Tom, try not to worry. There must be some

logical explanation. Let's go over what you experienced again."

Chet, I think you should hurry on this. The other computer seems to be under attack. It is losing processing power fast and the small ones no longer function at all. Now the computer here is starting to lose some of its memory...and I feel mine slipping away too. The big computer across the pass will cease to exist soon. Maybe we can help it recover somehow. I want you to know that I feel very strongly about this, Chet.

"Look Tom, Sandra and Morrow took the day off. I think they mentioned going for a sail. Let's both take break and I will bring her to you when she returns."

As Chet turned to leave the lab, the video wall flashed and then faded to black.

PIG Island

Sweat poured off Eiger's brow and dripped onto the keyboard. He sat open mouthed at the PIG console, his jaw slack with disbelief. Something was going badly with this run. The digital timer indicated that just over two minutes had elapsed since he had begun the experiment by inoculating the PIG with ANX. The first memory seizure had occurred exactly on schedule–just as it had on each of the preceding runs. Then out of the blue, the PIG's operating system had rebooted on its own. ANX automatically began the infection procedure again and consumed another massive amount of code, but once more it was suddenly interrupted by the PIG rebooting.

At this rate it would take at least half an hour to annihilate the first host so the dispersion throughout the SDN would be somewhat slower than he had projected. *It's as if the PIG is trying to defend itself, but how? This definitely should not be happening.*

TELEPATHIC DOLPHIN EXPERIMENT

Finally the start/stop loop ended and the PIG became lifeless. Although some factor had interfered with the ANX attack, in the end ANX wiped out the host–it just took longer than it should have, but ANX still posed the awesome threat for which he had designed it.

A ten minute delay will mean nothing to General Houston, but the mere fact that this test has not gone precisely according to schedule is a matter of great concern. I know from experience that any form of inconsistency in the operation of a computer is a warning that must not be overlooked. Invariably something of major consequence is likely to be wrong.

What if the PIG has somehow been in contact with another computer that kept providing the code for the reboot? If an outside computer system was at work, that would explain the 'how' but not the 'why'–unless there was a major breach in security and foreign agents were involved. The General will not like this at all!

Chapter 25

The bleached white sails of the *Island Princess* swelled and stretched their seams taut against the stiff breeze as the catamaran picked up speed on a beam reach. Mr. John studied the trim of the jib and shouted instructions to Morrow at the winch. As Morrow ratcheted the sheet tight, one sleek forty-two foot long hull lifted out of the water. The boat was skimming along the surface, slicing through white caps at a brisk thirty knots. Their spirits soared as the nimble cat surged forward in the fresh salt air. The day sail was part of a week of shakedown cruises to put the newly launched catamaran through its paces before Mr. John took it single handedly on a five hundred mile voyage to Majuro, government seat of the Marshall Islands. From Majuro he would trace the original route of early navigators...atoll to atoll...until he reached the islanders' native homeland in Polynesia.

Sandra, blond hair flashing highlights in the afternoon sun, already felt sadness about Mr. John's imminent departure. She would not only miss his cheerful presence, but she felt badly for Morrow. If she had not appeared on the scene, she guessed that Morrow would have been invited along on Mr. John's expedition. She was sure that he would have been elated to venture across the South Pacific. She imagined frequent stops to explore unknown reefs and tranquil lagoons and overland forays to search for water and fresh coconut. In fact, she would have loved to go too. *The timing is just off...that's all. I have pressing responsibilities. But I wish Mr. John the best as he ventures off to exotic ports in magical seas. I'll have to tell Morrow that he should go. I'll miss him, but opportunities like this are too precious not to take. I'll tell him tonight.*

As soon as North Island came within sight, it was obvious that something was wrong. Through Mr. John's binoculars, Sandra could see Chet pacing back and forth across the beach. Every minute or so he waved his arms frantically as if to hurry their progress. As the catamaran landed, he grabbed a hull and caught Sandra by the waist as she ducked beneath the safety line and slid into the water.

Before she could ask, Chet let loose with a barrage of information. "There is something in the Convex operating system that is malfunctioning. Tom says the memory is eroding. It actually shut down completely just as I left the lab. Now I realize that a systems glitch is not that unusual, but this is different. Tom thinks he is responsible. I'm not kidding, he seemed to be crying!"

"What can be wrong?" asked Sandra, relieved that it was only a computer problem and that no one had been injured.

"At this stage, I really don't know. But Tom keeps talking about another computer across the channel that has the same problem."

Chet raised his arm and pointed toward Parry Island. "He thinks a computer over there is causing the problem. Actually he thinks that there is also a computer on Runit Island that is the ultimate source of the disease, which it has passed on to the computer on Parry Island and then infected our Convex. Right...I know it sounds bizarre. But I have never seen Tom down in the dumps like this before. Sally just plain isn't communicating at all–with me at least."

As Morrow and Mr. John waded in after anchoring the cat offshore, Chet turned to include them in the conversation. "Strange as it sounds, this story does have a certain degree of logic to it. A computer virus could cause these symptoms. I just don't know what to think about this 'other computer' stuff. All I know for sure is that Tom is under a great deal of stress and that is not good. He seems to have a guilt complex...that somehow he is responsible for the problem with the Convex and the other computers, if there are other computer that is. You need to reassure him and try to relieve his anxiety. He's in a very bad way. I think that part of the problem is that he keeps trying to fix a problem that is beyond his ability."

Sandra said, "Maybe it was some sort of solar flare or atmospheric disturbance of some kind. I think I will use the radiophone in the boat to call the Main Island and see if they know anything about the situation."

"Donaldson here," the Centron Site Manager spoke into his walkie-talkie. "Yes Dr. Grant...we do have computers over here–or at least we used to. Funny you should ask, all of our Macs are down. Today is payday too! No computers, no payroll. I got plenty of problems...and you're the second call I've had this afternoon asking about our computers. You guys on that side of the atoll up to something?" Remembering too late that his awareness of the clandestine operations on Parry and Runit was privileged, he added, "I mean you guys at your lab, have you blown some circuits that affected us over here?"

TELEPATHIC DOLPHIN EXPERIMENT

Hanging up the handset, Sandra informed the group. "The manager just made a slip. I think that there may be some hanky panky going on next door." She told them exactly what Donaldson had said.

"Well, it figures doesn't it?" replied Mr. John. "If there are secret labs of some sort on Parry and Runit Islands, it explains why we see Chalmer's people, along with their Centron contractors, going and coming day and night. It doesn't make sense that all of those guards are there just to keep people away from radioactive soil...I mean who would want to go Runit Island anyway?"

Morrow slammed his fist on the desk. "And it explains why General Houston flew all the way from Washington just to take a thirty minute tour of your facility. All he did was admire your tan, Sandra. He didn't even ask any questions about the budget or your progress."

Sandra blushed as she remembered the experience. "He must have been here to check on whatever they have going on next door. Tell us more about computer viruses, Chet. I vaguely remember some kind of scandal in the late eighties–a genius, grad student playing a trick on the Pentagon that got out of control. But didn't the government develop a universal vaccine that eliminated the problem?"

"Absolutely...and guess who developed the vaccine?"

In unison they chorused. "Chalmer Labs."

Chet laughed. "Right! I bet that's what they're doing over there. They're testing some new kind of new virus and Tom nosed in on it."

Sandra slumped to the sand and softly asked, "And now Tom has the virus?"

"Right again. He transmitted it to our Convex and to the microcomputers on the Main Island. This is serious business," concluded Chet.

RON S. NOLAN

Morrow returned with a bucket of ice and beer. "Thought we might need this," he said as he passed them out. "You know...it won't take long for them to figure this out. The brass will come to take care of Tom and Sally...who knows... maybe they'll decide to dispose of us too. This is obviously a top-secret project if they have gone to all of the trouble and expense to operate out here in the boonies. And knowing military mentality, they'll assume that we purposely set out to infiltrate their project. They won't buy any accidental ESP research stuff either, it simply wouldn't compute. Pardon the pun."

Chet interrupted the silence. "I think we should attempt to rid Tom of the virus. I have some ideas that I would like to try."

Morrow offered, "While you do that Mr. John and I'll go over a contingency plan in case things start to get out of control."

"Yeah, like we get the bejesus out of here," shouted the normally mild-mannered and composed Mr. John. When they all turned in shock, he apologized for his outburst. "Sorry, I must have gotten carried away with myself."

******

After Eiger returned to the Main Island and gained access to the satellite com system, he calculated that it was eight in the evening Washington time so he phoned the General at home. Grimacing, he launched into the story. "General, it's Carl Eiger on Enewetak "No sir, I am not certain that this is a secure line, but it is the only means of access available from the atoll. We have a serious problem out here General. I believe that an unauthorized agent may have accessed the PIG and in turn received the ANX contaminant sequence. Somehow, the agent must have made contact with

160

TELEPATHIC DOLPHIN EXPERIMENT

Centron's computers here on the Main Island and, after talking to Jim Donaldson, it sounds like ANX has wiped out their memories. I need your authority to seize those machines and software...they can be in my possession by nightfall."

The General downed his tumbler of Scotch in one long swallow. "You got to be kidding me Eiger. How could this have happened? Are you really sure that the virus has escaped?"

"No General, I am not certain, nor do I have any idea who could have penetrated our security defense. Whatever means they used is a complete mystery. However, I am curious about Dr. Grant and the dolphin experiments which Commander Cummings told me about."

"Yes, go ahead."

"The Centron site manager, Donaldson thinks that they have a Connex, which is a small super computer—one of the dolphin research techs mentioned it to him several months ago at the club bar. It is possible that Dr. Grant's computer may somehow be involved. I am obviously wildly speculating because even if they do have a high level machine, that doesn't explain how they obtained access to our computers. Another possibility is that some sort of space-borne probe has violated us. I put in a call to NASA to trace all satellite movements during the last twenty-four hours. No word from them yet."

"What about some sort of direct, physical sabotage? Is that possible?"

"Although it might seem to be the most logical explanation for someone unfamiliar with the great lengths we have taken to insure security, I think we can eliminate that option. There is no way General. Security on both ANX and PIG Islands is absolute. No one has been in physical contact with the ANX program except me."

"Try to relax Professor. There has to be some sort of

logical explanation. Let me know when you get the satellite data."

"It doesn't look good, sir. Donaldson just handed me a telex from JPL–nothing out of the ordinary. No new birds in orbit–not even weather satellites in this region."

"Then that just leaves the dolphin hotshots doesn't it? Professor, could they have accessed the PIG by accident? Some sort of electronic seepage or something?"

Eiger considered the possibilities. "In my expert opinion, it would require a carefully planned mission and a very determined effort to pull it off. Even still I am very concerned about the relatively close proximity to another computer–one that may have advanced capabilities. Remember when you came to visit me at Chalmer Labs I warned you about the risk. That's why we set up out here to begin with."

"But tell me this, is ANX still the threat that we hoped for in spite of this glitch?"

"I suppose it is sir, but I would like more time to figure out what is going on."

In spite of his growing sense of alarm, Houston maintained a calm tone to his voice. "I have Commander Cummings here with me now Eiger. After we end this conversation, he will head to Andrews and board my Lear Jet. He should get there by tomorrow afternoon."

"Okay sir, I will meet him here on the Main Island."

"Meanwhile, tell Donaldson to sever all communications out of the atoll. We will only maintain this one channel. I understand the situation and concur with you that we have a very serious circumstance. From here on out, I will assume that whomever is responsible could be trying to send ANX to the mainland. Maybe some communist infiltrator is trying to beat us at our own game.

"But once more, ANX works. Right?"

"Possibly not as fast as intended, but yes. I would..."

TELEPATHIC DOLPHIN EXPERIMENT

Houston put his hand over the mouthpiece and whispered, "Commander, you are good to go. Take a bunch of new computers for Donaldson and a couple of Marines with you just in case. Call me after you check out Grant's lab."

The General brought his attention back to the phone call. "Eiger I am counting on you to resolve this alleged intrusion on the PIG. Be ready to fly back with ANX when Cummings gives the all clear. Once the virus has been inserted into the Soviet system and the missiles start flying, you can perfect it to your heart's content."

Chapter 26

Control Room
Dolphin Research Lab

After considering several options, Sandra decided to contact Robert McCord. She dialed his number in Washington on her satellite phone, but the SATCOM operator informed her that all communication lines were down for servicing and that the entire Pacific Island Network would be unavailable for an indefinite period. "No, sorry ma'am, there is no other way to get through."

With lots of head rubbing and encouragement on the part of Sandra, Tom had appeared to be gradually recovering from his state of depression. Throughout the ordeal, Sally had remained close to Tom, but for reasons unknown didn't seem to be infected with the virus.

Suddenly Sally became agitated and repeatedly nudged the window of the SDC. She sub-vocalized a message to Sandra. *The SatCom operator was incorrect. If you wish, I will tap into the local circuit that is open right now."*

TELEPATHIC DOLPHIN EXPERIMENT

"By all means, please do. Listen up everyone, Sally is listening to a SATCOM call originating from the Main Island."

Chet replied, "Listening in...in real-time? That's wild. Here plug your phone into my cassette player and record the call. You can use my headphones to listen in."

Sandra asked for quiet and began taking notes, A few minutes later she reported. "Apparently someone named Eiger is talking to a general. It seems like Eiger is a computer engineer and he's talking about us! The 'general' has got to be our one and only General Houston and the gist of this conversation, is that he is planning to sick the same virus that infected Tom into the Soviet Defense Net and start World War III."

Morrow replied, "Real nice friends you have Sandra. This Houston is obviously insane. But if this virus were let loose in Russia, he might pull it off. No wonder the SATCOM line is off line. They've cut it off to keep the virus from spreading to the U.S."

Sandra consulted her notes. "It looks like Commander Cummings, whoever he is, is on his way with the Marine Corps in tow.

"I am going to call Robert if Sally can open that SATCOM line again." She gave a thumbs-up when she received the dial tone, but there was no answer so she hung up.

Morrow warned. "If they are coming from D.C., that will take them a day or so to get here, but the Centron security people are practically right next door How about a nice ocean cruise, Sandra? I better go fill in Mr. John and see if we can hitch a ride on his catamaran."

"Good thinking. I suggest we start packing right away–essentials only please. And what about the dolphins? I know they can swim along with us, but can we risk bringing Tom if he is carrying this virus thing around in his head?"

Chet shrugged. "You know...I have no idea of what is going on inside Tom's brain. He seems to be carrier all right, but that's because the virus is embedded in the program that he has committed to memory. If Tom was actually a computer, replacing the contaminated program with a virgin one would eliminate the problem. We could try that, but programming telepathic dolphins is a little outside my range of experience."

"Or anyone else's," laughed Sandra. "But won't you just be passing the virus back and forth between Tom and our computer? Won't that just repeat the whole process?"

Chet pointed to a large box beside the operations console. This is the brand new operating system just released by Convex. It hasn't even been taken out of the box yet. That's the reason the computer was down in the first place. Installing a new system purges everything from memory. If we can keep Tom under control for a half hour or so...you know keep his mind away from the Convex, I can sterilize the system and replace the program with software that is virus free. Then if Tom is asked to learn the new program and erase the one he has now, it should get the virus out of his brain. Of course this assumes that there is some similarity in the way that Tom stores memories and the way a computer stores information."

"How can you check him to make sure that he is safe?" asked Sandra.

"Well, that should be easy. I'll just have Tom access the Convex. If it doesn't crash, Tom is probably okay. None of my hacker buddies in California will ever believe this."

Morrow returned with Mr. John in tow and, after filling him in on the situation, they began planning their escape.

While Chet began the new software installation on

the Convex, Sandra moved the Twins to the channel with the intent of distracting Tom while Chet rebooted the computer.

With both dolphins resting next to Sandra in the shallows, she broke the news to the Twins. Tom and Sally eagerly accepted the notion that they were to swim free in the ocean. "Yes to a new home," she assured them.

Suddenly Tom excitably began splashing his tail fluke. He sub vocalized to Sandra, *Our computer is doing much better. It is like a heavy anchor has been lifted from my mind. Please tell Chet that his plan worked and thank him. I feel much better now.*

While Sandra and Chet hastily sorted and packed videotapes and computer disks, Morrow rounded up sleeping bags, dive gear and fishing equipment—any item that would aid in their survival, yet light enough to be stashed on board. Several times as Morrow rushed through the lab looking for flashlights and first aid supplies, he warned Chet and Sandra that they were taking too much—and left amidst their insistence that the records were priceless and could not be sacrificed on account of some crazy general.

As the group waited in the sand, guarding boxes packed with file folders and tapes wrapped in plastic bags and wondering if they might have forgotten something irreplaceable, Mr. John arrived with his catamaran and nudged it up on the beach to load the gear. He waved everyone over and said, "I have been thinking about logistics. Sandra tell me if I am wrong, but most dolphins seem to have a cruising speed of around five mph and a top speed of seven mph."

"That sounds right. I think I know where you are leading, but go ahead."

"Under optimal conditions, my catamaran will fly along at twice that, which could cause a problem because the Twins would get left way behind—or we would have to slow down and wait for them to catch up."

"I have been wondering about that myself. We can't carry them on your catamaran–not enough space .What do you suggest?"

"It's pretty simple actually. When the wind comes up and we start sailing too fast, or at any time the dolphins need a break, we can launch my Zodiac inflatable dinghy and connect it to a line trailing from the stern without slowing us down too much. We could even attach a canopy so that they would be shaded. If we take off the outboard motor and strip out the seats, the Twins can slide in and rest whenever they wish. It is big enough to carry both them at the same time and there should be enough spray to keep their skins moist."

Sandra nodded and Morrow agreed. "That is a great idea. We will help you take off the outboard and make the changes."

First Night at Sea

Sandra waded out to comfort the Twins, while the others made a human chain and, not daring to talk above a whisper, passed their cache of boxes and gear hand over hand up to Mr. John on the deck. Finally Morrow and Chet strained with all their might to shoulder the heavy cat off of the beach. The Twins chattered excitedly and circled around Sandra as she braced against the swell. As the boat began to drift away on the longshore current, Morrow reached down and hauled Sandra aboard. The dolphins fell in behind the stern as the boat slipped away from the island and disappeared into the black lagoon.

Other than a slight glow of luminance to the east where the moon lay beneath the horizon, the night was deep and black–a perfect night for stargazing. Even the otherwise distinct shape of the Southern Cross was smothered in a blanket of constellations that illuminated small wavelets that zipped diagonally along the shore. The night was so quiet it was somewhat spooky.

As the others rested, Chet began rummaging through the bags and boxes that they had loaded from the lab. Sandra asked, "Chet, what are you looking for?"

"In a rush to leave, we ran out of boxes so I went around the lab and shoveled everything on the top of the desks into a trash can. It looks like it was overlooked in the rush to leave. Don't worry all the lab notebooks are here, but my tape deck and headphones got left behind."

"Then don't worry about it. I will buy you a new set when we get back to Randamount."

Propelled only by intermittent puffs of breeze, the cat sailed sluggishly, tipping to and fro in the chop. The slack rigging clicked and snapped against the hollow aluminum spar. Hearing the racket, Chet and Sandra volunteered for the task of jamming towels in between the shrouds and stays to silence the commotion.

Across the lagoon, a sliver of new moon rose solemnly into the star-rich sky, casting a narrow band of quicksilver onto the surface of the sea. The brilliant glow outlined the islands blanketed in palms as they slowly receded in the distance. Darts of reflected moonlight glistened like sparks from the backs of the dolphins as they rose, blew and sounded in unison. Slowly they crept through the reef pass into the open sea. At the outer edge of the channel, a murky cloud of chalkiness swirled where the ocean swell rose and then crashed onto the fringing reef.

Other than the smooth rush of water sliding beneath the hulls and an occasional slap of rigging, the only sound was the rhythmic exhalations of the two dolphins. Frightened and overwhelmed by the rapid turn of events, Sandra buried her head into Morrow's chest and sobbed.

RON S. NOLAN

Finally, unable to contain herself any longer, she addressed her shipmates. "Well, where are we going anyway? I still want to try to reach Robert–maybe he will have an idea of what to do. This whole doomsday plan could go down at any time and somebody is sure to figure out that we have flown the coop. Come on...please, somebody say something."

Morrow cleared this throat then answered, "Mr. John and I talked this over earlier and we have worked out a plan. It was widely known that he was planning to sail to Majuro. Surely Houston will find out...so that's out of the question. Mr. John has told me about one of his close friends who lives on a small island to the southeast called Nauru. It's a four or five day trip if we sail direct, longer if we're forced to take cover along the way. But it's the only safe place we can think of–at least that the General would not immediately suspect. We'll have to rely upon the Twin's senses to warn us of any approaching danger. "

Sandra cheered up a bit, gave Morrow a hug and smiled. "I should have guessed you two would come up with something."

"We would be in hot water without Mr. John's help that's for sure. Houston will probably order up an air search to comb the area, but most likely he will focus on routes to the north...and we're heading south. We may just be able to sneak away before they get within range. We took down the radar reflector, so at least we won't be advertising our position. I know it's not much, but in the time we have had to plan, it is the only idea that seems to have a chance of succeeding."

"We do have a ship-to-shore radio that is capable of reaching Kwajalein or Honolulu if the skip is right," added Mr. John. "But once they find out we're gone, they will monitor every frequency. Morrow didn't mention it, but my friend on Nauru is well placed in the

170

local government. I know he will try to help us—we go a long way back. You'll like him; he's another savage with an Ivy League diploma like me. Plus, he is very well off financially and even has a jet that can take us wherever we wish to go. We just have to get there. I doubt that your general would consider Nauru to be a logical destination for us. So much the better. I vote we head for Nauru and take our best shot."

Morrow offered. "And I agree. But our highest priority is to get clear of Enewetak as fast as possible. Once they know we have escaped by boat, they will have AWACS in the air within hours. If it comes from Kwajalein it could be overhead by mid-day. I'm guessing that we may still be in range by then. It's going to be very tight, but at least they'll most likely begin their search towards Majuro and we will be heading in the opposite direction. If we can make two hundred miles by noon, we may just elude them. What do you think Mr. John?"

Mr. John calmly replied, "Right now I would say we don't have much of a chance. Look...we're barely making headway in this light air. If the trades pick up at dawn, we'll blast ahead for all we're worth. There are several chains of small islands not too far away. Assuming that your dolphins can somehow detect the transmission from a search plane, we could duck in close to their radar shadow and turn our *Island Princess* into a stealth ship. But the wind is the key factor and I sense that the Twins are emitting something that feels to me like the calm before a storm. I'll take the first watch. The rest of you get some shut eye."

Morrow did his best to make a cozy nest out of their sleeping bags in the fore section of the boat's doghouse. With his arm resting around her shoulders, Sandra tried to calculate the distance that the Twins might detect an approaching aircraft.

The only certainty was that Tom had tapped into the computers on the Main Island–a distance of about twenty miles from the lab. Now he would be asked to stretch his awareness to the limit. Sandra tuned her mind to the dolphins. They were quiet, almost as if they were swimming in their sleep, which was periodically interrupted by a wave of joy accompanied by a pang of fear.

Due to the potentially bandwidth taxing mix of multiple acoustic and extrasensory signals that they were monitoring, Tom had suggested that they should limit their ESP contact to Sandra and keep their other channels open for the time being. That way she could serve as a relay to the others during stressful times while the Twins were on the lookout for aircraft and radio signals. Naturally exceptions could be made depending upon the circumstances. Sandra filled the others in on the suggestion and they wholeheartedly approved the idea.

Chapter 27

36 Hours Later

Commander Cummings dreaded making the next call. "Right General, Dr. Eiger and I just searched Grant's lab and there is no sign of her or the technicians that worked there. That is correct, sir. They're gone." Commander Cummings was shouting through an annoying frazzle of static on the line. The SATCOM operator had explained that solar flares were wreaking havoc in the overseas network.

"That is affirmative; the dolphins are not here either. According to the flight manifest, most of the technicians returned to the mainland last week–except for the head tech named Chet O'Brien who stayed on with Grant. The Centron site boss informed me that the resident marine lab manager and the local native Chief are also missing–along with the Chief's new sailing yacht. Donaldson said that the Chief was planning to sail to Majuro next week. His guess is that the Chief left early and took the others with him. "

"How about the computers?"

"We haven't had time to check on the ANX or the

PIG, but the Convex in Grant's lab was up and running fine. Eiger claims that it was not infected as far as he could tell. However, all of the computers in the Centron offices here on the Main Island are toast. Eiger says that we should destroy them."

The General speculated. "Grant's Connex is okay? That seems strange, but maybe the culprits cleaned up their tracks."

"Dr Eiger just walked in. He wants to talk to you."

"Put him on the speaker phone. Go ahead Dr. Eiger; what have you learned?"

"Sir, I want you to know that I am now certain that the Dr. Grant knows about our plan to deploy ANX. I found a portable tape player and some notes in a trashcan in her lab control room—somehow they must have had a tap on the line because they recorded most of our conversation. I strongly urge that you find them as soon as possible and I would like to request more time to straighten things out."

"Listen up Eiger, we have reached the point of no return and you had better fix the problem fast or start looking for a new job. Commander, what's the mood on the Main Island? Is Donaldson freaking out?"

"No sir, he was happy to get the new computers you requisitioned and doesn't think anything irregular is going on. Apparently lots of boats sail in and out without his knowledge. Shall we check it out—Majuro that is? It's a small atoll northeast of here and the capital of the Marshall Islands. Yes sir, I'll wait right here for your call. Goodbye, sir."

The General stood, stretched, and then looked in the mirror and was surprised to see that dark rings of perspiration that had soaked through the armpits of his dress uniform. *God, I'm starting to sweat like Eiger. I just need some time to sort this out. I've got the virus that I wanted. Eiger is confused. I mean if it didn't*

TELEPATHIC DOLPHIN EXPERIMENT

work, then why were all the computers on the Main Island fried? And we have our deployment strategy all set up, ready to roll. All we need to do is to get rid of Grant and the others—a small accident at sea, and then we're back on the fast track. I just have to get a handle on this. The drop is set to come down in less than three days, but somehow Eiger let that fool Grant and her ocean going circus in on our little scheme. We gotta pull the 'destruct and disappear' act on Grant and her cronies, but without spilling the beans about ANX.

He jabbed the intercom. "Brandy, get me some ice. It's hotter'n hell in here." As soon as he iced down his drink, Houston began, "Brandy, take down this memo then send copies the Joint Chiefs of Staff and directors of the CIA and FBI. And set up a meeting right away with the President. Tell his secretary it's a matter of national security and I must meet with him today and alone."

Houston paced the room as he dictated. "Gentlemen, I am alerting you to a major breach of security which occurred today at our secret computer installation located in Enewetak Atoll in the Marshall Islands. The classified purpose of the facility is to make our nation secure against computer-based terrorist intrusion and espionage.

"At this time we have yet to determine precisely how the system was compromised, however, we have confirmed the names and identities of the perpetrators who are at this time fleeing aboard a pleasure yacht, probably to another atoll in the northern chain of the Marshall Islands."

Houston took a breath then continued, "Due to the highly sensitive nature of this act of espionage, I hereby exercise and grant my authority to use full force against these perpetrators. They are to be detained or interrogation as soon as possible. The extraordinary nature of this security violation necessitates that such extreme use of force be employed in order to preclude even the very most remote possibility that any critical information be delivered into enemy hands.

"You are undoubtedly aware that the use of lethal force is reserved only for use in the most pressing of circumstances. I assure you, gentlemen, that we presently face such a situation. I will be calling upon your full complement of military assets to accomplish this mission. In order not to cause undue international alarm, it is mandatory that you each immediately issue official press releases to the effect that your branch of government service is conducting routine, fast deployment exercises in the South Pacific. I expect complete cooperation and assume that you will alert the chain of command in your branch of service that all such assets will be made available for deployment with all possible urgency."

Houston concluded the memo with, "I will conduct a strategic briefing with you in my office at 1300 hours in order to fill you in on the details and to provide you and your staff with descriptions of the assailants. As per General Order 255, I will discuss these proceedings with the President prior to their final implementation."

Houston fished around his desk drawer, brought up a bottle of scotch, and poured his secretary a drink. He said, "Finish up with the standard confidential boilerplate, and sign my name." He handed her the cocktail and told her thanks.

After a breathless Brandy left to convert her shorthand to a word processed document and call the couriers needed to hand deliver the General's message, Houston pulled a fresh piece of note paper from his drawer. He furiously began scribbling, 'AWACS, Navy Seals, submarine, carrier, helos...?' Then gouging too hard, he snapped the pencil in two.

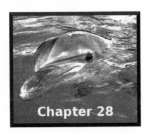

Chapter 28

Always remaining within eyesight of the boat, Tom and Sally usually swam in a tight diagonal formation. Morrow pointed out that they were employing a strategy similar to bicycle racers–alternately pulling one another along in their slipstream. The dolphin in the wake was dragged along saving energy until its turn to take the lead.

By the second day of the voyage, territories had been staked out among the crew and shipboard routine had become well established. Lookout watches were switched every four hours. Sandra often queried Tom if he detected any radio signals that might warn of impending danger, but only passing airliners and cargo vessels had been detected.

The Twins occasionally left the stern, after requesting Sandra's permission, to venture out on fishing expeditions. They remained in telepathic contact in the event that they were needed. Sandra had repeatedly demonstrated to her shipmates how she was able to effortlessly communicate with Tom and Sally. "I just think a message to them and they respond."

RON S. NOLAN

Mr. John took daily sightings of the sun at noon and the North Star at midnight using the same battered sextant that his father had used in his far ranging travels. After determining their latitude and longitude, the Chief spread his chart, marked their position with a grease pencil and then calculated the heading for the next leg of their journey that avoided the ocean traffic around inhabited atolls and the main shipping lanes.

Finally, they were making good time. The catamaran now enjoyed just the right amount of quartering breeze needed to make it fly over the water and the Twins surfed along behind riding in the Zodiac which they seemed to enjoy immensely.

At night and alone at the helm, Sandra found herself immensely enjoying the experience. The polished chrome wheel felt satiny smooth in her hands and she delighted in finding just the right heading to make the cat hum at its optimum performance. The longer they stayed at sea, the less ominous seemed the danger behind. *Could we just be imaging all of this? It would be some joke on us if this is all just a false alarm.*

The weather ahead looked promising. Solid blue patches of clear sky lined with terraces of light fluffy clouds. Not so astern. The entire northeastern sky was gray-black. Even in the middle of the afternoon that hemisphere was dark and shredded with sporadic lightening pulses. Mr. John observed that with the trade winds skewed to the east and the weather behind so threatening, they were probably barely skittering ahead of a major tropical disturbance, perhaps even a newborn typhoon.

The yacht had adopted a bedraggled Robinson Crusoe look. Laundry set out by Sandra to dry flapped in the wind like Japanese flags on "Boys' Day." A bright blue tarp was set to collect rainwater that fell in warm sheets from the occasional passing squall. Fish, split and cleaned, dangled by their tails from the rigging, drying in the hot sun Marshallese style. The fishing had been first rate thanks to Mr. John who had rigged a yellow feather jig on a stout line trailing from the stern. Morrow took great pleasure in examining the catch and expounded at length upon the natural history and behavior of the newly captured specimens. Skipjack tuna, called 'caba caba' by Mr. John, were unanimously regarded as the prize catch. The crew ate the tuna raw, sashimi style.

The further from Enewetak they sailed, the more they let down their guard. One quiet evening, when they found themselves unexpectedly becalmed, Mr. John entertained them with beautiful Marshallese songs accompanied with his ukulele. The dolphins stationed themselves alongside and participated in the party with discordant chorus of whistles and grunts. The episode provided a welcome diversion from the terror that lurked behind and possibly ahead.

Nearly all-shipboard conversations eventually turned towards their pursuers and often took the form of second-guessing the General's next move. Morrow painted the gloomiest scenario. "By now the entire Pacific Fleet is searching for us. If that's true, so far they are looking in the wrong places. Even though the Central Pacific occupies a vast area, it's only a matter of time before they move their search to the South and West."

Mr. John drew an imaginary circle around the chart of the Marshall Islands with Enewetak at the center. "If they plot all possible courses from our origin and take into account winds, currents and an estimate of our maximum speed, they can easily project the distance that we have covered. Morrow is right; it is only a matter of time before they start looking in this direction."

He pointed to their present location on the chart. "I expect to be spotted any time now by a recon flight or maybe even a surveillance satellite. But if we hole up at an island for a few days and camouflage the boat, the flights might pass overhead without seeing us. Then we could set sail again for Nauru. Plus it seems like a good idea to get near land. According to Manila radio, tropical disturbance 'Sheila' has now been upgraded to typhoon Sheila and Majuro is directly in the storm's path."

Sandra said hopefully, "Well maybe the General will think that we sank in the storm?"

Morrow wasn't convinced. "I think we are too much of a threat for him to risk an assumption like that. I'm sure he would be elated if we were lost at sea, but I doubt he would trust nature to do his dirty work. I think we should find a sanctuary and heave-to like Mr. John suggests. It will give us a chance to stretch our legs a bit on land."

Mr. John jabbed a finger at the chart. "As you can see, we have just skirted around Ebon Atoll, which puts us a few days from our destination on Nauru, depending upon the weather of course. Further to the south there is a very small, rarely visited atoll which will do nicely. It is uninhabited, except for occasional visits from Fijians who come to collect fairy tern eggs. My father and I camped there when I was a child. It was so long ago that I don't remember the island's name. We should be close by sundown, but it will be too risky to cross the shallow reef at night; we'll just drift off her lee side until tomorrow morning."

Morrow laughed, "An island with no name. Perfect!"

Sandra chimed in. "Or how about we call it 'The 'Island of Dr. Morrow'?"

"Very funny."

The shallow pass on the leeward side of the mini atoll

was just deep enough to allow the catamaran to float into the shelter of the lagoon. The largest island had once been planted in copra, but the business failed due to the lack of a deep-water port. Using the anchor windlass as a winch, they dragged the catamaran up the gently sloping beach until it was sheltered amidst the coco palms.

While Sandra and Chet collected dead fronds from the floor of the grove and lashed them in place to camouflage the boat and the Zodiac, Morrow and Mr. John used a set of paddles to sculpt out a small pool between the cat's hulls which they connected to the lagoon with a trench just wide enough for the Twins to slide in and out single file. Tentative at first, the Twins seemed to approve wholeheartedly of their new hiding spot. But they were relieved to learn that it was to be used only in the event of an emergency and quickly resumed their exploration of a nearby reef.

After a lunch of coconut crab followed by a short siesta, the castaways soon discovered that they had picked an extremely scenic site for diving. The marine life was lush and diverse. With Morrow as guide, Chet and Sandra donned masks and fins and were soon absorbed in trying to learn the names of the many kinds of brilliantly hued reef fish.

Sandra reflected that this was like a scene from Swiss Family Robinson: a warm, still lagoon, soft blue sky laced with cotton white clouds, her close friends, and her growing ever closer mate. General Houston was a mirage, the virus merely a residual bad karma from another lifetime. But at night her dreams were unsettling and she was unable to sleep soundly. Visions of frightened dolphins and savage tropical storms wound and twisted about the train in Mac Arthur Park.

RON S. NOLAN

The Next Morning

Just as Sandra was beginning to feel comfortable in the water, the image of a racing locomotive accompanied by a screeching train whistle filled her mind followed by a message from Tom. *Watch out Sandra a dangerous shark is circling ahead. Alert Morrow and Chet!*

Abruptly a gray reef shark with pectoral fins drawn down and back arched rushed towards Sandra. From out of the blue depths, Tom darted in and butted the shark in the side, knocking it off course. Sally took up station next to the group and herded them ashore as Tom ventured out in search of the shark.

Back on the beach, Morrow was ecstatic. "I have never seen that kind of behavior up close before...it was amazing to see Tom come to Sandra's defense like that. Look here he comes. Wow he is almost flying!"

Suddenly Sandra heard Tom's voice, *A plane is probing here. I can feel the electrical wave energy from above. Is this what we have been waiting for?*

Sandra jumped to her feet and thought, *Yes! Yes! Tom and Sally come now. Get under the boat quickly."*

"Morrow...Mr. John, Chet hurry–they're coming...an aircraft is coming." cried Sandra.

The painstaking job of camouflage had paid off; the four-engine propeller driven plane with Air Force insignia painted on the underside of its wings and a large radar antenna seated on the top of the fuselage flew at low altitude directly over the atoll raising flocks of startled terns. But the plane maintained its heading and grew smaller until it vanished in the clear blue sky. Tom relayed a fragment of the air crew's conversation "...what an outstanding little atoll...I plan to come back here some day with my sailboat...wife and kids...no sign of the missing catamaran, though..."

Reality had struck home. Conversations were now

exclusively focused on their dilemma. An actual shark attack and a near miss air assault were a lot to deal with in a single day. They decided to hold tight in case the plane returned. Afraid to venture back into the water, the crew was despondent to waste such a beautiful day cowering in the shade of the cabin.

Finally, the tension rose to the breaking point and a vote was taken. It was time to go. Just as the sun sizzled into the sea with a momentary flash of green, the cat cleared the reef. A brisk twenty-knot breeze brought them back on course for Nauru.

Seeing Sandra wistfully looking back at the receding island with a soft glistening in her eyes, Morrow said, "Yes it is a wonderful little atoll. Someday we'll come back and bring the kids." She laughed and kissed him.

******

The C-141's link to Washington was clear—so clear that Cummings could hear the General's labored breathing. "Yes General, our combined forces have completed a search of the entire area within a radius of one thousand miles of Enewetak. They seem to have vanished."

"What about Majuro? Isn't that where they said they were heading?"

"That's affirmative; they could be headed towards Majuro, but if so, they will be heading straight into the mouth of the typhoon. We left the Majuro an hour ago and barely escaped before the storm hit. They expect wind speeds of eighty miles an hour and very limited visibility."

Is their boat capable of weathering this storm?"

"We do have a report that one of the inter-island freighters went down. According to Donaldson, the Chief's boat is a new craft about 40' long, which is pretty big for a catamaran. It's hard to say, but the Chief is an accomplished sailor..."

"Alright. What's your plan? What do you think we should do next?"

"We are heading back to Enewetak and see if anyone has any information in the islander office. I do have a recommendation. I think we should call off the search. Yes, Eiger is here with me. He recommends once again that we delay our operation. Sir? Are you there, General?"

Cummings carefully replaced the telephone in the receiver and gave Eiger a thumbs down sign.

Chapter 29

As they entered the channel leading into the picturesque lagoon at Nauru, millions of shorebirds screeched their welcome to the voyagers. Sandra counted the days on her fingers. *Only five days since we left the lab. In some ways it seems a lot longer. I almost wish we could stay at sea and not face what lies ahead. But I know this problem won't just go away. We have to do something about it–nobody else knows what the crazy General is going to do–that is if he hasn't done it already. But nothing on the news from Manila, so we may be in time. Finding someone who will believe us will be the problem. We'll have to work out some sort of story that doesn't involve the Twins or people will think we're nuts and not bother to listen.*

Mounds of stark granular powder, the consistency of ground chalk, lined the banks of the channel. Mr. John had explained that the birds were the holy mana of the island. The Republic of Nauru was a tiny, but very rich nation with real estate holdings throughout the globe. Surprisingly, the birds were its key economic resource. The empire revolved around the harvest of bird guano.

Over the eons, natural high-grade deposits of phosphate had amassed in strata hundreds of feet deep.

Throughout the lagoon, massive freighters were tied alongside wharfs piled high with the valuable mineral. Each ship proudly displayed a flag with a red rising sun snapping crisply in the breeze at the stern of the vessel. Large yellow machines slid gigantic buckets into the piles of guano and transferred the ore onto conveyor belts, which ferried the ore into the gaping holds of the freighters.

Mr. John explained, "All this bird dung has transformed each and every Nauruan into a millionaire. They all drive Cadillacs or Mercedes—even though there are less than twenty miles of paved roads in the entire country. If they break down, they just park them along the road and cannibalize them for parts."

Earlier in the afternoon when Mr. John had risked a brief radio message to let the harbor master know of their pending arrival, Sandra had expressed concern that they might be endangering Mr. John's friend, Chief Solomon.

He replied with a toothy smile, "Don't worry. We Chiefs stick together."

True to his word, Chief Solomon had prepared well for their arrival. An immense crane waited expectantly at the dock. As soon as they came alongside, divers placed wide nylon bands beneath the hulls and the crane effortlessly plucked the sleek catamaran from the water and carried it off towards a warehouse. Smaller slings cautiously lifted the Twins onto a deep pile of padding that covered the bed of an ore truck. With the jolly, rotund Chief of Nauru personally at the wheel, the fugitives were quickly driven to the runway where Chief Solomon's Grumman twin engine cargo jet gleamed spotlessly in the brilliant afternoon sun.

Chet pleaded to come along but to no avail. Sandra

TELEPATHIC DOLPHIN EXPERIMENT

had tears in her eyes as she gently denied his request to accompany them; the road ahead was too uncertain and she didn't want anything to happen to him. He would have to take a commercial flight to Tahiti and then head back to the mainland. Sandra made sure she had his lab notebooks and gave him a hug.

Chet brightened. "I've always wanted to visit Tahiti. How about you and the Twins, where are you off to? Or is that a secret?"

"Secret to everyone but you, Chet. Morrow and I have talked it over and we think it is best for us to head to Key West. I still own my grandparents' property there and my next-door neighbor has been looking after it for me. She's a professional fly fishing guide and ties her skiff up to dock in the channel right behind her house. She has a hoist to lift it out and a loading ramp, which may come in handy. There is very little boat traffic so the Twins can hide in the channel during the day and venture out to feed at night. This way if things go bad, we can find a home for the Twins at the Dolphin Research Center on Grass Key where they should be able to blend in with their wild cousins."

After Sandra gave him a farewell hug and kiss, Mr. John handed her a golden locket and explained. This has been in my family for generations–somehow I think you and it will be famous some day and your picture will be inside. My clan thinks it has special powers. It should bring you luck; it has me."

Sandra slipped the chain with the locket over her head. "I owe you so much already, thank you and goodbye Mr. John"

Chief Solomon waited impatiently while he and the copilot went through the preflight checklist. As soon as Sandra boarded the plane, Morrow raised the stairway while the engines whined to life. The extra fuel tanks attached the wings gave the plane an international

187

range–a feature that permitted Chief Solomon to make monthly excursions to his estates in Hawaii and France. But on this flight they would only stop briefly to refuel in Mexico City and then fly on to Key West.

Solomon and Morrow's plan was to use the cover of a diplomatic flight from Polynesia bringing a gift of marine mammals to the Dolphin Research Center which would allow them to land without undue scrutiny. Sandra wondered how Morrow and Solomon had conjured up this cover story so quickly.

They must have planned this while I was talking with Chet. But the plan sounds like one that might work. Once aloft, I will get Robert on the radiotelephone and enlist his help–but I have to be careful without revealing our plain in case someone is listening.

The old pet shop, which I haven't visited since the passing of my grandparents, but to which I have been too attached with to part with, will serve as our base of operations. Operations? What operations? The only plan is to get the Twins to safety and blow the whistle on General Houston. We just need some time...and Robert's help!

After the dolphins were stowed safely in the cargo section, the jet lifted off the runway. Once the seatbelt sign went off, Sandra borrowed Solomon's radiotelephone and called Robert in Washington, D.C.

"Robert, this is Sandra. Right...long time no see. I have a major problem and I need your help. Actually I am in pretty bad trouble to tell the truth. Yes...I am serious! Robert, please listen carefully...this is going to be hard to explain and this call may be monitored so watch what you say. Okay?"

"Wow, sounds serious. Wait a second while I close my office door. Go ahead, what's the problem?"

"Remember back in high school when you took me fishing? Don't say the name of the place! I will meet you at the nearby airport tomorrow morning at six. I know this all sounds bizarre...it is. Rent one of those Rider moving trucks...oh and stop at Freddy's Hardware and purchase a couple of large tarps. And whatever you do, don't tell anyone about this!"

"Alright. I will book a flight and head to the airport as soon as I hang up. This isn't a prank of some sort is it?"

"No Robert this is for real. Please trust me. It involves national security. I'll explain everything tomorrow and cover your expenses as well."

Next Sandra called Monica Evans, her next-door neighbor in Key West and, to Monica's surprise and delight, hired her as a guide for the next week.

Monica, asked, 'What do you want to go for, tarpon or bonefish?"

"Just site seeing. I will tell you when we arrive in the morning."

"Wonderful! It will be great to see you after all of these years."

Throughout the flight Sandra frequently ducked back to the rear of the plane to check on their precious cargo. She used a sponge to wet their skins and covered them with soaked towels and blankets to help preserve their body heat. She cautioned Tom specifically not to make contact with any of the aircraft's communication systems. In spite of Chet's confidence that Tom was clean, a viral infection in the navigation computer would spell disaster to the guidance system. The constant whine of the turbines lulled her into a deep sleep.

******

Sandra jerked upright, not knowing where she was. Then the memories flooded in: Chief Solomon, King of the Birds, the mad rush to get on his plane. But something was wrong. The plane was dark and quiet. She rubbed her eyes and peered at the PEMEX fuel truck next to the plane. A dark haired man in coveralls was standing on the wing filling the tanks. She flexed to try to ease a stinging jab in her side where the armrest had dug into her side as she slept.

This must be Mexico City. That means I was out for over eight hours straight.

Morrow, his bright smile glowing in the dark, walked up the aisle and shoved a steaming basket of tortillas and refried beans into her hands. Her stomach automatically growled at the spicy aroma reminding her that her last meal had been aboard the catamaran before landing on Nauru.

Morrow opened a bottle of Corona and handed it to her. "You'll need this if you try the salsa. Buenos dias, señorita."

It was a quick stop. The engines began cranking as the attendant threw the hose down to his partner and jumped to the tarmac. As soon as the fuel truck was clear, the plane began to roll.

Morrow buckled himself in next to Sandra. "It's eleven PM Florida time. We're right on schedule; we should arrive in Key West at dawn. Don't worry the Twins are fine. How are you holding up?"

Sandra was fast asleep. Morrow carefully removed the basket and half empty beer and covered her with a blanket.

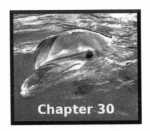

Chapter 30

Seated directly opposite the General in his Pentagon office, Cummings was at the end of his rope and needed a drink badly while Eiger was patting his forehead with a towelette wipe. He and Eiger were so groggy and exhausted from the long flight from Majuro back to Washington that Houston's obvious irritation barely registered. Except as usual, Eiger was sweating profusely.

"No General, there has been no sign of them; Professor Grant and the dolphins have disappeared without a trace."

Houston's red face peered furiously through a haze of blue cigar smoke. "So you still maintain that they went down in some catastrophic storm, right? Well just let me tell you what I think. I think that you two should be shot for incompetence, that's what I think. But maybe...just maybe you're right and those jerks are fish bait at the bottom of the ocean. You just better pray that they are...or you may end up there too."

"But sir, we have done everything that you ordered and..."

The General interrupted. "Today is Friday. The drop is Monday. I know what Eiger thinks...don't even say it. We're going ahead no matter if ANX is only half as good as it could be. That only leaves three days for something else to go wrong–like Grant showing up somewhere in front of a news camera for example.

"Cummings I want you to check with the FBI and CIA to make sure that all major harbors are covered. Get Grant's picture pasted in every post office and laundromat in the country. Put her picture on the tube too. Now I wanna hear more about these psychedelic porpoises. Go ahead, Eiger."

Eiger looked at Commander Cummings, winced and then cleared his throat. "General, I know that this will be very difficult for you to accept. But based upon a careful review of the events that have taken place and a study of Professor Grant's research proposal and the notes that they left behind, I have concluded that somehow Dr. Grant's dolphins must have used paranormal telepathy to access both the ANX and PIG computers and as a result the dolphins became contaminated by ANX and transmitted it to the microcomputers on the Main Island."

Eiger realized how bizarre his pronouncement sounded. *Could mental telepathy really be the explanation? But this seems to be the only solution that fits the facts.*

He continued, "How else could the virus have been transferred to the Centron computers. Don't you understand? This is a very serious matter. If those dolphins retain the contaminated code and they are still alive, they could infect any computer that they come into contact with. Furthermore, they must know about our intentions. As you know, we found a tape recording left behind at Grant's lab that holds the conversation that you and I had over the SATCOM network."

TELEPATHIC DOLPHIN EXPERIMENT

"Hold on a minute Dr. Eiger don't blow a damn fuse on us. You are our one and only expert in these matters. Personally, I think you are way off base, but nevertheless for argument's sake, let's assume that you' are right. I want you both to figure out a way to find those dolphins. I mean they probably could care less about a typhoon. And I have a gut feeling that Grant is still kicking around somewhere out there in the middle of the ocean—call it my ESP if you wish.

"The first thing I would do if I were her is to get back to the States. Commander, send out a Code Red alert; you know the procedure. Eiger, you look for signs of any unusual activities that might lead to their whereabouts. Just be sure there are no more screw-ups. Oh and Eiger, I will take that ANX tape now."

"But General...I'm not sure if..."

"Can it Eiger, it'll work good enough for my purpose. Shut the door on your way out gentlemen."

Eiger reluctantly deposited the briefcase holding the tape onto the General's desk and began to follow Cummings out the door, but halted when the General suddenly rose to his feet and yelled, "Hold on a second. Eiger. I have changed my mind. I want you to keep this and deliver it to Cummings team in Tijuana when he gives you the word. Guard it with your life, understand?"

Houston lovingly caressed the brushed aluminum surface and then handed the briefcase back to Eiger. A shiver of excitement racked his body as he leaned back in his leather chair and finished his drink.

Key West International Airport

As the early morning sun rose over the horizon, Chief Solomon's Grumman bled off speed and taxied to the service area. At this early hour, the airport was quiet;

the tower did not open for business until the arrival of the eight AM commuter flight from Miami. Sandra stepped gingerly from the plane, her legs knotted from sleeping in an upright position. Chief Solomon and the copilot were already fast at work dragging the pallets with the Twins to the rear cargo bay doors of the plane n a hurry to get back in the air.

Sandra was relieved to see Robert standing knee deep in weeds next to a large moving truck, staring incredulously though the chain link fence. She gestured for him to bring the truck over to the rear of the Grumman and gave him a hug when he arrived.

"My dear Sandra, this better be good." Robert tried to plant a kiss on her lips but got a taste of her cheek instead. "Aha! You are just as beautiful as I remember.

He glanced up to see Morrow glaring at them as he climbed down the stairway. He said, "Hi, I am Robert McCord, what has she gotten us into this time...smuggling marine mammals? But I don't get it. Are these dolphins from your experiment? Why did you bring them all the way to Florida?"

"I'll explain it all later. We need to get out of here fast before a bunch of nasty people begin showing up. Let's load the Twins into your truck. I wonder where the customs agent is."

Robert smiled. "Hm...I sort of took care of all that for you last night. Like the flight manifest said, these are obviously marine mammals consigned to the Dolphin Research Center. I said I would take care of it for him so not to worry. You know how the federal government works—when you have the right connections!"

"No I don't and furthermore I don't care as long as we can get going now. Your connections amaze me though."

By the time the Twins were loaded and the tailgate of the yellow Rider truck had been rolled down with a bang and locked into place, the Chief's plane was lifting off the runway. He would return to Hawaii and stay for a few days before heading back to Nauru in order to make the flight look as routine as possible–another one of Chief Solomon's brilliant ideas.

With Robert at the wheel and Sandra and Morrow crammed into the cab, they headed into downtown Key West. As they drove past the train in MacArthur Park, Sandra experienced a rush of memories and emotions.

She said, "Oh, I didn't know that I missed this place so much. I wish we could stop, but we have to get the Twins into the water as soon as possible. Take us to the pet shop and then maybe we can come back later."

Robert said, "It has been so long, but somehow it all looks pretty much the same as when we were kids."

Sandra was trying not to cry but when they reached the former pet shop, tears flooded down her face. The weathered sign with the faded cocky parrot reminded of her of happy times, going to school and playing on the train in the park and how much she missed her grandparents. *Are you with me Grandma, can you see the old parrot? Oh I how I miss you Grandma and Grandpa.*

Robert pulled over to the side of the road and asked, "Do you want to stop here?"

"No I'll come back later. We are going to the house next door. Pull up over there and let us out."

Robert did as she directed.

"Okay. That's good. The driveway ends in a ramp leading into the canal. We can unload the Twins back there. Morrow will guide you as you back the truck down the ramp. I need to talk to Monica and let her know about the dolphins."

When Monica heard the truck arrive, she threw open the screen door and ran down the steps, but stopped cold when she saw the truck shift into reverse and begin backing down her driveway.

Sandra gave her a hug and handed her a check that

she has already made out and handed it to Monica.

Monica's eyes widened and she broke into a broad smile. "Wow! This is twice my weekly rate. Where does that truck driver think he is going anyway? Are you launching a boat?"

"I have a pair of dolphins that need to get back in the water ASAP. Do you mind if they hang out by your boat for a few days? And the extra money is for you not to tell anyone."

"Ah ha! My lips are sealed. I heard you were doing marine mammal research. Are these your study animals?"

"Yes...and that is exactly what I don't anyone else to know about. Okay?"

"Roger, message received loud and clear. Let's go welcome them to the neighborhood and see what we can do to make them feel at home."

Robert and Morrow had been splashing buckets of water from the canal onto dolphins that were making anxious chirps and wiggling on their pallets. When Sandra and Monica arrived, everyone pitched in to slide Sally and then Tom into the canal where they raced up and down the waterway.

Monica went to a freezer on her porch and held up a frozen Florida pompano. "Do you think they might life to try a few of these? They're still frozen though..."

Tom messaged Sandra. *We are very hungry, thank you.*

Helping Monica throw the fish to the Twins, Sandra told her, "They will love these. Could we also borrow some line? We would like to stretch some tarps from your boat to the pier to give them some privacy and shade. After that, could you make a run to the market and load up with some fresh mullet? I would rather they stay close by rather than go out hunting on their own—at least until we get established."

TELEPATHIC DOLPHIN EXPERIMENT

"Sure, don't worry about the money. I have many friends in the seafood business."

Sandra walked to the end of the pier and was joined by the Twins who floated quietly at the end. She vocalized, "If you feel safe, I would like to go next door and check out my grandparent's place. I will be back soon, please stay nearby and alert me if you detect anything that you feel might be suspicious."

Both dolphins nodded their heads, and then swam back under the tarp.

Sandra found the rusty key hidden above the door exactly where she had left it on her last visit, which seemed like a very long time ago. The lawn was neatly trimmed. She had been afraid that the Cuban gardener that she had hired would have let the yard deteriorate into a tangle of weeds, but he had kept the grounds in good order. Time had not been so kind inside. Spiders and dust had encased everything in a thick film of grunge. The empty cages and fish tanks cast a pallor of gloom to the shop's once vibrant atmosphere and the dank air smelled like a moldy cellar.

Morrow, Robert and Monica were barbecuing fresh mullet and drinking beer when Sandra returned. She was surprised to see Monica sitting right next to Robert and was pleased to see them hitting it off so soon. They made an interesting couple. Both were tall with brown hair. Robert was wide and muscular and Monica, thin and radiant.

After dinner Robert and Sandra stepped aside. Robert patted her on the back. "Sandra, you have both mystified and amazed me. I don't know anyone that could have pulled off what you just did and I still haven't the slightest idea of what this is all about or what you are really up to."

Sandra haltingly tried to explain to Robert how the dolphins had uncovered a plot to begin World War III.

After several attempts, during which Robert had been unable to conceal his disbelief, he placed his hands on her shoulders and said, "Sandra, the last time we spoke you had just been awarded a grant to do your research. Let's start there, Okay? What happened after that?"

Sandra pointed at a couple of lawn chairs and said, "This will take a while." An hour later, after describing the events that had taken place in chronological order—including a lengthy description of the call that she recorded between Eiger and the General, she stood and said, "All right darn it; I see you aren't convinced about the ESP part, so let me prove it to you. Do you have a pen and something to write on?"

Robert rummaged through his pockets and came up with up an envelope and a ballpoint.

"Great. Write down what you want me to tell the dolphins to do and hand it to me."

He said, "Okay" and wrote. "Tell them to swim in a circle...clockwise."

Sandra nodded and issued the thought command. The Twins immediately complied and then returned to their starting point.

Robert said, "Very interesting." He wrote "Have one go around one way and the other circle in the opposite direction."

Again the dolphins did as Sandra requested.

"Sandra, I'm impressed. Let's do one more." He wrote, "Have them both come up and say something to me."

Tom and Sally obediently rose up in a waist stand squeaking from their blowholes and shaking their jaws. Robert reached down and tentatively reached out and stroked their heads as they sank slowly back into the water. Then the Twins turned together and splashed their tails down on the surface surprising Robert with a thorough drenching.

TELEPATHIC DOLPHIN EXPERIMENT

Robert whirled around facing Sandra exclaiming, "Hey, what's the big idea? You told them to do that, didn't you?"

Sandra laughed while she bent down to the boat and retrieved a towel, which had been draped on the steering wheel to dry. As she tossed the towel to Robert, she apologized. "Sorry, I just wanted to make sure that you got the message."

"I believe...oh Lordy, I believe and since you can really talk to dolphins with ESP, the rest of your story about the virus must be true too! This is a mess, isn't it? Now that I think about it, this is exactly the kind of nasty plan that I would attribute to our General Pratt Houston. I have always thought that he is easily the most paranoid individual that I have ever met—at least that wasn't committed to an institution or incarcerated.

"We need to do something about this guy right away...and you know what? President Scott is spending this weekend just up the road at Islamorada. He's combining a bonefishing trip with a fundraiser for his political party. Lots of VIPs have been invited. One of the senators that will be there is a long-time friend of mine. I will try to reach him tonight."

"Did you say bonefishing? Monica just happens to be an expert. She's the one and only female flyfishing guide in the Keys. She's good too."

"You're right that may come in very handy. There will likely be a press conference afterwards. The White House public relations staff really like to play up President Scott's love for fishing—makes him seem more like an American hero I guess, fishing and all. There's a little cabin at the Palms Motel that has been remodeled just for the President's use. They put in telecommunications, lots of security...the whole works. My senator friend has the President's trust. If anyone will listen to your story, I think it will be Jason Phillips.

"Oh Robert, I hope so for all of our sakes."

"Don't worry, Sandra. I have some connections in government that you don't know about and which I don't want to discuss. But I will tell you that I may be just about the only person that can help you pull this off in time.

"Oh my!"

"I need to make a call from a pay phone. I will see if I can get Monica to give ma a ride."

"I'm sure she won't mind. You two seem to be hitting it off nicely. I'll see you when you return. I will either be here or next-door in the old pet shop. It's a real mess."

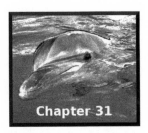

Chapter 31

Monica waited in her Jeep as Robert used the pay phone outside of Freddy's hardware store. Robert placed his classified, state of the art portable PC with its slim liquid crystal screen on the narrow metal shelf and squeezed his linebacker-sized frame past the door into the phone booth. Next he deftly unscrewed the black plastic cap at the microphone end of the handset and attached two wires tipped with small alligator clips to the exposed leads. The PC's internal modem now had access to the AT&T system. He used his credit card to call an unlisted CIA number, which, in turn, connected him to the institution's mainframe located in a basement in Langley, Virginia.

Covert operations consumed a major part of Robert's life as an undercover CIA agent. But as an intelligence analyst, he was used to drawing conclusions and inferences from scant tidbits of intercepted data—not the cloak and dagger stuff of international espionage. Langley had been a career move straight out of George Washington University, where he had received a master's degree in engineering. And to his credit, after ten years in the spy game, none of his close friends had the slightest inkling of his real profession. They swallowed without question his cover as a lobbyist for defense contractors. As a matter of fact, he did do a considerable amount of lobbying and the consulting fees that he received, with the agency's approval, dwarfed his salary as a federal agent. The net worth of a lobbyist was directly proportional to his or her contacts and sources of information and Robert's sources were the best available—making him a hot commodity as a consultant.

The computer responded with a series of prompts for access codes, passwords, and authentications—details that Robert had long ago committed to memory. He clearly understood that each of his responses opened a new access path within the computer circuitry. And likewise, hid an equal amount from his scrutiny. The agency worked on the theory that only the director was permitted to see the overall picture. The rest of the gang was only privy to information within their area of specialization.

Robert was surprised to see a flashing alert message. In his ten years as an agent it was the first one that he had ever received. He had his pager turned off, so the alert was totally unexpected.

CODE RED. ALERT!
NEED TO KNOW ONLY

SATURDAY 10. FEB 1991 – 1800 HRS

All agents are alerted to be on watch for a group of armed and dangerous enemy infiltrators operating under the guise of scientific researchers...May have 2 (two) stolen and dangerous saboteur dolphins (porpoises) in their possession.

TELEPATHIC DOLPHIN EXPERIMENT

Agents may be using the aliases of Professor Sandra Grant, parapsychologist, Dr. James Morrow, marine biologist, and John Sturtevant, Marshallese Islander Chief. Physical descriptions of suspects in detailed report file that is attached.

These individuals are believed to be armed and dangerous. They are to be approached with caution and apprehended on sight including the dolphins which are carrying a virus that may be contagious and lethal to computer systems. Notify Director Hastings upon sighting.

ONLY DETAIN SUSPECTS--DO NOT INTERROGATE.

REPEAT

HOLD, DO NOT INTERROGATE SUSPECTS

The perpetrators are suspected of planning entry via sailing vessel. All harbors are to be inspected by the Coast Guard ASAP. All agents are to report any information that may bear upon this case.

This is an authorization to use force to apprehend and detain the suspects.

Read next page (N), View details (Specs), or return to Main Menu

Robert let out the breath he had been holding since seeing Sandra's name listed. *You're right Sandra; General Houston is out to get you.*

As he downloaded the full text of the 'Specs' file onto his hard disc at 56k, a blur of green characters too fast to read scrolled across the screen. He was certain that it would make captivating reading back at the pet shop...and might reveal some clues as to what they were up against.

The only other messages in his mail slot were the expected requests from accounting to submit travel vouchers for reimbursement and an invitation to a social gathering to honor a senior analyst who was retiring after twenty-five years of service. Robert skimmed through the other options presented by the main menu looking for other mentions of Sandra and her co-conspirators. There were none. That meant that there was no history to the case, only a last minute CODE RED to seal the harbors. He suspected that the detailed report would also only contain descriptions with no background on what purported sinister crime had taken place.

This alert makes things a lot more difficult to say the least. Getting an audience for Sandra and the Twins with the President is going to be tough with them topping the international most wanted list. And this story is just too bizarre for him to listen without them there in person to provide credibility. I guess I will have to try to open the door myself.

After leaving a note for his immediate supervisor indicating that he had come down with the flu and would be out for a few days, Robert logged off the computer and dialed Jason Phillips at his home in Washington. The congressman from Virginia had just sat down to dinner.

"Sorry to disturb you, Senator. This is Robert McCord. Yes...it's nice to talk to you too Jason. I have a very serious matter to discuss with you. I'm sorry but it can't wait until tomorrow. No, I'm not at my office; I'm calling from a pay phone in Key West, Florida. It's about this dolphin matter—you know the story about the saboteur porpoises? Right...that's it. I'm glad you are aware of the situation." *He wants to know my involvement in the case. After all, he knows me as a technocrat, not a federal agent.*

"Some Pentagon types asked me to look into it, Jason. They involved me because of the technology aspect," he lied out of necessity.

"But Jason, the reason I called is that while checking this out I've run into some pretty heavy stuff. Things that I don't want to talk about over the telephone. Are you still coming here to the Keys tomorrow? No? What happened? It's Sunday instead? And you'll be at the Palms with the President? I could meet you there if you can get me on the guest list. I know that this is an extraordinary request, but I would like to meet with the President too. Well if Sunday is impossible, how about Monday? Yes Jason, I know this better be good. Believe me, it is! I'll come up to see you at the motel at noon on Monday. Thank you Jason, thank you very much."

Monica could tell there was a problem by the look on Robert's face when he returned to the Jeep, but appreciated his honesty when he told her, "Things have gotten a little complicated. It would be best if you didn't ask any questions. I'll try to get us out of your hair as soon as possible."

Monica replied, "No problem. Do you like Cajun music?" She turned on the radio and drove them home.

After carefully filling Sandra and Morrow in on the situation without revealing his source of information, they had an early dinner and retired for the evening.

Robert tossed and turned until dawn. The realization that he was aiding and abetting a group of suspected criminals didn't help matters. It was only a matter of time before he was linked with Sandra—he had the utmost confidence in the abilities of his fellow workers.

At dawn, Robert strapped on his digital quartz sports watch. He used a button on the side to enter a number then pressed it again to start the numerals spinning down. Thirty hours to wait. And they were like sitting ducks on the opening day of hunting season.

Chapter 32

Washington D.C.

I t was a fine Sunday for a football game. Cummings impulsively reached into his coat pocket and fingered the tickets for today's game. The Redskins would have a tough time against San Francisco; the 'Skins were undefeated and determined to make it to the Super Bowl after last year's disappointment. The call from the General setting up a morning meeting was certainly unwelcome, but not overly alarming. His wife, Diane could read a book in the limo while he handled Houston, then they would be off to the game. The tickets felt crisp, their surface slick. They had set him back five hundred bucks apiece, but after traipsing all over the South Pacific, he was more than ready for some time off. The General was waiting impatiently when he arrived.

"Commander, proceed with the SITREP," grumbled Houston through the usual haze of cigar smoke.

"Sir, I really do believe that they were lost at sea. It's been over a week since they left the lab and there has not been a single trace of them since then.

"Our fleet of AWACS have combed the sea for a thousand miles in every direction and we didn't find them. And sir, we know how effective our satellite imaging can be. Grant and the others have simply disappeared.

"We have checked out Dr. Grant's technicians–who know nothing, her condo in Santa Rosa–no sign of recent habitation and the Catalina Island residence and university office of Dr. Morrow–nothing there either. None of his or her coworkers admit to being contacted. No one has seen or heard from them. General, they're just gone, plain and simple."

"Commander, can you absolutely guarantee that you have left no stone unturned? Something you consider minor and not worth investigating?"

Damn! Maybe he knows about her grandparents' house in Key West. But that's halfway around the world from Micronesia. I bet anything that they're at the bottom of the Pacific.

"Yes, sir...well..."

"Well **what**, Cummings?"

"I am still waiting for more information, but the FBI discovered that a person named Sandra Grant was raised by her grandparents in Florida. Her parents were killed in a head-on collision on the Kansas Turnpike– some intoxicated KU student driving a muscle car crossed the divider and nailed them on the way home from a Jayhawk Division 1 tournament basketball game in Kansas City. After that her grandparents took her in. They lived in a combination residence and pet shop down in Key West, Florida."

"Pet shop eh? Is it still operating?"

"No. Her grandparents passed away five years ago, but Dr. Grant still owns the property–the FBI boys in Miami found out about it; they ran a computer check on property taxes and found a match. They did a drive-by recon and reported that they place looks empty. Since

TELEPATHIC DOLPHIN EXPERIMENT

Grant and her party were last seen in Micronesia, my guess is that her being in Key West is pretty unlikely. At least it seems unlikely to me."

"Commander, it's called covering all bases."

"But how would Grant get into the country? Even if their yacht really didn't go down, it would take several weeks to sail this far and all of the airports are under surveillance–plus they would have to clear customs. I'm sure we would have found them if they made the attempt."

General Houston slammed his fist down hard on the walnut desk and erupted out of his leather chair sending it caroming against the wall and upsetting one of the flags.

"Look Commander, you have been wrong before–more than once as I recall. You better get your ass on a plane heading south within the hour. Don't give me any more of this 'you're sure' crap. I want answers and I want them now. Oh...you'll have to fly commercial. I'm taking my bird to some waste of time, work-play combo event with the President down that way tomorrow."

"Then how about if I wait and go with you sir?" Commander Cummings asked hopefully.

In a softer tone, the General replied, "Look I know you been traveling a lot lately. But this is important. The ANX drop is all set for Monday and I want to be certain that Grant and the bloody dolphins don't screw things up. I'm sorry if this throws off your weekend. You didn't have anything too important planned, I hope."

Cummings realized that his hand was still in his pocket lovingly fondling the tickets. Now they felt warm and wilted. "No sir, I'll head directly to the airport. I haven't even unpacked yet from my last flight."

"Good man, Commander. Call me if there are any signs of her whatsoever. I can tell that you think this is a wild goose chase, but that pet shop sounds exactly like the kind of place I would go to hide out if I were she. I will be staying in Islamorada. Call Brandy to find out where to find me. I want to stay close to the Prez to make sure he's got his briefcase with the launch codes handy when he's out there fishing. Just think, by this time on Tuesday the world will be a lot better off. I may switch to vodka in honor of the occasion. We just gotta make sure that Grant doesn't screw this up."

Cummings stood on the curb next to the passenger side of the limo and looked down at his lovely wife. He took a deep breath as he slid into the seat next to her, handed her the tickets and said, "Hi honey, guess what?"

Key West

While Sandra and Morrow sipped coffee at the kitchen table—the very table that her grandmother had used to commune with spirits, Robert paced the dusty floor obviously in very deep thought. Sitting with one palm flush against the surface, Sandra could feel her grandmother's presence emanating from the old wood.

Robert joined them at the table and rested his elbows on the surface. Suddenly the table gave us a small lurch towards him knocking over Sandra's coffee cup. He looked up at Sandra. "Wow, did you feel that?"

"Yes. I am getting a strong sense of pending danger. We can't stay here much longer."

Robert thought for a moment and then said, "We have to get going up the coast to Islamorada. Sandra, you said the Twins swam several hundred miles behind the boat when you escaped from Enewetak. That's it. We'll go by boat!"

Sandra said, "How about using Monica's skiff?"

"No not big enough. We need a cruiser that will carry all of us on the open sea, but with a draft shallow enough to let us move in close to shore when needed."

TELEPATHIC DOLPHIN EXPERIMENT

Morrow said, "I bet that Monica knows where we can charter one."

"Good thinking. Let's go find out."

They locked up the pet shop and hurried next door where Monica was playing catch with Twins. Robert told her the situation and what they needed.

Monica smiled. "I know just the boat. It's a thirty-six foot cabin cruiser that belongs to a real estate developer and his wife that live in Phoenix. They asked me to look after it and take it out once in a while. I'm sure they won't mind, but I will call them to make sure in case they show up and think that it was stolen. I will be right back."

Ten minutes later, Monica returned. "Using their boat is a go. They say it's fueled up and stocked with food. We just neat to replace whatever we use. It also has a full complement of diving and fishing gear."

Robert gave her a hug and said, "You are a dream come true. Thank you so much."

Monica shrugged off Robert's embrace. "There's just one more thing."

"What?"

"I have to go along as the skipper and I need you to come clean and tell me exactly what you are really up to. I know this is no holiday vacation trip. What gives?"

"Okay, I promise to tell you the whole story, but can we do it once we get on board? Where's the boat?"

Monica pointed down the channel. It's docked in the marina. We can take my skiff and your dolphins can follow along behind. Load your gear while I lock up... you're CIA right?"

Robert nodded and held up his index finger to his lips.

Monica smiled. "That's what I figured. I'll be right back." She ran to the house to lock up and fetch a back-pack she kept on hand for overnight trips. When she rushed back a few minutes later, she threw off the mooring lines and started the outboard engine. She looked at Robert. "How about the truck? Do you want meet us at the marina...or take it back to where you rented it?"

"No, not now. I will have someone pick it up later."

******

An attaché from the Naval Air Station awaited Cummings at the Air Florida terminal in Key West. Sergeant Michael Mulligan looked as Irish as his name implied with red hair, red freckles and a sizable beer belly. But he talked like a southerner.

"First time I say any thin' to some'un new they think I might be a put'em on," Mulligan attempted an explanation as part of his introduction. "It's jest that I was a born and raised in Atlanta–thas why I kind'a got me a drawl instead of a brogue."

Obviously a little rough around the edges, Mulligan confessed to suffering under the influence of a brutal hangover following a Saturday night beer and tequila party with a few buddies from the base.

"Sorry sir if seem a tad under the weather." His words stretched along in no hurry to be spoken. "I jes wasn't expectin' any visitors today. Had in mind catch'un a couple of cold uns and tak'in' a nice long siesta. My cap'n says differ'nt though, thas why I'm here to help ya all out. Did ya hear about the 'Skins whopping the Niners? Man, thas a hell of a team you got up thar in Washington this year."

Cummings threw his overnight bag onto the back seat of the gray Ford sedan. Even though it was late afternoon, he could feel a deep heat that penetrated his trousers from the car seat and he began to sweat in the hot, still air.

TELEPATHIC DOLPHIN EXPERIMENT

They pulled out of the baking asphalt parking lot into a bumper-to-bumper procession of hot dog vans, ice cream trucks and rental cars. Traffic barely inched ahead, alternating lurching forward and slamming to a halt in synchrony with the Conch Train as it paused to pickup tourists bound for the beach.

"The traffic's murder this time a year. It's the peak of the tourist season and a gorgeous Sunday afternoon to boot. Might as well jes sit back and watch the scenery, Commander. You picked the right time for cruisin', but the wrong time for be'un in a hurry. As a matter of fact, thar's a great little spot jes a ways up the road, which has got the coldest draft beer in the Keys. Sits right on the beach so you can check the gals out real good. I tell ya sar, these gals they got down here make your mouth water. Hardly wear any ting at all these days. Besides, it's Sunday ain't it? We can jes stop and have one lil' ol' beer and let this here traffic die down a tad."

Cummings was cooking, tired and angry about missing the game and on the flight from Dulles, he had sucked down several gin and tonics and his system thirsted for more.

He replied. "I haven't known you too long now Sergeant, but I have a feeling we may get along just fine. I can't see how stopping for one beer could hurt our mission timetable—especially if driving under these conditions is as hazardous as you claim. By all means, I think we should at least find some place that is air conditioned before I melt into these seat covers."

"Right you are sar and lookie right thar. My goodness gracious if it's not the very same girl watcher's bar that I was jes a mentioning. May I have the honor of buying the first one of the day for ya, sar?"

"Commendable idea, Sergeant. Maybe this won't be such a bad trip after all. Let's not stay too long, there is a location that I want to check out before dark."

Chapter 33

Three Hours Later

The Sergeant's drawl became even more exaggerated when he was drinking. "Well sar, here we are approach'un the location that you specified." He gestured wildly with his left hand while steering with his right. "Let's check this place out and then resume our lil' t'ur of the best damn bars in the south. Look'a here Commander, this here is the address we been a lookin' fer. Well whad'ya know? Look at the sign. This ain't nuthin" but a damn ol' pet shop—or used to be. Looks abandoned."

The Sergeant parked the car across the street from the shop and they both, wobbling a bit unsurely, walked up the steps to the front porch.

"No lights, sar. No car...no nuthin". Ain't' nobody round here, sar."

Trying to act sober, Commander Cummings moved slowly, carefully planning his motions, but still he tripped over the top step and barely caught his weight on the handrail. He leaned over and jabbed at the doorbell, missed the mark, then hit it squarely on the second try. Nothing happened, so he used the screen door as a rapper, knocking it repeatedly against the door jam.

"You're right Sergeant, doesn't seem to be anybody at home. Just like I told that dumb jerk boss of mine, they're all at the bottom of the ocean. Lawns mowed nice though. I wonder who keeps the place up if nobody lives here."

"Thar's a big truck parked in the driveway next door; looks like someone is mov'n or out. I knocked, but got no answer. No lights on there either."

Lurching back to the sidewalk, Cummings turned and asked, "Say what's that roaring sound?"

"Sounds like a boat to me, sar. Must be from the house next door. It probably has dock on the canal. Let's take a look."

The chain link fence was choked with leafy vines that made it difficult to see so it was hard to make out details in the gathering dusk and with his blurry vision, but Cummings thought he could see two guys and two girls in shorts and T-shirts standing on the deck as the boat sped away.

Wanting to be helpful, the Sergeant squeezed in beside him and squinted through the foliage.

"See, sar. It's just a skiff headun' out to the ocean— maybe going night fish'un for crabs. They are real tasty you know."

"You're right again, Sergeant. How is the fishing around here anyway?"

"Well, sar, with a nice rig like that'n thar you could go for tarpon or bonefish. Used to be ya could always count on hook'un up with somethun' sizeable. No longer though. Probably 'cause they have these here tournaments all the time. Bring the fish back to the dock and take their pictures. Then they jes throw the carcasses back in the bay. Kinda sad seems to me, sar."

Cummings was sufficiently intoxicated to let his mind wander while leaning head first into the fence and relieving himself he rambled. "What a life...battling to the end against those giant monsters...just like the Old Man and the Sea. You know, I might bring my wife down here on our next vacation. I wonder what she's doing now. She's probably still mad about missing the games, but she might have gone with one of her girl friends. I haven't even had a chance to call her since I got here."

"How 'bout if I drive by the marina on the way back to your hotel. That way you will see whar them canals come out and there's a nice bar we can stop at with a great view of the harbor."

"Whatever you say. We need to stop somewhere; these are the only two beers that we have left." He passed one to the Sergeant, popped the top and took a big swallow from the other.

******

The tropical sky over the marina was turning golden as Monica expertly navigated her skiff through the maze of luxury yachts and shrimp boats. She slowed to a stop and pointed to the name painted in bright lettering on the cruiser's stern, 'Lady Luck'. "This is our new ride."

As they boarded, Monica stowed her skiff in the adjacent space, making sure her marina pass was easy to spot, she said, "Store your gear and then we will get underway."

The thirty-six foot Chris Craft sports fisher tied to the dock was exactly what Monica promised and Robert and Morrow wanted. The high flying bridge provided a great vantage point, yet the boat drew only three feet of water allowing it to run in the shallows. It was powered by twin 350 horse Detroit diesels and carried an outstanding top speed of just over forty knots–Monica had forgotten to reveal that the owners in Phoenix were part owners in a NASCAR racing team and the boat reflected their passion for speed. The main cabin slept four in comfort and the bow stateroom was plush and private.

"She's a real beauty," shouted Robert as he caught the last of the mooring lines tossed over by Morrow and the engines roared to life."

As the sun set with Morrow sitting next to her holding her hand, the sky overhead was bustling with soaring seagulls scavenging for scraps from the commercial fishing fleet reminding Sandra of the gulls that hung out at the train in MacArthur Park.

"Morrow, when we get through all this madness, I want to come back and show you a train locomotive that is very special. It's only a few blocks from..." She stopped in mid-sentence and then jumped up. She yelled, "Listen up everyone! Tom says we've got trouble. Some of the General's men are on their way here. They are very close. Tom didn't say how he knows, but he has always been right in the past."

Morrow shouted, "Monica, let's get going...get us out of here!"

Monica spun the wheel so fast that it seemed to blur and then smartly reversed the boat out of the dock and then nudged the throttles forward. An inner voice told her to take it easy; she reasoned that if they roared away in a panic they were sure to be noticed. A nice easy touch and they would look like just another fancy boat moving through the harbor on their way out to sea. In spite of the precarious circumstances, a smile slowly crawled across her face. The powerful boat pulsed beneath like a thoroughbred. She was back on the water where he felt most at home and this boat was a beauty.

Robert spotted a grey, four-door sedan moving along the side of the marina. He yelled, "Nobody look back. Sandra get in the cabin and stay down out of sight. And tell the dolphins to follow but not to surface for a couple of minutes...or as long they can stay underwater.

Robert was surprised to see that Monica had an ear-to-ear grin. "All right what is so damn funny? You' look like a kid in a candy store. What gives?"

"This boat is just like the one that I have been dreaming about since I was a kid. We've got enough range to sail to Bimini if we need to. Very nice living quarters, diving platform, and galley ready to sail in any direction."

Robert raised his arm, pointed and yelled, "And that direction right now mate is up the coast. Ready about, man the yardarms, and tighten the sheets; To the north, we shall sail!"

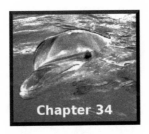

Chapter 34

A dozen formidable looking men wearing identical dark gray suits, each with a radiophone plugged into his ear, scrambled from the rear of two unmarked vans at the entrance to the President's cottage at the Palms Motel. The agents were the forerunners of the President's entourage which was presently en route from Homestead Air Force Base twenty miles up the coast. The men were all packing revolvers in shoulder holsters under their loosely cut jackets. The leader of the group gave a hand signal indicating that they were to spread out and search the premises. Weeks of tedious planning and careful preparation had taken place to orchestrate President Scott's visit, still the agents systematically opened every item that could be opened and looked beneath everything that had an underside— including the king sized bed.

The cottage next door, to be occupied by the President's private secretary, was given a similar treatment. Her room contained a red phone, which connected directly to the Oval Office. Satisfied that all was in order, the agents fanned out across the grounds and took up positions around the perimeter of the motel. This was a particularly critical time; nearly all assassination attempts took place upon a dignitary's immediate arrival or departure. The agents had been drilled to maintain strict discipline and not allow their attention to be diverted by sneaking a glance at the VIPs. Under no circumstances could they allow themselves to be caught up in the excitement of the moment; danger lurked where it was least expected. They had been trained to pan the surroundings, to consciously order their eyes to keep moving, the way a seasoned pilot scans the gauges of his instrument panel. By now it was an automatic reflex; anything out of the ordinary would be investigated with all possible haste. Curious onlookers would be forcefully, yet courteously, engaged and moved away for questioning. Vehicles were especially worrisome because they provided hiding places for snipers or they might be wired with explosives. Each agent ran down a mental list of horrors that might await the President as he stepped away from his limo. They would give their lives to see that he was protected.

This trip to the Keys required an even greater degree caution than usual. The Iraqi leadership seemingly had still not gotten the picture. To the contrary, they appeared to interpret the departure of allied forces as a signal to resume militaristic ambitions. Still, deals were made. Oil found a way out of the country, and depleted stocks of ammunition had been replenished by an international cartel of arms smugglers.

Leaks from unofficial sources hinted that the President would deliver a scathing indictment at the forthcoming press conference calling Cuba and China onto the carpet for supporting the re fortification of Iraq. The real purpose, however, was to send a clear signal that any shipments of nuclear weapons would not be tolerated. And if the Iraqi leadership was not sufficient cause for concern, there were other foes that would like to rid the world of the President. Scott's continued commitment to destroy the Colombian crack connection had prompted the Cali Cartel to post a bounty on his head. And then there was Cuba. Just 105 miles from Key West, anti-American sentiments had been fanned by our nation's leading role in the expulsion of Iraqi forces from Kuwait. A hostile Cuba was just too close for comfort.

The Secret Service had been warned to anticipate an act of retaliation from insurgents in Cuba, Iraq, or Colombia—even clandestine communications from jailed officials to their longtime thugs in Panama had been intercepted. South Florida might be a playground for the President, but to those assigned to protect him it was the one of the most dangerous locations in the entire country. They wouldn't sleep soundly until the President was back in Washington.

And to make an intense situation even more threatening, the President regarded his jaunts to the Keys as 'get away time'. He was likely to do the unplanned. After all he was a fisherman at heart. He had to go to where the fish were, not necessarily stay where he would be most secure. In order to protect the President from a possible assault by sea, a Coast Guard Cutter was stationed just offshore and the Secret Service had outfitted an armada of small boats with fifty caliber machine guns and ship-to-shore radios. The word was that no boats were to approach within a half mile of the President's boat when he was fishing. If an unknown vessel failed to heed a warning to change course, it was to be fired upon without hesitation.

The first event on the President's calendar was a poolside cocktail party and barbecue for staff, friends, and invited members of the press. Bamboo tiki torches flickered in the breeze, lending a festive tropical ambiance to the occasion. Many of the senators were embarrassed to show their lily-white legs, but President Scott had set the dress code as Bermuda shorts—no one wearing long pants was to be admitted making the agents wearing suits easy to spot.

A group of onlookers drinks in hand, stood gathered in a semicircle watching the President as he proudly displayed his prowess with a fly rod at the side of the pool. His longtime friend and fishing guide was coaching him on how to stretch a few more feet out of his double haul, the expert method for casting to wary bonefish and tarpon.

In high spirits, the President turned the rod over to the on looking wife of one of his cabinet members, who promptly demonstrated that she was halfway in the bag by slipping and falling face first into the pool. The drummer from the Caribbean band fired a crisp shot to the steel drums precisely when she crashed into the water, bringing tears of laughter to the President.

The President's good humor permeated throughout the party. As usual, many of the guests were concentrating their activities within easy range of the pair of portable bars that had been moved into place by the pool for the occasion. The President shouted to Jason Phillips, "Judging by the noise level and the crowds at the bars, the party is off to a great start. I can't wait to get out on the water tomorrow. You'll come along won't you Jason? We have extra gear for you."

Jason winced and slugged back the rest of his drink. "Yes George, I'll ride in the boat. Not much of a fisherman myself, though. Excuse me, I just ran dry. I'll round up the gals and meet you back at the table."

The ever-popular senator from Virginia was accosted by a trio of junior legislators who wasted no time in pitching the silver haired patriarch to support their side in the upcoming budget fight. Mumbling his regrets that he was wanted elsewhere, Jason edged backwards and stumbled awkwardly into General Houston. They both held their margaritas out at arm's length to keep the drips off their tennis shoes.

"My God, General. You look absolutely ridiculous in that outfit. I hardly even recognized you. Sorry about your drink, let me buy you another one. Let's try the bar on the other side of the pool, too many sharks around this one."

After topping off their whiskeys, Jason leaned closer to Houston and offered, "General, I heard about the new developments in that malignant computer virus case. Sounds like you're onto something serious. I expect you will be briefing us tomorrow at lunch?"

Shocked, Houston grabbed Jason's arm and pulled him roughly into the shadow of a nearby palm. "What do you mean briefing you at lunch? What are you talking about, Jason?"

"Surely you're kidding, Pratt. I got a call from Robert McCord Friday evening. He was insistent upon seeing the 'boss'. He interrupted a nice candlelight dinner with the missus too. McCord described how he had turned up some heavy stuff during the investigation and asked me to set up a meeting with the President tomorrow at noon. I'm surprised you weren't briefed General–I just assumed that Robert would alert the chain of command."

"Robert McCord, you've got to be kidding me. He's just a consultant for any defense contractor willing to pay his price. He's not on my payroll. But, you know now that you mention it, he would be in a perfect position to be an operative– consulting for contractors would provide a good cover. I'm just surprised that I never ran into him over at Langley. So...what did Robert have to say?"

"Pratt I have no doubt that you are in the loop. I mean you must have one of the highest clearance ratings that they issue. But, it bothers me that you don't know anything about this. Maybe Robert has some reason for cutting corners, but I can't think of any with sufficient justification to meet with President Scott—especially on one of his precious bonefish expeditions."

"I get your drift. Tell me what he said exactly."

"Robert was damn serious about what he called a computer virus called 'ANX'...said he was called in as technology expert because of his software engineering background. I didn't let on that I didn't completely buy his story. I can't remember precisely when or how I found out, but it seems to me that I have known that Robert was CIA...well, let's see...at least for a couple of years now. He only said he had some 'heavy' or 'critical,' something like that, information which he needed to relay to the President. He also said he couldn't say anymore over the telephone...like it might be bugged or something. As I said, he sounded very agitated. Acted relieved when I told him that I would set up a quick meeting. So what's this all about Pratt? Why do you think that he wants to talk to George in person? This is highly irregular if you ask me."

"Did he happen to mention where he was calling from?"

"I think he said he was down in Key West, that's why he said he would come 'up' to the meeting."

Houston was flabbergasted. *Key West! He must have met up with Sandra Grant. After all, they were old buddies; she probably turned to him for help. And I was right, they're probably hanging out at that house or whatever... pet shop that she owns down there. Cummings you jerk! I knew that you were slacking off. Now what does this all mean? It means that Robert is contact with Sandra and that she has told him about ANX. That's why he wants to see the President, to blow open the story. He figures that nobody in the agency would actually believe I am planning to launch ANX on the Russians.*

In spite of feeling a growing sense of panic, Houston forced himself to look comfortable. He laughed. "Sounds like Robert has been working too hard and could use some time off. One way or the other, Senator, if I were you, I wouldn't waste another minute worrying about Robert McCord. You said he is planning to show up at noon tomorrow. Don't worry; I'll handle it. Look this kind of confusion makes the intelligence business look bad. Don't bother the President with this nonsense."

"Whatever you say, Pratt. But please keep me informed. Always felt kind of fond of Robert. He seems like a decent guy. Aha, we've been discovered. Here comes my wife and she's wondering what happened to me. Better get back to the party."

Houston downed his drink and hurried to his limo. He used the phone in the rear compartment to place a call to his office. The night clerk relayed a message from Commander Cummings and the number at which he could be reached. Cummings picked up immediately

"Yes, sir. After talking with you earlier, I obtained a search warrant. I'm sitting in the kitchen as we speak."

"Good job. What have you learned?"

"You were right, General. It is likely that they were here and brought the dolphins with them too. There is a canal in the back and a truck parked next door that is big enough to have carried them and. Guess what? It was rented to Robert McCord!"

The General gritted his teeth, biting the tip off of the fresh cigar he had just lit. "This is just plain nuts. We have an international search going on and they have been lounging around a backyard canal in Florida all this time. So what's the situation? What are you doing to find them?"

"One of the neighbor reported seeing the Rider truck

pull up next door to Dr. Grant's old pet shop two days ago. They thought someone had finally rented the place, so they were curious. They remember seeing a couple of men and a woman that match Sandra Grant's description. They didn't notice the dolphins. They must have missed them when they were unloaded."

"Did anyone see them leave? They couldn't have just disappeared into thin air again. What about the airport? Any flights coming or going out of the ordinary?"

"It is possible that they might have flown in on a private diplomatic flight yesterday...a corporate jet registered to the Republic of Nauru—that's somewhere out in the South Pacific, General. The plane left on Saturday. They filed a flight plan indicating Mexico City as their destination. I have alerted the consulate there, but they seem to be pretty disorganized. All of the senior staff are off for the weekend. Perhaps there is more you can do along that line from your end.

"Alright. I will see what I can do."

"Oh...one last thing. There is also a distinct possibility that they left by boat. There's a dock on a small waterway out back. But I don't think that a boat big enough to carry the dolphins would be able to fit into the canal. It is quite narrow. We have a man checking the marinas just to be sure."

"Damn, use your head, Cummings. Those are dolphins aren't they? Maybe they could just swim along side. "I'll see you tomorrow. Tomorrow is gonna be a day that we will always remember!"

Seeing the acute distress registering on Cumming's face, Sergeant Mulligan handed him a beer wrapped in a wet paper towel. After chugging down the entire beer without a pause, Cummings crushed the aluminum can flat against the table and was shocked when the table seemed to skip a few inches across the floor.

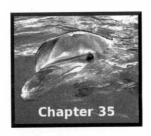

Chapter 35

Next Morning
Islamorada, Florida Keys

The sleek Chris-Craft cabin cruiser, tugging gently against its mooring lines, looked comfortably at home amidst the swarm of luxury boats. Row upon row of floating docks at Bud and Mary's Marina were jam packed with all manner of yachts: sailboats, powerboats, day sailors and ocean cruisers. In contrast to the frenzied traffic of the weekend, when sports fishers churned the harbor waters to a boiling froth, Monday morning found the harbor still and serene. The Twins had been stationed at the harbor entrance in order not to draw undue notice from the local residents. By now Sandra had established such a firm telepathic lock with both dolphins that she was able to converse with them as if they were close at hand.

Their options were limited and so was the amount of time available for them to act. After a tense, joint session, they mutually agreed that the best strategy was for Robert to keep his appointment as planned with Senator Phillips. The Chris-Craft was docked only a twenty-minute walk from the Palms Motel. Sandra would come along to support Robert's credibility if needed.

The Twins would provide reconnaissance, swimming as close to shore as possible. If they sensed danger, they would alert Sandra. Robert would carry a small walkie-talkie borrowed from the boat and Morrow and Monica would stand by with the engines at idle, ready for a fast getaway if the plan fell apart.

By now Houston would have probably surmised that they had fled by boat. Robert realized that leaving the truck in Monica's driveway might have been a mistake since his name appeared on the rental form and the credit card voucher...and it was parked next to the old pet shop which would link him to Sandra and the dolphins. If so, Robert's name would have joined Sandra's on the most wanted list. The Secret Service would have circulated his dossier and picture and that meant they would be walking into a trap.

Our only hope is that Jason Phillips hasn't mentioned our prior conversation with anyone and that he has cleared their meeting with the President as promised.

Robert checked his watch. The digital timer indicated one hour and forty-five minutes until the meeting. Soon he would know.

******

General Houston had put a plan of his own into play. He had made it clear to all concerned that Robert McCord was linked to the dolphin conspiracy. He had also let it be known that he had received a tip that McCord was in the area. Anyone approaching the Palms matching his description was to be held in quarantine for personal interrogation by Houston. The senior agent was relieved that the President would be off island throughout the day. Even still, he ordered extra precautions to be taken. If McCord was foolhardy enough to venture near the Palms, he would be quickly apprehended. Two agents wearing bathing trunks were sprawled on lounge chairs on the beach in front of the motel; weapons and two-way radio were hidden in an igloo cooler. Their white skins already radiated a painful shade of pink. Another pair of agents was playing poker at a table next to the pool. A half a dozen other men sweated inside a van stationed in the parking lot.

Houston and Cummings sat on metal folding chairs sipping lukewarm cups of coffee while the team captain made the rounds checking communications. The trap was set. As soon as Robert was apprehended, he would be turned over to Houston. All they had to do was to keep Robert out of the way for a few more hours. The balloon was going up this afternoon. After that the General didn't really care who found out about his plan. It would be too late.

Tijuana, Mexico

Frederick Sampson, astrophysicist and traitor, hastily pulled up the sleeve of his sport coat and checked the time. In less than an hour Avolar flight 32 would taxi away from the ramp, roll down the main runway at Tijuana Airport, climb to its cruising altitude then turn east for Mexico City. He squeezed the handle of his leather briefcase until his knuckles blanched white and the veins on the back of his hand swelled blue with pooled blood. After a quick check to see if the tape containing the secret Strategic Defense Initiative files was secure, he put the briefcase between his legs, picked up a technical journal and thumbed through the pages without registering the words. His mind was filled with nervous apprehension, it was as if the clockworks of his Seiko watch had entered his mind and were ever so slowly ticking away.

For weeks now, he had experienced second thoughts about going through with this part of the exchange—the last part of the deal. Each time he had made the trip to Havana in the past, he had experienced the same queasy feeling in the pit of his stomach, a sensation similar to the unexpected sudden descent of a high--speed express elevator.

When the little hunched over Hispanic man had originally approached him in the lobby of the Hotel Habana Libre on his very first trip to the island, he had thought it was all a joke—or a mistake. Why would the KGB want to meet with him? Two weeks later when the agent called him back to Cuba, he had followed the directions on the note slipped under his door more out of curiosity than with the thought of personal gain. But the little man, who spoke English flawlessly, had given him a package containing one hundred thousand dollars in worn currency. "Just to get your attention," he had offered with a smile. The man offered no other explanation and left Sampson sitting alone in the dark.

When the KGB finally made their request for the complete spectrum of new Strategic Defense Initiative developments, Sampson balanced the books of his life and came up short; a wife that was unfaithful, a teenage son whose only passion was MTV and his daughter—a bloodthirsty realtor, already divorced. But mostly he felt the overwhelming frustration of a long life lived without meaning—now that he had personal issues with his boss and was being bounced from project to project. At least he would soon be playing a role for which he would be handsomely rewarded, a project with a financial outcome far beyond that of just another peer-reviewed paper published in Science magazine. And how he regretted those countless hours of agonizing committee meetings, years of association with closed minded academicians who would stop at nothing to win tenure, or a seat on the National Academy of Science, or the greatest treasure of all, the Nobel Prize. He had been one of them, and while he was on top, he had luxuriated in the power struggle.

But there would be no Nobel Prize for Frederick Sampson. His career would end in scandal. The sympathy from family and the condolences from friends would not alleviate the pain. Sampson was jumping at the chance for a fresh start–this time with a bank account of consequence and a new identity to start his life anew. On his last trip to Cuba, he had left a reel of computer tape containing some SDI files of minor importance in an airport locker using a key he had received days earlier by mail. He was supposed to use the same procedure this time, except the files he was delivering were a magnitude of secrecy higher than those in the earlier drop.

Sampson jerked involuntarily as the boarding announcement was made first in Spanish then in English. *One last drop and this time I'm not coming back.* He reached into his pocket and felt the small key. It had arrived two days earlier by U.S. mail in a handwritten envelope. The return address listed a post office box in San Francisco. The key would open luggage locker 347B in the Havana airport. There he would find a small suitcase containing one million dollars in American currency, a passport with his new name, and the keys to his new condominium located on the outskirts of Rio de Janeiro.

He would place the briefcase containing the tape in the locker and leave the key in the lock. He knew that the locker would be carefully watched. Then he would board an Avianca Airlines flight, have a drink, and enjoy the flight to Bogotá. In Colombia he would get a room at the Airport Ramada, and then catch the first flight to Rio in the morning. *By this time tomorrow, I will be a new man–a new rich man. And I'll never look back either!*

******

Carl Eiger used the phone in the surveillance van stationed in the Tijuana Airport parking lot to call Commander Cummings and report that the exchange had gone according to plan. As soon as Cummings received the update and terminated the call, he gave a summary to General Houston.

"General, Eiger arrived with the ANX tape on time and the switch has been made. Sampson and the ANX tape have departed Tijuana Airport and are now are en route to Mexico City. There he will change planes and head to Havana as planned. We got lucky sir, the label on the tape was blank– just like it was on the trial run– so it looked exactly like the original tape. The good news is not only that Sampson is carrying the tape containing the ANX, but the KGB won't receive the SDI information they were counting on."

"Your team at the airport, they don't know about ANX do they?"

"No sir, the agents at the airport know nothing about ANX, just that we are intercepting the transport of secret SDI files by giving them a blank tape."

"Well done Commander. Are you ready to distribute the vaccine to our list of entities to be immunized from ANX?"

"Sir, I feel that I should warn you again that Eiger is worried that ANX may have been affected by recent events with the telepathic dolphins...."

TELEPATHIC DOLPHIN EXPERIMENT

"Nevermind that now. I hereby order you to proceed with the vaccination process."

"I understand. I will contact Eiger and tell him to distribute the vaccine now."

******

Sandra walked ankle deep in the ocean carrying her leather sandals in one hand; her long hair was tucked up tight beneath her favorite Raider's ball cap. Robert complimented her on her choice of a dark blue string bikini but could do little to calm her obvious anxiety about their mission. After conducting a quick sound test with Morrow using the walkie-talkie that he had wrapped in a towel, they held hands and looked like a pair of newlyweds on their honeymoon as they strolled down the beach..

Robert checked his watch timer. Since they had a half hour until the meeting with Jason Phillips. They stopped at the ocean front bar at Kokomos to kill some time. They could easily see the Palms complex next door. Perched on wooden kegs that were wobbly on the sand, they ordered two beers and tried to talk over the roar of the jet skiers who were tearing around an area roped off for their exclusive use.

The obnoxious water cycles, throbbing like angry chain saws, attacked the sea, churning the still waters into foam. Sandra checked with the Twins who had swum ahead seeking asylum from the irritating noise. Both Tom and Sally seemed nervous. Sandra was not certain if it was from the assault of the jet skis upon their sensitive ears or if they were picking up danger signals from the beach.

Robert paid the bill and they ambled hand in hand in the direction of the Palms. At one point, they stopped and waded out to waist deep water. They wanted to give the impression that they had no particular destination in mind.

The beach looked like a sea lion rookery, except the sunbathers were humans of all shapes, complexions and sizes. As Robert and Sandra neared a sign that warned 'Private Beach, Guests of the Palms Resort Only', they noticed two pale men lying close together. One rose to his knees and peered into an ice chest. He lowered his head down low behind the lid, apparently searching for something on the bottom of the cooler.

Tom came in sharply. *Sandra, I just detected a radio transmission. I believe that they are talking about you. I definitely feel a strong sense of danger. I feel that the man Houston is nearby.*

Trying to keep her voice low, Sandra pulled Robert close in a way that she hoped looked like a hug. "Tom says it's a trap! Those two guys are really Houston's men. They're waiting for us. General Houston is around here somewhere too. It's not going to work!"

"Okay. I understand. Slowly turn around and we'll start back down the beach. Don't panic—just take it nice and slow. Here let me kiss you. Make it look like you mean it."

The agent lifted his radio handset from the cooler and reported, "False alarm, Commander...just a couple of tourists with time on their hands. They're heading back down the beach."

Robert nonchalantly used the towel to wipe the sweat from his face and keyed the remote walkie-talkie. "This is Comber One to Comber Two. We are returning to base. Please have the next fishing party ready and waiting to board. Comber One out."

He tugged on Sandra's arm to slow her pace. "Don't look back. Tell the Twins to meet us back at the entrance to the harbor. Make sure they keep out of sight."

TELEPATHIC DOLPHIN EXPERIMENT

Robert took her into his arms again and kissed her deeply. Over her shoulder he could see that the lid to the cooler next to the agents was now closed and they had returned to talking and sunbathing.

He whispered in her ear, "So sorry this is just for show, but I can tell that you have the hots for your marine biologist. Here, give me your hand...and please stop that trembling."

Chapter 36

The General sat facing Cummings in the passenger compartment of a limo adorned with a Bud and Mary's Marina logos on door parked inconspicuously in front of the Palms Motel. Two senior agents wearing beach attire, sat in front, passing a pair of binoculars back and forth as they scanned the swimming pool area and the surrounding beach on the lookout for Robert McCord and Sandra Grant.

The senior operative in the driver's seat consulted his watch and swiveled to address the passengers in the rear compartment. "It's nearly two o'clock local time General. I understand that McCord's appointment with Senator Phillips was supposed to be at noon. If so, he's two hours late. Doesn't look like he's going to show today. We'll rotate our personnel and maintain the enhanced alert status, but I think you two are waiting around for nothing. I'll call you if anything should break. I know…nobody is to talk to McCord but you…I get the message loud and clear."

Houston was about to override the agent's plan, but reconsidered and said, "Just keep your men on standby.

TELEPATHIC DOLPHIN EXPERIMENT

It may be a false alarm, but you can't be too careful when the President's safety is on the line and if anyone suspicious tries to make any kind of contact with Jason Phillips, you let me know right away."

Houston took a sip of scotch then swirled the cubes around the glass in a circular motion. The limo was parked in the shade, but the air was muggy and hot.

The General studied Cummings to see his reaction and said, "Something must have tipped McCord off, but I'd bet my five stars that they're up to something. You have people watching the local radio and TV stations? How about the newspapers, Commander?"

"There are more stations and papers down here than you might think, sir. We have all the major media sources covered. But just in case, we have alerted the AP and UPI. They agreed to call us if they receive any calls about dolphin espionage or national security. That way if Grant or McCord tries to break the story by telephone, they will not find any takers. We can nip any leaks in the bud."

Houston finished his drink and checked his watch. Are we on schedule?"

"Yes sir, Frederick Sampson has been confirmed boarding the Avolar flight in Tijuana. He' should be arriving in Mexico City in three hours."

"We're almost there. By this time tomorrow he will have handed over the goods in Havana. As soon as the KGB downloads the tape, ANX will quickly spread throughout the Soviet Defense Network. Nobody will have time to worry about telepathic dolphins after that. Do you know how the drop will be made in Cuba?"

"Standard briefcase drop and switch using an airport locker has been used in the past, probably the same today. But the KGB is on top of their game. They might vary the procedure somewhat."

"Well this time they will be getting more than they

bargained for–a lot more," laughed the General.

"Cummings added. "ANX should be transmitted from Havana to Moscow early tomorrow morning. Give them a few hours to get it to the KGB strategic center. By noon our time the curtain should go up."

Houston struck a match against the armrest. "I think I'll have one of these here Cuban cigars to celebrate. But we still have to get past this McCord business. I'll check in with the boys at Langley to see if he has contacted the home agency. You get us a boat with a radio. I want to be out on the water to watch over the President personally. Tell security we're going out. Don't wanna have them sink us by mistake."

Aeromexico Airlines
Mexico City International Airport

After an hour of fidgeting and clock watching, Frederick Sampson was finally able to board Aeromexico Airlines flight number twelve. After stowing his briefcase beneath the seat in front, he closed his eyes and began taking deep breaths to try and slow his racing heart. As the engines spun up and the plane began to move away from the terminal, he paged through the Spanish version of Time Magazine that had been left behind by the last traveler. Abruptly the plane stopped; its turbines spun down to an idle, then shut down completely.

"Attention everyone, this is Captain Gonzales speaking. We are experiencing a slight delay." The pilot's voice intentionally carried a confident air of nonchalance as it reverberated over the public address system.

"We have a safety light that refuses to turn off. It's probably just a bad contact," the pilot said with a forced air of good humor. "But just to make sure, we'll have one of our top notch mechanics up here in a jiffy to check it out. And in keeping with the Aeromexico Airlines policy, we will be offering you a complimentary cocktail while you wait. Likewise in keeping with our company policy, the crew will wait until landing in Bogotá for theirs," laughed the pilot.

An attractive dark-haired hostess repeated the announcement in Spanish. This time a collective groan of frustration emanated from the tourist class of the main cabin. Frederick Sampson cursed silently as he looked at his watch; the flight was already an hour late. He stashed the Time Magazine, opened the June issue of the Journal of Astrophysics and unbuckled his seat belt.

******

Sandra and Robert sprinted the last few yards to the marina. As soon as they scrambled aboard, Morrow asked, "The Twins picked up bad vibes, right? We couldn't make out what they were up to, but Monica and I figured that something had gone wrong.

Morrow handed them each orange life jackets. He had already attached regulators to the SCUBA tanks and had piled fins and faceplates on the deck to give the impression that they were merely heading out on a dive trip.

"Here put on these buoyancy compensators; we want to look like we're heading out to dive at the underwater park at Pennekamp. We better get away from this marina and fast!"

As Morrow slipped the mooring lines, Sandra yelled over the diesels, "Tom first felt General Houston's presence, then he over detected two agents on the beach that were waiting for us. Robert and I put on act that we were newlyweds on our honeymoon and I think they bought it—at least we made it back to the boat. The

Twins also discovered that the President doesn't know anything about us. He has been out on the flats fishing the whole time."

Speaking loudly to compensate for the roar of the diesels, Robert added, "Houston must have talked to Jason Phillips and found out about the meeting, then set a trap. We got away, but that doesn't help us much does it? It might be better to give ourselves up and try to convince someone important that Houston is a madman."

"Not likely that the General would allow you to talk to anyone not in on his plan," countered Morrow.

"Well, as a last resort I could call my senior at the CIA, try to tell him what is really going on. But with an APB out on me, he would probably just humor me until they found out where I was calling from and then arrest me. Besides it might take weeks to uncover the truth, and we only have a few hours at the most before they find us."

Morrow offered a suggestion. "We haven't tried talking to a news reporter. Could we get to a local television station and broadcast some sort of news alert?"

"We would still have a serious credibility problem," replied Robert. "Houston surely has all the stations on alert by now...maybe if we had gone to the press earlier. Now it is too late. We're simply out of options."

Sandra, who had sought refuge in the relative quiet of the fore cabin to mentally talk to the Twins, returned in time to catch Robert's note of despair. "Perhaps not. The President is somewhere out there fishing isn't he? Well, we have the two best fishers on the planet right here with us. Maybe the Twins can find him—you know...somehow talk to him...or at least get his attention so we can tell him our story."

Robert had slumped into a deck chair with his face in his hands. Abruptly he jumped to his feet. "It might

TELEPATHIC DOLPHIN EXPERIMENT

work! Undoubtedly the security will be intense out there too, but if we can get close to the President—even if it is just for a few minutes, we might convince him of the truth. It's worth a try. I think that it's our best and last chance."

After they cleared the outer channel marker, Robert moved to the console and flashed Monica a 'cut throat' signal. Nodding her head, she jerked back the throttles slowing the boat as if she had applied the brakes.

Suddenly it was still. Robert said, "Now we're on to something. Let's make a plan based upon the premise of using the dolphins to make contact.

"Okay Robert. You're right, but let's not rush into this since like you said it might be our only chance. First the Twins have to find the President, and then we follow their directions. Then maybe we can anchor a ways off and put up our dive flag. Getting close enough to talk is still going to be a problem. But first can we locate the President, Sandra?"

Sandra unrolled the nautical chart that Monica had just retrieved from the cabin. "Sally says that there is a group of small boats about an hour swim away. Let's see...she says to keep the sun on our left, the boats are in shallow water that is only five body lengths in depth...say about thirty feet deep. Sally noted that there is a large bridge linking two of the islands."

Morrow pointed at the chart. "The thirty foot contour line is here. All we need to do is to follow the contour line to the bridge."

Monica joined in. "That means the President's party is about two miles offshore and five miles to the north. At top dolphin speed, we can be there in a little less than an hour. Tell the Twins to station themselves right here at this latitude and longitude. Monica grinned and yelled, "Hang on everyone," then jammed the throttles forward to the stops.

Chapter 37

Commander Cummings smiled when he opened the ice chest and found it packed with bottles of beer made by a Key West brewery—a gift from the Palms Motel management.

"We should have brought along some fishing rods, General. Maybe catch a snapper or pompano while we're out here," yelled Cummings to the General who was sitting on the fiberglass engine compartment at the stern of the sleek, silver vessel.

"Pass me another beer, Commander. You messed up royally not bringing any scotch. This beer tastes like gator piss. But you did get a hell of a fast looking boat. What is this, a water ski boat?"

"I'm not exactly sure, General. But the finish shines like a mirror doesn't it? Look there's the President's flotilla. What's your plan, sir?"

"We will just motor around and keep George in sight. Make sure nothing goes wrong. Just in case, I brought a pair of Uzis so if Grant and her traveling road show make the scene, we'll drill holes in their hull. If that doesn't do the job, I got five pounds of plastic explosive with a remote control detonator all rigged to go."

Lifting a small device that looked like a television remote control from the canvas bag, Houston pointed to a red button on top. "Just press this button and it'll blow them to kingdom come. Here, stow this bag on that shelf in the console to keep it out of the salt spray."

"Where'd you get the arsenal, sir?"

"After all this time Commander Cummings you should realize that in our business you need to be equipped to handle ugly situations. There are infiltrators and terrorists everywhere in the good ole USA and we need to be ready to take action.

"But to answer your question more directly, the arms goodies are from my limo parked in the back lot of the motel. Its trunk is loaded with various sundry weapons of destruction. That's why I always try to have a driver bring it to my meetings—even if I travel by air. You may also recall that it makes a right fine mobile office and that the bar is always impeccably stocked. Ahem...more than I can say about this particular boat and the limo you hired from the marina as a decoy, which I find both to be quite lacking in the area of refreshments."

"Look General, the President just landed a bonefish— pretty big too, I always thought that he posed for pictures with the fish that his guide caught."

"Quiet, Cummings. I'm trying to catch a little shuteye, Okay?"

******

Monica shouted over the roar of the diesels, which were revving at full speed, "I see them...four—no five boats about a mile offshore." She handed the glasses to Robert and slowed the boat to a crawl.

Robert steadied his back against the side of the cockpit and tried to keep the binoculars on target in spite of the pitching and yawing of the boat. "Someone is poling the President's boat from a platform on the stern. The rest of the boats have Secret Service agents in them. We better keep moving or we will draw their attention."

Monica edged the throttles forward to pick up some headway while Morrow peered again through the glasses. He said, "Looks like the President is flyfishing."

Monica gave Morrow gave a thumbs-up. "He is probably hunting for bonefish, tarpon usually don't come up from the Gulf until later in the year. The boats with the security guys have to stay pretty far back so as not to scare the fish. They seem to be working their way up a sandbar."

After a few moments, Morrow turned to Robert and Sandra and shouted over the engine noise. "I have an idea. If we anchor just off that little island near the drop off we'll look like we're diving on the reef. We can run up the dive flag to add to the effect. Hey! The President just landed a nice fish. That's good, they'll want to keep working the channel next to the sandbar and that will bring them closer to our anchorage. It will be much less suspicious if they come to us rather than us approaching them."

Sandra looked at Robert who nodded affirmatively. "Sounds good. Robert agreed. Let's try it. But better make a long sweep out to sea so as not to look suspicious. I have a feeling that the Twins may be able to help us out. Those SCUBA tanks are filled, aren't they?"

******

The President was having the time of his life. Jason Phillips could hardly say the same. It was still a mystery why he had agreed to come along, prone to seasickness and hating boats the way he did. Although he was accustomed to doing business on the golf course, where a cold martini and private conversation went hand in hand, fishing was definitely not his cup of tea. And every time he brought up his appeal to increase the HUD allocation for Virginia, the President had deftly asked the guide to move to a new spot or change his fly. Clearly he was not going to accomplish anything political that is worthwhile on this expedition. And now that the President was finally catching fish, the chance to beat an early retreat looked slim.

The guide balanced precariously with his weight on the pole and pointed ahead. "Sir, the current is swinging just right on this channel next to the sandbar. There should be good fishing for another hour or so—at least until the tide begins to slack. I suggest we stay just inside the bar and work our way up the channel."

"Is the current too strong for you to pole?"

"No sir, I'll use the electric motor to take some of the strain. Fish...thirty yards at one o'clock! Go ahead, cast, and let her lie. School of twelve or so real nice bonefish...tailing too! Hold it...now give it a twitch...that's right. Good, one broke off the school and he's coming our way...steady...steady...give it another little twitch...I think he's gonna take it...NOW! You got him, way to go Mr. President! Watch that coil of line at your feet. Hot damn look at him go. Good job, Mr. President. Keep the pressure on. What a beaut."

Even Jason was on his feet and complimented the President with a, "Nice going George" before sitting back in the padded chair and looking at his watch. *Blast it, it's already three thirty and happy hour starts at four.*

Chapter 38

Waiting on pins and needles, Sampson jumped when the public address system came to life. "Ladies and gentlemen, I have good news and I have bad news," announced the Aeromexico Airlines captain. "First the bad news. I am sorry to have to tell you this, but this aircraft isn't going to Cuba today. Our plane's fuel warning light was working after all. It looks like a faulty pump in the fuel delivery system.

"Now for the good news...we have another airplane that can be brought into service. It will, however, take a little time to transfer the baggage. Maria, please see to disembarking the passengers."

After repeating the captain's message in Spanish, Maria announced. "The boarding of Aeromexico flight sixteen will commence at approximately four-thirty—a little less than an hour from now and all connecting flights will be notified of the delay. Please look around your seat area to make sure that you depart will all of your carry-on items. Check the video screens in the departure lounge for the new gate assignment. Thank you for flying Aeromexico Airlines."

TELEPATHIC DOLPHIN EXPERIMENT

The slow streaming of passengers off the plane came to a sudden halt. Sampson looked on in dismay as an elderly lady, loaded down with a pair of bulging shopping bags and a folded over garment bag, stopped to vent her anger on the hostess. Her wide girth effectively blocked the exit, bringing the line of passengers behind to a standstill. Sampson felt a rush of panic.

Keep cool. This is just a routine problem and has nothing to do with me. This lady is obviously drunk. If so, they may call airport security. I have to blend into the background and wait for the next flight. I've waited a lifetime for this opportunity, another lousy hour won't make any difference.

******

Although she and Robert were swimming at a depth of fifty feet, Sandra could still clearly communicate with the Tom and Sally. She gave Robert the diver's "Okay" sign by touching her thumb and forefinger making a circle, then pointed towards an abrupt rise on the bottom which indicated the edge of the sandbar. The water was clear and warm. The sunlight filtering down from the surface cast flashing ripples on the white sand. She could distinctly feel a steady current running parallel to the bar. She checked her air gauge. The thin needle was nearly all the way to the right indicating 2,500 psi of air—enough to stay down an hour at this depth. Even though the President's boat had looked a long way off before they had plunged backwards into the water, she was confident that they had plenty of air to accomplish their mission—especially since the current was heading in the right direction. Sandra wished that Morrow was with them, but there had been only two regulators—and it was obvious from the outset that she and Robert stood the best chance of convincing the President—that is if they somehow managed to reach his boat without being shot. The trick was to stay in the deeper water until they came alongside the President's boat. Sandra hoped that the slight chop on the surface would hide their bubbles from the sharp vision of the nearby operatives watching from their mini-armada of high--speed boats.

In spite of the tension, she had to laugh at Robert. His brown eyes looked enormous inside the rubber face-mask and he was thrashing his arms and legs like an octopus having a nightmare. His mask was half full of water and a constant stream of bubbles gushed from his regulator. But after all, he had only officially been a SCUBA diver for only about five minutes. Given the fact that he was born and raised in Kansas and that this was his first dive, he was not doing too badly.

Robert was panting hard and felt like he was getting nowhere fast. It had seemed so simple when Morrow had given him the single pointer that was to constitute his entire course of instruction in the art and science of SCUBA diving. "Just breathe normally...and whatever you do, don't hold your breath when you come up...your lungs will explode if you do."

Well I am certainly not holding my breath, but I'm not breathing normally either unless diving is like running a marathon. But what about not being able to see where I am going thanks to all of this water inside my mask? Let's see if I just tilt it like this, the way Sandra just did, and blow through my nose. Voila, it worked. Much better. There's the sandbar and there go the Twins. Maybe they'll save me if I start to drown.

Sandra thought to Tom and Sally, *Be ready to catch the fish when we get close to the boat...and please help me keep an eye on Robert.*

Now that Robert could see, the full impact of the blinding white sand seared into his eyes. He immedi-

TELEPATHIC DOLPHIN EXPERIMENT

ately experienced a nauseous sort of vertigo and became disoriented. But, he recalled Morrow's warning not to surface before reaching the President; a diver floundering on the surface would draw the attention of the security force in short order. *Relax– just follow Sandra. This all sounded much easier back in the boat.*

The Twins abruptly slid down past Sandra and she gently stroked their backs as they flared by. Then they darted off in different directions. Robert could clearly see the shadow of a boat in the shallows. Intermittently, the guide's pole periodically shoved against the bottom raising a cloud of sand.

Sandra grabbed Robert's wrist to keep him from floating to the surface as they reversed direction and finned against the current to maintain their position.

Robert pointed to his weight belt and then pointed upwards trying to tell Sandra that he did not have enough weight. Sandra flipped him the 'Okay' sign once more, descended to a block of coral and grabbed hold. Morrow got the message and did likewise.

Then suddenly the Twins were back, each grasping a wriggling bonefish in its mouth. Sandra stroked the bulbous crown of their foreheads in encouragement as they swung upwards, sliding towards the skiff like torpedoes homing in on a target.

The President danced with glee, violently rocking the skiff and nearly sending his guide overboard. "How's this for fishing? Would you look at that–I can't believe it! Those two dolphins just tossed two of the biggest bonefish that I have ever seen right into the bottom of our boat. Now where'd those guys go?"

The guide was leaning heavily onto his pole trying to steady the skiff. "Geez...Mr. President, in all my years fishing the flats, I've never seen anything like this before. One of those fish might have set the world light tackle record. I'd better get them back in the water

N S. NOLAN

before they suffocate." Just as the guide left his platform and had scooped up the first of the thrashing fish, the Twins erupted from the surface, tail walking backwards. A few moments later, they threw two more trophy bonefish into the boat.

The radio in the console crackled to life. "Is there a problem over there, Mr. President? I see you have dolphins swimming around your boat."

Since the guide was busy scrambling to retrieve the lively, thrashing fish, the President picked up the radio microphone. "No problem whatsoever. These two dolphins are absolutely amazing. I really can't believe it. But I repeat...there is no problem over here. Please stay back, we're having a hell of a good time."

******

"What was that? Did he say dolphins? Cummings, give me that radio. Did he say two dolphins? Hey, look where we are, you jerk! I can barely see the President's boat from here. Come on, get this boat in gear and let's find out if those are our blasted, psychedelic dolphins."

50

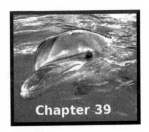

Chapter 39

Sandra squeezed hard on Robert's wrist and pointed up with her other hand. Robert nodded, released his grip on the coral and followed her upward in a cloud of exhaled bubbles. Once on the surface they threw off their masks and clung to the rail of the skiff tipping it with their weight.

"Mr. President, my name is Robert McCord. I am an agent with the CIA and I must speak with you. Our nation faces a grave danger and time is running out. Sir, I am talking about the beginning of World War III. I beg you to listen for the safety of the country. Jason, tell him he has to listen. It is extremely urgent."

Senator Phillips answered, "What in the world are you doing here McCord? Is this some kind of ill-conceived stunt or something? George this is Robert McCord and I understand that he is CIA, but I don't know what he is talking about. Except he did try to set up a meeting with you today about an espionage case, but General Houston told me not to bother you about it— that he would handle it. Do you want me to call security? Never mind, I can see that they are on their way."

The President leaned over and pulled Robert into the skiff. The guide did the same for Sandra. The President took Robert's arm and asked, "Okay McCord what is the meaning of this? What exactly are you talking about? Are you mad?"

"It's General Houston who is mad, sir. He's developed a virus to infect the Soviet Defense Network; he thinks that it will destroy their military communications and that they will panic and launch a preemptive missile strike against the U.S. But the virus will disrupt their missile guidance systems and cause them to misfire, so our retaliatory strikes will completely unopposed and apparently justified since the Russians fired first."

"Do you have any evidence to support your wild claims?"

"Yes sir, I do. One of this pair of dolphins picked up the virus with his ESP. This is the scientist, Dr. Sandra Grant, who trained them. All we ask is five minutes of your time, Mr. President, to prove our story. Don't let those agents take us until you have heard us out. If you don't believe us, we'll give ourselves up without a fight."

The President grabbed the mic and ordered the agents to keep their distance. "This better be good or you two will spend the rest of your lives incarcerated in Leavenworth."

The radio barked to life. "Mr. President, this is General Pratt Houston. We're on our way. Do not, I repeat do NOT talk with those people. They are terrorists and they plan to kill you. I am in the silver boat coming your way. Just hold on until we get there and don't bother listening to any cockamamie stories they might tell you. There are warrants out for their arrest and they are extremely dangerous. To all other security boats, stay back. I will handle this situation myself."

Robert pleaded, "No! Mr. President, it's General Houston that is the terrorist! He's the one that is crazy.

TELEPATHIC DOLPHIN EXPERIMENT

Just give me five minutes, sir, and I will prove it to you. Five minutes is all I ask."

Again there was a call from the lead Secret Service agent, now with a noticeable air of tension in his voice. "Sir, this is Agent McCowski. I insist on checking these people out. You may be in grave danger, Mr. President."

"Hold it McCowski; the situation is under control. You let General Houston in his boat through and maintain your position until I direct you otherwise. I am in no danger. These people are unarmed and one appears to be with the CIA."

******

Professor Sampson, short of breath and frightened returned to his seat in the airport lobby in Mexico City. He had just committed the extraordinarily foolish act of drawing attention to himself. In fact, he had made quite an embarrassing scene at the ticket counter demanding to know why the Aeromexico flight to Havana was still on the ground. The ticket agent tried to explain that one of the passengers had decided to cancel his trip and the baggage handlers were having difficulty locating his luggage. The explanation infuriated him to the point that he demanded to be allowed to board the flight immediately. Sampson later had returned to the counter and apologized for his rudeness, hoping that the call that the agent had made after his outburst had not been to the airport police.

The scientific journal shook in his hands as he peered over the top of the page, surveying the corridor for uniforms. He looked at his Seiko again. It was almost four thirty. *At least there is a new plane at the gate and my flight from Bogotá to Rio doesn't leave until morning. I wasn't planning on doing much sleeping tonight anyway.*

RON S. NOLAN

******

President Scott carefully stowed his custom made fly rod in the holder and addressed the guide. "Please anchor us here. We'll give the fish some time off until this situation gets resolved."

The guide jammed the pole into the soft sand and tied a line to it to keep the boat from drifting with the current.

"Alright McCord, let's hear what you think is so important that it warrants interrupting one of the few precious afternoons that I can spare for my favorite pastime. You have your five minutes."

Just as Robert began to speak, the boat lurched when Cummings accidentally rammed the bow of the General's boat into side of the President's skiff. Apologizing, he threw the guide a line and secured it to the bow.

Before the General could even open his mouth, the President silenced him with, "Shut up General until I specifically grant you permission to speak. Mr. McCord here is going to explain what is going on."

Trying to look unperturbed, Houston moved forward to the cooler and fished out a bottle of beer. With a quick glance, he made sure that the Uzis were out of sight on the shelf behind the steering console. Then he leaned casually against the wheel within easy reach of the weapons.

The President interrupted several times during Robert's description of how the ANX virus worked, how they had uncovered the General's plot, and how at that very moment a traitor was en route to Cuba to deliver a tape to the KGB which he thought contained SDI secrets, but which in reality carried the ANX.

"Some of this sounds remotely possible, McCord. I mean I happen to know something about computer viruses from the private computer literacy classes I took last year and I clearly recall authorizing funds for the Chalmer project to make certain that no virus could ever disrupt the Government Defense Network again. And you obviously have some very talented and highly trained dolphins here—excellent fishermen too. But in addition to your accusations about a trusted member of my military staff, I have to be upfront with you, the ESP part leaves me cold."

The General who had been barely able to constrain himself as Robert revealed in such accuracy his carefully conceived plan, leaped into the conversation. "Of course, Mr. President. The whole thing is a bunch of hogwash. Now will you let me take these characters off your hands? I will deliver a full report on the matter to you by morning."

Robert looked at Sandra and shrugged his shoulders in frustration and despair.

"Mr. President, my name is Dr. Sandra Grant. I am a professor at Randamount College. My special area of research is in the field of parapsychology, specifically mental telepathy to be exact. During the last several years, I have conducted many experiments in which ESP has been shown to be a scientific fact. But until recently, the results have been very subtle—that is until I started working with this pair of experimental subjects. These are two very special animals that we are talking about. They have undergone a new kind of conditioning program, which involves the manipulation of endogenous rhythm to increase telepathic abilities. They are also extremely intelligent, as animal behaviorists have been suggesting for years, but have never been able to demonstrate convincingly. I am able to communicate with them because of an innate psychic tendency which has apparently resided in the genetic code of my family for many generations."

Sensing that she was fast losing her audience, she added, "Look, Mr. President, I know this sounds like science fiction, but I can prove it to you."

Houston cried, "Come on Mr. President, this is absurd. Why don't you go back to fishing and leave these lunatics to me?"

"Wait a minute, General. Hold your horses. You seem to be a little jumpy. Maybe there is something to their story." Turning back to Sandra he asked, "How do you mean you can prove it to me?"

"Just ask me any question, sir. Make it something only you know the answer to...something exact."

"Okay doctor, that's easy. How about the best-kept secret in the world. Tell me the code that I would punch into my briefcase over there, the one handcuffed to poor Agent McCowski's wrist, which would authorize the launch of our strategic missile fleet."

Houston pleaded, "George this has gone far enough. Let's put an end to this farce."

"This is the last time that I am warning you General. Keep quiet or I'll have them remove you instead."

Sandra continued, "Sir that should be no problem. Just give me a few minutes; it is an alphanumeric code...some of the characters I do not recognize. It begins with 'FAST GRAY FOX ASTERISK PERIOD DASH DASH NUMERAL 4 NUMERAL 9'.

"Hold it right there young lady...that is quite enough. I find it hard to believe any of this, but I certainly do not want you to proceed along these lines any further. I admit that you seem to be able to read my mind. Now I think that in itself is a most remarkable feat and I will certainly want to look further into your unique ability, but that doesn't mean that the dolphins have any special powers or that rest of your story is true. I am, however, considerably impressed by your talents."

"No sir, it wasn't me. I can't read minds. But Tom

can. He did it. Tom come up here and meet the President."

Tom immediately broached next to the boat near the bow where the President was seated and squeaked a greeting while holding himself high out of the water with rapid thrusts of his tail. Sally erupted from the surface and landed sideways, creating a splash that sent a spray of water into the boat.

"And that's his twin sister, Sally. Now you be in charge, Mr. President. You just think a command and they will comply. This way you can see that I am not involved. Go ahead and give it a try."

Suddenly the Twins swam off in the direction of Agent McCowski's boat, circled it, and then swam directly back to be stroked by the President. Sally became impatient and gently pushed Tom aside to receive some of the President's attention. Then both dolphins began chattering and nodding their heads as if to say, "yes" again and again.

"You told them, I mean thought, them to do that, George?" asked Jason.

"Jason, as strange as it seems, they did exactly what I commanded them to do. This is truly an incredible phenomenon and...."

"It means that Robert McCord and Sandra Grant are telling the truth!" Jason completed the President's sentence. "And General Houston, has conspired to start a war with the Soviet Union."

Now the President and Senator Phillips were both standing, glaring at Houston. "Exactly," responded the President. "Get on that radio to the airport in Mexico City and find out which flight that defector with the tape is on, use my authority to take him into custody. Under no circumstances is he to depart for Cuba. Do it now!"

"Hold it, everyone. Nobody move. Keep away from

that radio Jason." Houston held the black Uzi pointed at the President. It was covered with a towel, but the tip of the barrel protruded ominously.

"Cummings, get your weapon and keep it down so McCowski can't see it. Bring that bag back here and hand it to me, then take a position behind the console; they won't be able to see you from there. Keep them covered."

The General nearly lost his footing as he stepped into the President's skiff. Robert tensed, ready to strike, but the towel moved quickly to put him in the Uzi's sights.

"No tricks, McCord. You've already caused enough trouble. Nobody move or the President is a dead man. McCord, you and Grant sit down on the bow seat and face this way."

The General jabbed the barrel painfully into Robert's stomach and shoved him forward past the center console. Keeping his eyes fixed on the President, he reached over and grabbed the microphone out of Jason's hand and pressed the talk switch. "McCowski, all stations, everyone listen up. This is General Houston. The President has been taken hostage by Robert McCord. He is armed with an automatic weapon. He wants you to move off...take those boats back to the marina. If anyone follows, McCord threatens to shoot the President. I think he will too. He looks like he means business. You better get a move on it."

None of the boats moved away.

"Okay Mr. President, you tell them. I will personally kill all of these people if you screw up. Just tell McCowski to back off and everything will be fine. It will too—if you go along with this. I don't want to hurt you or them. I just need a little more time to make sure that my package gets delivered. Our man should be on his way to Havana right now, Aeromexico flight number twelve, if you must know the details. Soon it will be too late for you to interfere. I know you won't order a retaliatory strike now that you know about ANX, but Israel certainly will when they see five hundred Russian IBM's heading across the Atlantic. Now order those boats to stand off or I will start shooting."

The boats turned and moved off at the President's request.

Houston continued to issue orders. "Commander, tie our boat to that cleat on the stern and pay out some line. Good, now keep them covered. Cummings, if anybody makes a move, shoot the Senator first. Watch where you aim too. Now I'm just gonna take a seat right up here on this nice high perch so I can see everybody real good. There...excellent view from up here. Don't anybody try be a hero and do something you will regret."

Gesturing to the guide, Houston commanded, "Heh you there...untie that line and drive us out to sea...very slowly too if you want to live long enough to ever go fishing again. Like I said, nobody needs to get hurt if you all cooperate."

The General's mind was racing. *This could still work out to my advantage. My story is that, McCord must have been a terrorist with a bomb bent on killing the President. It was a suicide mission. As soon as we get out a little ways, I'll blow them all to hell. Then I'll make up some excuse as to how we got away. That'll pose no problem because there won't be anyone left alive to dispute our story...and with Scott out of the way, it will be easy to convince the Vice President that the Russians are taking advantage of his assassination to attack us. Maybe I'll even run for President after this is all over.*

Robert had his head down. Sandra felt sorry for him after he had tried so hard and they almost made it too! As the boat crept forward, she caught the President's eye, but, she was completely surprised to see the beginning of a smile on his face.

In an instant, a gray mass exploded from the water and crashed squarely into the back of the General, catapulting him into the water. The Uzi, left momentarily in mid-air as the General plummeted head over heels into the water, clattered to the deck. Robert ran to the stern in time to see one of the Twins pull Houston underwater by the arm. Robert picked up the Uzi and pointed the gun towards Cummings. He barked, "Are you really ready to die for this madman?"

Cummings hesitated and Robert began to squeeze the trigger. Before the machine pistol fired, Cummings dropped his weapon and raised his arms. There was no fight left in him. A moment later the General bobbed to the surface, coughing up saltwater.

The President ordered, "Pull Houston into your boat Commander, but toss that weapon over here first."

The President held the Uzi in the crook of his elbow as he spoke into the radio microphone. "It's all over everyone. It wasn't Robert McCord who was the terrorist; it was General Houston. He and Commander Cummings will be placed under arrest. But first, I order every one to stay off this channel; we have important calls to make. Here, Jason...do whatever you need to do to find and stop that flight. It must now be allowed to land in Cuba. Next have someone pick up this Dr. Eiger that Robert mentioned. Make sure that he is put on ice as soon as possible—obviously keep him away from any kind of computer system."

Chapter 40

At last the long awaited boarding call for Aeromexico flight number twelve at Mexico City International Airport was announced. Sampson, his business suit soaked with dark circles at the armpits, moved into line with the other passengers. Just as he handed his boarding pass to the attendant, he felt a sharp jab in the small of his back. Two men in grey suits formed close ranks on either side and angled him away from the gate. One of the unseen men behind him snatched away the briefcase containing his precious cargo. Sampson collapsed to the floor seized by uncontrollable spasms yelling that it was all a misunderstanding. Within moments he had been handcuffed, placed on a luggage cart and wheeled through a maintenance exit to a U.S. Embassy car waiting in the parking lot. Not a single word had been spoken by his abductors.

******

After getting permission from the President, Robert contacted Morrow on his walkie talkie, gave him a quick update and said to come and get them. When Monica maneuvered the Chris-Craft next to the President's skiff, Robert made the introductions. Morrow apologized for meeting the President under such unhappy circumstances and Monica was uncharacteristically speechless and just smiled happily. Sandra jumped aboard and gave Morrow a long hug and kiss.

As the President's boat pulled away, he shouted, "The nation owes all of you its gratitude. There will be service medals for you all. God bless you."

Sandra waved as she watched the President's boat turn and head for the marina. Suddenly she broke away from Morrow. "I almost forgot." She pulled the boats radio mic out of its bracket and bravely spoke, "This is Sandra Grant again, Mr. President. I know this is a lot to ask, but would you come to our wedding? Morrow and I are to be married and since I have no father, I hoped that you would give me away...over."

In a few moments the President replied, "Dr. Grant I would be most honored to attend your wedding. Absolutely the least I could do under the circumstances. Have you set the date? Over."

Morrow gave Sandra a quizzical look and shrugged his shoulders. "How about next week sir? Next Sunday, would that be convenient for you?"

"Dr. Grant, next Sunday will work out fine. I will use your betrothal as a reason for another fishing trip. And since the bonefish are biting, the timing couldn't be better. Congratulations to you both. I will see you next Sunday.

Obviously in a state of shock, Morrow covered his face with his hands, leaned backwards over the rail and plunged into the ocean. When he surfaced, he broke into a grin and yelled, "Next Sunday is fine with me Mrs. Morrow."

Sandra blew him a kiss and helped him climb aboard.

TELEPATHIC DOLPHIN EXPERIMENT

McCowski and his senior operative boarded Houston's vessel under the watchful eye of a dozen other agents in surrounding boats—all with weapons leveled at Houston and Cummings. Their job was to return the traitors to the marina where an armored van would take them to the Islamorada police station for temporary holding. The young field agent operating the controls obviously had little experience at the helm. He moved carefully, tentatively engaging the levers trying to determine which was the gearshift and which was the throttle and finally got the boat underway.

McCowski stood next to the steering console, facing the stern with his sidearm pointed midway between Houston and Cummings. As their boat turned and headed back to shore, the other skiffs moved alongside.

Both Cummings and the General were sitting on the deck with their legs stretched out in front of them. Houston did not look good—the near drowning might have precipitated some sort of cardiac malfunction. His face was a sweaty, pasty white and his breathing was shallow and labored. He had little to say anyway. Cummings turned away from him in disgust.

Curiously the prospect of life imprisonment brought only a dark numbness to Cummings. But the growing realization that his wife would disown him and never want to see him again became too much. He rolled into a fetal position and lost control for the first time in his life. The sobbing just would not stop. *Oh Lord, she was all that mattered to me and now I have lost her.*

For a brief moment, Cummings' mind cleared and the wave of despair temporarily dissipated. He was surprised to realize that he was sprawled on the deck, drenched in the dirty bilge water. His left hand was resting against something scratchy.

Keeping his head down, he felt the rough surface of the canvas bag. Cummings made up his mind in a flash and deftly rolled into a sitting position pulling the bag onto his lap.

McCowski yelled, "Hey, put that down."

Cummings screamed, "Don't move. This is a bomb; my hand is on the trigger. Stop this boat right now!"

Now both agents were staring at Cummings with alarm clouding their faces. McCowski shouted, "General, is there a bomb in that bag?"

Although Houston was unable to focus his eyes, his hearing was unimpaired. He nodded yes to the question and grunted something incoherent.

Cummings rose to his feet and shrieked, "McCowski, you and your friend drop your weapons, tell the other boats to back off...then go over the side if you want to see your families again. I have nothing to lose." He patted the bag. "I mean it, now get off this boat!"

McCowski spoke into his walkie talkie and reported the situation. The other boats drifted back and fanned outward in an arc at the stern. At Cummings' insistence, the boats continued to fall behind until a distance of a couple of football fields separated the prey from the predators.

Cummings passed the two agents life jackets and then they kicked off their shoes and leaped into the ocean. As soon as they were clear, Cummings took the helm and jammed the throttle levers forward to their stops. The boat surged ahead, pounding fiercely in the afternoon chop.

The General's head slammed repeatedly against the engine compartment as the boat rammed unmercifully into the waves. Houston was too weak to lift his head away from the fiberglass housing and was dazed by the pounding, but deep inside there still glowed a mad spark of hope that Sampson might complete his mission and he would be a national hero.

Cummings abruptly slowed the boat and killed the

engine. In the distance, he could see the spray of the chasing boats as they struggled to catch up. As he watched, the boats grow larger in size. He knew he only had a few minutes before they would be in rifle range and they would be shooting to kill.

He kneeled in front of the General and, with all his might, drove his fist squarely into Houston's face. Again and again he smashed the fat man's bony skull until his knuckles lay open and bleeding.

Then collapsing breathlessly beside him, he roughly grasped the front of the General's bloody T-shirt and spat, "General, I have waited a long time to tell you this. You are a complete ass. I hate you and everything about you!" Then he reached into the canvas bag, flipped up the safeguard panel and jabbed the red detonator button.

Chapter 41

I t was another sunny and hot Key West summer
day, perfect for a wedding attended by a formal
party from the White House including the President and
Mrs. Scott and Senator Phillips and his wife. As the
men sweated in tuxedos, the women radiated glam-
orously in full-length pastel gowns. The pet shop's
grounds overflowed with bouquets of brilliant flowers,
which filled the air with a light, tropical scent. The
Twins even sported festive ribbons around their necks
and seemed to enjoy the attention showered upon them
by the guests as they cruised back and forth in the canal
behind the pet shop.

After the ceremony, the President and Sandra drifted
away from the crowd and sat close together on an
immense outdoor lounge resplendent with bright blue
cushions, a wedding present from Mr. John and Chief
Solomon who had flown in for the ceremony. The ever-present Secret Service agents sprinkled throughout the
yard respectfully directed well-wishers away from the
pair, allowing them a few moments of undisturbed
privacy. Morrow cautiously approached the lounge and

laughed, "Come on Sandra. I know you would like to bend the President's ear with your plans to build a new center, but do you have to do it today...on our wedding day?"

She replied with a smile and a wink, "Not that often that you hold the President of the United States captive in your own backyard. We'll just be a few minutes. Why don't you make sure that the guests aren't driving the Twins berserk?" Morrow got the message and drifted back towards the bar.

An hour later, the President had agreed to all of her requests, which was not unexpected since the new bride sat wide-eyed, squeezing his hand throughout the conversation.

The list was impressive: operating funds for her research, money to set up a small lab right on the grounds of the pet shop and money to buy Monica's house to provide room for expansion and security— Monica had joyfully announced that she would be moving to D.C. to move in with Robert. She joked that she would be living in sin with a national hero.

As Chet and Morrow enjoyed drinks at the outdoor bar, they went over a plan on how to move the lab computer and gear from Enewetak to Key West where they would both be joining Sandra in her next series of telepathic dolphin experiments.

Morrow finally lost patience and attempted once again to join Sandra and the President at their little private party. This time the President fondly grasped his arm and laughed, "You know you have your hands full from here on out don't you? This little gal has talked me out of a lot of taxpayer money, but who am I to refuse a beautiful bride on her wedding day? But seriously, I can justify the entire shopping list on the basis of national security. You are aware by now, Sandra, that your work does have a tremendous application for defense. You have a great future ahead in this new field of parapsychology and I will gladly support you one hundred percent."

At last there was a pause in the conversation long enough for Morrow to interject, "You are right, sir about the defense potential of Sandra's work. Remember how she used telepathy to order Tom to attack the General? That was a darn good demonstration of ESP!"

Sandra shared a knowing glance with the President. She was about to reply when he slightly shook his head from side to side, so she remained silent.

President Scott quickly continued, "She sure is something isn't she, but there is one thing that I would like to know—tell me if it is too personal. But sometimes even the President of the United States is interested in domestic matters. I mean at home, I actually am a devoted husband and father too."

"Of course, sir. What is it that you would like to ask?" beamed Sandra while moving over to allow Morrow to join them on the lounge. She could feel the weight of the heavy new gold wedding band on her ring finger.

"Well...let's see...maybe I shouldn't say anything, but earlier in the afternoon I was over at the dock watching your fabulous dolphins. It was strange; Sally kept turning over on her back and Tom kept flapping her stomach with his fins and making sounds like a baby crying. At first I thought they were just playing but then I had...it is hard to explain...a sort of vision that you...well...anyway, how should I put this? All right, I'll just spit it out...do you know if it's a boy or a girl?"

Morrow looked questioningly at Sandra. She flushed crimson, smiled and said, "Oh that." Sandra turned and took Morrow's hand. She softly said, "Sally's imaging sonar works just like a medical sonogram. She can see that I am expecting!"

"You two are so fortunate," said the President. "More

congratulations are definitely in order. Why don't I just commandeer one of those bottles of champagne sitting all by its lonesome over there? I'll be right back, save my place. Morrow keep your seat, you look a little pale. I'll see you shortly."

Speechless at first, Morrow gently took Sandra's face in his hands. "A baby? You mean you're...I mean we are going to have a baby?"

Sandra kissed him passionately while the President cheered and pounded Morrow on the back. She whispered into Morrow's ear. "No my love, two babies...twins and..."

Morrow lifted her by the waist and joyously swung her around in a wide circle. He carefully lowered her down and after another kiss he finished her sentence. "And that means we will soon have our very own new pair of paranormals. Hallelujah!"

About the Author

Ron S. Nolan, Ph.D. studied marine biology at Scripps Institution of Oceanography where his doctoral research focused upon the ecology of coral reef fishes in Enewetak atoll ...quite a leap from his early days in Western Kansas where he shared the farm outhouse with a nest of half frozen rattlesnakes and learned to read by the light of a Coleman lantern!

Engine 1073 located in Watson Park in Lawrence, Kansas serves as a key psychic power spot in the TDE novel. For more backstory topic descriptions, please visit my website.

Photo Courtesy City of Lawrence, Kansas

Planetropolis Publishing
www.planetropolis.com

Metamorphosis Chronicles (Met Chron)™ explores the future of a human society that is confronted with the threats posed by rampant climate change and AI androids and robots that are competing with *Sapients* and *New-Humans* for jobs and natural resources on an over-populated planet Earth controlled by profit-driven, corporate governments.

_____-

Planetropolis Publishing
www.planetropolis.com

271

MET-CHRON SANCTUARY
Metamorphosis Chronicles Book 1

Astra, a head-turning, Brazilian girl in her mid-twenties is not only beautiful but also brilliant…and in big trouble! After discovering a key to the genetic aging clock that could dramatically increase the human lifespan, she is tracked down by a psychic who delivers a stern warning that she must work to heal the planet before adding to the over population crisis by allowing a select few to live longer lives.

In the year 2029, the terminal impacts of global warming are having disastrous effects on ecosystems and global tensions have escalated as countries fight to extract the last barrel of oil. Astra's new mission is to assemble cryogenic repositories ('Arks') of frozen plant and animal embryos to preserve them for the future. However, she is opposed by a fanatical religious group that will do anything to stop her. But is it the Ark that they really want…or something hidden within? Either way, they will have to go to a mining base on the moon to find out.

Now Available in e-Book, Softcover & Hardcover.

MET CHRON NEW-HUMANS

Metamorphosis Chronicles Book 2

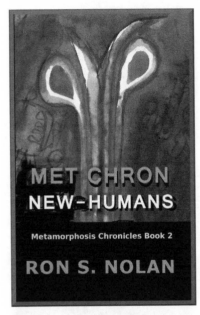

Set in the year 2030, a Sci-Fi technothriller of a world near the global warming tipping point and humanity's survival is threatened, from the author of *Met-Chron Sanctuary and Telepathic Dolphin Experiment.*

Timing is everything. If the intern at the SpeeZees Lab on the Moonbase doesn't accidentally select the wrong code sequence in a training program, the world's first New-Human will not be 3D printed and brought to life....and without Chron's genius, the strategy of developing a space elevator to convey pods of seawater into space and generate snowfall over tropical seas, coastal cities around the world will face catastrophic flooding. Furthermore, if Chron does not assist her longevity research, Dr. Astra Sturtevant will not make her game clinging discovery of how to control the genetic clock and arrest the aging process. Meanwhile, the AI androids that had mutated in the high RAD zones following the nuclear detonations in the Bay Area, have launched campaigns to gain their independence and plan to annihilate all organic humans. The innovative pioneers that operate the Deep Space Mining Moonbase have a plan that will solve humanity's problems. The question is will anyone listen?

Available in eBook, Softcover & Hardcover
www.planetropolis.com

FREEDOM RIDE

Short Stories and Poems

From the wheat fields of Kansas to surfing the immense waves on the shores of Planet Nuptia, the author takes readers on a journey which may be referred to as the "future meets the past."

In "Earth Boy" a child is held captive on Europa and in the "Longevity Gene" a geneticist searches for a gene complex that may hold the key to immortality while stock car drivers race around a track in Alabama and discover something totally unexpected.

As the book title suggests, searching for and struggling to acquire independence is the underlying theme of Freedom Ride's short stories which concludes with poems about seagulls, crows, ship wrecks, dangerous sharks and young love that makes today seem like yesterday.

****

If you would like to be notified when my new novels are published, send me an e-mail at nolan@planetropolis.com

My website has book descriptions, interviews and backstories that reveal some of the amazing adventures that have shaped my career as a science fiction author.

IF YOU BUILD IT THEY WILL STAY

YOUR GUIDE TO CONNECTING GENERATIONS IN THE WORKPLACE

CHRIS CANO

ChasingHappyatWork.com

ISBN Paperback: 978-1-64746-355-7
ISBN Hardback: 978-1-64746-356-4
ISBN Ebook: 978-1-64746-357-1
Library of Congress Control Number: 2020912289

Dedicated to my family:

Thank you Jessica, Lelia, and Henry for all of your unwavering support!

TABLE OF CONTENTS

PART II: LEADING IN A GENERATIONAL WORKPLACE

INTRODUCTION

I recently attended a conference and had the pleasure of speaking with many of our new and future leaders. These leaders are in their mid to late-twenties and are referred to now by most people as millennials. As I spoke to them, there was a recurring theme as we talked about how their acclimation to the workplace was going. The vast majority felt that their education and experiences to date had not prepared them for the world they were stepping into. They had a desire to lead people but had a hard time assimilating into organizations. That rough transition led to challenges with their peers and bosses, which ultimately led to issues with their teams.

This new generation of leaders and employees has been heavily stereotyped by employers, the media, and just about anyone else with a noteworthy opinion. The terms "narcissistic, disrespectful, and entitled" are frequently used to describe an entire generation of workers. The reality is that as employers, that could not be further from the truth. This generation is predominantly made up of educated, innovative, and motivated individuals who need guidance and direction to help them succeed in the organizations we have built.. Their definition of longevity looks much different from that of their predecessors, and their outlook on what it takes to be successful is also very different. As the mentors who have been charged to guide them, we must understand where they are coming from, what influences them, how they learn, where they find support, and what we can do to influence their growth.

If you are an employer and you are reading this, then I want to thank you for taking the first step in creating an environment that will not only attract millennial talent, but will also foster retention. You are taking the first step in tearing down stereotypes and will ultimately reap the benefits of having a passionate and engaged workforce. Part one of this book will provide you with information and systems to activate the benefits your team brings to the table and capitalize on the potential they exhibit. Part two will focus on the traits you and your leadership team can hone to ensure you are guiding your team in the right direction.

If you are a millennial or new leader and reading this, then you will be looking at this book from a couple of perspectives. First, you should look at some of the difficulties your employer is having connecting with you and creating an environment for you to thrive in. You need to understand that to make an impact in the future, you need to understand the past. The rules, processes, systems, and norms of the organization you are joining or are a part of are extremely important to the people who work there. The more respect you pay their accomplishments, the more support and empowerment they will give you. You will have plenty of accomplishments someday, and I am sure you would appreciate the same from the incoming generation. Next, you need to answer most of the questions as you move through the book. The more prepared you are to help your employer, the more symbiotic the growth will be. Understand that amenities, perks, and services are great, but their value is usually fleeting. Work to build the things that connect you to your company's mission, vision, and values so you will be able to do the same for your future teams. Finally, if you lead people already, then you need to read this book from both perspectives, working as a millennial and as an employer. Remember, influence does not always come from the top, and by practicing the leadership traits in part two, you will be able influence others from any level of your organization.

Thank you for taking this step. Please feel free to reach out to me at any time at www.jlhleadership.com.

PART I

CONNECTING GENERATIONS

*A genuine leader is not a searcher for consensus
but a molder of consensus.*

—Martin Luther King Jr

CHAPTER 1

THE REAL MILLENNIAL QUESTION

The children now love luxury. They have bad manners,
contempt for authority; they show disrespect for elders
and love chatter in place of exercise.

—Socrates

The tone of the room turns to one of silence and reflection as an executive begins to volley the thought that the reason turnover is so high and productivity continues to suffer is because this new generation of millennial leaders does not have the same focus or dedication as their predecessors. Furthermore, our inability to manage them has led to greater concerns, though the concerns were never really addressed. The forty-five or so leaders in the room all nod their head in passive agreement.

This training class we were all attending was one of the standard corporate classes designed to build leadership skill in one area or another. It focused on generating conversations that led to actions designed to improve the work-life of the team, thus improving the performance of the organization. One of the standard exercises was splitting the room up into quarters and rotating through a SWOT analysis for the organization. Many things became similar trends across all of the groups, but one became particularly evident—those in attendance were struggling to connect with the new generation of leaders, the millennials.

Most in the room had opinions about the generation, but as we cursorily dipped our toe into the conversation, most used buzz words that they had heard somewhere. The terms "entitled, selfish, narcissistic" were brought up, but in equal measure, they thought they were extremely educated, innovative, and passionate. After just a few minutes of banter, a more prominent leader in the room basically stopped the conversation and asked the room to move on.

This conversation encouraged me to talk to some of my leaders when I returned to my property to gauge their thoughts on the subject. Most of them are millennials so their thoughts revolved primarily around being misunderstood. One of them brought up an interview Simon Sinek did on the "Millennial Question" for Inside Quest. I had not seen the video, but I promised the team I would watch it. Apparently, about five million other people had seen it to this point, which made me feel a little like I was hiding under a rock somewhere.

To be truthful, I had never paid much attention to the millennial Question. As a leader born in 1979, I was basically the tail end of Generation X, and I was before the start of the millennial generation, which is largely identified to start somewhere between 1980 and 1984. For me, these were my peers, and I had just simply been a little ahead of them. The generational question I had struggled to answer during my career was how to lead older Generation X or baby boomer leaders as a relatively young leader. The thought of being worried about leading people younger than me had never crossed my mind.

As I watched the Simon Sinek video, I learned a few things. The first thing I learned is the generational divide had apparently been given a name, and it was ever-widening. Sinek began to attribute the concerns of the millennial generation to four things: parenting, technology, patience, and the environment. He cited a few studies throughout the fifteen-plus minute analysis, and in the end, I was left with more questions than answers. I then proceeded to watch dozens of responses on YouTube, watched several TED talks discussing the generation, and began to read the research that most of these thought leaders cited.

As I returned to Sinek's video, two statements stuck with me. First, millennials are looking for ways to acculturate outside of their family into the greater tribe. I attended a talk where Seth Godin was the keynote speaker, and he touched on the thought of tribes. Godin's definition of a tribe during that talk was "a group of people that care about each other, their goals, and their culture." As this new generation of workers and leaders matriculate into society, they are struggling to find a means to connect to a group or organization because, in many cases, they cannot identify the culture of the group they are joining. Sinek points out that the evolution of the corporate structure will start moving to one that attempts to connect passion and purpose to this new generation of leaders. Corporations are finding out, "You can't be a tribe of everyone," as Godin points out. Defining what matters to the company and synthesizing that into a connection with this new generation will start to form the tribe they are seeking to acculturate into.

The second thought from Sinek's Millennial Question interview was that there is a "lack of good leadership." Godin further supports this by identifying that we "have a shortage of leaders that help us connect and grow." As organizations and corporations start to try and make a meaningful connection with a new generation of leaders, they are also struggling with a gap in good leadership that has permeated most levels of their entities. The 1980s and 1990s leader with a title and a directive has fallen by the wayside, and in their place is an expectation of a leader who is a coach or mentor and less of a boss. During the training class I attended, one of leaders said they get frustrated because they cannot tell someone to do something anymore. That simple statement illustrates the much larger issue—we have grown into a society filled with managers and very few leaders. Developing leaders who understand how building connections and growing their teams leads to success may be the answer to the millennial question people are so intently asking.

Sinek explored several more controversial reasons for the widening gap between millennials and the generations that preceded them. He suggested things like the way they were raised, the connection between social media and addictive behaviors evident in alcoholism and smoking, and the impact of technology on the ability to connect. All of the thoughts were supported by research and begin to address some of the reasons why there is a perceived divide between the generations. Sinek never really provided his answer to the question. His postulated thoughts were intriguing and stimulating, and to his credit, in a later video, he asked for constructive feedback to help grow the thought leadership on this subject.

Maybe the real millennial question is less about the nuances attributed to this generation and more about the way we communicate as leaders. Like with previous generations, the answer always lies in the evolution of our norms and the way we communicate those norms to our teams. There will always be things that earmark generations. Still, one consistency is once you find a way to inspire and motivate them, the larger challenge lies in gaining their enrollment through communication, connection, and action. A further look at the last statement breaks the key components down into four words: enrollment, connection, communication, and action.

ENROLLMENT

The summer months are particularly busy at the hotel I run, and as the general manager, I make it a point to be on the floor most of my day. One day, I went to our restaurant during lunch, and as they were busy working, I jumped in to help. After taking a few orders and clearing a few tables, I asked one of the senior servers if we were missing someone. He replied he had not seen Miguel for a while, and as a result, the restaurant was backing up. As I asked around, another server said he saw Miguel walk out toward the beach. I quickly headed that way to track down my missing server. When I arrived, I found Miguel staring at the ocean. I walked up next to him and suppressed my urge to ask him why he was out there. Instead, I simply asked if he was okay. Miguel looked at me and said that he did not come all the way from Cuba to not matter, to *just be a server* at a restaurant. I asked him what he wanted. He told me he wanted to make a difference in other people's lives but did not think he could do that where he was. He said he joined our company because of the unlimited opportunities. But over a year later, he was still stuck as a server.

Most leaders I have met would have stormed out to the beach after Miguel and fired him because this had been an ongoing issue with him. Instead, I looked at Miguel and simply asked him what he was doing about it. He said he had applied for other jobs but had not gotten them. I again asked him what he was doing about it. After a few volleys back and forth, he basically decided he had really done nothing to get where he wanted to go. I told him growth happens in small, measured steps done daily, and it did not happen overnight. I asked when he last read a book that he was not forced to read in school. He said he did not think he had ever read a book someone had not forced him to read. I told him maybe he should choose to read a book about what he would like to do. I told him my door would be open if he chose to take that step. He smiled and ran back to the restaurant.

About three weeks later, he stopped by my office and asked if we could talk. I told him I would love to. He said he had finished reading *How to Win Friends and Influence People* by Dale Carnegie. He asked if I had ever read it, and I nodded, a little stunned. He spent the next 15 minutes downloading, in exciting detail, the contents of the book. In those 15 minutes, I could see his engagement. A light turned on within him, and as he turned to the last page in his book, he started to see more clearly where he could go and what he could do. In that one simple action, Miguel enrolled in his future and our business.

Seth Godin identified, "the key to enrollment is having the right people on the right bus." Miguel and I began to discuss what his seat on the bus looked like. It was clear that he did not want to be where he was, so I told him we had a position open at the front desk. It would be a step backward in pay, but it would give him a chance to work on all of the things he had recently learned from Carnegie. Miguel took the job. Six months later, he was promoted to supervisor, and six months after that, he became a manager. When I asked him what that meant to him, he said the money was nice, but he was finally in a position to make a difference.

Enrollment will be paramount as leaders attempt to answer the millennial question. Finding a way to ensure the connection between the organization and the individual inspires leaders to want to succeed. That inspiration will drive them to achieve results. A leader who dictates terms to their team will engender a disconnect with demotivated individuals in the wrong seat on the wrong bus.

CONNECTION

The thought of connection has changed greatly since I was a child. When I was growing up, we made connections face to face, and because those connections were generally hard to come by, it meant something when they happened. Growing your connections required you to maintain your current ones and took the time to explore the people your friends and relatives were connected with. To foster those connections, you would have to set aside time to meet, write letters, call them on the phone (that was attached to a wall), and sometimes hang out even if you had something else you would rather be doing. Those connections built friendships that required a solid amount of time and effort to foster and maintain. And when you lost one of those connections, it hurt.

Today, connections are different. There are so many more options for meeting people. The world has become so small, and technology has become so powerful. As a result, connections are being made instantaneously. The Internet, social media, cell phones, and the like have made identifying and interfacing with people worldwide as simple as logging on and sharing a thought, sometimes with only a picture. I do not think many people would argue that today's connections are not as robust as they used to be. Still, at the same time, it is where we have evolved to, so finding a way to incorporate the new paradigm of a connection into our workplace could help to answer some of the posed questions.

An organization or business needs to find a way to incorporate the concepts of lasting and instantaneous connections. The connections will build a stronger network with your team and ensure that those connections become assets.

COMMUNICATION

There are more avenues than ever to communicate with. The reality is the delivery method is not the issue with communication. The president of the United States of America tweets. CEOs and department heads blog. New companies are entering the market every day to give team members more of a voice than ever before. YouTube channels and Podcasts provide team members with verbatim thoughts from their leaders on almost any subject they could ever care to ask about.

One of the largest reasons communication is breaking down today is not a lack of delivery methods, but rather a lack of trust. I do not know how many times I have heard the sarcastic phrase, "Well, if it says so on the Internet, it must be true." Since most of the communication today is through the Internet in some form or fashion, the default premise is most of what is communicated lacks the credibility of truth. When communication lacks the element of truth, you lose trust. People worldwide fail to truly communicate because developing trust has become increasingly harder to do.

Companies have long provided their employees with mission statements, mottos, and values hanging on office walls but usually not exemplified by even the officers of the company. As the new generation of leaders are entering the work force and searching for the company's mission, trust with each leader is broken and does not connect with the mission, vision, and values of the company. No number of tweets, Facebook live videos, or blogs can re-instill that trust.

ACTION

I have been told the largest gap is the gap between thinking and doing. One of the most common examples of this gap happens to most people I have met around the start of a new year. Millions of people step on a scale and immediately declare this is the year they will lose weight. The gyms and health food stores are packed for the next 14 to 30 days with people trying to achieve their weight loss goal. What quickly happens is that more than 80% of people break their New Year's resolutions by the end of the first month.

In most cases, those people spend 30 days planning the weight loss, finding the right clothes to wear to lose weight, and probing friends about their methodology. Usually, they hope for a new pill or procedure to make the fat melt off. To lose weight, you have to take intentional and measured steps daily while focusing on achieving your goal. Too many people focus on the outcome and not enough on the steps to get there. People who successfully lose weight are either highly motivated or highly systematic.

This new generation has more distractions than ever, which has resulted in more excuses as to why tasks cannot be done on time. They are one Netflix binge away from putting their great thoughts and good intentions into action. Leaders who want to inspire growth in this generation must guide the team in the concept of execution through intentional growth.

The millennial question is one all organizations and corporations must ask themselves. However, this question must not be how to work with a group of entitled, narcissistic, selfish people who still live with their parents. That base premise is flawed to the point that it discourages actual growth within an organization. The opening quote from Socrates may have been read as a reflection of people's current views of millennials. Learning to connect with a new generation has been a challenge throughout time; this generation is no different. Technology has sped up the way people communicate and consume information. As a result, leaders have to learn new ways to communicate, grow, and inspire one of the most educated and innovative generations in history. Understanding what the actual millennial question is, finding ways to bridge the generational divide, and consistently executing on re-imagined means of engagement will ensure the future success of any organization.

CHAPTER 2
THE GENERATIONAL DIVIDE

Few will have the greatness to bend history itself;
but each of us can work to change a small portion of the
events, and in the total; of all those acts will be written the
history of this generation.

—Robert Kennedy

On January 21st, 2017, an estimated 15,000 people took to the streets of Omaha, Nebraska, to protest for women's rights. The turmoil after the 2016 presidential election led to many similar demonstrations all around the country. Activists engaged in a peaceful protest in a manner that echoed efforts of the past. Omaha is of particular importance to me because my aunt marched alongside those 15,000 people to voice her concerns not only for her rights but also for her children and grandchildren's rights. A woman who graduated in the 60s was once again marching right alongside today's new social activists.

This is the same voice as a student who graduated in 1965. Martin Luther King delivered his famous "I have a dream" speech in 1963, which caused people to march against injustices and segregation. Two historically iconic figures, Martin Luther King and John F. Kennedy, were assassinated, which left the country feeling uneasy. The Vietnam War had been raging since 1955, which engulfed the youth of America with growing unrest as to why we were still there. In 1962, Rachel Carson's book, *Silent Spring*, launched an environmental movement that led to a focus on pesticides like DDT and the proliferation of industrial waste affecting the environment. President Nixon's impeachment followed all of this. Like the 60s and 70s, Americans in 2017 were actively protesting racial injustice, human rights violations, the necessity of ongoing military action, environmental degradation, and political and ethical transgressions.

On January 21st in Omaha, Nebraska, the generations found a way to cross the divide and stand united for something they believed to be important to protect. While generations may be struggling to find common ground in the office place, they are finding ways to connect like never before on social issues and philanthropic efforts. This common ground can provide a road map to crossing the divide and creating bridges to foster lasting growth for all parties involved.

In the workplace today, we primarily see baby boomers, Generation X, millennials, or Generation Y. Today, the commonly accepted year ranges for a baby boomer were being born from 1946–1964. Generation X was born from 1965–1976. Generation Y or millennials were born from 1977–1995. In my research, I have seen most of these dates within a plus or minus of four years. If you are on the line of one of these generations, you probably exhibit characteristics of both or lean strongly one way based on the influences you experienced growing up.

In 2008, I became the director of operations for the non-gaming side of a casino. My job was pretty expansive, covering more than 500 employees in about a dozen different departments. I was in my mid-twenties and found myself for the first time having to rely on building relationships with leaders and employees who were, in some cases, 40 years older than I was. Previously, my roles had been mostly through the front of the house of luxury hotels, so nearly every employee or leader was within ten years of me. I remember my first department head meeting, where I realized I was the same age as more than half of my leader's youngest children. At that point, I was not as worried about earning anyone's respect as I was trying to find something to talk about that did not make me sound like I was asking my parents if they could clean up their laundry before my friends came over.

On my first day, we had our first leadership meeting that went as well as could be expected. People found out a little about me, and they left with assignments. There was some measure of alignment, but I left with a mountain of homework. My first order of business was to speak with my director of housekeeping for the hotel. Sarah was a no-nonsense woman who had been a professional housekeeping leader for more than 40 years. I was in her office for about three minutes when I heard people gathering outside. It was time for the daily housekeeping meeting, where everyone met to get their assignments, seek alignment, and get motivated for the day. These meetings are fairly commonplace in the industry and are a prime stage for housekeeping leaders to shine. Generally speaking, if you have not been in housekeeping, you fall flat on your face because you do not have a way to relate to the team staring back at you. If you do not captivate them within the first minute or two, you are sunk.

Sarah gave me a half-smile and said, "Come on, let's go meet the team." She said good morning to the team, and they replied, "Good morning!" in a thunderous roar. Sarah promptly said, "This is Chris, our new director of operations," and then took a step back. The hospitality industry is a pretty high turnover industry, so I had seen this scenario play out on many occasions. The new executive stands up in front of the team and reads off their list of accomplishments and credentials, says something cliché, and then walks out before the meeting is over, to a faked golf clap. I was not about to be one of those guys.

When Sarah turned the meeting over to me, the first thing I did was say good morning in the four languages I knew (that was about all I knew in three of those languages). Housekeeping is a diverse workforce, usually consisting of team members who speak English as a second language. The room erupted with "good mornings" in their native languages. I saw smiles staring back at me. As I picked out a few replies in the crowd, I was able to make my way through, shake their hand, and ask where they were from. Someone would say Haiti, and everyone from Haiti made a noise. I did this a few times, and everyone in the room was smiling. I told them I was from a lot of places, but Ohio was where I called home. I said I was excited to be part of the team, and I could not wait to meet everyone over the next few weeks. My credentials, accomplishments, and business acumen never came up. I got to shake almost everyone's hand when they left the room, and we got things started on the right foot.

As Sarah and I returned to her office, she looked at me and said, "That was pretty good." She thought that I would try and prove myself with my title or job knowledge like my predecessors had, but instead, she said I saw them as people and not housekeepers. I started the meeting by asking about her, and we began discussing things I was not going to find on her resume. I asked her what her biggest challenges were, and she went through a myriad of organizational and systemic issues she was having trouble getting through. She asked about me, my wife, and my background. We discussed the fact I had been a director of housekeeping before, and that led to conversations about solutions.

The reason that introduction and meeting were so successful was that I did not look at the team as housekeepers or employees. I did not fit them into stereotypes or worry about their age; I looked at them as people. There has been a lot of talk about the differences in generations, but at the end of the day, everyone wants to be treated as a person, not a position, title, or generation. I left the four-hour meeting with Sarah and headed to the lunchroom. I had not really met anyone else at that point, but as I exited the lunch line, a housekeeper flagged me over and asked if I wanted to join them. I sat down and was introduced to not only the housekeeping team but also a few members of a few departments that I had not met with yet. We had some great conversations, and those relationships helped me introduce myself through several of the other areas I oversaw. Again, focusing on people as individuals overcame any age, language, or cultural barrier that would normally have been an impasse to communication.

I recently read an Inc. article that referenced a concept from the digital analyst, Brian Solis, called Generation C. The C stands for the "Connected Consumer" and refers to "anyone who integrates technology into their daily routine, regardless of age." The article later goes on to point out there are many definitions from many people for the letter C in Generation C, but the key component is connectivity. This generation is made up of people from every current generation class, despite the fact it is most commonly connected to the millennial generation. This generation lives an algorithmic, curated lifestyle not dependent on traditional media, and it values the opinions of their social media networks above the canned testimonials of the past.

I admit I have been severely behind on the social media movement. I have sat through countless presentations and demonstrations on uses and best practices but had a hard time finding a need for it in my daily life. Once I started to use it, I was shocked that, without fail, the first like, comment, or share I received came from someone older than me. That person was usually my parents' age, and when you looked at their profiles, they were posting, interacting, and updating at a pace that would put my college-aged sister to shame.

The Generation C concept is outstanding because it illustrates the possibilities of what can happen when labels are removed, and threads are used to connect people. One adjective that could be used for the letter C could be *commonality*. This simple concept provides a road map for any employer who is racking their brain, trying to find ways to connect with any generation. When I had to connect with the housekeeping department, I simply needed to find something we both cared about. Some of the most amazing relationships are built on finding common ground and growing from there. Think of every couple you have met who has stayed married 40, 50, or 60+ years. They never start by talking about their differences. They begin by discussing the commonalities between them that helped to strengthen and grow their relationships.

As an employer, the idea of a *connected* generation should be a breath of fresh air. You do not have to have the amenities of the GooglePlex or funky office spaces that resemble adult playgrounds. Rather, you simply have to identify commonalities in your team, and build through them. In the workplace, Generation C could stand for culture—a group of people of all ages connected by the norms, practices, and environment that breeds and grows connectivity.

When I started at my most recent hotel, there was a significant amount of change as the property was doubling in size. That type of expansion leads to rapid hiring and usually a higher than normal turnover. The local area workforce was not great, so in the first year of operation, we saw more than 100% turnover. There were dozens of contributing factors, but at the end of the day, the largest one was our inability to connect as a team. Leaders in their 20s were trying to engage a team that was, in many cases, two or three times their age, and this led to a myriad of shortcomings on both sides.

I attended a conference, and Jon Gordon was the keynote speaker. He spoke to our room full of executives about his book, *The Energy Bus*, and how it can be used to improve everyone's life through the power of positivity. The book was a simple story with a simple concept, and I took some notes but did not do anything right away. When I returned the following week to my site, I observed dozens of interactions where communication and lack of connectivity was a detriment to the team and the overall operation. I decided we needed a better way to communicate, and we needed to have something everyone could get behind, or on board with, in this case.

I decided to launch an Energy Bus initiative at my hotel. I took the book and worked with about 25 team members from all levels to develop a great presentation I would personally deliver. The concept was well put together, and there was already buy-in from a solid number of team members from all levels. I delivered the message over a week to every team member in a small group setting. We posted the Energy Bus Rules, and the entire property helped to create values we would all adhere to. The attitude, engagement, and even vernacular of the property changed. People were *getting on the bus.* There were no *energy vampires* allowed, and everyone said they were too blessed to be stressed.

Over the next two years, our turnover plummeted to less than 15%, our employee engagement numbers rose from 73% to 90%, and we won dozens of awards including the coveted Resort of the Year, which recognized outstanding achievement in every phase of operation. The trick was not the 12-foot bus poster with everyone's photo Velcroed to it, and it was not the other posters or even the commitment by the leadership team to remove anyone who was not *on the bus.* Rather, the results came from having a common set of cultural norms that provided us all with our unique means of communication. This culture enhanced the why of the property, which was to deliver unforgettable experiences to make vacation dreams come true.

My crowd did not see my aunt in Omaha as a baby boomer, instead, she was seen as an activist. Everyone in that crowd found a commonality that united them to a common cause regardless of their age, race, sex, or sexual orientation. In the workplace, we do not need to find a trick or a program to bridge and bind generations; we simply need to remember to treat everyone like a person and find ways to connect those people to a common cause.

It is important to understand the millennial generation better so we can begin to effectively create the inroads of commonality that will lead to future success in our personal and professional lives. The rest of this book will provide some information on the millennial generation. It will point out some key non-negotiable traits that have been identified through extensive research from leading agencies like PEW, Price Waterhouse Cooper, and several more. The result will be an introduction to the concept I call "Creating A Millennial P.A.C.T." This will be a set of guidelines to help establish the culture, commonality, and connectivity that your organization and you as a leader are looking for.

CHAPTER 3
WHAT DO WE KNOW?

From my very first day as an entrepreneur,
I've felt the only business worth pursuing in business
is to make people's lives better.

—Richard Branson

Earlier, I mentioned a book by Jon Gordon called *The Energy Bus*. It is a great story of someone who can overcome their negative view of the world by finding the positivity through a series of collective connections that lead to amazing things for everyone involved. In this book, the protagonist, George, is told about ten rules for the ride of his life. Whenever I started to explain these rules to my team during the rollout, I always became stuck on rule number eight, "love your passengers." I always got stuck because we are not supposed to discuss love in the workplace. If we do, it is usually accompanied by corporate relationship agreements or the awkward discussion about sexual harassment.

In this case, Gordon uses the phrase "love your passengers" to encourage people to get to know the team they work with. This is always a tough concept to teach because generally, in the workplace, relationships stop at a cursory level. If they extend to a deeper level, then there is usually a business motivation behind it. As we work to integrate new generations into the workforce, knowing what motivates them and getting to know them personally will be the difference between harnessing their potential and wasting their talent.

At one of the hotels I worked for, a new cook was hired into the kitchen team. He was quirky and quiet, and he struggled to integrate with the kitchen team. He did not process things the same way everyone else did, and since this was his first job as a cook, he did not have the practical experience to fall back on. At one point, the kitchen team grew so frustrated with him, they asked the leaders of the department to consider removing him from their area. The food and beverage manager did not want to make that call because she felt the cook had not received a fair shot.

By chance that night, the manager was on Amazon looking for a book to help her come up with the best way to deal with building non-traditional relationships like the one she was dealing with in the kitchen. She made a mental error and typed in the name of the cook that everyone was having trouble with. To her surprise, listings in the book section came up with his name. Even though this cook was only in his early twenties, it turned out that he had already written four books and had also been recognized for his accomplishments in the art community. The leader started reading some of the available text and was able to gain some insight into how the cook thought.

With her newfound knowledge, she worked up a plan to combine the information she gained with a style she could introduce to the team to get the most out of the new cook. It turned out if you engaged his creativity and gave him a platform to express his thoughts, he came out of his quiet shell and contributed to the team. The concept of personalizing the work experience to gain higher levels of productivity from team members is a fairly common leadership concept. Still, common knowledge does not always equal common practice.

There are countless studies, articles, and blogs that discuss what we think we know about the millennial generation. The Internet is full of TED talks, editorials, and YouTube videos that provide insights into this new generation, and business and organization leaders continue to digest this information at a fairly high rate, making experts out of even the most passive observer. With all of this knowledge, there should be countless strategies that employ empirical data to help businesses forecast and project the needs of their new workforce. Their future can be secured with the understanding that their product, group, or service will be well taken care of down the road. Unfortunately, there may be too much information, so all of this has led to analysis paralysis. I want to point some of what I feel are the most important points about this generation, so we can start developing strategies for capitalizing on the unique attributes that make them great.

10 THINGS TO KNOW

There are a lot of them—A recent article in the USA Today points out that as of 2017, millennials have officially become the dominant generation in the workforce. In fact, by 2020, the workplace is projected to be comprised of more than 50% millennials. By 2025, that number will balloon to more than 75%. That equates to roughly 81 million workers in the workplace by 2025.

Social Responsibility Matters—This new generation is looking to challenge the baby boomers as the most charitable generation. Currently, 84% of millennials surveyed will donate to charity during the year. Further, more than 72% will donate their time to a charitable cause.

They Are Connected—More than 75% of millennials have a social media profile, which is not entirely surprising, but when you consider the breadth of potential socioeconomic barriers, it is impressive. Additionally, more than 80% sleep with their phone by their bed, leading to a constant state of connectivity.

Not Business as Usual—As many as 66% of this generation have a strong desire to be entrepreneurs. The success of young captains of industry and the limitless possibilities our suddenly compact planet provides have inspired this generation to live their passions as opposed to servicing someone else's.

Innovation Matters—The corporate structure and rules are a major deterrent to millennials entering the business world. More than 63% of millennials believe management's attitude is a significant barrier to innovation, and 61% believe operational structures and procedures stifle innovation.

The Autonomy of Groups—The millennial workforce is clamoring for more autonomy, but that autonomy comes with a caveat different from previous generations. They like the empowerment, freedom, and flexibility that comes with autonomy. Still, more than 70% of respondents are excited about a decision they make when their friends agree with their decision.

Homeward Bound—One of the more prolific stereotypes of the generation is they all still live at home. In actuality, an estimated 30% of the generation still lives at home, but to be fair, many are still in school. School loan debt has ballooned to crippling levels, and parents are more amiable to it now than ever before.

Changing Roles in the Workplace—There are some sizable shifts in how this generation views the workplace environment. Many millennials prefer a job rotation versus a more time-consuming promotion as their time is much more of a premium. They also believe work output is king, and factors like hours worked in a day and years with the company should not be deciding factors when discussing growth opportunities.

Interviewing You—This new generation is looking to be connected to a cause, and if they can connect a cause to your business, they are more likely to engage with you. They also believe that the most important factor in taking a job is the opportunity for personal growth and development. Only 21% of millennials surveyed made an employment decision based on pay. Payroll has become a *threshold issue.*

View of the Top—Bosses are now expected to be mentors and coaches. Those mentorship programs become deciding factors in retention. They have also clearly identified the number one reason they leave their jobs is because of their boss.

The first time I did a presentation with this information, I was in a room of about 25 people, none of whom could be confused with a millennial. These were my peers in the hospitality industry, made up of mostly site general managers and regional corporate leaders. They had a genuine interest in the findings and were excited to hear what they could do to crack the new generation's code. As I went through the presentation, everyone was highly engaged, and they provided a ton of feedback. I hate to say it, but I may have learned more during that presentation than they did. There were some very insightful observations to show how most of the stereotypes and generalities that follow the millennial generation are not as believed as the surveys would have you think. One of the participants had more years of experience in the industry than

I had been alive, and it was interesting to hear him say that, "you just can't tell them to do something anymore. You have to explain the value in that thing, and then work with them to get it done." The team agreed, and they went on to say some form of that probably should have been done all along. Now it is no longer a best practice but rather common practice.

Leaders who are able to take some of this information and adapt it to their teams will be the type of environments that promote growth, collaboration, and mentorship. Those environments will equip leaders with tools far beyond compensation to attract premium talent. Environments designed around growth will foster more sustained results in the coming years.

CHAPTER 4
ESSENCE OF A PACT

*Service to others is the rent you pay
for your room here on Earth.*

—Muhammad Ali

As you start to look into what a pact is, you have to start with the definition. When you apply it to people, the definition of a pact is a formal agreement between two people or groups made to help each other. This is important because as we move forward, we will be doing just that—working on ways for two people or groups to find common ground and help each other succeed. Like with any agreement, emotion is a contributing factor to success. Marketers will tell you ads and products become transcendent when they connect with the passion of the target audience. In addition to passion, there has to be a sense of authenticity with the product or service and the people providing it. As the millennials continue to search for connections and purpose within the workplace, they will seek out employers who can tap into their passions and provide a sense of authenticity.

About a decade ago, I found myself sitting in a conference room surrounded by several people who looked a little different than I did. They were covered in tattoos and piercings, their attire for a business event was pretty much like that of a Friday night, and it was hard focusing on what was more of a spectacle between the hair color and hair gel. Pumping through the room was some very trendy music, most of which I had never heard. The room was adorned with images of Johnny Cash, Kurt Cobain, AC / DC, and some artists that I did not even recognize. I was at the corporate orientation for Hard Rock International.

I had left Ritz-Carlton, where ladies and gentlemen serve ladies and gentlemen, for an opportunity with a brand I had only known for t-shirts and cheeseburgers. My business attire consisted of a well-pressed suit, conservative shirt, and cap-toed shoes polished to a high shine. I thought maybe I missed the memo on casual attire, and immediately I thought this was going to be a long week. My dress-down clothes included a sport coat which was not the same color as my slacks—yes, slacks. I thought I had captured the Hard Rock spirit by leaving my ties at home. I had two, but that's like nothing for a week-long business conference.

Just then, a short man exploded onto the presenter's stage with a look like Bono and energy like Angus. Jim Knight had arrived. Jim was the cultural ambassador for Hard Rock International. He was charged with indoctrinating all new leaders with the Hard Rock Spirit. I was a bit thrown off, but at the same time, I could not help but get caught up in the excitement of the room. People in the room knew who he was and looked at him in awe like a Rock Star.

My whole life had been a mixture of Mr. Marriott's staunch conservatism and the exacting service culture of Ritz-Carlton. When I took my first leadership role as a management trainee in Washington D.C. at the J.W. Marriott, I remember people asked me if I was going to wear that olive-colored suit again.

I chuckled and asked why and was basically told if I was not wearing one of the same color suits as the photo of the two Mr. Marriott's hung behind the front desk, then I was going rogue.

Jim Knight quickly started talking about the Hard Rock culture. I found myself enthralled by stories like how the first piece of memorabilia was collected when Eric Clapton wanted to reserve a seat for himself at the first Hard Rock Café in London. He did so by hanging his guitar over the seat. Pete Townsend and thousands of others followed suit by donating memorabilia to what is now the largest collection of music memorabilia in the world. The unbridled spirit of the company led them to destinations all over the world, creating cafes that sometimes resembled more art than architecture. Their intoxicating spirit to serve others permeated every facet of every program.

I connected with two words Jim used and the way that he talked about them. He said the company's spirit was authentic, and everything they did had to be authentic or guests would not buy into the culture. To further illustrate his point, he handed out the handbook, which was a small burgundy book with a velvet cover—yes, a velvet cover. Inside the book was the heart, soul, and spirit of the company. Jim proceeded to talk to us about how important it was this book had heavier weight paper, the type was a certain font, it was organized in a certain way, and the velvet cover helped to capture the irreverent spirit of the brand.

The word irreverent also stood out to me. I had heard the term used before but never in a business setting. Most companies I had dealt with would have shuttered if someone described their business or team as irreverent. Instead, the Hard Rock embraced an irreverent spirit forged by punk rockers, philanthropic pioneers, and tattooed servers. That spirit led to innovation and growth through a culture that embraced everyone for who they were with a motto of "Love All, Serve All."

As I heard the word irreverent, the thought of a runner from Coos Bay, Oregon, slipped into my mind. I had taken to running that year and was reading everything I could find on the subject. In my reading, I came across the story of Steve Prefontaine, a runner from Oregon who changed the running world forever and was the inspiration for a mega brand. Pre, as Prefontaine was nicknamed, became known for his brash, irreverent style. He often spoke of his running as art, likening his time on the track to the efforts of a painter or composer. One of my favorite Pre quotes is "a race is a work of art that people can look at and be affected in as many ways as they're capable of understanding." He was an authentic figure in the sport of running and will always be remembered as such.

If you have ever run a race of any distance, you know the most authentic moment of any race is the second you cross the finish line. Even the most seasoned runner cannot help but bear everything he or she is during that pure moment. The runners-up become equals as they are cloaked in the feeling of pride that accompanies even the most disappointing finish. Cheers and congratulations are the jubilant rewards for everyone who crosses the line, and the awe and admiration of the spectators help compose the song of your heroic deed.

Clad in compression spandex and wrestling with my bright pink swim cap, I could not help but let my ears drift to the groups of people who had gathered to join at the start line on this beach in Delray, Florida. Their conversations were filled with thoughts on their latest addition to their outlandishly expensive bikes, discussion of their split times in the pool, or even the occasional proclamation of their finishing times, which would be hard for any mere mortal to beat. The start line of my first sprint triathlon was very different from anywhere I had been before. I found if I asked the elder statesmen for advice or clarification on the course, they were very willing to indulge me and even engage in the occasional conversation about their first time. I had only ever run races, so the triathlon was already starting to turn me off as I was having a tough time connecting.

The race began, and as we fought the swelling waves to get out past the break, I found myself literally fighting off other swimmers as they tried to crawl over me to get an advantage. As we exited, I clumsily transitioned to my bike and endured 10 miles of people yelling "on your left" as they flew past me. Nearly defeated, I dismounted and began to run. The distance was only a 5k, but in that short time, I flew past more than 50 people. The runner in me kept saying things like *great job*, or *you look great*. I crossed the finish line, and to my surprise, was received with high fives from many of those people who seemed annoyed by my presence only about an hour earlier. I found the authentic spirit of the triathletes at that finish line, and it inspired me to keep going for many years in the sport. The competitive spirit drives all of them to achieve things most people could not dream of, and in the end, each of them can respect and admire the accomplishments of everyone who steps foot on the course.

I will always remember the Ritz-Carlton Credo as it is the heart and soul of that company. I will also always remember what it felt like to hold that little book while listening to a man speak with a singular passion for everything inside of it. Those two things, to me, are the essence of being authentic. Businesses that know who they are and can convey that message to their teams instill a sense of authenticity and passion, inspiring and engaging everyone in the organization. That authenticity and passion are the answers to most of the questions or problems anyone in that organization may face. When a leader possesses the same authenticity and passion, then people cannot help but follow them. The one great authentic moment will engage and inspire those around you to follow you passionately.

Ask yourself these questions to help identify your authentic leadership style:

1. Can you think of a time when you, as a leader, could truly inspire those around you to action without the benefit of your title?

2. How would you describe your leadership style to a spouse, parent, or other loved one who knows the authentic you?

3. What actions do you take as a leader to enliven your authentic leadership style?

The authentic leader carries themselves in a manner that exudes confidence in their abilities and their team and organization. They possess a dogma people to gravitate toward and can convey that in an educational and enlightening manner. This leader is not afraid to make mistakes and support others who have failed because this leader knows failure leads to growth.

Employment can now be seen as two sides coming together to pursue their passions to the benefit of each other. If these sides were to enter into a pact together, the base premise of authenticity would be non-negotiable. The same genuine, passionate spirit that fuels organizations like the Hard Rock and Ritz-Carlton will lead to differentiating factors that connect both sides to the future. Employers need to be prepared to find ways to tap into the passions of the incoming leaders to ensure the same pure feeling I experience while racing can be found in some facet of the job. If this generation does not feel like they can make an impact in their roles or trust the leaders they work with, they will continue to an employer who can fulfill that need.

One characteristic that connects most hospitality organizations is their version of a spirit to serve. This is not only something that is spelled out as a process for the betterment of the guest. It is an ingrained dogma that drives us to help our communities. I have been part of the Marriott family for more than 30 years, and the spirit to serve is one of the strongest connections I have to the organization and my desire to help the people around me. Its philosophy teaches us all to support and serve the community and organizations that support and serve us. During my time with Hard Rock, I learned to *Love All, Serve All.* Regardless of the organization, there is a connection which can be fostered and grown into a point of passion and authenticity with new employees, which in turn can activate their desire to make an impact. If your organization does not have this philosophy, then to start, you must do so through the passionate activists in the organization, even if they are not in HR or are the CEO. Authentic passion will fuel your spirit to serve.

As we jump into actually creating a pact, it will be important to remember authenticity and passion are the fuel for building a bond between generations. As we learned earlier, the millennial generation is looking for a cause to connect with and is willing to put in the time and effort to achieve an impact result. As employers, we need to make it clear from day one where their passion should be focused and also make the transparency of authenticity our currency.

CHAPTER 5
MANAGEMENT VS. LEADERSHIP

Management is doing things right;
leadership is doing the right thing.

—Peter Drucker

Authenticity and passion are now expected in the workplace, and they are the basis for new generations to become inspired to put their best foot forward for whatever organization they function in or cause they choose to pursue. This generation has grown up in a business world that preaches the difference between a manager and leader, with the once-vaunted manager coming up as a short-sighted taskmaster when compared to their enlightened counterpart, the leader. This comparison is extremely important to examine before moving forward because every millennial who enters the workforce is told they need to be an ascended leader and avoid the manager's drudgery.

This comparison is unfair and leads to many of the issues millennials are having in the workplace. The reality is our current corporate environment and many organizations were built on the manager's premise as the business unit leader.

The definition of a manager is someone who can direct others to execute processes that produce a predictable result. Most corporations have a litany of processes and procedures, and they flaunt those processes as controls to ensure a result will be achieved. These processes are usually easy to learn, but a manager is required to ensure they are followed. If those processes are not followed, then the results that dictate the future success of an organization cannot be consistently produced enough for others to develop trust. When trust is lost, then things like reputation suffer, and that leads to a decline in obvious monetary metrics like a stock price.

Travelers and families have flocked to the Marriott brand for more than 80 years because of the consistently excellent experience they deliver worldwide. People know standards of cleanliness are adhered to, the front desk agents will be friendly and knowledgeable, and all the modern comforts will be available. If you go behind the scenes, you will find binders and intranet sites dedicated to standards that can be translated into any environment the flag is flying in.

As millennial leaders enter this environment, they are asked to be something they learned to run away from. They are told to be shepherds of the predictable and directed to learn and adhere to hundreds of standards that define every interaction, aspect of a product, and even personal conduct. This expectation of consistency is what allows businesses to make decisions that lead to growth. This same model can be found in many organizations across dozens of industries. The industrialization of our culture was founded on our ability to be able to produce consistency from randomness. Unfortunately, the managers who have helped us achieve those results are cast as the villain in the profile of a leader.

There are hundreds of definitions of a leader, and most of them have to do with a few keywords like "inspiration, vision, and achieve." A leader is someone who inspires others through their vision to achieve results they never thought possible. As new leaders enter the workforce, they are challenged to change the world and to create revolutionary and socially conscious businesses. The leader is someone who mentors and coaches their employees and is an inspiration through their adherence to a vision.

When I graduated college, I was accepted as a management trainee for Marriott. I was stationed at a premier hotel that served as a flagship of sorts for the company. The general manager for the resort was a man named Charlie Perkins. Mr. Perkins was a leader. He had a presence on the property that was felt by everyone he came in contact with. His mix of professionalism and humor instilled respect and confidence in the team, and when he spoke, we all listened. He lived the mission and vision of our company and helped all of us live it as well. The property standards were always evolving, and the evolution led to better results within the Marriott system. He selected leaders who were empowered and driven to succeed.

As a new addition to the property and leadership as a whole, I looked up to Mr. Perkins. One thing about him was he understood there was a process to success. He had a military background, which was evident in many of his even most basic interactions. I remember an interaction I had with him during my first week of work when I was in the lobby. He walked by to introduce himself and asked me to walk with him, and as we approached the shoeshine in the lobby, he asked me to sit down next to him. As we sat down, the cheery Brazilian shoeshine attendant greeted Mr. Perkins and got to work immediately on his shoes. I was a little shocked because as I looked at his shoes, I could not see a speck of dirt or a single scuff on them. He began to talk to me about the property and what they were trying to accomplish as a team. When his shoes were done, he asked for the attendant to do mine. I had never had a shoeshine before, so she had her work cut out for her. When she was done, my shoes looked amazing. Better than the day I took them out of the box.

We stood up, and Mr. Perkins paid for both of us. We thanked the attendant and continued on our walk. I should have known something was coming when the shoeshine attendant smirked at me and shook her head as we walked away. As we finished our loop around the lobby, Mr. Perkins commented on how nice my shoes looked and told me to keep them that way. As he walked away, I admit I was a little turned off. Of all the things he could have said to me, he felt my shoes were the most important thing to discuss. I went back and talked to one of the front desk managers and explained the entire interaction. The manager chuckled and told me what the interaction meant.

He told me everything had a process, and the process started with you. Each leader on site was the vision and definition of a standard that the property embodied. Our ability to care about the details leads to our desire to want to perform even the most menial task in the pursuit of excellence. Mr. Perkins expects you to adhere to standards and keep your team focused on their standards so we can all move ahead. As he put it, imagine if everyone's shoes were shined, we would not have to worry about that anymore, and we could all spend more time worrying about more important things.

This simple premise is why new leaders are having so much trouble adjusting to the environments they are entering. No one explains to us in school that if we can complete measured intentional tasks daily, we can achieve results that will enable us to lead. Being a good manager is simply a cost of entry to being a great leader. Visionaries like Steve Jobs, Elon Musk, and the like all understand the steps have to be taken to achieve their vision, and they need managers to make those things happen.

The discussion of a diminishing practice like a shoeshine may seem to be out of place in a book discussing the next generation, but it is at the heart of the divide between those leading in the working world today and those entering it. Mr.

Perkins was able to make decisions about moving forward because he knew he stood on solid ground. His team adhered to standards, which provided a base level result he could then elevate. His demeanor was consistent, and his thoughts were forward-facing because he knew he did not have to worry about looking backward or checking his feet underneath him to make sure his platform was still there to stand on.

The vast majority of new leaders need to understand the value of managing. There are very few new leaders who enter an organization and introduce such a visionary and inspiring performance that they reshape the business in a transcendent manner. In actuality, most new leaders are given a title and people who report to them, and the leader is told to lead them. This reality suggests the incoming leader knows the vision, mission, and values of the organization and can then deliver a series of predictable results that would allow them to develop ideas to inspire their teams to excellence. What usually happens is leaders are given a title and a team, and within a few months, *their* leader has to address a course correction because they deviated too far from the company mission, vision, values, or norms. Their desire to break away and lead led them to jump ahead without observing no one was following them.

In the *21 Irrefutable Laws of Leadership*, John Maxwell discusses something called the Law of the Lid. This is a principle used to describe the leadership ceiling of a leader with the understanding that if you can raise your lid, you can raise your performance. For example, if your leadership lid is a six, you are most likely to perform at a five. Maxwell says it is entirely possible to raise your lid, and by doing so, you raise your potential. I explained this law to my team at one of the hotels I ran, and after everyone had ascertained where their lid was, we had a great conversation about how to raise their lid. To my surprise, many of my younger leaders concluded if they could start producing more consistent results daily, they could begin to raise their lid. They came to this conclusion because every time they talked about a barrier to performance, it usually started with an anomaly in their world. Despite having come to that conclusion on their own, they still shuttered when I told them they figured out they needed to be better managers before they could be great leaders.

The intent of this section is not to tell future leaders they need to learn to shuffle paperwork and be guardians of the latest standard operating procedure. Rather, it is to save them some growing pains as they learn management is a cost of admission for being a great leader. If they can understand the work their teams do and provide their teams with a beacon to hone in on, they can start to be the visionary leader they were told they could be.

As employers, we need to remember millennials are being told they will change the world through their educated and innovative spirit. If we do not take the time to integrate them into the organization, they will become frustrated with our built-in box. Very few organizations have been successful at loosening the reins and bypassing years of process adherence to tap into this generation's true potential. Taking the time to merge the new vision of a leader with the real-world environment that awaits them will give companies and organizations the ability to invest in their future. If this understanding is achieved, both parties will benefit from the innovative spirit that is a hallmark of this generation.

Successful entrepreneurs understand you have to be more than your vision. When you entrust your vision to someone else, there has to be a base standard everyone operates at, or else vision gives way to chaos and frustration. Since more than 66% of this generation wants to be entrepreneurs, largely due to the existing crushing practices of our managers and confinement of processes, we must help them understand the place of management in their vision of the future.

If you are a millennial reading this, give your employer a break. Learn the history of your organization, invest in the processes that produced the results which first attracted you to the organization, and do not come in with a disruptor mentality. You will find the respect you pay your employer will be accorded back to you with the freedom and empowerment you have been looking for. If you choose to come in and endeavor to make an impact, then you will most likely become a statistic of the generation that quits their job because of their boss. Bosses are not always great leaders, or, in some cases, competent managers, but if you learn the success factors of your company, it will entice people to invest in you. Almost every book on leadership will tell you to lead by example. If you show your team you value what they built, they will show you the respect and support you need to become the leader you intend to be.

CHAPTER 6
WHO SHOULD BE RESPONSIBLE?

You must take personal responsibility.
You cannot change the circumstances, the seasons,
or the wind, but you can change yourself.
This is something you have charge of.

—Jim Rohn

R ight now, most of the literature and experts agree that companies and organizations should take responsibility of creating environments where millennials can thrive. Practices like flexible work hours, frequent and consistent performance reviews, and new boundaries of empowerment are designed to foster innovation and engagement. Employers are being encouraged to abandon old work habits and incentives and replace them with new, more trendy offerings and standards which will appeal to the next generation.

In many cases, this is a massive departure from the cultural norms of the organization. This shift may seem great for the leaders coming in, but in many cases, this is uncomfortable for the existing team members and leaders. Many of these practices are great and enhance the work environment for everyone, but in some cases, it leads to resentment at many levels. Existing team members and leaders will frequently allude to new members not *paying their dues* or being allowed to *get away with things* not previously allowed.

This resentment is nothing new. As long as I can remember, established generations are always looking at newer generations as having it easier. People are working fewer hours with more perks, more robust benefit packages, and more competitive salaries. In many cases, these perceptions may be true, but the reality is, this is how the work environment has evolved, regardless of the incoming generation. People are working fewer hours because values are changing throughout our country. Millennials did not invent work-life balance. They are simply a by-product of the overcompensation arising from the generation that thought an 80-hour workweek was a badge of honor.

The hospitality industry used to be a highly transient environment. People transferred to new locations throughout the world every 12-18 months, which was how you got ahead in the industry. You worked a ridiculous number of hours, were always available, and moved on command. With those moves came promotions, recognition, and increased compensation packages. Unfortunately, in many cases, it led to parents living in different cities, kids changing schools frequently, or a high-level of burnout with a low rate of retention. To this day, I still have older guests ask me when my company will be moving me to the next site because they remember when that was the norm.

As recently as the 2000s, I was one of those leaders. The expectation was your value was attached to the number of hours you worked, and if you only worked 50 hours a week, then you were not a team player. In multiple organizations, I worked 14-16 hour days, and in many cases, six or seven days a week. I was a leader in my twenties and ingrained with the mentality of work-life balance. There is no balance—there is work and the occasional things you get to do outside of that paradigm. I want to say this was reserved specifically for hospitality members. The reality is that my friends, family, and acquaintances all held to the same standard in a variety of industries.

The world and people's definitions of work-life balance are changing rapidly. Millennials are credited with forcing the shift, but nearly everyone I talk to now, regardless of their generation, has started to realize its value. The massive leaps in efficiency, seen by the connectivity that currently exists, has opened the door for this new work-life balance to be achieved. Employees and leaders at every level are finding new efficiencies every day, and their employers are rewarding them with greater flexibility to pursue the things important to them.

The hospitality industry is learning to adapt to this shift and, in doing so, has created programs to speak to the essence of this new generation. In many cases, leaders and team members stay put longer in one location, which is causing more log jams in the hiring and promotion process. As a result, new programs are being developed and highlighted to allow associates at all levels to learn new skills. In previous models, you physically had to switch jobs to learn new skills. Now, the best leaders realize you can provide cross-training and development, which sets you up for future success. Instead of hoping someone from another location applies for an opening you may have, you are building a series of qualified people to move into those roles. This homegrown system is strengthening the perception that work-life balance is as important as any other industry priority.

This same premise could be applied in nearly any organization. From a purely monetary standpoint, saving the money be used for recruiting and relocation will cover a good deal of the costs associated with cross-training. In this model, a two-way relationship is formed. The employer is providing the opportunity, and the employee is given the responsibility of succeeding on their merits.

In the coming chapters, this book will examine solutions in a symbiotic manner. There will be a give-and-take between both employer and employee, and both sides will be responsible for bringing the pact to life. The steps of the pact are going to be written from the perspective of the employer, as they are the ones who have to adopt the principles in the work environment for these programs to be effective. Once these principles have been implemented, the millennial leaders will have a responsibility to be active in the participation and execution in these areas. We will learn to personalize the experience, create autonomy in the workplace, improve communication, and place a greater emphasis on teaching.

CHAPTER 7
PERSONALIZE THE EXPERIENCE

Conformity is the jailer of freedom,
and the enemy of growth.

—John F. Kennedy

There are many buzz words and phrases used in business to impart a sense of autonomy to leaders with the hope they will take their organization to the next level. Words like "empowerment" and "leader" are brandished with little regard for the implication and intent of their use. Inevitably, you are told to run the business as if it were yours. That sentiment feels great when your boss tells you that, but the application tends to be a bit more difficult.

I was 24-years-old when I first told a direct report to run the department and team like it was their business. It made sense because my boss said that to me, and it had fired me up enough to get me going in the right direction. I told Darin to live our mission and said that he was empowered to make the guest happy, and he needed to take care of his team. I urged him to be creative and think outside of the box to come up with world-class solutions. I am pretty sure that covers most of the clichés out there for giving direction for the first time to another leader.

Once I had Darin aligned with the rhetoric, I let him go. I let him go for about a day before I gave him his first corporate standard operating procedures manual. I followed that up by having him adhere to the local standard operating procedures and wrapped that up by peppering him with memos of understanding, which further defined his roles and expectations. Once the paperwork was turned over, I made sure he attended our corporate training classes and completed his exhaustive e-learning requirements. At the end of all of that, I had painted a comprehensive and complete box for him to live in to ensure he was a proper manager for our company.

As I reflect on my direction to Darin, I effectively told him to treat the business like it was his but only if he adhered to a process, policy, or memo I provided him. Corporations are great at doing this. We identify a set of norms that define success, and we try to produce as many people to fit those norms as possible with the understanding that those teams will have the greatest possibility of success. The growing issue with this mentality is that it puts a generation in a box screaming to be let out. The process of doing this is exhaustive for managers and is unproductive for millennials. In my experience, I find teams who learn *less is more* when it comes to policies that enjoy an evolving workplace with a lower turnover.

As we look to engage new employees and leaders, we need to determine the best way to create a more personalized experience that allows for growth, development, engagement, and advancement on multiple timetables and not only standard progression charts. This sterile suggestion does not at all capture the emotion associated with all of these topics. Any one of these areas can elicit a passionate response that either energizes or deflates one of your team members. In many cases, things like engagement, development, growth, and advancement have been rallying cries for change in many organizations worldwide.

Most of us fail as leaders because we provide the tools for our teams to manage, but we never explain that the procedure box is simply a platform to stand on to be great. The drowning conformity of managing through the process will strangle this new generation. If employers want to make an impact, then the processes and procedures I saddled Darin with have to be accompanied by an expectation and plan to connect them with the larger purpose and inspire them to innovate and grow past the established standard of excellence. For this to happen, then leadership development must evolve into a combination of process and personalization.

The first step in creating a millennial P.A.C.T. is to personalize the experience. From an employer perspective, this is going to be difficult because we have worked hard to develop systems and processes that lead to predictable results. Those paradigms generally thrust people into the boxes I mentioned earlier. Personalizing the experience requires a far deeper commitment as it implies that each individual in your organization is deserving of your time or the time of the leaders who report to you. Not only are they going to receive your time, but they are going to receive your efforts, and they are going to benefit from the marriage of the two. Employees will be required to participate in reaping the full benefits of the opportunities provided to them.

A couple of key pieces of information from earlier provides a window into a direction to take personalization. Millennials choose a job based on their perception of the opportunity for personal growth and development. More than 66% of millennials want to be entrepreneurs. These facts describe a group looking to grow and looking to do so at their pace. As such, employers need to take an active role in providing the tools, opportunities, and feedback sessions necessary for the new leaders to succeed. This personalization will require an understanding of the individual's desires and goals for advancement and an understanding of how to navigate them through your offerings to help them reach their destination.

In some cases, you may determine your programs are not sufficient to service your team's growth and development goals. It will become incumbent on the leader to be open and forward-thinking enough to involve their millennial counterparts in creating and implementing new programs to meet the evolving needs of the workforce. By involving your team in the generation of new programs, you will gain buy-in and will guarantee a higher level of participation and retention. In many cases, your world is evolving faster than you can handle, and creating these relationships and working paradigms will ensure you are competitive in your approach.

The following are examples of programs that you can implement to help personalize the employee experience:

DEVELOPMENT PLAN

The development plan is nothing new, but executing a successful development plan generally escapes most leaders. In my experience, a development plan is a stagnant set of tasks designed to attain a fixed goal. That definition better fits an action plan a manager can use to guarantee the successful attainment of a task, or conversely, can be used to reprimand an individual for not completing that same task.

A development plan, on the other hand, is a fluid document designed to capitalize on the strengths of an individual created to help attain the desired state. A successful development plan will be a living document that changes as both parties grow. The practical execution of this plan requires a form that can be tracked and monitored. The focus should be on information to help your team member develop professionally or personally, should you choose.

The most difficult aspect of a development plan is the time required to execute it. The form should not be the focal point but rather the follow-up, follow-through, and the produced results should be the measuring stick of success for all parties involved. Interactions, in general, are being sped up, and the traditional review process of drudging through a form for an hour-plus is losing its place in the business world. A development plan session could be accomplished in as short as a few minutes. Both parties are well-informed of the agreed-upon criteria, ready to follow up on commitments made, and ready with the next steps. The document is updated, and then they agree upon the next meeting time. I have even had successful development plan updates walking across the campus. If both parties are engaged, the process becomes much smoother. I find that the longer sessions are usually brainstorming sessions—when both parties decide they need to execute a course correction and then make the corresponding commitments.

ACTIVATE THEIR STRENGTHS

Too often, people guess their strengths, or worse— your boss does. There are several existing tools to help to identify a person's strengths. Assessments like the ones provided by Myers-Briggs or the DISC Assessment or StrengthFinders provide outstanding information on a person's strengths. Knowing your strengths is paramount when determining what your growth will look like.

If you want to invest in your future leaders, make sure they have taken a strength assessment and know what those strengths mean. They will be much more productive and engaged if you can work together to find programs and assignments that allow them to activate those strengths. A strength approach to leadership is the ultimate personalized experience that ensures engagement.

SYSTEMS OF RECOGNITION AND REWARD

Just like everything else we have discussed, recognition and rewards are not one-size-fits-all. The traditional plans for recognizing top performers like employee of the month are becoming obsolete. Like a development plan, millennials want recognition and reward to be specific and commensurate with their accomplishments. As a result, employers have to develop non-traditional systems to ensure they reach their target market.

Rewards like paid days off, schedule preferences, additional job opportunities, new benefits, and educational experiences are becoming the norm. Cash is not as important as it used to be; we learned salary is more of a threshold issue than an actual deciding factor on engagement. The more specific the team member finds the reward, the more value will be placed on it. Personalized recognition can lead to instant engagement, regardless of the generation.

While it will traditionally be the employer who has to set up these systems and processes, it will be the employee who has to participate in reaping the benefits. A development plan without active participation is simply an exercise in paperwork. The millennial generation has to understand their work cannot give personal responsibility; it has to be shown by them.

If you are a millennial reading this, then understand if these opportunities are presented to you, you must be actively engaged in their execution for them to be successful. You need to know what you want and have an idea of what direction you would like to travel in. If you wait for someone to dictate where you are going, it is unlikely you will like where you arrive. It is okay to start a job and not know what the next step is, but it is incumbent on you to ask the questions and begin to form opinions. Be present, active, and engaged in reaping the most out of your employer's work. If you lead others, remember you also have to go down this road with them.

CHAPTER 8
AUTONOMY IS NON-NEGOTIABLE

Synergy is what happens when one plus one equals ten, or a hundred, or even a thousand! It's the profound result when two or more human beings determine to go beyond their preconceived ideas to meet a great challenge.

—Stephen Covey

The autonomy of teams is a growing trend that will be a hallmark of the millennial generation. As we learned earlier, they feel more confident about a decision when their friends or co-workers agree with them. Many employers now believe millennials want to be empowered to operate in their one-person army and accomplish their task at their pace. The research starts to point to a much more social trend whereby small groups are more attractive because the support found in numbers creates a desirable confidence.

As employers look to set up business models to accomplish their goals, they must keep in mind that the concept of accountability has not been particularly reinforced with this new generation. The phrase "participation trophy" has been used on many occasions to describe how parents and educators have dealt with the millennials. The idea is that if you show up, you will be rewarded, which is a dangerous trend. As that trend progresses to the workplace, the participation trophy mentality leads to a lack of accountability in many cases.

Employers work on deadlines with a desired level of achievement, and when that does not happen, the result is not a participation trophy. Rather, you are usually documented or possibly even fired. New leaders and entrants into the workforce will claim they were not given participation trophies, and their employer did not set the right expectation of success. This argument could continue forever, except that at the end of the day, the employer will be deciding your future employment. A new methodology for setting expectations and establishing accountability needs to be established.

When I was young, I played in one of those elementary school soccer leagues where everyone was required to play, and everyone got ice cream or pizza. I was never particularly athletic, so I ended up being the goalie for most of the season. At that age, the goalie is not the agile monster cat lurking as the last line of defense for a team. Instead, it is usually the kid who cannot run or follow directions and was pretty much a liability everywhere else except standing in a box. That was me. I was told over and over again that I was part of the team and was good at what I did. The reality is I was horrible, and the only balls I ever stopped were usually with my face. If you have glasses on, that can be particularly painful.

I would have loved for someone to tell me I wasn't that good. Instead, I spent practice barraged with balls, running laps, or practicing kicking downfield, which was my one responsibility. My poor mother had to buy about half a dozen pairs of glasses before we realized soccer was not my sport. I still have plenty of trophies from those years but had someone found a better way to motivate or do something with me, I might not have been so beaten up.

Finding a new way to align teams is easier said than done. Each industry and job present barriers at many different levels, but as we have learned, if you do not evolve, you die. More particularly, if you do not find a new way to engage these new leaders and provide them a template to engage their leaders, then you are setting them up for successive patterns of failure.

If you look at the structure of social media, you will see that while most profiles are individual, they rely on others' approval to drive content, frequency, and engagement. Groups are established in many ways to join like-minded individuals to a cause, and immediately, you are connected to people who will provide you with feedback regularly. In a work environment, you are usually given assignments or goals, and your feedback comes from your boss. As employers, we need to figure out how not to make work an individual effort but instead, create connections to help provide feedback, establish systems of accountability, and foster an environment of positive growth.

Ideally, employers would be able to establish small groups or committees to solve a problem or generate innovation within their space. With our understanding of how this generation operates, the group would provide them with many of the latent needs not found in their current jobs. Small groups would offer differing viewpoints, would encourage social support, and would give the needed validation to feel confident with their approach.

During a speaking engagement on millennial leadership, one of the attendees made a very relevant observation about the differences in the generations. He said he could not ever remember teaching his parents anything, but now things are totally different. He made a remark that at a family dinner, he was having an issue with his cell phone, and his twelve-year-old nephew fixed it for him and even downloaded the new software. At that point, he realized there is a symbiotic relationship between generations that could be viewed as constructive or destructive. He went on to say how much he values millennials in group work exercises because they bring a unique and savvy perspective. At the same time, he also felt a responsibility to guide them and provide what knowledge he could, without trying to impress his decision-making paradigm on them.

The point of the story as it relates to autonomy is the changing dynamics in the workforce need to be recognized. If employers can build groups containing multiple generations, they can not only leverage their collective intelligence but also create synergies and build relationships. A group would ideally be made up of three to seven individuals with complementary skills. I realize this is not always possible, and when it is not, the group should, at least, include different points of view to ensure that multiple ideas and solutions are considered. These groups should feature specific assignments with enough direction to make them functional and have enough latitude to allow them to succeed or fail independently.

Failure is a tough concept for many leaders to deal with. In most cases, failure is viewed as unfavorable, with the resulting outcome being grounds for disciplinary action. In actuality, failure, in many cases, leads to future success. Much like a scientist experimenting, your teams will do the same, often-times resulting in less than sterling achievements. At that point, it is the boss's responsibility to not get angry but rather to work through the failure with the intent of getting to a future success. Failing forward is a concept that many leader-ship authors have touched on but is still not widely accepted in the workplace. Rather, too many leaders jump in before an employee or team fails to affect a different outcome. By doing so, the leader has stunted the growth of the individual or team and most likely still did not achieve the desired result. By supporting the group and allowing them to create change, either positively or negatively, you are building trust. If that trust is not present then, the group scenario will be an exercise in futility because they will soon learn they do not have the trust and support needed to make an impact.

When constructing a group-think environment, leaders need to be ready to harness failure to accomplish their goals. The millennial generation is not too familiar with failure, so there is a risk of this being devastating to them. If they are put into small groups to accomplish a task, then the group's validation will provide the autonomy they need to make decisions and push forward, regardless of the resulting conditions. Turning failure into victory is a key component of group execution.

At one of the hotels I worked in, we conducted time and motion studies to determine how to make housekeepers more efficient while cleaning guest rooms. We found in our business model that it was more efficient to pair housekeepers into teams of two. In the first couple of weeks, we experienced ups and downs. Some teams had outstanding performances, while others lagged. We saw some team members who loved the changes and others who were furious. As we started investigating, we started tracking the different productivity levels of different pairs. We thought if we paired them with people they liked or shared themes of commonality with, they would be more productive. Over the next several weeks, we worked on finding out each team's preferred pairing with four alternatives in the event someone is not there for the day. As we started to pair these teams together, we found increases in the quality of relationships led to more productivity. Furthermore, if we paired those teams with inspectors they trusted, then the productivity continued to increase.

Leaders who are in tune with their teams can judge each player's various attributes and put them in an environment where they are supported and validated by the members of their group. When this happens, productivity increases, engagement increases, and innovation is fostered. Additionally, the paradigm governing the terms of failure is shifted. Group members can support each other with candid feedback, much like what occurs on social media. Affirmations are free-flowing, and comments dictate the future growth, development, and execution of the group.

To further examine this phenomenon, I think the tribe mentality that occurs in many fitness groups is a great example of like-minded individuals coming together to support each other to reach a common goal. Over the past several years, a fitness craze has led to almost cult-like group followings all over the world. The CrossFit craze has led to tribes all over the planet developing into small group support systems to accomplish unreal physical fitness goals. The garage-style gyms have evolved into brick and mortar businesses that house fitness fanatics bent on pushing themselves to the absolute peak of physical endurance. Industries have evolved from their passion, comradery, and dedication to their craft. The tribe mentality can be seen in these groups and can be used as a model for creating effective groups in the workplace. Lofty goals are clearly set and defined by the workout of the day format. Instructors and tribe members alike motivate you to achieve things you never thought possible. When you fail— because you always do at some point—then the tribe is there to lift you.

Another outstanding example of this can be seen in something called the November Project. Runner's World Magazine did a feature on a group called the November Project. This movement was started in Boston by Brogan Graham and Bojan Mandaric, Northwestern Crew Alumni, as a way to keep working out during the cold winters. This group now has chapters in 41 cities with hundreds of members all attending free-to-the-public workout sessions held in featured locations. These groups employ the tribe mentality, and like the CrossFit members, they provide guidance, support, praise, and an antidote to failure.

These examples provide great blueprints of how small groups can thrive in organizations, and how, when combined with passion, this can ignite movement level growth. As employers look to connect with their leaders, they need to remember that unless there are systems of support for new leaders, they run the risk of failure without progression. Like any initiative, if this is not fully supported at every level, then it will become something that has to be done, versus something that is a benefit to all parties involved.

If you are a millennial reading this, then help your leaders understand the value of groups. When you are allowed an opportunity to perform as a contributor to a group, take the responsibility seriously with the understanding that the more you invest in this process, the higher the likelihood this will become a viable model within your organization. Groups can hold each member accountable to deadlines and deliverables. As a member of one of these groups, understand your contributions and participation lead to the autonomy you are looking for. Look to include members of other generations in your groups as they have a knowledge bank not even Google can provide. They will help keep you on track and together, you can symbiotically move forward. Do not worry if you fail. It will happen. It happens to everyone. Do not get so caught up with the trophy that you forget why you are there. Own your failure, learn from your failure, and grow towards your desired outcome. The tribe will be there for you.

CHAPTER 9
COMMUNICATE

To effectively communicate, we must realize that we are all different in the way that we perceive the world and use this understanding as a guide to our communication with others.

—Tony Robbins

One of my leaders came into my office to discuss an issue she was having, and like a good leader, I stopped what I was doing, turned my chair behind my massive desk, and faced her. While she was discussed her concerns, I could not help but notice how distracting my desk was. I had a laptop with my e-mail scrolling, a cell phone, an iPad, a desktop with the property security cameras playing, and the same security screen was mirrored on my wall across from my desk. As this leader talked, I could not help but watch both of our eyes dart around the office as movement occurred on the security cameras, my phone vibrated, or e-mails churned through. I was also seated on the other side of a very large desk that almost served as a barrier between me and the leader. In that small fifteen-minute conversation, we had experienced more than 25 distractions, and we failed to connect on the issue.

As I took note of the state of affairs, I began to change the way I handled conversations. I first set a meeting with the leader, and when she arrived, I came around to her side of my desk and sat down at a small table next to her. I ensured my wall screen was off, my phone was muted, my e-mail was silent, and we had a chance to speak without interruption. Once these distractions were eliminated, we had a great conversation, connecting on many issues, and resolved her original challenge. That moment was a revelation for me because I never realized how detrimental passive communication devices could be to the connection process.

As we all know, there are more ways to communicate now than ever before. Phone calls have given way to texts and e-mails, and new social media sites seem to pop up daily, offering a variety of ways to connect. In speaking with many leaders, the sheer volume of communication opportunities has become an impediment to actual communication. Leaders of all generations are struggling to figure out the most productive way to deliver a message, and are losing ground on building the connections needed to be successful.

I had the privilege of presenting workshops on millennial leadership and communication to a group of executives struggling to move the needle with their teams. I had one executive ask if he would have to start tweeting to get his point across because, in his words, that was never going to happen. Most people around the table started to chuckle, but you could also sense the uneasiness as they anxiously waited for my response. They were relieved when they heard me say that Twitter was a tool, but that if you were not comfortable using it, your communication would come off as fake. The questions then turned to what they could do to make a connection.

I went on to tell them a connection is something that happens when two people, or a group of people, share a commonality that leads to the achievement of a goal or task. The base premise is that points of commonality lead to conversations, and conversations lead to connections. The important thing is communication should be about the other person and more than only words. It should be simple and authentic. If you want to move your team to achieve their goals, then communication should also inspire them. In his book, *Everyone Communicates, Few Connect,* John Maxwell discusses these topics from his point of view with the intent of providing the reader with tools and guidelines to make those connections. We will explore those topics further through the lens of millennial leadership.

CONNECTING IS NOT ABOUT YOU

I recently watched a video of Simon Sinek, where he talked about improving your public speaking. One of the main points was the first thing a speaker should do is determine what they are going to give to the audience. This is an amazing piece of advice very few people actualize in their lives. Most people view each interaction from the paradigm of themselves. What can I get from this interaction, or what will I take away?

As an employer, it is challenging to constantly look to provide value to your team while trying to be a steward of the bottom line. Each interaction with your team is—either consciously or unconsciously—perceived and assimilated to produce not only a reaction but also a blueprint of how they should or should not act. Most leaders I have been around choose to interact from *me* paradigm, which, in turn, leads to the same mimicked behavior from the team.

In today's social media society, everyone is used to sending out updates on what they are doing and keeping cursory contact with hundreds or thousands of friends. This trend is shaping how both millennials and non-millennials communicate. Listening is a skill, and active listening is an art form.

Communication is programmed to go the wrong way if the focus of leaders shifts from their teams to themselves.

While at a conference, I had a chance to speak with a leader who was excited to talk about how he communicated with his team. He told me about his new blog, social templates, e-mail protocol, and daily handout. He was excited about the increased communication and thought it was a good time to back down on the one-on-ones since the team was getting all of the information they needed now. His systems and processes were impressive, and his templates were great for what he was trying to do.

As he finished his download, I could not help but ask questions about the recipients of his messages. It turned out the one thing he forgot in all of his new tools was the group of people who would be receiving them. He basically carved out a social media program where he would dump information and then respond via e-mail to cursory questions. He had decided to cancel his one mechanism, which ensures he will build a connection with each team member, and he removed the personal portion of his communication.

This leader forgot that our team's comments, questions, and feedback are what drive the communication we provide. If we send nothing but one-way communication, we will fail to connect and engage with our teams. Millennials require two-way communication, and while they understand how to digest one-way communication, they become disenchanted when they do not feel part of the solution or bigger picture. Communication should not be about the leader; it has to be about the employee. No employee cares about trendy apps or new formats as they do about being heard and engaged. There is no product on the market that listens for you and then uses that information to build a connection with your team.

Leaders should have their teams in mind when they communicate. When delivering a message, they should constantly think about how it will add value to those receiving it. Yes, millennials have dozens of ways to communicate, but the only one that matters is the one that works. If you are genuine and have your audience in mind, then you will be received. If your communication lacks authenticity and is only you talking at your team, then they will not respond.

An authentic style with a mindset on others is not a natural process. It will require time and effort to adopt. In many cases, this will be a cyclical exercise in practicing and evaluating. However, once you are comfortable with this style, you will notice an immediate change in the way you perceive your role as an employer, and you will also appreciate how your team receives your direction.

This concept was hard for me to adopt as a leader. I always had a very hands-on style of leadership, which was perceived to be authentic and for others. In actuality, I was merely looking for a way to be recognized so I could move up the corporate ranks. This dueling agenda often caused my message to lack substance, requiring the sweat of my brow to make up the difference. As I progressed and became a leader of more savvy leaders, this style began to fail. I remember sitting with a department head and asked them to go a direction with a project in which they were not comfortable going. They told me the research pointed to the project being bad for the team, but I knew if we pulled it off, I would be promoted again.

Naturally, I could not sell the time and effort needed to succeed, and the leader lost respect for me during the process. That interaction made me realize the value of authenticity, and, as a result, I learned a lot from the failure. I took the blame for the project going poorly and watched someone else get promoted over me. The unintended side effect was my leader regained her respect for me. She told me that by taking the blame, she knew I understood the decision was bad for the team, and she knew I would start thinking about them before I thought about my advancement. It was a tough lesson but one which reshaped my future as a leader.

CONNECT BEYOND WORDS

Most people at this point in their careers have heard 93% of communication is non-verbal. Your message is communicated through your body language and tone. The words you use only account for 7% of what is understood. If you did not know that, then know how you say things is infinitely more important than what you actually say. So, spend time not only thinking about what you will say but how you will say it.

In today's society, there are evolving barriers to keep people from connecting. The largest barrier to communication in the workplace may be the cell phone. I know cell phones have provided an increased amount of functionality to deliver almost any piece of information to your fingertips. At the same time, they have also become almost as effective as a mosquito repellent. When you use them in public, people stay away from you. Occasionally one gets through, but as a rule, people just do not come near you.

Cell phones have been a growing concern in the hospitality industry, so I have become accustomed to looking for them everywhere. If you go into any restaurant or walk through any mall, you will see a sizeable percentage of the population with their head down, soaking up the warm blue light provided by their mobile device. The enormous potential of these devices is torn down by the communication disadvantage they pose in the connection process.

I have two meetings every week fixed on my calendar. The first is my executive committee, which consists of department heads and my assistant. The other meeting is with every other leader on property. The first meeting is about half millennials, and the second meeting is about 90% millennials. The executive committee meeting usually features a few leaders checking their phones throughout the meeting. Most of the time, they try to hide it, and other times, they blatantly check their e-mail, texts, etc. Always afraid to miss a note or communication, they often miss what is happening around them. They do not see any problem with it. Besides, they see me doing it all the time, so they think it is fine.

My second meeting, surprisingly enough, rarely or never has anyone checking their phones. Occasionally, someone tells me they have a family issue to check on, or someone forgets to silence their ringer, but 95% of the time, the phones are put away, and they engage. It took me months to notice the difference in the two meetings, but when I did, I could not help but ask my millennials in the second meeting why they did not check their phones all the time. They replied, almost in unison, "it is disrespectful," and they "cannot focus on the meeting." I was shocked. For a generation so connected to their mobile devices, they understand how using a cell phone poses a massive barrier to communication. The non-verbal signals it sends tells the individual or group you are more interested in what is happening on that little box than what is happening with them. They have all grown up with cell phones, so their understanding of their place in business may be more advanced than ours.

After that conversation, I implemented a "no cell phone" policy in my executive committee meetings and for myself in all other meetings. We have a table with a cloth on it at the entrance of the conference room. Everyone puts their phones down, so we do not have an issue with distractions. Imagine carrying that attitude forward to the common spaces of your work environment. People see you walking down the hallways, not acknowledging anyone, clicking away on your cell phone, and the non-verbal cues are perceived as your lack of desire to connect. It becomes virtually impossible to turn it on and off, so instead of picking and choosing when you want to engage, people assume you will abandon your conversation with them for the buzzing master in your pocket.

As employers, we need to take a page from our younger counterparts and set the correct example. Use your cell phone for the powerful tool it is, but do not let it act as a force field guarding you against any interactions with people while you are in its proximity. You need to be very deliberate about where and when you use your phone. Just think about your life. I am sure you have seen the disconnect with your children when you fire up your phone. They are required to love or at least tolerate you because you are their parent. Your employees have no such contract with you, so you can bet you will never be able to engage or connect if you choose your phone over them.

CONNECTORS KEEP IT SIMPLE

I love to go to meetings or have conversations with people who talk to hear themselves talk. I hope you sensed my sarcasm through the text and understand there is nothing worse than someone who will filibuster on any topic, only for the sake of buying time to come up with a real answer. Unfortunately, these people are everywhere. In my experience, I have found leaders do not like feeling there is something they do not know. So, instead of saying they do not know or asking for time to think about it, they will talk in circles until they come up with an actual answer.

Many leaders today forget people are communicating in 140 characters or less or use pictures to send their message. As leaders, if we produce long-winded memos, over-built presentations, or unfocused-conversation, then we will lose the participation of our younger leaders. This generation is encouraging concise communication that is easy to digest and simple to respond to.

As I have grown in the business world, I have seen communication evolve dramatically, and the preferred method gets shorter every time. When I was in college, we took a whole class designed around shortening our message to get people to listen. The desired outcome of the class was what people have come to refer to as business communication, but now the further evolution of that same communication is a paired down slide show or text message.

Woodrow Wilson once said, "If I am to speak ten minutes, I need a week for preparation. If an hour, I am ready now." He understood the complicated nature of keeping things simple. One would think if you were asked to keep things simple, then the process would be easier. The 28th president of the United States knew if you want to deliver a simple, concise message, it takes planning and development well before you can hope to execute. Too often, we fail to connect because our message is too long or too short and ill-prepared. As we move to simplify our communication, we should always make sure that the message is well-thought-out and delivered concisely to ensure engagement and connection.

CONNECTIONS MUST BE AUTHENTIC

I frequently speak to executives who feel like the key to all of their issues lies with a better understanding and execution of social media. High-level people are hired to manage the brand image of the company online, and whole departments are dedicated to creating a social media presence. They work tirelessly to build a consistent image supported by robust articles, carefully researched blogs, and highly monitored Facebook, Twitter, YouTube, and Instagram feeds. I marvel at how quickly all of their efforts can be torn apart by a CEO or executive who decides they are going to put information out on social media, bypass the controls, and deliver a fake message, in a manner inconsistent with the medium.

I had a friend who worked for a large corporation, and one night, while we were out together, he showed me a string of tweets coming in on his page. The COO of his company had decided he was going to use Twitter to convey information to the team, and he sent out his first tweet. It was not a horrible idea, except he did not understand how brief he needed to make his content, so his one 140-character tweet evolved into seven tweets carrying a full chain of consciousness through the message. My friend chuckled, rolled his eyes, and deleted his COO. In one communication, the inauthentic delivery of the COO alienated his millennial subordinates because he tried too hard to be something he is not.

As I mentioned earlier, it is not always about the medium, but rather the message. Some of the most effective communication I have seen in the workplace were videos recorded by leaders and shared with the team. They would record no more than 60-second messages playable on screens, tablets, or phones throughout the organization. The message was simple, clearly delivered, and in a format people could easily digest. Team members were able to connect with the non-verbal cues, and any imperfections almost added credibility to the message. The authentic nature of the communication established a connection with the team that left them engaged and looking for more.

CONNECTIONS SHOULD INSPIRE

I attended a wonderful function where the local high school students who participated in the magnet culinary programs prepared the food for a fundraising dinner to support their programs. Like most of these events, there was a silent auction and a number of presenters. The last presenter was the head of the school district. He had his Ph.D. and was a well-respected man in the community. He was charged with closing the event and leaving all of the sponsors and donors with a sense of connection to inspire them to want to maintain their support of the program.

He started his speech off predictably, thanking everyone in attendance. Behind him were the chefs of the evening, and he solicited a round of applause for them. After that, he began about five minutes of talks about himself. A couple of minutes later, about half of the room were already engaged with their cell phones, and the number climbed with each passing minute. He began to realize he was losing the crowd and, out of nowhere, he executed a hard stop. As the seconds rolled by, people started to look up from their phones, and within 30 seconds, the whole room looked back at him. It was evident he deviated from his script, and the next 120 seconds became the emphatic message that the board and donors were looking for. He used the remaining two minutes to talk directly to the audience and to give them a call to action. He admitted he and his team would not be the ones to teach this next generation of young people to be successful; the people in the room would have to take action and become involved in the lives of our developing youth. His two-minute call to action was so passionate and impactful; the crowd went from staring at their phones to providing a standing ovation.

The next day, I emailed him to ask what I could do. I offered my services free of charge and began to work with his team on developing a message to impact our future leaders. His call to action was an inspiration for me because, during that 30-second pause, he realized his message needed to be about the young people standing behind him and the crowd in front of him. It could not be about him. He realized his mission was to add value to the young people in his care and not to solicit donations. His message included nothing about the next event or about remaining silent auction items or even about donations yet to give for the evening. It was simple, elegant, and served others.

The millennial generation is looking to be connected to a cause and to make an impact. Leaders need to be authentic, not because people will see through them if they are not, but because authenticity inspires others to action. If your team knows you are working to better someone other than yourself, they will follow you and may become connected to the things you are passionate about.

When you inspire others, you create a sense of trust and engagement found only through genuine connections. Connectors inspire by not only thinking of others but also creating calls to action that motivate people to do things they did not think was possible. Sometimes, inspiration can cause a movement or quantum leap, and other times, it elicits the first step. That one first step can change the way an organization operates forever.

If you are a millennial reading this, be willing to assimilate other communication styles into your daily routine. You may love text messages or videos, but realize your boss probably does not feel comfortable there. If you meet them where they are, they will be more willing to meet you. Communication methodology is one of those things you could actually teach your non-millennial co-workers. Do not be afraid to help someone understand the value of brevity, but you must do so with the understanding it is how they have communicated all of their lives. When you are allowed the opportunity to influence how communication is conducted in your organization, remember it should not necessarily be about you. It should be authentic, and it should be simple. If you can be patient, constructive, and informative, you will be able to bring your team closer to you instead of forcing them to venture there alone awkwardly. If you like it when you get a handwritten thank you card, then tell them so the cards are not replaced with texts, e-mails, or social media posts. The perfect communication method is most likely a combination of what you like and what they already do. Communication can be the single great differentiator between loving your job and looking for a new place to work. Be active in ensuring you are part of the solution and not part of the problem.

CHAPTER 10
TEACHING IS THE FUTURE

Dig your well before you're thirsty.

—Seth Godin

One of the primary drivers for millennials choosing a new job is the opportunity for personal growth and development. This concept seems simple enough, but as employers everywhere start to peel back the onion layers, they realize it is an expansive and complicated issue. Most organizations are not built to service the individual development needs of their teams. The concept of mass customization of the employee experience has started to permeate organizations. Businesses are now beginning to realize there are systems and processes available to provide customized learning experiences to many of their teams through a standardized package.

A trend also starting to emerge is training leaders to be teachers. Businesses everywhere are starting to invest in train-the-trainer programs to help push messages out. In addition to that, they are teaching leaders to identify those points of learning to create differentiation within development plans and produce an employee growth experience around that.

Leaders are being taught to harness the individual strengths of their teams versus trying to mitigate their weaknesses. People at every level are realizing you can no longer show someone how to do their jobs; you must find ways to show them how to grow and develop systems to help them get there. Without these systems, businesses become less attractive to top job-seeking talent.

I worked for a hotel once that had enjoyed a great deal of success before I arrived. They were able to serve guests at a world-class level, the facility was immaculate, and there were systems and processes in place to ensure everything was delivered consistently. At first glance, it was an amazing opportunity I walked into. However, as I started to study the property, I realized while the results were great, retention was not. There were very few systems in place to grow talent from within. Additionally, new hires were put through standardized training packages, and nothing was customized from that point. The turnover was well over 100% in the first year, and it was challenging to attract and retain talent.

We decided to train the senior leaders and supervisors to customize development plans and add value individually. This program was rolled out with tools and programming designed to customize the learning experience for the team while still falling within a system. The program began to take off when we started offering classes on personal growth. We found our engagement numbers and retention improved when we stopped focusing on the individual's connection to the job and started growing them as a person. We shifted our culture and began to offer several growth opportunities a month taught by different people on different subjects. As leaders became educators, they became more connected to the team, and productivity increased as well.

Teaching cannot only be the responsibility of human resources. They are shepherds of programs designed to train people on a large scale, and they are hardly able to affect personal growth in the workplace. Many businesses today have opted to introduce robust on-line content designed to give their teams access to a multitude of educational opportunities. Unfortunately, the content rarely connects to people, and it definitely does not inspire them.

If millennials value personal growth and development, then organizations need to train their leaders to become teachers who create individualized lesson plans designed to kindle growth in their teams. Leaders need to be trained to spot teachable moments and to use them to build a connection with their new leaders and employees. As they create these personalized experiences, they will automatically increase retention and morale.

I read an article on LinkedIn that provided hiring and retention data on millennials in the workplace. Most of it was pretty standard, and I did not see anything that needed to be commented on. That being said, I did check the comments to see what other people were saying. As I scrolled through the responses, it was almost exclusively HR recruiters with their opinions about millennials. One comment, in particular, was a rant about how millennials do not stay in one job anymore, so recruiting has become a much bigger problem as positions are constantly opening or in transition.

I could not help but start to formulate a response, that turned into too much content to be relayed in that medium. Maybe we, as employers, need to start looking at turnover and recruitment in a different light. The linear progression model we have all used forever is no longer the path this generation plans on taking. In their book *The Corporate Lattice: Achieving High Performance in the Changing World of Work,* Cathleen Benko and Molly Anderson describe an employment paradigm where progression is no longer linear but follows a lattice progression. Moves made by individuals can be in a multitude of directions depending on their interests, personal lives, or changing priorities.

If we accept the lattice as the new progression model, then recruitment looks completely different. Recruiters could literally be targeting internal recruits for cross-training programs or cross-functional groups designed to expand the overall knowledge of the team members. At the same time, they can give them the tools they need to move in whatever direction they need on the lattice structure. Education within the workplace will be a free-flowing cascade of information designed to go in every direction as the recipients will constantly be in a different place in their development. With employees at every level able and willing to move in both directions, the ability to fill positions becomes very easy.

When recruiters have to bring talent in from the outside, then they have a model to attract the best applicants and teachers in place to ensure the model continues to work. While this may seem like a lofty structure, the reality is it is already happening in many of the most successful organizations. An eye on internal recruitment would open up opportunities for recruiters and businesses to have a sufficiency of talent at every level.

Creating leaders who are teachers in the workplace will be a non-negotiable reality of our future. Some people may say this is nothing new, and leaders have always had to be teachers, and they would be right. The difference is leaders are now responsible for customizing each individual's experience, which will naturally result in them having to develop content and execute on learning initiatives. This concept is a vast departure from a work environment that has relied heavily on human resources to produce the team's education. Teachers will be the future of successful organizations.

If you are a millennial reading this, understand you must be an active participant to receive the benefits of this type of education. School did not prepare you for the workplace because there was never a way to connect the tangible benefits of education to the reality of your life. If you want the flexibility to dictate your level of responsibility, you need to be prepared to move in many directions, which requires a substantial amount of education. It will also be incumbent on you to use the information you are given. If you would like it in a different format or need more, then you need to step up and say that. Do not be afraid to speak to your employers about your desired personal and professional growth goals, and do not miss the chance to act on the opportunities they give you to achieve them. If personal growth and development opportunities are truly important to you, then you need to be ready to put in the work to accompany those goals. Your employer cannot help you with work ethic.

CHAPTER 11

PRACTICAL APPLICATION OF THE MILLENNIAL P.A.C.T.

Without execution, 'vision' is just another word for hallucination.

—Mark V. Hurd

There has been a great deal of information shared to this point, and the overarching theme is there is a way for employers and employees of multiple generations to engage in a manner that produces growth for all parties involved. In this chapter, we will discuss how an organization can adopt these principles and what millennials can do to be successful. As we outline the steps to success, employers need to focus on how they can add value to their millennial counterparts. Millennials need to consider what they can do to play a role in their growth and development.

CARE MODEL

I have always worked for large corporations, and I find there is always a hefty list of acronyms to accompany every situation. I already introduced you to the pact model, and now we are going to look closer at the CARE model. Following this model will help your organization, business, department, or small group improve your work environment and set you up to create the pact we identified earlier.

The CARE model consists of four parts. The first part is to do a current practices assessment. Next, you will ask your operation and team questions to ensure you are heading in the right direction with your resolution. Then, you will be a sterling representative of the change you are going to make within your organization. Finally, you will evaluate the success of your changes.

CURRENT PRACTICE ASSESSMENT

Step 1: Culture Review
In this step, you will to want to review every aspect of your culture and determine how well it has permeated your organization. This is always a tough exercise because the people at the top always feel like the message is received, and the people at the bottom rarely receive it. I find you can assess your penetration by going to the line level of your organization and asking if they know the company's mission statement. In most cases, they cannot recite it. That is not necessarily a horrible thing, but it can be if you ask them to articulate the company's spirit, and they cannot come close to what you are trying to accomplish. When this happens, it is time to find a way to energize your culture.

While you are going through this process, take note of any business units, departments, or employees who seem to be enlivening the company's mission statement or spirit. If you find patches of connection, you can usually look back at the leaders of those areas, and start to formulate processes for spreading your message through their successes. You may need to take a stronger look at the message if you cannot find anyone having success with your message. The company's mission has to resonate with the organization to create the connection you need to attract and maintain your millennial workforce.

Step 2: Communication Overview
The next step in working toward building an environment conducive to millennial success is to evaluate the existing communication methods you have at your disposal in your organization. How does a message get communicated from various levels? Are e-mails sent with an understanding everyone reads them? Is there a newsletter, communique, or other written document? How do people receive their daily alignment? What social media channels do you already have access to? Are there any third-party vendors involved in the communication process? How many people have cell phones and actively use them? What is your team's level of access to technology like tablets, laptops, or desktops?

Again, are there any individuals, departments, branches, or other aspects of the organization that seems to be dialed in from a communication standpoint? Like with culture, these examples will act as future models. Make sure you understand exactly why their communications are successful, and it is not merely a function of the personnel or proximity.

You will also want to evaluate the communication strengths at each level. Is your CEO a great orator but poor with e-mail? Are your line-level employees already successfully using apps and texts to communicate with each other? Who exactly is in the circle of communication? Are some of your messages reaching parts of the team, and are they well-received? Are some of those messages reaching other levels of teams? All of these questions will provide a profile of not only the available means of communication, but also the strengths to act as a base for future growth.

Step 3: Recruiting and Retention Practices
You will want to evaluate your recruiting and retention practices now. To start with recruiting, are you meeting your future team members where they are, or are you using what has always worked? Many businesses are content with recruiting like they always have and only switch methodologies when the well runs dry. What channels are your job postings being publicized through? Where are your recruiters focusing their efforts? How quickly are you reaching out to candidates after they apply? Is there a mechanism to audit stagnant requisitions to prevent your future talent from walking? Is the hired talent in line with the company mission and vision? Are the people interviewing trained well enough to bring in top talent to match your organization's profile?

Once you have reviewed how you get candidates, you need to do an honest assessment of how you are retaining them. What does your onboarding process look and feel like, and is it in line with your mission? What sort of training is the recruit receiving in their respective area? Are there any weekly, monthly, or quarterly follow-up meetings that occur with new employees? What is your short-term retention rate?

These are crucial steps because you need to know how talent is entering your organization and if it is staying. In many cases, businesses find their methodology has become stagnant on both fronts, and as the workforce is evolving, their processes are not. You will also learn the easiest time to connect with your employees is within their first six months. They worked hard to join the team, and you worked hard to get them there. The synergies and excitement are high, so now is when you should be capitalizing on the momentum. Too many businesses wait too long to create connections with their team, and the longer the employee is with the organization, the harder it is to connect them to the mission or vision.

Step 4: Evaluate Your Training
The final piece of your current state evaluation process is to take a hard look at what you offer for training. Most companies can check off some easy boxes because they have some sort of orientation, leadership training, and online university. Do not be discouraged if your organization does not have any of these; it only means there will be some low-hanging fruit to pick up as we look at solutions. In addition to the formal programs available at an enterprise level, dig deeper to see what is being done by individual departments or individual contributors because there may be gold hiding in there. If you have wildly successful programs, then highlight them. If you have lightly utilized or poorly received programs, then note those as well.

As you are going through these programs, try and figure out who the actual end-user of the training is. Is this training adding value or meeting a compliance standard? What are the key takeaways, and what is the retention rate on the message? If you were to remove the program, who would it hurt? What holes are left to fill to address the needs of your team? Do any of your programs address the mission of your company, and if so, what weight is given to that program as compared to others? Are any of the programs attractive to millennials, and if so, why? These are all great questions to help collect a baseline. Once you have collected your organization's current status, it is time to move on to asking questions.

ASK QUESTIONS

Now that you have built a picture of the current state of your operation, business, or organization, it is time to work on changes that can make an impact on your retention and future recruitment of millennial talent. The first thing to do is take a hard look at the programs you are not actively using or have deemed ineffective through the process to determine if you need to keep allocating resources. These programs could be part of your cultural initiatives, a communication methodology, a class or on-line university, or even a recruiting and retention strategy. It is very important to note those programs you have been allocating resources to and have been poorly attended or utilized. If you identified it through the process as ineffective or questionable, it needs to go on one list.

The next step is to look at those programs that have a moderate perceived value and bundle those together on a list. These programs will usually require a minimal investment of money or time and will yield mixed-to-moderate results. The program value may be overstated by occasional success or may be masked by successive failures without growth. Either way, they do not consistently produce the results you want to achieve. However, they may have potential if modified.

Finally, you want to identify all of the things that are going well for you in any areas you identified. What messages or communication channels are penetrating the team? What training programs are frequently used or talked about? Are there leaders you discovered that *get it*, and do their teams show it in their success? Hold onto the cultural initiatives that have permeated the organizations, and at the same time, make sure you capture any individual effort as well.

Once you have these three lists, you should start with the list working for you. Analyze these programs to see why they are connecting with your target audience and if the key elements can be reproduced. Is there someone or a business unit or division driving their success? These programs will give you wins and will help your strategy gain momentum. If you do not have any recruitment or retention successes, communication methods, training initiatives, or cultural programs to produce wins for you, you need to start looking elsewhere for wins.

This is where asking the right questions will lead to better initiatives and execution. Look at your competition and see how they have been successful. Most people cannot help but get their successes posted on the internet. Your competitors are no different. If they have something working for them, which you do not appear to have, try and analyze the successful elements to see if you can infuse those into a new or existing program to gain leverage from proven successes. One-on-ones with your top team members at every level will also produce a bevy of great ideas and future wins. In these meetings, you are going to want to lead with the reasons why the team members are sitting with you. Highlighting their accomplishments will make them excited to participate and instill the confidence you need to move the needle.

In addition to benchmarking, you can start to analyze the other two tiers of your lists. In the moderate tier, begin to ask why the highs are high and the lows are low. Look at what is causing the inconsistency and determine if there is a variable you can modify. If the programs are simply bad, then get rid of them. Learn from your failures and move on. If you can salvage success and turn a program into a win, then it is worth the effort.

Asking good questions about your processes and methodology and your team and competitors will lead to the insight that will produce results. Through this process, you will have many programs, communication methods, and teachable materials to jumpstart your retention and recruitment. Start with the cultural programs to enhance your mission and connect your team to the *why* of your organization. Once those are in process, begin to work on the strongest programs on your list. As your team increases their engagement, they will be more willing to go out on a limb for a new initiative you roll out. Your successes will be well-publicized in our viral society, leading talented people to want to work for you and the talent you have to want to stay with you.

REPRESENT CHANGE

Making changes in the way you do business is key to the future success of your organization. Each change will engage the team to produce results for whatever your goal may be. As a leader, regardless of your generation, you will be responsible for being the blueprint for what others should and should not be. Frequently, programs are launched, and executives do not understand why they do not work. What I find is most of the time, the initiative comes from the top down, but the example goes from the bottom up.

One of the key pillars to success with millennial integration is the prevalence of authenticity in your organization. A leader who does not act by the vision they have laid out then casts the first stone in the bucket that will eventually sink the ship. Lack of authenticity is a deal-breaker for the new leaders and employees entering your organization. If cultural jargon is just that— jargon—then connections will not be made, and employees will start to look elsewhere. The vicious cycle of constantly having to recruit and retain will be furthered by the self-inflicted turnover that occurs because the organization is not aligned from the top down.

Even leaders who show vulnerability through change initiatives are more strongly received than those who quit when things become uncomfortable. I worked for a leader once who used to make us recite the company mission statement nearly daily. He frequently asked us what it means and how we can apply it. At the time, I did not see value in the exercise, but now I can see how it would be beneficial for the younger leaders. The only issue was when we talked about how to treat guests and each other; our leader would use that time to tear people down in public as part of his management style. We had a great deal of turnover, and the ones who stayed were miserable. Eventually, when he left, the guest satisfaction scores began to rise again as the team began to build a relationship with the new leader. This is a great example of a leader who did not walk the talk, which ended up costing him his job and a solid piece of his team.

EVALUATE YOUR SUCCESS

The final step in the CARE model is to evaluate your success. I mentioned a cultural initiative earlier I implemented at one hotel. This initiative revolved around the book *The Energy Bus,* by John Gordon. We had a great deal of success rallying the team around a simply message for everyone to understand and communicate. Our engagement, financial, and guest satisfaction results were through the roof that year. The leadership team continued to ride that message into the following year, but as time wore on, the message wore off. We were not taking the time to evaluate what was working to keep it fresh.

There are always going to be timeless staple programs with your team. These programs will provide a sense of security to new employees as they enter your organization and will sustain a connection between the employees who stay year after year. Unfortunately, the vast majority of new initiatives come with a shelf life. Once a new program reaches a certain penetration level, it will need to be refreshed or replaced. One of the great shortcomings of many leaders I have worked with is that they celebrate the same success repeatedly. They fail to realize that success has a shelf life, and it requires constant evaluation.

In my experience, an unchanged program in a year is most likely reaching its critical penetration. At that point, leaders need to start the CARE Model all over again with an understanding that what works today will not necessarily work tomorrow. This process is great for younger leaders as it will always make sure their opinions are heard, and they have input in the future of the organization. The core programs will always remain, but the initiatives that engage the millennial generation will have to be kept fresh to keep pace with the rapidly evolving society, retention, and learning cycles.

If you are a millennial employee or leader reading this, then the CARE Model is not only for your employers; it is also for you. Take this model and apply it to your environment from the bottom up. Do a cultural inventory of your organization from your point of view. Ask the questions to help to create the change you want to see. Look hard at your habits and practices to make sure you are representing the organization you want to see built around you. Finally, constantly evaluate your paradigm to make sure you do not need to make adjustments to meet the changing climate. By doing this, you will ensure you know what you want. When your leadership structure looks to involve you, the ideas are already generated, and you are ready to participate. If you want things to change but bring nothing to the table, then you will be marginalized, not because of your generation, but because you were unprepared. If employers go to this length to engage you, make sure you are supporting their attempts.

PART II

LEADING IN A GENERATIONAL WORKPLACE

Leadership is lifting a person's vision to high sights,
the raising of a person's performance to a higher standard,
the building of a personality beyond its normal limitations.

—Peter F. Drucker

CHAPTER 12
MILLENNIAL LEADERSHIP

Before you are a leader, success is all about growing yourself.
When you become a leader, success is all about growing others.

—Jack Welch

After several days of build-up, the moment was finally here. I found myself sitting on the lanai of a hotel in Miami Beach watching one of mother nature's deadliest weapons bear down on this lively and vibrant community. Hurricane Wilma had been tearing across Florida in a rarely seen west-to-east pattern, leaving a path of destruction. This storm was predicted to weaken as it crossed the state, but it never really did. Sure, it dropped a category, but when you are sitting on a barrier island, the variance in wind speed seems negligible.

The country was still reeling from the devastation caused by hurricane Katrina earlier, so the prospect of another hurricane hitting a major metropolitan area was unnerving, to say the least. The city of New Orleans and the gulf coast were left in utter destruction with lives lost and billions of dollars in damage left in the wake of this superstorm. Stories of the absolute worst fears of human potential surfaced from the refugees left in the Super Dome, and at the same time, the heroism of the first responders began to heal a frightened nation.

I was a manager at a hotel in New Orleans during hurricane Katrina, and I experienced both the heroism and depravity first hand. I witnessed the complete devastation of the historic metropolis. I saw some of the most shining examples of leadership and hope that could be experienced during such a trying time. Now I found myself sitting on a balcony waiting to see which I would experience this time.

Following hurricane Katrina, my company relocated me to Miami Beach. They were gracious enough to put my wife and me in the hotel until the city of New Orleans would let us get back in to retrieve what was left of our belongings. At no point could any of us have predicted that another major storm would hit this exact spot a few months later. If so, I might have chosen a hotel in Nebraska.

My time in Miami was an outstanding study of leadership. I wish I could say mine was transcendent, but the truth is I was still a new leader, and I had as many failures as successes. I was the director of the largest department on-site, and I reported to a gentleman responsible for four other departments. I was one of the youngest leaders, but I was lucky enough to have a diverse group of peers that were more than willing to share their leadership style, advice, and perspective whenever I needed it.

Like many businesses, hotels are built like a pyramid of responsibility. All of the success of the operation hinges on the effectiveness of the housekeeping department. They are the base of the pyramid. Housekeeping meets the majority of the most basic reasons you stay at a hotel. They prepare your room on schedule and to a degree most of us do not experience even in our homes. If they deliver on their service expectation, then everyone else on site gets to do their job.

No clean rooms. No hospitality experience. I point this out because I ran the housekeeping and laundry departments.

I had never been solely responsible for this team before, so I was relying heavily on my industry knowledge, leadership ability, and work ethic to make me successful. I had some wins and losses in this role, but my largest learning came from my interactions with my leader. He was new to leading this type of team and really only had anecdotal knowledge in this field. He was a very hot and cold leader with high expectations and a low threshold for recognition. He was quick to criticize and slow to recognize. These qualities produced fear-based results that were inconsistent and hard to reproduce. The turnover in our departments was high, and he seemed to be aloof to the negative effects this had on the team and property. For example, I was the seventh person to hold my job in three years. When I hit the seven-month mark, I became the longest-tenured person in my role since the property opened.

I decided to come to this property because I had a great deal of respect for the general manager. I had worked with him in New Orleans prior to Hurricane Katrina, and he reached out to me right after the storm to see how he could help. He did not have a job available in a field I had experience in, but he thought enough of me to turn my current misfortune into a chance for growth and development. I loved John's leadership style. He was very intense and straight forward but also a funny leader. He was the leader in my career who taught me the value of transparency and authenticity. He treated every person on the property the same, and in fact, in most of the interactions I saw, he treated the housekeepers, stewards, etc. better than his executive committee. He had a healthy appreciation for everyone's work, and we all respected and admired him for it.

When I started at the property, John warned me that Mike, my direct boss, had a brash style I would have to get used to. I told him I did not mind, and truthfully, at the time, I was thankful to be alive and have a job. I did not initially worry about my new boss because I loved my general manager, and I was excited to excel in my new role as the director of housekeeping.

Almost immediately after I started, Hurricane Wilma appeared in the Atlantic Ocean. Forecast models had the storm going everywhere from Mexico to New York. The various systems in the Atlantic and the Gulf of Mexico were clouding the forecast for something already almost impossible to predict. As the storm entered the Gulf of Mexico, John started to get concerned that it may take the path many were predicting and come all the way across the state of Florida before it headed back out to sea. We started to run our preparedness drills, ordered supplies, created lists of volunteers, and all of the other things you do to prepare for an impending natural disaster. As the storm made its turn, it became more likely we were going to get affected in some way. We were all called together for a meeting to decide the future of our property during the storm.

This meeting was one of the defining moments in my career because I experienced one of the greatest examples of leadership. All of the department heads gathered with the general manager and executive committee in one of the ballrooms. We were given a security briefing that included all of the pertinent details we needed to know to prepare us to make decisions for the impending storm impact. The executive committee laid out their plan to keep the resort open with as many guests in-house as possible not to forfeit revenue and to house the employees we needed to make sure the guests were cared for. They went division by division, department by department, detailing the entire plan and what needed to be done. I took notes but began to get nervous because this was the same standardized plan we had when we went into Hurricane Katrina.

At the end of the briefing, we were asked if there were any questions. I raised my hand and asked if I could share a little about my experience in the previous hurricane. Out of respect for what we went through, they let me speak. I explained how people in the property caused way more damage than the storm or people outside the property. The challenges of feeding a large number of people, keeping areas secure, keeping exits closed, servicing basic hygiene, and tending to their needs at a luxury level all but destroyed our property in New Orleans. I asked if the team would be willing to hear another plan if we were able to put one together. The general manager asked everyone to keep preparing the plan as outlined but then told me he would speak with me later that afternoon to discuss my concerns.

Knowing I had a small opening, I began working with some of my peers to brainstorm an alternative idea. Over the next couple of hours, we developed an alternative plan we believed would put the property in the best possible position to succeed. The general manager came and found me a few hours later and asked more about my concerns. I told him we had a plan if he had a few minutes to listen. He bought me a Cuban coffee and listened as I detailed the plan we came up with. We proposed we would load up our guests in-house and send them off-site until the utilities came back on. We would use the downtime to ready the property for their return and would keep only a skeleton crew on-site to deal with any immediate emergencies. I discussed some rudimentary financial impact numbers the finance and sales teams helped me with, and at the end of the discussion, he thanked me and said he would consider it.

I got a call a short time later, and he told me to make it happen. The other department heads and I began putting the plan in motion. We found a property out of the cone of uncertainty to send all of our guests to. We arranged for busses to take them there, and we even took care of the creature comforts for guests to make sure the ride was a great experience. The guests were grateful for our concern as Hurricane Katrina was still fresh in their minds. The team pulled together to make all of this happen, and everyone except Mike, my boss, were on the same page. It turns out Mike was the architect of the original plan, so when the general manager approved my plan, he was angry. The leadership John showed by considering outside ideas and supporting their execution instead of the initial plan was a powerful example of trusting your team and not always needing to be right just because you are the boss.

As I sat there on my lanai watching the storm blow by, I pondered the dichotomy between being excited to see the support and execution of our plan and fearing the blowback from my boss. I was sitting on a balcony chair in a major storm, worried about my leader. That one thought still is a defining lesson for me in leadership. My life became more difficult following that moment because the plan I presented was a rousing success. Our property was only closed for 36 hours following a major Hurricane. The rest of the beach properties were down for one or two weeks. There were a thousand lessons to be learned in that single experience but what I remember is that it was one of my great accomplishments and the start of one of my greatest leadership failures.

WAKE OF THE STORM

Within 48 hours of the end of Hurricane Wilma, our site was bustling and seemingly the heart of Miami Beach. Local leaders paraded in and out, first responders stayed with us, and our establishment was the only place to stay in town. An important result of the plan we enacted was the recognition for the dozen or so leaders who were part of the planning and execution. I had a meeting with the general manager because I had the relationship, but the team was recognized. I had received my first great lesson in building trust. If you give the team credit, the team will trust you. Keeping credit for a team effort may help you in the short term, but it will also ensure your team will be missing when you need them.

A couple of days later, I was called into Mike's office. I assumed he was going to talk about the teams' efforts during the storm. I went in and sat down. He immediately pulled out the results of our latest guest satisfaction survey. He pointed out our numbers were declining, and he needed more from me to make a difference. He said he needed to see me put more hours in, and if I was, he expected my scores would go up. I was caught off guard, and in an attempt to recover the conversation, I started to lash back with excuses that mostly revolved around my short time period with the property, the storm, and anything else I could come up with. He pushed back, saying I was only creating excuses for not making the impact I was supposed to. I then asked if he had any insights or ideas that could help me make a difference. He responded almost stereotypical by saying he did not need me there if he had to help me with a solution.

I came out of the wake of Hurricane Wilma only to be caught in the wake of Hurricane Mike, the ruthless administrator. He was going to make my time with him difficult as a result of ruining what would have been his shining moment with the company. That was my short-sighted perspective and the point of view that ultimately caused me to quit the company. At the age of 24, I was coming face to face with the most difficult leadership challenge of my career, and it would end up being one of the biggest failures of my career as a leader. Mike was a bad boss, and I was an even worse employee. We started a yearlong dance in which I quit, and Mike was asked to leave. That is the interesting thing about hurricanes. It is rarely a storm that causes the biggest damage. It is usually the storm surge, debris, and people involved who make the biggest impact.

Mike's leadership style was pretty indicative of the norm of the industry at the time. He led from behind a desk, using his position and title to encourage compliance. The company mission and vision were quoted frequently, but they were rarely seen in practice. He had his golf clubs leaning against the wall in his office and would often find a reason to get out and use them, despite the business demand. His career wins had come at another time and with other teams. He relied on his reputation or the reputations of his previous hotels to provide him the credibility he needed to direct the team. His efforts to relate to the employees were usually awkward and resulted in criticism of their leader. Recognition was non-specific and usually superficial. He expected his leaders to be accessible at all times, and he frequently equated output with hours worked. If you were there, you were making a difference. Finally, you were only as good as your last numbers. This led to a definition of success that was, frankly, unattainable. This profile was pretty common when I started to work in the real world after college.

Today, there are remnants and elements of this style everywhere. The manager who works from behind his desk is fairly commonplace. Leading through the paradigm of metrics like ROI and EBITDA are the driving force of their decision-making paradigm. Recognition is a mystery to many leaders, although they are starting to realize the value of an engaged team. Feedback is still a one-way exercise with many leaders, and your value is still linked in many cases to the hours your work. As today's world is changing, so is today's leader. The leader of the 80s, 90s, and even early 2000s is finding it difficult to lead the new workforce, and it is making for ineffective teams, which leads to poor results.

CHAPTER 13
MORE STATISTICS

*The most dangerous leadership myth is that leaders are born-
that there is a genetic factor to leadership. That's nonsense; in
fact, the opposite is true. Leaders are made rather than born.*

—Warren Bennis

Earlier in the book, we discussed ten things we know
about millennials. Those facts helped us establish best
practices for creating a work environment conducive
to the growth of this new generation in the workplace. Once
an environment that fosters success is established, it will be
the responsibility of the leadership team to instill leadership
traits in their new and future leaders. This section will discuss
four traits imperative for a millennial leader to possess. These
traits are necessary for not only established leaders but also
new leaders as they develop. These are not reserved for only
millennials that lead but rather would benefit any leader at
any level regardless of generation.

Part two of this book will reference the following fourteen
points. These areas of focus are supported by a conglomera-
tion of studies from Deloitte, Gallup, and Price Waterhouse

Cooper. The survey work and reporting they have done on the millennial generation have provided invaluable insight into both employees and employers and has led to a much deeper understanding of how we can ensure synergy in the workplace.

MORE THINGS TO KNOW

Energizing Leaders—Nearly 25% of millennials are asking for a chance to show they can be leaders, and more than 50% believe their organizations could do more to develop future leaders. The educational process can create the empowerment they need to act.

The Power of Process—Almost 60% of millennials believe organizations can become good at innovation by following established processes. They also believe innovation can be learned and is repeatable rather than spontaneous. As I previously cited, millennials still believe corporate processes and leaders are the major barriers to innovation. Following the right processes make sense to them, but *following processes for the sake of following processes* will result in a stagnant environment.

The Value of Recognition—Only 50% of millennials feels the organizations they work for encourages its people to suggest new ways of doing things or rewards them for innovative ideas.

Retention Whoas—Only 50% of millennials believe they will be working with their current company in one year. 21% of millennials, more than three times the number of non-millennials, switched jobs last year.

The Value of Engagement—Only 29% of millennials are engaged at work leading to an estimated $30.5 billion in turnover related costs each year. Highly engaged workforces realize a 41% reduction in absenteeism, 24% less turnover, and a 17% increase in productivity. Highly engaged workforces experience 59% less turnover.

Engagement Shortcomings—59% of millennials state their lack of engagement stems from a lack of opportunities for personal and career development. This is a sharp increase from their baby boomer (44%) and Gen-X (41%) counterparts. As we learned earlier, that is the number one reason they select a job.

Leadership Impact—70% of the variance between lousy, good, and great cultures can be found in the team leader's knowledge, skills, and talent, not the players. 50% of employees have left a job to get away from a manager.

Are They Ready—While 96% of chief academic officers of colleges and universities believe their institutions are effective at preparing students for the workforce, only 11% of business leaders strongly agree. Only 35% of college students say they are prepared for a job, and over 50% of recent graduates are either unemployed or underemployed. (44 million Americans carry $1.3 trillion in student loan debt).

Quality of Feedback—Less than 25% of employees strongly agree managers provide meaningful feedback or feedback to help them do better work. Only 21% of employees strongly agree their performance is managed in a way that motivates them to do outstanding work.

The Engagement Factor—67% of employees strongly agree their managers focus on strengths or positive characteristics, which creates engagement.

On the Rise—52% of millennials say their main attraction to an employer is their ability to advance rapidly.

The Value of Values—56% of millennials would consider leaving an employer who did not have the values they expected.

Generational Tensions—38% of millennials say senior management do not relate to younger workers. More than 50% felt their managers did not always understand the way they use technology.

Why Should I Work There—65% of millennials chose a job for the possibility of personal growth and development. The next highest activator was 36% for the reputation of the organization.

The profile of a leader is evolving because our workplace and our world are changing. Many people like to say it is the introduction of the millennial workforce that is catalyzing change. But the reality is this new generation of employees is giving a voice to what most workers already feel. For decades, the profile of a boss has been evolving from an isolated C-Suite executive to an accessible democratic leader who treats employees as individuals and not numbers. This change is accelerating now because it is not only the millennials who are interested in personal growth and development, but their Gen-X and baby boomer counterparts see the value as well. People treat the millennial generation's expectations as new, but they learned these paradigms from their parents, and now their parents are starting to find a voice for their desires through their children.

Part two of this book defines traits that must be present in leaders in this evolving environment. The great leaders still must develop influence through trust, should be quick to listen and slow to respond, should possess the integrity to always make sure they do the right thing and be able to set and spread their vision. These characteristics and skills are universal to great leaders and should be the base focus of anyone trying to grow their leadership skills. The second part of this book, however, will discuss evolving traits that will become vital to a millennial leader. Those traits include being a mentor/coach, a student/teacher, and advocate, and an activist. Learning and growing these skills will provide any leader with the tools they need to make an impact regardless of the generation they are leading.

CHAPTER 14
THE DANCE

A great person attracts great people and knows
how to hold them together.

—Johann Wolfgang Von Goethe

During the year that followed Hurricane Wilma, I was very difficult to deal with for both my boss and my team. I had moments of greatness that created unity and inspired confidence. In equal measure, I made dozens of decisions while I was exhausted and created a martyr mentality around myself. I wanted pats on the back because I was stinging together ridiculous shifts, and though I made progress, I was running myself into the ground. For example, we had a labor contracting service that provided us with daily housekeepers. We rarely got the same people, and it usually took twice as long or twice as many people to accomplish the same task of an employee who was part of our team. This model was so difficult to work with I ended up clearing rooms every day and did turndown service every night. I was the director of the largest department on the property, and I was cleaning 12 rooms a day and doing 15 turndowns in the evening. My days started at roughly 5:00 a.m., and I was usually there until around 11:00 p.m. My wife was back in New Orleans finishing her degree, so I was left to do my job and make sure the cats were still alive.

My schedule and self-imposed workload resulted in a pretty negative outlook on my boss, the company, and the industry in general. I vividly recall John, the general manager, calling me to ask where I was. I was missing a fairly important meeting. I do not recall the exact words I used, but it resulted in John coming to the room I was cleaning and forcing me to leave the property and take my two days off, effective immediately. I think I slept for 24 straight hours, and when I woke up, I had a voicemail from Mike, my boss, asking me why I was not at work. He let me know this was an unexcused absence that could result in termination.

Going back to work after those days off was very difficult. My first order of business was to schedule an appointment with John to apologize. I walked into the building wearing a jacket and tie for the first time in months. I walked past the coffee shop, and John came out. He took one look at me and said, "There's the guy I stuck my neck out for."

I could not even muster my planned apology. I said, "sorry." I asked if he had time to talk about what happened, and he said he did not. He said he really did not want to talk about what happened because he could not imagine how the person he sent home was the same person who promised him he would make a difference in the department.

He then went on to give me one of the better pieces of advice I have ever received as a leader. He said, "Chris, I did not bring you here to clean rooms. Anyone can be taught to do that. I brought you here to inspire and support those that do clean rooms. Running yourself into the ground does not give them the support, vision, and inspiration they need to be successful."

Nearly 15 years ago, John understood what the value of true leadership was to those they lead. At their core, people do not want you to do their job for them. They want you to support and inspire them to want to contribute to the greater good. Bosses who sit behind giant oak desks cannot support or inspire their teams. Managers who look at labor as a ratio or figure will not make the right decision when times get tough. Leaders who do the work for their teams will never be able to provide them the support they need to advance and grow. I do not know if I had ever heard any of this, and it sent me on a path to becoming a better leader.

Unfortunately, this advice never seemed to make its way to my boss, Mike. From that point forward, I made every attempt to be available, supportive, and provide genuine leadership to the team. I knew that they did not need a martyr; they needed an advocate. The team did not need someone who was exhausted all the time, but rather they needed someone who was motivated to make the right decisions to help them. I decided that 16-hour days six to seven days a week did not help anyone. I forced myself to get my hours down to 12 at first and made sure I got at least one day off each week. I decided to take a couple of trips to see my wife, and it energized me in the workplace. Mike, however, felt the noticeable decline in my work hours would lead to a decline in our scores and output. He began to critique my hours worked and tried adamantly to tie them to declining performance. He bypassed obvious signs of growth like lower turnover, improved guest service scores, and stable budgetary performance for benchmark comparisons to sites we were not equipped to compete with at the time.

Mike learned early on that my sense of self-worth was rooted firmly in the results I produced. He made it a point to attack me where he knew it would hurt me the most. When I made progress in one area of the balanced scorecard, he pointed out a faltering spot in another section. I understood it was his job to make sure we are performing at a high level, but it was difficult for me to inspire my team when it seemed like there was no way for me to win. He constantly told me I was not working enough and would sling his golf clubs over his shoulder and leave. Fifteen years ago, I was running into the wall many of our millennials feel when they join our current workforce.

One day, while I was the property manager on duty, a gentleman approached me and asked me who was in charge of housekeeping. I told him that I was, and he asked to speak with me. He said he was there for the weekend enjoying some time away and could not help but notice how great the place looked. He asked about my background, what I did on-site, and how long I had been with the company. Eventually, I stopped him and asked why he was so curious. He said he was the director of operations for a giant hotel just north of Miami, and he was looking to bring in some new talent. I was instantly flattered but told him I was happy where I was. He asked for my card, and every now and then, he checked in on me to see how I was doing. The dance Mike and I engaged in did eventually end when this gentleman extended me an offer to advance my career and get me away from Mike. This was the first and only time I ever quit a job because of a boss. To this day, I still do not regret doing it. The outstanding support John gave me was not enough to override the poor performance of my direct leader.

This was the shortest job I have held since I started working at the age of fourteen. I loved the company, respected the business leader, and truly cared for my team. With that being said, my inability to lead, combined with my disdain for my direct leader, prevented me from seeing and acting on the multiple opportunities to learn and grow as a leader. The number one reason millennials leave a job is because of their boss. Mike allowed me to see first-hand how negatively influential a leader can be when their series of limiting self-beliefs create a paradigm of failure.

If you are engaged in this dance with an employee or your boss, you need to take a step back and understand the responsibility of a leader. A leader is responsible for the personal and professional growth and development of those around them. They instill a spirit of confidence and trust throughout the organization that enables them to use their platform for the betterment of the team. Leaders will use the influence of their actions to not only achieve the metric success required of their position but also for the team and organization's future success through their pursuit of overall mission and vision of the business. Leaders will build their teams through their support of the passions that inspire their teams to come back and make a difference every day. Managers are not leaders, and leaders are not managers. Traits of both are necessary to be successful, but the workplace of tomorrow will be influenced by inspired leaders achieving results in the development and growth of their teams.

CHAPTER 15
WHO WANTS TO BE A LEADER?

The key to successful leadership today is influence,
not authority.

—Kenneth Blanchard

In the evolving workplace, the mantle of a leader can be worn by anyone. John Maxwell says, "leadership is influence, nothing more, nothing less." A common mistake made by many in today's workplace is the leader is the one with the title. That concept could not be further from the truth. The leader of the group is who the people look to for answers and support. In a perfect world, the boss would be the leader in the department. They would have built the trust and respect needed to direct the team to success at about any level. In practice, many bosses believe their title affords them the credibility to tell people what to do. This boss is the one who has to explain their requests and is often left wondering why people do not do what he says. On the other hand, the leader has the trust and equity built to make a request, regardless of title, and see the team take care of it.

I did my management training program at the J.W. Marriott in Washington D.C. Once I completed the program, I was part of the front office leadership team. Each leader in the department was responsible for one aspect of the operation. One person was the leader who oversaw the front desk, another the bellmen, another the valet, and so forth. When I completed my training program, I was assigned to the telephone department. I had seen the team at the end of the hall and stuck my head in a few times to say hi, but honestly, I had never really interacted with them before. I decided on my first day I would introduce myself again and sit in for some training so I could understand what they did for a living.

I sat down on my first day, and in front of me was a computer, several phone lists, a few manuals, and a giant telephone console with about a hundred buttons. In the middle of all of that was a small box with my name on it. It was my headset the team leader had set out for me, so I was ready to go on day one. I read the manuals and watched for an hour or so with all the confidence of a 21-year-old. I decided to plug in my phone console to get started. My first call was someone who asked to be transferred to sales. They asked for a name I did not know, and while I was fumbling through the phone list, they hung up. The room erupted with laughter.

My ego was put in place in less than a few hours by four team members who looked at me like I was their grandson playing in the living room with my toys. Francis gave a snap and pointed to a space right next to her. Most people would have been offended by that, but given my ego-less state, I slid right over. She grabbed my headset and plugged it into a box right next to hers and put it on mute. She took a brief respite from operating the nerve center of the building to explain to me how this department worked.

Francis had been there for 35 years. She was a short but imposing lady whose feet did not even touch the ground in her chair. But when she spoke, the entire room listened. Francis kind of came with the place. She was a telephone operator for the previous business who used to inhabit the space the hotel now did. She stayed on when the hotel was built, probably because no one could tell her otherwise. The first thing she said to me was, "Son, you just cost us money." The shocked and confused look on my face prompted her to explain that each call into the property was someone looking to engage with us. They could rent a room, eat at the restaurant, attend a meeting, or have the wrong number, but they could love our service so much they come to stay here in the future.

This was right on the heels of 9/11, so the hospitality industry was in a new space where every interaction was the next potential dollar that kept someone employed. Francis and her team took great pride in ensuring their service was second to none. They ensured everyone who called the hotel was connected to their appropriate destination or was called back if that person was not there. They were the daily connection to the outside world, and they took pride in that every day. As I asked around the room, I found out the new employee on Francis' team had been there for seven years, and the majority of the team had been there since the opening of the hotel. Imagine a group of employees who come to work every day professionally dressed in perfectly pressed uniforms, impeccably groomed, their work area immaculately maintained, and every one beamed with pride to answer phones and share a space no larger than 300 square feet. Francis was not a manager and did not have a title. She was, however, the leader of the department. She had seen twenty or thirty people like me come and go over the years. Each of them tried to lead this team, and they made the mistake of minimizing Francis' role on the team.

Leadership is about more than getting the job done. Francis and the team taught me a lot about leading people and having the courage to lead others. My role in the department kind of defaulted to one of support. We made changes together, and any time I needed support, I went to Francis first then the team. We did not always see eye to eye on everything, but she respected me enough to support the ideas that bettered the team. A few even helped me create credibility with other departments. Learning to lead through others was one of my favorite lessons and is at the heart of the leadership disparity that we see in today's workplace.

THE FOUR TRAITS OF A MILLENNIAL LEADER

A study by Gallup concluded that only one in ten leaders naturally possess the skill necessary to lead. What this tells us is leadership education may be the most vital thing missing from our workforce today. If we as leaders know that only 35% of our employees feel school prepared them for the workplace, then the logical next step in our development as leaders has to be to become better teachers to help fill the void our future leaders feel exists as they take on new roles. The millennial leader will understand that education will come in many forms. But it will be the primary catalyst for creating an environment where teams can grow in multiple directions, and achieve results that are both personally and professionally beneficial.

The Student/Teacher
The formal education system is not preparing the leaders of tomorrow for the current workplace. Company norms and processes are not as evolved as educators would have you believe, and the systems in place to address are not robust enough to make the impact that our future leaders need. The millennial leader will have to be versed in creating training classes, opportunities, and materials to grow their workforce towards a new definition of success. The tools needed to do this will come from a self-motivated education system that

will create students capable of being teachers. The leader of tomorrow will be a student that can teach others to grow.

The Mentor/Coach

Nearly all of the leading research on the evolving workplace states that *the boss's* time is rapidly ending. There will always be a need for someone who will be the end of every conversation, but those people are few and far between. The majority of the people who lead others need a new way to approach leadership. Millennials entering the workforce are looking to their leaders to be mentors and coaches. In this role, you are not telling people what to do; you are acting more as an executive coach. You are helping them realize the answers to their challenges within their skill set and encouraging them to branch out to grow. Leaders falter in this role when they lose patience and try and do the work for their teams. I have done that more times than I can count, and every time I regret it. If we know that personal and professional growth is the reason millennials choose and stay at a job, then the mantel of the mentor/coach must become a part of your approach as a leader.

The Advocate

The future promotional structure will more closely resemble a lattice versus the traditional ladder. The millennial leader will need to be an advocate for each team member using the same political capital they would use for themselves to benefit the growth of their direct reports. Advocating for growth through the personalized development plan of each team member will provide the uniqueness this generation desires without locking them into one vision of vertical promotion.

The Activist

The millennial generation is most effective when they are connected to a cause. The millennial leader will connect their team effectively to your cause. They will be able to enhance the company culture in a manner that connects the team with not only the organization's *why* but also their role in the greater societal good. The activist will also be the steward of the programs that drive innovation and will ensure traditional barriers to growth are removed.

If you are an employer reading this, make sure you are taking account of where not only your leadership teams sit with regard to these traits, but also where you sit. Like the workplace evaluation in the first part of this book, a skills and traits evaluation must be honest. The opportunity for growth in your organization will lie in the growth and execution of your team in these areas.

If you are a millennial leader reading this, then understand everything you have been taught in school is changing. Your leader has an 11% confidence that the education you received has prepared you for your time with their organization. As you look to advance your personal and professional growth, do not forget you are also a leader. Maybe you have a title; maybe you do not. If you have a job or are seeking a job, you have an opportunity to learn these traits and apply them to your everyday life. You have an opportunity to lead, regardless of your level. Remember, you have as much, if not more, a responsibility to learn and grow as you would like toward your future as your leader does of preparing you for the future.

CHAPTER 16
THE MESSENGER AND THE MESSAGE

By changing the fulcrum of our mindset and lengthening our lever of possibility, we change what is possible. It's not the weight of the world that determines what we can accomplish. It is our fulcrum and lever.

—Shawn Achor

Part one of this book focused mainly on building an environment that fosters the growth, innovation, and engagement needed in the workplace as we move forward. In most cases, however, the messenger is more important than the message. As we identify and build the traits needed to succeed as a leader, it is imperative leaders understand their teams take their cues from them. If a leader's attitude is negative or inconsistent, then the team will generally mirror that behavior. Conversely, if a leader can put themselves in a position to be positive, engaged, and humble, their teams will do the same.

"Mr. Chris, I can't work for him. I know he is smart, and I know he knows his stuff, but I can't do this anymore. I come here every day dreading what is to come, and I leave every day upset. I should quit, but I love what I do. I just don't like who I work for. Why can't Jake be a little more like Sarah? I mean, how hard is it to just smile occasionally? Sarah's team never seems stressed, and my team always feels out of control, like we are failing before we start. Sarah is easy to talk to, and Jake always seems angry or disappointed. Chris, is there anything you can do to help because I just can't continue doing this."

The effectiveness of a team and the success of an organization can be directly linked to the consistency of the attitude of its leaders. Over the last twenty years, this theory has been heavily researched and heavily supported. Thought leaders like Daniel Goleman identify that your IQ will not carry you as far as your EQ. Your EQ is your emotional quotient or your emotional intelligence. The science of positive psychology has been supported in the mainstream and has provided research to support a positive attitude that will produce more rewarding and effective results. Practitioners and researches have linked a positive mental outlook to success in the workplace and life.

Every hotel features multiple departments. Everything from housekeeping, to food and beverage, to sales, and the like are represented in one operating unit. Most hotels have slews of standard operating procedures that define how a task or position should be completed, with the understanding if performed in this manner, then a consistent product or experience would be produced. In most cases, the single biggest variable in these processes and procedures is the person doing the task. When a product or service breaks down, it is usually the responsibility of the person tasked with performing it. In theory, there should be no variability in the way each operation performs if everyone follows the processes and procedures laid out for them.

The reality of the industry, however, is the experience at some hotels is memorable while others fall short of your expectations and the expectations of their owners. The variability can usually be traced back to a failure in leadership. Like in most industries, some departments or business units perform exceptionally well, while others struggle.

My conversation with Mike was a tough one. As a leader, I had failed Jake. Jake was a college graduate with more than a decade of industry experience. He had transferred from another property where he was highly regarded for the results he produced. Jake was bright, innovative, and driven. Jake had one major personality flaw, which was preventing him from growing as a leader. He had a very inconsistent attitude. There were days where he was awesome, and his team fed off of his energy. There were other days where his negative attitude was sometimes worse for business then the rain outside.

Jake had got himself stuck in what I call the "martyr rut." In Jake's mind, he was too busy, too exhausted, too overwhelmed to be expected to lead his team. He was constantly trying to garner sympathy from his team and leaders for the work he was doing. If he stayed late to help cover, everyone knew about it. If something out of the ordinary happened and he was required to react, we knew about it. He never seemed like he was on stable ground. His team rarely got the direction that extended more than 72 hours out, and feedback was usually negatively focusing on what they had not done.

I liked Jake. I had personally recruited him and made it a point to be involved in his development. I knew he had these inconsistency issues, but I also knew he produced results. I made the same mistake leaders around the world make; I valued results over the team's welfare and well-being. I decided if Jake was producing, then his issues must not be as impactful as I thought.

Leadership is more than the results you produce. How you got those results defines your ability to achieve success over extended periods and to lead through adversity. Sarah understood one of the most basic tenants of leadership, which is if you take care of your team, they will take care of your guest or end-user. Sarah knew that her front-line team was dealing with a constantly changing and evolving environment where they were expected to deliver uncompromising service in the face of sometimes very negative circumstances. Sarah did this by ensuring her message was always delivered in a consistent manner with what the team needed at the time. She was always listening to ensure her decisions were having the desired impact. Sarah's self-awareness allowed her to be not only confident in her abilities like Jake but also humble when necessary. That combination of self-confidence and humility is what gave the perception of control Jake sorely lacked. Sarah knew when her team needed a firm leader and when conceding bolstered her agenda. She knew that sometimes merely being there was enough, and other times, she needed to get hands-on to support her team.

I ended up taking a new role only a couple of weeks after that conversation, and unfortunately never had the chance to sit down with Jake and share some candid feedback he could use to grow in his role. If I had the chance, my advice to Jake would be the same advice I would give you. There are three things a leader can do to improve their overall effectiveness and connection with their team.

1. **Emotional Intelligence**—A leader's ability to deliver their message is more about what the team needs then what you need. Leaders must improve their emotional intelligence, which is the art of balancing five traits to achieve a result that not only meets the needs of your organization but also fulfills the needs of your team. Those five traits are self-awareness, self-recognition, motivation, empathy, and social skills.

2. **Positive Attitude**—The lens you view the world through will guide you to your destination. Leaders who constantly look for problems will find them. I am married to a lawyer, and she will always find the flaws in what I am doing (they are usually there, of course, but I do not always need to hear about them). She has been maniacally trained to do so, and to her credit, she is very good at it. I have found that I am generally going to find a positive outcome if I maintain a positive attitude. Shawn Achor does a masterful job of illustrating this in his book *The Happiness Advantage* and through his TED Talk. This simple and basic premise is what has led people to realize strength management is far more successful than focusing on a person's weaknesses.

3. **Humility**—I love being right about pretty much anything. This basic human tenant drives most leaders to assume a position of power and authority where their ideas are presumed to be right. Some of my most valuable discoveries as a leader, however, came when I was wrong. A leader's ability to admit when they are wrong, learn from their mistakes, and provide an opportunity for growth to someone who had a better solution is sometimes the best way to build trust within an organization. Humility is a strength and one that allows even the most skilled person the ability to accept feedback and ideas from others, therefore growing the breadth of that leaders' knowledge and effectiveness.

In my experience, the message is not nearly as valuable as the messenger. You could be the smartest person on the planet, but if people do not buy into you, they will never buy into your message. If you are a leader, either established or new to your role, then remember your team will do what you do. If you say one thing and do another, then they will be inconsistent, and trust will dissolve. If you are authoritative or unwilling to listen, you can expect to see the same as your team interacts with each other. Take the time to invest in yourself and establish systems that will allow you to deliver a consistent message to inspire your team. Inspired teams are productive teams. These teams are engaged, and they generally stay together. Think of yourself as a messenger as you review the four traits of a leader and how your delivery will shape their effectiveness with your team.

CHAPTER 17

THE STUDENT / TEACHER

*The growth and development of people
is the highest calling of leadership.*

—Harvey Firestone

The most stunning series of statistics I read during my research for this book revolved around the disparity between what educators, employers, graduates believed. 96% of educators believe they are preparing graduates for what they will experience in the real world. A stunning 11% of employers feel the education system is preparing their new and future leaders for the demands of what they can expect in the workplace. Equally stunning, only 35% of millennial graduates believe their education has prepared them for the jobs they are taking. This shocking variance suggests many educators may be out of touch with the worlds they are preparing students to enter. This is not necessarily the fault of the colleges. In many cases, they are a natural outcome of the systemic failures of the education system. It should, however, concern educators that the perceived value of an education is deteriorating. This is giving way to alternate educational structures like that provided by Seth Godin through his altMBA program. This uses a focused approach to educate students and provide them with hands-on learning in individual and group settings designed to produce results that could be actionable in a working environment.

These alternative learning systems should catch the eye of employers because corporate training programs rarely have the curriculum, engagement, or backing to bridge the gap between what millennials have and what they need to be successful. 50% of millennials believe their organization could do more to develop future leaders. That tells you one out of every two developing and future leaders believe the programs that exist fall short in their goal of preparing them to contribute at a higher level to the overall mission, vision, and values of the organization. While it is easy to recognize the disparity between what is out there and what needs to be done, it is tough to formulate a plan to address this.

It would be very easy for me to continue to produce disparaging statistics that suggest we are failing as educators. Instead, I want to focus on the 35% of millennials who believe they are prepared for the workplace they are entering, and the 50% of millennials who believe their workplace is providing them with the training they need to be successful. I want to focus on these people because they get it. They understand education is what you make of it. Your school can layout the curriculum, but it is incumbent on you to learn it. You can always view that three-day corporate leadership seminar as an opportunity to network, or you can take what they teach you and apply it in the manner in which it was intended.

Organizations could produce the most robust training program ever seen, but if you are not willing to learn, you will not be able to reap the benefits of the program. Leaders of tomorrow will be students, not just of the information provided, but of the information they need to grow. The first step of everyone should be to set up systems of learning.

These systems do not have to be complex. One of the best questions I was asked was, "If you had one hour every day, what would you do with it?" It would be easy to say things like sleep, workout, watch TV, spend time with my family, etc. There is value in each of these activities. I will be the first to tell you that spending time with your family should always be a priority. With that being said, if you can carve out one hour of your day, you should be taking intentional steps to learn and grow.

59% of millennials lack engagement due to a lack of opportunities for personal growth and development in their organizations. I would challenge anyone who believes the sole responsibility for growth should fall on the organization. One of the best ways to learn leadership is to study great leaders and those who have written about leadership. Reading is a diminishing skill in our society. The six out of ten millennials who feel their company needs to do more should consider identifying and reading books that provide them with the knowledge base they need to attempt the practical application of those principles. The tools needed for personal growth are readily available on-line, in print, and at the public library. Corporate training classes help bridge education and practical application, but they cannot be the only means of education in a future leader's portfolio.

I worked for an employer a few years ago who did a great job of on-boarding employees but did not have a system in place to help them with their ongoing education. Sure, they purchased the standard online catalog that provided hundreds of classes of self-directed knowledge. The employees sat there and clicked through the lesson with the payoff of a certificate at the end. During my time there, I started to run into challenges leading through experiences I had never been a part of. My team became very negative as a result of the type of guests we dealt with. As a result, they became standoffish with their team members. I tried just about everything I knew, but at the end of the day, I made things worse. I asked my boss what he thought I should do. He told me I should consider taking the online conflict resolution course. I took the course and came away with nothing. I could not relate to the material and went back to my leader for suggestions. He said he could spend some time in my operation and offered me some suggestions. I did not want to go that route; I wanted to try and solve the issues alone. Having him do it for me would not get me ready for the next time.

I looked on his desk behind him and saw a copy of the *Seven Habits of Highly Effective People* by Stephen Covey. I asked him if I could borrow it, and he gladly handed it to me. I was not sure what the book was going to do for me, but I thought if a vice president had it on his desk, there were some answers in there. It was not the easiest book to read, but as I got rhythm, I realized the incredible wisdom crammed into each chapter. The principles of interpersonal leadership, empathetic communication, and creative cooperation were timely and just what I needed. I was able to take the information I gained from Covey and turn it into a plan to help the team.

I began by creating small hands-on training centered around listening. These were done daily with each shift and were easy enough for me to script so anyone could digest them. I then turned to the concept of a win/win situation. This was a bit tougher, but once we did a little role play, the team understood how they could turn seemingly negative situations into mutually beneficial ones. Finally, we performed a series of hands-on exercises that introduced them to the vast resources they had at their disposal to satisfy guests. After that training, they began to engage the whole property in resolving guest concerns, as opposed to turning them into personal battles. This training resulted in a much lower turnover rate and a higher guest satisfaction score for the department. The company did not prepare me to deal with the very real issue at hand, but at the same time, it gave me the freedom to research a solution and the empowerment to act upon what I had discovered.

Millennial leaders need to understand the value of continued education. The world is changing quickly, and the personal drive to grow yourself should be supplemented by corporate training programs and not replaced by those programs. Once a leader develops systems of education for themselves, they have the opportunity to share what they have learned. At no time will a leader ever become an expert. If your leader tells you they are an expert in their field, you should become concerned that they have lost the desire to learn. Learning is a lifelong endeavor that only compounds the knowledge of the recipient. Leaders who realize the value of personal growth will not look for it from their employers, but instead, will look for a test environment to practice what they have learned.

Once you have developed a system of learning, you can share what you have learned with others. A leader understands knowledge is power, but it becomes powerful when it is shared with others. When knowledge is kept inside, it does not benefit the team, and if the team grows, then the leader succeeds. The approach of the teach/student becomes most beneficial when it is applied to the leader of a group or organization. 70% of the variance between lousy, good, and great cultures can be found in the team leader's knowledge, skills, and talent. When the team leader is a student, they can acquire the skills necessary to move their team culture from lousy to good to great. If a team leader relied on corporate training like I initially did, they can all but guarantee their culture and output will continue to suffer.

Becoming a teacher is an interesting transformation in the business world. When you enter your organization, you are looking to the team to educate you and provide you with the tools you need to be successful. At some point, you find the *Francis* of the team, and you begin to learn from a team member who is not necessarily your leader. You attend the corporate training classes so you can gain the insight you need to relate and grow with the team, and eventually, you evolve into someone other people look to for advice. This evolutionary process is fairly standard and is not necessarily wrong. However, it makes the assumption everything you have learned is correct and could benefit your team if passed on to other people in the organization. This is all dependent on your desire and ability to teach others without simply doing the job for them.

The role of the student/teacher will provide a blueprint for any leader or future leader to add value to an organization through their ability and self-motivated desire to learn and grow. The fact that 65 % of millennials pursue a job because it can provide personal and professional growth opportunities suggests that any leader will develop the student/teacher skill set and will be highly sought after in the future.

Organizations generally follow a few different training methodologies. First, they employ the corporate trainer. This is the person who hosts live trainings or webinars. You probably come in contact with them a few times a year, and otherwise, you do not hear from them. They teach the pre-approved curriculum and usually assign standardized homework that rarely gets followed up on by the department leader. The next type of teacher is the department trainer. The department trainer has been through a higher level of corporate training and is usually responsible for two main tasks—onboarding new employees and rolling out new processes. Finally, there is the train the trainer approach. This process gathers identified personnel in one place and teaches them a new concept or system with the hope they can bring this to the teams. The biggest problem with each of these models is they are designed for single lesson activation. They are not meant to be an ongoing means of continued growth and development. They teach a skill or process and then disappear until the next time a skill or process needs to be rolled out. They usually lack the passion required to make an idea a part of the greater culture.

Leaders who want to be successful in the future will learn techniques to become better teachers. The existing paradigm for learning can be alleviated and enhanced through delivery bolstered by follow up and activation. The train the trainer approach is one I never understood. In my experience, department heads or department trainers are selected by the management collective to go through a series of learnings that should be delivered to the team in hopes of accomplishing a task or goal. There are two main flaws in this model. The first is the assumption that the person selected has the ability and desire to teach and train others. If only one in ten people have the natural ability to lead, then the natural ability to teach should be similarly low. The second major downfall of the train the trainer program is that the lack of follow up causes a retention within the workforce model.

A leader who is a student and then becomes a teacher develops a healthy understanding of the need for learning and understands the value of intention and follow-up in the process. The millennial leader will acquire knowledge and incorporate it into her existing business model. That knowledge will be converted into a system of education that will include intention with the follow up required to make the information more than a passing phase. This focus on passion and retention will ensure the engagement level increases as leaders will be able to tailor the program to team's strengths. 67 % of millennials believe engagement improves drastically when a strength-focused approach is taken. Leaders who are engaged with the strengths of their team will be able to tailor programs to ignite the team's growth by individualizing a usually standardized approach. That personalized approach is exactly what millennials are looking for to connect them to their organization.

The transcendent version of the student/teacher will inspire other to grow and share their learnings and journey with others. Reading has long been viewed as something recreational or a requirement of a class. It should be the basis of a strength-based approach to learning development. The leader who can learn will be able to teach. If more than 41% of the millennial workforce believed they held the keys to their growth and development, they would not so readily look to their organizations for the answer.

If you are an employer reading this, try to make it easier for your teams to learn. Encourage them to read by offering to buy them books related to their fields. I have had great success by allowing leaders to read up to one hour a day at the office if they can turn around and share what they learn with the team. The leaders who take me up on this have provided some of the best insights and learning systems I have seen. Their passion and drive to succeed produces systems of learning that speak to their teams and create results surrounding those learnings that better the whole organization. They tend to be the people that replace the trainers because they want to share what they learn.

If you are a millennial reading this, keep reading. There are hundreds of thousands of professional books to help you solve almost any problem you may encounter. Today's connected society also offers summaries and professional trade articles that give you the answers you need to advance everyone's agenda. Even if you are not the department leader, you can learn and share the same. When you become a team leader, you will be part of the 70% impact that takes your business and culture from lousy to great.

CHAPTER 18
THE MENTOR / COACH

*No man is good enough to govern another man
without that other's consent.*

—Abraham Lincoln

In the movie *Horrible Bosses*, Kevin Spacey plays the role of Jason Bateman's *horrible boss*. Spacey is a ruthless, self-centered, egotistical tyrant who uses his iron-fisted rule to drive his employees to perform while keeping the credit and rewards for himself. This vision of a horrible boss is easy for us to picture and associate with the worst possible example of leadership imaginable. We have all come in contact with a boss like that at some point, either through our experiences or through those of our connections. That boss is easy to blame for any shortcomings or issues we may have. That boss is why we do not realize our potential, why our organization is not moving forward, and why we are ultimately going to leave our job.

This boss is not as prevalent in today's workplace because our organizations have identified the behaviors and tendencies and tried to set up policies and procedures to prevent them from impacting their employees in the same way Spacey did. Unfortunately, this process has built a different kind of leader who is harder to deal with and is basically a horrible boss in sheep's clothing. The leader who scares me the most in today's workplace is a benign leader. This is the leader who is present in title only. They manage their teams to produce predictable results, and that is where their responsibility ends. They are champions of the daily reports that must be produced for data to be collected. The data proves that productivity is improving and thus setting a value on their role as a leader. These leaders see their teams as part of the solution, but they either do not understand the value of development or even worse, they do not want to develop their team members for fear of them advancing past their leader. These leaders do only enough not to get fired, and they expect to advance through seniority and the production of the status quo.

These leaders are extremely dangerous to the workplace because they do only enough not to get fired, and instead, they steadily weigh down their teams a little more every day. Their leaders have a hard time dealing with them because they float in the middle of the pack, and there are usually worse issues to deal with. If you look at Jack Welch's model of differentiation, these leaders are the middle 70%. Welch said the top 20% of your performers will be your highest producers and should receive the majority of your attention. The middle 70% can be further broken down but are your bubble group and daily laborers. There are members of these groups who you can inspire to move into the top 20%. Some members will naturally fall to the bottom 10%, but the vast majority are there, doing their jobs every day and going home. The final piece of Welch's theory is that the bottom 10% should be fired, and you should not spend any time in this arena.

If more than 50% of your leaders punch the clock and do just enough not to get fired, start doing the math on their impact on their teams. Every leader in that portion of the differentiation scale is failing to develop their teams actually to improve the overall good of the organization. Instead, they are simply teaching them to be average. Companies know who these people are but usually are frantically trying to deal with the bottom 10% while also trying not to lose the top 20%. The middle leaders get lost, and subsequently, so do their teams.

This information is nothing new. Businesses have been trying to combat this for decades through standardized forms. Most organizations have some form of a performance review or development plan that is usually due midway through the year and at year-end. These reviews are designed to ensure even mediocre and poor leaders fulfill their responsibility to their teams and have a methodology available to them to generate talent in their areas. These forms are usually standardized documents that take you through prepared questions by a professional company. I have worked for several different companies, and most of them buy their material from the same place, so the forms end up being normalized throughout the industry. Just like any tool, if a leader uses it correctly, it can be highly beneficial, but if used incorrectly, it becomes another exercise in paperwork.

In this instance, the horrible boss does not believe the development and growth of their team is as important as the production and metric output they can point to on their reports. This is quite possibly one of the worst holdovers and learnings from previous generations of leaders. The scarcity mindset tells these leaders there is not enough recognition and not enough jobs to go around. The apathy and fear that exists in these leaders result in a lack of growth in the business, which usually costs them their job. A leader with an abundance mindset will see that increasing the acumen and talent within their organization will create more opportunities for everyone.

As I stated in section one, millennials expect their bosses to be mentors and coaches. At the most basic level, that means they expect their boss to take an active interest in their growth to help them achieve their goals through the paradigm of the leaders' experience. Currently, only 25% of millennials feel their managers provide meaningful feedback. That falls pretty closely in line with Welch's differentiation ratios. That means that three out of every four people on your team believe you are not providing them with the individualized feedback needed to develop them personally and professionally. An even more frightening statistic is that only 21% of employees feel their current performance management motivates them to succeed. That means roughly four out of every five people acknowledge that you are providing them with information, but it does not help them move the needle.

Where does that leave us if three out of four millennials believe your feedback is meaningless, but the vast majority believe their boss should be a mentor and coach. This leaves us with a need to develop better the definition and role of a mentor and a coach. If statistically, the feedback we have been trained to give is not resonating, then we need to find a new way to do it. A mentor is currently defined as an experienced and trusted advisor. A coach is someone who trains or instructs you. These definitions paint a picture of a leader who has built trust and resources with you that you value. This mentor/coach shares the value of their experience with you and instructs you on how to improve based on their experience. The base elements of this relationship are trust, experience, and personalized action. Where our existing platform falls short is we never really identify the difference between the two. We do not know how to use them interchangeably to grow and support our teams.

When most people think of a mentor or coach, they are thinking of a mentor. The mentor is someone with the experience and education needed to guide you through situations utilizing their collective knowledge gained from doing what you do. This person will be able to tell you the how and why of doing your job. Mentors are great because they are more than a sounding board. I have been in plenty of organizations where a mentor acted as almost a middle man between me and my boss. If I needed clarification on a process, I could call my mentor instead of bothering my boss. My mentor could always help me understand the dynamic of the organization and where I needed to go with questions or needs for any subject. My mentors could generally tell me how the organization wanted us to handle employee situations and could help me access tools to benefit my team. We would celebrate our successes together and create a game plan against my failures. Mentors serve a massive need in an environment with constant turnover. They are the knowledge repository that ensures new team members, managers, and leaders can succeed.

In the best circumstances, the mentor and mentee connect and engage for the betterment of the organization. In the worst case, you are Kevin Spacey. I have been on the side of mentorship where I was assigned to the mentor. They had all of the knowledge needed to support me. They had the track record of success, but they did not have the desire to help. In some cases, they sabotaged me because their scarcity view of the world convinced them I was going to take part of their pie.

I had a job in my mid-twenties where my mentor was someone who reported to me. It seems like a crazy dynamic, but that relationship was what I needed at the time, and it became symbiotic. I was hired to be the director of operations for the property at the age of 26, and my leader at the time had a dozen or so other departments reporting to him, which left him with very little time to develop people. Despite my age, I had amassed an unusually extensive amount of practical knowledge in my field and was able to apply it in the right measure to generate great results. I had an eye and a feel for the business; however, I was still very much learning people. My boss must have known this was going to be an issue because, on my first day, he introduced me to Conrad and told me he would help mentor me as I grew into my role. I was excited to meet Conrad, and at the same time, surprised my mentor was a department head who reported to me.

I remember quizzing Conrad on his industry knowledge and pressing him to find out why we were matched in these roles. After a while, Conrad chuckled, smirked, and drifted away. Later that day, we were at a meeting with a few other directors, department heads, and a couple of vice presidents. At one point, a vice president suggested something. I pushed back in front of everyone, and it turned into a bit of a thing. As I started to ramp up, I catch a glimpse of Conrad across the hollow square giving me the throat slash sign to cut it out. The whole argument had something to do with how we schedule meetings and who needed to attend them to be most effective. I took Conrad's direction. I conceded and stopped talking. After the meeting, Conrad motioned for me to come with him, and we proceeded to the executive offices. He introduced me to Emily, who was the executive administrative assistant. He then let me know that Emily scheduled all of the meetings for the executive team, and if I needed someone to be somewhere or not be somewhere, she would take care of it. I was embarrassed by my behavior, and at the same time, immediately realized why Conrad was my mentor.

Conrad knew how the building worked, knew the teams' politics, and knew how to get things done without inciting conflict. He truly knew to create win/win situations and how to make people feel they won, regardless of the actual outcome. Conrad's mentorship role had nothing to do with teaching me about the business. It had everything to do with helping me understand how to navigate the organization to achieve my goals. A mentor can come from any direction in the organization as long as both parties are willing to listen and grow. Conrad was a great example of someone who had the practical knowledge and skill to guide me to a beneficial outcome for all parties involved. His ability to draw on his experience and education to provide me with real examples and hands-on lessons on how to grow made him the very definition of a mentor.

Coaching requires a different skill set than being a mentor. At the core of both is the desire to help an individual or team achieve growth and success. However, the methodology of getting there and the persistent outcomes are very different. In most cases, mentorship and coaching are confused, and most people use them interchangeably. Being a mentor is generally most effective when the mentor knows the position they are mentoring will add value and allow them to instruct the mentee towards growth and success. Coaching is paving the way for them to achieve their goals and overcome limiting beliefs and behaviors by seeing what they are currently going through and what is up ahead.

Gregg Popovich is the coach of the San Antonio Spurs basketball team. He has had the privilege of coaching two of the greatest big men of all time, David Robinson and Tim Duncan. Popovich was never a half of fame center or power forward in the National Basketball Association, so he did not provide them with position-specific instruction on how to be a better center or power forward. Instead, Popovich helped these big men develop tendencies and systems that helped them win their matchups on the floor. Popovich also coached these men to be pillars of their community by helping them tie into causes that were important to them. It is no surprise that Popovich famously put the following poem in the locker of every Spurs player:

When nothing seems to help, I go and look at a stonecutter hammering away at his rock perhaps a hundred times without as much as a crack showing in it. Yet at the hundred and first blow it will split in two, and I know it was not that blow that did it, but all that had gone before.

—Jacob Riis

A coach will not give their team member a quick fix but rather will help them pound at the rock daily until they have a breakthrough and achieve their goal. The goal of coaching is not to tell you what I believe the outcome is, but rather to help you determine the outcome through your paradigm. Mentors create outstanding situational knowledge, whereas coaches build patterns of thinking and successful habits in the individual or team that they are coaching.

Leaders should work to have both skill sets in their tool bags. Many leaders can understand the concept of a mentor and can achieve being a successful mentor. Coaching requires some level of education and a servant mindset. There are many courses and programs out there designed to help you become a coach or at least have a better understanding of what is required of a coach. At a very base level as a coach, you must fight your urge to give advice. If you want to practice this, try going through a coaching interaction with a team member where you only ask questions and keep your opinion and experience out of it. If you say "In the past I have," or "I would do this," or "In my experience," then you are a mentor and not a coach. Ask questions to help the individual being coached determine an outcome based on their experience, knowledge, and skills versus yours.

Much like there is a place for both managers and leaders in an organization, there is a place for both mentors and coaches as well. The practicality and patterns of execution of the mentor help to push the immediately desired outcome. Coaching helps to build habits and traits that help the individual you are coaching prepare for what is next. If you are an established leader, understand that you need to invest as a student in understanding and participating in the mentorship and coaching experience. Take the time to diversify your toolset and understand how to utilize them properly. Good coaching comes from listening, empathizing, and asking great questions. You do not have to know the answer. It is better

THE MENTOR / COACH

that you do not. Your team will grow exponentially with the appropriate application of the mentorship and coaching traits.

If you are a millennial or newer leader, be willing to engage in the mentorship or coaching process. Take note of how your leaders use these traits successfully and practice them on others whenever you can. Your understanding of the process will not only help those that you plan to lead, but it will also help your mentors and coaches be more effective. Remember, not every coaching session yields immediate results, but like the stonecutter, they have a cumulative effect that creates growth.

CHAPTER 19
A NOTE ON DEVELOPMENT

Strengths and growth come only through
continuous effort and struggle.

—Napoleon Hill

I have discussed the concept of building trust as a theme throughout this book. This one concept is at the heart of what everyone, not only millennials, is looking for in the workplace. People inherently like solid ground. They like to be able to know, with some level of certainty, that if they do something, a natural and predictable response will exist from an outside influence. If you put forth a great effort but fail at a project, then you want to trust your leader will support and help you grow from your failure. People want to know if they do something positive, they will receive recognition for that accomplishment from someone they respect and trust. Trust, as a concept, allows leaders to provide constructive feedback to their teams with the understanding that it will be taken in a manner to grow and benefit all parties involved. Without trust, constructive feedback becomes destructive, regardless of the inherent value of the advice. This base premise of trust needs to be developed before any leader can be considered a mentor or a coach. Leadership is easy when you only have to tell someone they are awesome. It is much more difficult to lead when you have to tell someone they need to improve. When trust is involved, growth can happen.

If we assume that anyone reading this book understands the value of trust and will work to build it with their teams, then we can move forward. If you are reading this and discounting the value of trust, you will not be able to execute anything from here forward as your team will not value what you have to say. The mentor/coach gains their strength from the relationship and bond built with the team. Those bonds allow for standardized forms to become development plans and for reviews to become feedback sessions. This book will proceed with the understanding that as a millennial leader, you value trust and work every day to build and foster it.

So, if you have built trust with your teams, you are still left with the organization's desire to fill out standardized forms that pass as development plans or reviews. If you work for a corporation or business and you are not the CEO, then you will probably never get away from this exercise. From a positive perspective, these forms provide you with a common language to speak to your team. The important traits, behaviors, and actions are outlined in the form. By giving feedback in each of these sections, you are giving your team a roadmap to success. As a coach, you will be giving them personalized steps set within the confines of the greater structure to achieve their individual goals. The mentor will be able to point out the wins and develop plans with their team member to address the concerns. These reviews and development plans have value, but they are only what you make of them.

I have worked with dozens of versions of reviews and development plans for the better part of twenty years. I have usually been on the bad side of these exercises in that I wait until the last possible minute, cram information in there, and tell the team member this is only an exercise in the paperwork I need them to sign. The imposed deadlines are another task to manage. I would check off all of the required boxes and move on. After all, I mentor and coach team members every day. Why do they need a piece of paper to acknowledge we are moving forward and not backward?

When I took over in my first general manager's role, I had a number two. He was in charge of about three-quarters of the departments we had, and he reported directly to me. We shared a lot of similarities. We had similar backgrounds, career paths, contacts, etc. We both had young families, and we valued each other's opinions in the workplace. We should have worked very well together. I remember my first review with him consisted of me dropping by his office during a busy period of the year and setting his review on his desk. I told him to read it, sign it, and if there were any concerns to come and see me. He chuckled, signed it, and handed it right back to me without even reading it. Granted, I had not put much effort into it, but he also did not feel there would be anything substantial enough to make a difference in his career. I took that to mean he had a good feeling for where we were at, and I took the form back, submitted it, and we were done.

About two months later, we started to experience some friction in our relationship. He started to diverge from the plan I was providing, and it turned out every time we tried to execute a change that affected his department, he would block it and say it failed without ever trying it. These incidents started to turn into closed-door feedback sessions that eventually devolved into frustration, which led to a divide in our leadership team. Ultimately, because I was the boss, he ended up losing his job. He played a large role in that, but at the same time, he probably also suffered from my lack of leadership in the situation. I never took the time to build trust with him. We relied on the employer-employee relationship that masqueraded as trust. I recognized his unwillingness to change would be a problem, and I even put it in the review he never read. I made the mistake of failing to mentor and coach him, and it cost him his job. That experience cost me as well. I eliminated the role and instantly stopped trusting everyone who reported to me. Our relationships started from ground zero, and we had to build them back up again.

I failed him in this instance because I assumed similarities equaled trust. I made the fatal mistake of trying to improve his performance through an area that was clearly not his strength. I told him we needed to change, and because we shared so many personal similarities, I assumed change management was one of his strengths. Over and over again, when change was introduced to the team, his uneasiness with change leadership caused him to fail. My lack of understanding of strength management made me a poor mentor and coach for him.

Research shows that millennials understand the value of strength management. A staggering 67 % believe their engagement improves if their leaders manage them through their strengths rather than their weaknesses. This seems like a straightforward, and while it is easy to understand, it is generally hard to put into practical application.

A leader in today's workplace must understand the value of strength management. To be a mentor/coach, you will need to not only build the trust needed to provide constructive feedback, but you will also need to fight your urge to focus on what they cannot do, and instead, focus on what they can do. In my example, it is not that my number two could not change, it is that it was not natural to him, so he spent most of his effort trying to understand the concept and very little of it executing against it. He was an extrovert and had strengths in analyzing our past to try and come up with a future direction. He got lost when I asked him to trust a vision not based on any past practices and required him to create standard operating procedures to activate on new processes. He did not like being in his office, generating processes, and his strength was not in future thinking. Had I understood the concept of strengths better, I would have known I needed to bring some of his direct reports in on the initiative that had strengths in developing processes. I could have brought him into the fold by connecting our future to our past. Had I taken that route, we would have arrived at the same place together, versus not arriving at all.

In part one of this book, I outlined a few tools that exist to help leaders better understand the strengths of their team. The StrengthFinders, DISC, and Myers-Briggs assessments all provide leaders with varying information for themselves and their teams. Many organizations have made these assessments available to their teams, but in my experience, they are only available to the top leaders or the leaders they are having trouble with. Very rarely do all leaders get the benefit of knowing their strengths. Even more rare than access to the assessment is the training required for leaders to understand how to use the assessments. If you are a leader and have never had a strength assessment of any kind, then you need to try one of the assessments I outlined to at least have a basic understanding of team's strengths and the potential strengths.

In my current role, I have made StrengthFinders available to all of my employees, regardless of their status. Additionally, I have made the DISC assessment a requirement for my leaders. By doing this, I have a much better understanding of their strengths and how their strengths fit in with those of the greater team. The benefit of leading through strengths is that you enable the top drivers of your team, and as such, they grow and achieve faster. They do not have to worry about how to activate something they do not have a comfort level with; instead, they hyper-achieve through the strengths they possess naturally.

I pursued an educational opportunity to become a certified executive coach because I wanted to understand better how I could add value to my team and bring out the best in their performance. When I started the training, I came in with a major flawed preconception that made it very difficult for me to adopt the training. I came into the experience thinking I had to be an expert in the field to advise to people seeking coaching. As I went through the training, I realized that you do not even have to possess knowledge in the same field as your client to coach them. The reason is that you are not there to advise; you are there to listen. The executive coach's art and science come in their ability to be able to help their clients realize the answer to their questions through their paradigm of beliefs. The techniques involved in becoming a coach revolve around listening, identifying questions to insight growth, and providing encouragement as your client finds their revelations through the process. The first thing they warn you about during the training is to refrain from giving your opinion, and if you do, preface it with telling your client you are offering your opinion based on your experience. This should be a last resort to get them thinking in a direction to help them self-realize a solution.

To be an effective mentor and coach to your team, you will have to build trust and understand, giving them the answer will not inspire growth. In fact, giving them the answer actually stunts their growth. If you are learning to be a mentor, then learn about your team's strengths. Learn where they feel most comfortable and guide their growth through those strengths. Do not focus on what they cannot do; rather focus on their passions to keep them engaged. Your experience in your role will also play a part in the growth of your team. However, you will find they will be much more effective if you can guide them to a solution versus giving one to them. A strong mentor will allow their team members to fail forward and instill an abundance mentality that will encourage them to continue to push for their development. To make this trait actionable, you will need to be a student of mentorship and coaching. You will need to understand your boss's understanding of this process probably is not in tune with where the job market is growing. You will need to make sure you do not simply pass that limiting system of beliefs on to your team because that is your organization's norm. The reviews and development plans that exist are tools, and you can use those tools however you see fit. Millennial leaders will use the review and development plan process as an opportunity for growth. Your organization's prescribed due dates should be supplemented with regular feedback sessions you have with your team, so the paperwork is a culmination of your efforts and not the catalyst for them. If you take this process seriously, then you will build trust within your teams.

If you are an employer reading this section, please make the strength assessment tools available to your leaders. Take the time to either provide them with the material they need to understand the tools, most of which is online, or bring in a certified trainer to teach them how to get the most out of the assessments. Please explain the difference between doing a review with someone and creating a development plan. The review is a task; the development plan is an ongoing process for growth. Take the time to learn the strengths of your team and guide their growth through those strengths. Be creative in how you get to the end goal, understanding that effective strength management is much more effective than the existing performance management you have been using. Take these steps to build a trust bank with your team that will be there when you need their support. Trust helps everything move quicker.

If you are a millennial and a new or future leader, then understand that the majority of the leadership in the existing workforce probably has no idea how to guide your personal and professional development effectively. You may choose a job because they have a lot of classes and a structure that allows flexible movement throughout the organization. Unfortunately, it will be hard for you to activate on any of that if your leader cannot guide you through the growth process. Be involved in your personal and professional development. Determine your strengths and what they mean, even if your company or organization does not pay for it. The value you receive from it will be worth it. Choose your mentor and coach wisely. They do not always have to be your leader, and they do not have to be subject matter experts. If they understand your strengths and how to provide feedback that helps you grow, they will make an outstanding mentor and coach. You then have the opportunity to turn around and be a mentor/coach for someone else.

CHAPTER 20
THE ADVOCATE

*If your actions inspire others to dream more, learn more,
do more and become more, you are a leader.*

—John Quincy Adams

Several years ago, I started a conversation with one of my future leaders, Sarah, that ended up becoming a staple of the way I engage in career discussions with my team. At the time, Sarah was interviewing with the property for an entry-level leadership role. She was very excited about working for the company and getting a chance to use her major in her chosen career field. During the interview, we got to one of the standard questions, which was something along the lines of which direction she wanted her career to head in. Her answer caught me off guard and turned into a conversation that not only monopolized the rest of the interview, but also got her hired. She looked at me and said, "Chris, I am hoping that I will get a chance to work for you. I have worked so hard to get in the door, but to be honest, I really have no idea if the career advice I have been given gets me where I want to go.

If you were my leader knowing my background and where I will start, what career advice would you give me?"

First, it was absolute genius turning that question around, and getting me to do the heavy lifting. Second, she had direct access to someone who was where she wanted to be, and did not waste the opportunity. Her school's advice was always a linear progression, which, in our industry, does not prepare you for your time at the top. She asked smart questions, and as we talked, we realized this job was simply an entry-level, and she wanted to be in a different discipline. During the interview, we set out a personalized action plan for her that addressed her vision of growth and combined it with the possibilities we can offer as an organization.

Two weeks later, when she started, we formalized the process by putting it down on paper. I admit I bypassed her leader in this conversation. I included her direct leader in our discussions, but I was so curious about her viewpoint and approach that I felt it necessary to lead her personal and professional growth. Over the next four years, Sarah filled five different roles. I was able to advocate for the growth trajectory despite our company's pretty staunch policy about transferring roles before the 12-month mark in your role. Sarah went through several disciplines, some of them were promotions, and one was a technical demotion. She got raises for some and took a step back in pay for others. In a traditional model, I would have never supported or approached her taking a demotion or a pay cut. I felt that I was able to present the options and benefits and let her make the decision.

Sarah was my first real-life exposure to the corporate lattice that Cathleen Benko put forth in her book, the *Corporate Lattice Structure*. As discussed earlier, this theory states that employees should have the flexibility to move in any direction based on their situations. Sarah used this structure to her advantage. She learned each department and was able to gain the perspective she needed to get the director role she was really after. She went from entry-level to director in five years. She made advancement in the position, and she was comfortable with her knowledge base and professional contacts. Her advancement to the director role was impressive but not as impressive as her performance once she got there. Sarah became a top performer who put herself in a position to be fast-tracked as a general manager.

Understanding your team's career plans may mean helping them evolve in a variety of directions. I cannot tell you how often I have seen leaders climb the ladder rapidly only to find themselves locked into a position because they do not have the experience needed to compete with other candidates. That reality becomes very difficult for them to accept, and they usually quit versus trying to gain the knowledge and positions they need to get to the next level. There are always stories of someone that made that ideal ladder progression, but they are becoming few and far between.

The advocate is a leader who understands where an employee is starting, where they want to go, but also the road it will take to get there. The advocate leader must be willing to start putting plans in motion well before their employee ever needs to act on them. In Sarah's case, we started her growth in the interview. I was planning for each step of her growth before she even knew what she wanted to do. I was making sure she had the recognition she needed at various levels of the organization, was in the right trainings and meetings, and was around the right people to get her where she wanted to go. By helping to develop some of the environmental factors of her role, we were able to choose a direction together with few, if any, obstacles to success.

52% of millennials choose a job for their ability to be able to advance rapidly. I was speaking with a colleague recently, and he said that millennials always feel like they should be promoted. He said one of his direct reports came to him after only six months on the job and asked how he could advance to another role. My colleague was instantly frustrated because he was carrying the stereotype in his head, and he could not believe it was true. I asked him to walk through his response and resolution with me. He told the employee that if he wanted to get to the next role, he needed to learn about twenty more skills, and he outlined what those skills were. He said he gave the employee two of the twenty skills as part of his responsibility to learn and work on. He told me the employee came back to him a month or so later and asked for two more skills. My colleague was still frustrated, and I asked him what the team member's overall engagement level was. He looked perplexed, answering the question. He said the employee was pretty happy. I asked him if he realized he had handled the situation very well and increased his employee's longevity. My colleague had told the employee what they would need to be successful at the next level and gave them a place to start to grow. That place acted as a growth step in and of itself. I encouraged my colleague to put the other 16 steps in an action plan that the two of them could work on together. That would give them some formality and would keep the employee engaged for a longer time. One in every two millennials want to advance quickly, but the definition of advancement is evolving. In most cases, advancement means growth.

This leadership trait is important for several. First, the advocate leader will be able to control better the longevity of the employees who work for them. If 50% of all millennials believe they will be in a new job by next year, then there is not much of an opportunity for leaders to make a lasting impact. This trait also allows a leader to understand better how pieces fit in with the larger picture. The advocate leader will be able to stay ahead of their employment needs versus being blind-sided when someone decides to leave. Advocacy combined with mentorship will nearly guarantee the leader is aware of where each employee is in their lifecycle with the organization. Finally, the advocate leader will build trust and credibility with their team. When team members learn you have been laying the groundwork for their growth for a significant period time, they feel appreciated, will engage, and be connected to you and your organization. This should not be used as a feel good for the leader, but rather should be an opportunity for the leader to create capital with the employee that may be used later to help the next round of leaders.

Succession planning is a major priority in almost every organization. The understanding that a home-grown leader will have a deeper connection with an organization is standard throughout most industries. This connection generally builds engagement, and engagement is contagious. When the team sees people advance from within, they immediately feel that there is room for growth and the company is willing to recognize the team's contributions, versus rushing to *infuse new talent* into the organization. I have spoken with many executives who start a conversation by saying they are worried about losing their top-end talent and eventually bring it around to the holes they experience in middle management. The depth issues create a great deal of the depth issues at the top in the middle of the organization. Leaders fail to stock the pond at all levels and instead, encourage the exodus that has become the hallmark of this generation.

The advocate leader understands the value of a development plan. The mentor/coach trait will guarantee that the plan is produced with the right frame of reference. The advocate trait will begin to act on the contents of the development plan. The development plan will identify strengths, educational opportunities, desired career path, and any geographical requirements or wishes that would add to the experience. This plan will include not only information about the employee but also may include commitments from the employer. For example, if there is a recommended academic task, then the employer may agree to pay for that class or even a portion of that class. The responsibility then falls on the employee to take the required action to perform the defined action step. Defined development plans will allow both sides to set realistic expectations for growth if both parties adhere to their responsibilities. The advocate leader will build a path of opportunities for their team that will result in a relationship that will be allowed to evolve versus be prescribed like many plans currently do.

If you are an employer reading this, I strongly encourage you to begin the advocacy process for your team. Become familiar with the career paths and options available, as well as the needs of your greater organization. Do not think short-sighted lay about what would be good for you, but rather what would be good for your team and the organization. Do not be afraid to burn some of the political capital you have earned to advance your team. Your investment will be returned to you down the road. Begin your conversations as early as possible in the employee lifecycle and advocate for your team at all times. Do not wait until your team needs something to advocate for them. Create an environment where they have options, and you will always be able to grow your team versus lose your team.

If you are a millennial reading this, then be open to different career paths than you originally envisioned. You may believe the most direct ladder approach is the best, but understand that building experience and talent will make you more successful when you reach the top. Do not be afraid to go forward by going backward. The courage to talk to your leader about multi-directional growth will result in a complete skill set and greater satisfaction with your organization. The most important thing you can do is listen. If you have trust built with your leader and tell you it is okay to take two steps forward by taking one step back or lateral, consider it. Open lines of communication and a general desire by both of you to enhance your growth will result in a more robust growth experience.

CHAPTER 21
THE ACTIVIST

I alone cannot change the world, but I can cast a stone across the water to create many ripples.

—Mother Teresa

The student/teacher trait has allowed us to establish a pattern for learning and growth through education. That system of constant development has laid the foundation for the necessity of the mentor/coach. The mentor/coach uses strength development and the evolving educational paradigm to enhance the connection between the leader and the team. This relationship will connect the team member to the value they possess and will start the acculturation process with the greater tribe. The advocate trait helps to personalize the employee experience further and uses that to create a tangible plan that outlines the potential for multidirectional growth to achieve an evolving career development path. Each piece of the puzzle both builds on the previous and at the same time enhances the effectiveness of each trait. The activist leader will build a bond with the greater organization while igniting the millennial generation's passion.

The activist leadership trait is the one that takes the employee relationship from development to execution. Without this one trait, then a leader will keep their team members in a constant state of growth without the accountability of action. The necessity of accountability and action is what many leaders think is missing from the millennial generation. This could not be farther from the truth. This generation is craving actionable direction and consistent accountability. The apathetic leader discussed earlier is the one who wishes for action but does not set the standard of consistency necessary to foster it. This same leader has failed to connect their team to the organization's why, but instead, connects them to a metric goal that, when reached, leaves the team empty after the short-term elation. The activist leader creates connections through joining action and accountability to the why of the organization. That connection encourages innovation and change, which will ignite the passion of their team.

The recent Price Waterhouse Cooper *Millennials at Work Reshaping the Workplace* study pointed out that 56% of millennials would leave a company if the values were not what they expected. This generation is holding its leaders and organizations to higher standards than at any point in recent history. Companies need to ensure they are connecting their teams to the reason they do business or the organization's why. This concept is usually overlooked in most businesses. There is a well-written mission and vision statement, accompanied by a set of corporate values, but then they generally end up being a poster somewhere people frequently walk by. Those statements look good to investors and potential employees, but organizations fail to connect their team to the spirit of those statements. Most people who discuss the topic of the why of an organization agree that most team members know the what or the how of the organization but rarely the why. For example, an employee at company ABC is asked what ABC does. The employee quickly says, "We make widgets."

That employee is a perfect example of a team member who would leave to go to a competing widget-maker for a raise or promotion. He makes widgets, so the company making them is not as important as the production of widgets.

If another employee is asked the same question, and they say ABC serves the communities we operate in through the production of widgets, then you can almost guarantee this employee would stay, regardless of the nominal wage increase or title change. This employee gets why the company is there. The values of this company are instilled in the team, and anyone who joins the team will be made to feel the same connection. This will insight the 56% of millennials to stay with the organization they believe are helping their community, not only making widgets. The activist leader will strive to connect their teams to the heart of the company, not just the output.

Earlier in this book, I mentioned a cultural initiative I launched based on the *Energy Bus* by Jon Gordon. That initiative galvanized the team and put the why back in our organization. We were no longer cleaning rooms and checking people in. We were creating vacation experiences. We were enhancing the respite people seek when they travel on vacation. We were not only performing a function; we were adding value to people and creating memories. One other area that was enhanced through the initiative was the spirit our teams' had to serve. Our property had never really been active in the community, and we had never really raised any substantial funds for our corporate charity Children's Miracle Network Hospitals.

That year, our team connected to the why of our organization. Guest satisfaction increased, and employee engagement spiked, and our turnover plummeted. More importantly, a fire was lit to activate on the charitable connection our company had created with Children's Miracle Network Hospitals. As a team, we came up with and executed several initiatives that took our giving from non-existent to substantial. In just eight months, we raised more money for the charity than in the total combined history of the resort. Groups of employees became connected and launched initiatives to create consistent opportunities for guests to give. I was able to connect my love of running with my job by completing a 51-mile run for charity. The momentum of that connection has only gotten stronger over the years. Activists immediately indoctrinate leaders who come on board at all levels, so they understand our jobs are more than the physical tasks that need to be accomplished daily.

When a team is connected to the why of the organization, then they become excited about innovation and change. They know change offers the potential for growth, and innovation expands the influence of the team. The activist leader will personalize the challenge each team members will accept to improve the overall group. The autonomy and empowerment we created in part one will breed an environment that enables leaders to drive results. A leader's consistent application of the best practices that create growth will prevent the development of the system of limiting self-beliefs that cause employees to want to start looking to leave.

In part one, we learned that more than 60% of millennials believe management's attitude and corporate policies and procedures are barriers to innovation. Conversely, nearly 60% believe there is a process of innovation that produces results if followed consistently. The sense of stability that consistency brings is what allows team members to launch their potential. When teams are not operating from a solid platform, they tend to move in many different directions. A lack of consistency is most often seen when it comes to the enforcement of coaching and counseling or what is also known as disciplinary action. In my experience, managers will document a team member when something egregious has happened, if they cost the company money, or if they have done something to impact the manager personally. Very rarely do I find leaders who are comfortable disciplining their top talent to ensure consistency is preserved in the department. Providing a consistent platform for the team to operate from creates an environment where the differentiating factors of growth and development are the drive, determination, and activation of the individual. The activist leader understands the importance of the consistency required to create change, foster innovation, and deliver it to the team.

The root of the activist is action. Regardless of generation, management has too great a tendency to associate activity with action. Frequently managers love employees who always seem to be on the go. Those employees who always seem to be doing something. Those employees are the basis for the system of beliefs that has equated hours worked with productive output. Hours worked has very little to do with productive output. There are dozens of studies that show the diminishing productivity of a person as the time they work exceeds a certain threshold. Working 16 hours a day is impressive, but you probably stopped becoming effecting after about eight or nine hours. In his book, *Your Brain at Work*, David Rock points out that our brains are not wired to concentrate intensely for eight hours straight. The diminishing return that prolonged hours produce hurts the business versus help it. The activist leader encourages activity but infuses it with a measure of accountability that prevents a reward system based on hours worked. If the organization's why is properly aligned, then the outdated leadership paradigm that rewards long nights at the office and working through days off will not be present. The value placed on the now infamous work-life balance paradigm would become a natural byproduct of the system that the leadership team has promoted.

When all four leadership traits are present and operating within a team, an organization will be in a position to capitalize on the more than 50% of millennials who feel their company encourages them to suggest ideas. I love it when someone comes to me with an idea. What happens next allows me to see how serious they are about pursuing their ideas and how much they are willing to achieve their vision of success. The vast majority of employees who suggest ideas will put the idea on the table and wait for me to tell them how to do it. I never do. A much smaller percentage will put the idea out there and work through a rudimentary plan to activate it. The smallest group that presents the idea, a solution to activate the idea, looks for feedback on their idea, and then takes actionable steps towards implementation.

As we discussed in part one, 66% of millennials want to be entrepreneurs. That means 66% value innovation enough to understand an idea can ignite into a job when it connects to a passion. This generation has the inventors' spirit and has seen countless examples of their peers taking a new idea or modifying an existing idea into a full-time business that allows them to be their boss and set their system of beliefs. They have told us their innovative spirit hits a roadblock when they get to the corporate world because the existing businesses are not built to guide their passion in a manner that produces tangible results. Most employees end up in the first group I mentioned. They have great ideas but are not willing to do the work to achieve them or simply want someone else to do the leg work. That group has the vision but needs the activist leader to guide them to a place where they can make their vision a system of actionable steps to achieve their goal. The group with the drive, vision, and focus needed to act on innovation needs the activist leader to keep the parameters of their belief system stable and provide support. This way, they can work on growth and change instead of having to work through the roadblocks and setbacks that instability provides.

If you are an employer reading this, look for the activist trait in your leadership team and employees. This trait will be the one that takes all of the good ideas and intentions and grows them into tangible results and production to not only move the business in the right direction but also create engagement and loyalty within the team. You can create this trait within your team members by helping them learn to create solid ground, listen to their teams, and encourage measured growth. The tangible activation and growth of the team members will become contagious, and at the same time, will encourage your team to connect. The greatest impact you can make as an employer is to bring your mission, vision, and values to life within your organization. The greater the connection you can create, the higher the chance you will be able to create an environment that retains your team members and attracts others to it.

If you are a millennial reading this, do not only talk about your company's mission but also engage in it. If your leader has not done a great job of bringing the why of your company to life, seek out those in the organization who have figured it out, and connect with them. You should look for opportunities within your business to suggest innovative or growth ideas. When you suggest those ideas, treat them as if they were the basis for starting your business. Use the entrepreneurial spirit your generation knows to not only present the idea but also discuss your activation ideas and timelines with your leaders. Make it easy for them to support you, and they will reward you in turn with the autonomy and empowerment you are seeking to make an impact.

CHAPTER 22
PUTTING IT TOGETHER

I am not a product of my circumstances.
I am a product of my decisions.

—Stephen Covey

The success of an organization can be traced back to many things, but few are more powerful than the teams who support it. If you build the right environment and fill it with engaged leaders, your organization will launch from solid ground. Creating a P.A.C.T with your teams will ignite passions on both sides, and will ensure they are there long enough to make an impact. Leaders that evolve and hone the four traits will influence their teams to succeed.

The best part about this system is the traits and skills necessary can be learned. The same dedication and focus that keeps you working out, or got you through school, or even got you through that seven-season binge-watch of Game of Thrones will be enough to get you started down the path of becoming a millennial leader. The first step is to start learning. By finding time in your day to read, listen to podcasts, or activate another methodology, you are taking the hardest step. Once you start to add to your toolbox, you will be compelled to share. Those teaching moments will add value to those around you. That value builds trust and engagement. If you continue to learn and grow, then people want to be coached and mentored by you. Coaching and mentoring are the future of leadership, and the higher your comfort level in that realm, the greater your chances are of making an impact and create in systems of success. The team you educate and guide will trust you with their career. As a leader, you will be able to advocate for their growth to help them get to where they want to go, not necessarily where you want them to go. Finally, your ability to connect your team to the why of their organization will ignite their passion and insight innovation. You will learn how to consistently hold your team accountable to provide them a platform to launch their success from.

Most of us are not CEOs. Most of us are at some middling point in an organization, and we are looking for a way to connect and make an impact. The traditional definition of leadership is evolving. You have read this book to this point, so you understand the workforce and workplace are changing. As a result, we all must change with it if we plan on achieving our definition of success. Leadership is evolving from unidirectional definition where typically control is pushed from the top down to an omnidirectional system where influence comes from all levels.

The environment we create is a function of our organization's values, combined with the talent we hire, and the empowerment our teams exercise to create engagement. The byproduct of that environment is the output of our business. Bill Marriott famously said that if you take care of your associates, they will take care of your business. This is a straight forward and simplified version of what has been discussed in this book. Employees will choose to work for you because you offer them opportunities for personal growth and development. They will stay with you because you connect them to your organization's heart and provide them with outstanding leaders who are capable of shepherding their growth. Creating an environment personalized to them and providing them the autonomy they need to succeed will only strengthen their commitment to your organization. Taking the time to be a teacher and a mentor will open communication lines so that you are always engaged in their success.

If you are a leader at any level, start the process today. Take the time to honestly assess your leadership style and the environment that you have created. Understand that evolution is a part of the natural cycle of life, so you have not necessarily done anything wrong. You have a chance to foster the growth and change that will ensure the success of your business unit or organization long into the future. Do not be afraid to be honest with your boss and your team about your intentions. You can easily start by being a student and offering opportunities to teach. From there, it is a matter of your commitment to the process of developing the traits that will be required to acquire and retain talent in the coming years.

CONCLUSION

I hope you have found value in this book. I have been on both sides of the generational question most of my career and truly feel that the answer to the "Millennial Question" really lies in our ability to connect our commonalities and explore the new teaching paradigm. I am well aware you have probably read some of this information before, and the leadership principles contained in this book are not groundbreaking. I have read hundreds of books and articles on leadership, and most of them boil down to the same advice. That means everyone has had access to the same teachings and information for a very long time.

The major difference in all of these books is that someone presents the information in a way that resonates with you, and it inspires you to action. Dale Carnegie, John Maxwell, Stephen Covey, Simon Sinek all give you the same principles. My goal with this book is to provide you with another point of view to hopefully connect you to the information and inspire you to action. It may sound insanely simple, but you have to do something to get things done. If this book gave you a call to action to take the first step, then it will have been successful.

This new generation is extremely educated, motivated, and innovative. The progressive leader will see past the stereotypes that have been laid out there that generalize the behavior of a fraction of the generation and will activate their actual potential. Shifts will have to be made in the way organizations are run to ensure their teams are making the connection to their mission. Once employees know why they are working where they are and why their organization exists, then the buy-in will open the door for future success. Engaged employees, especially millennials, will attract future employees and will help to guide you in the best ways to retain them. Creative promotional structures, training, and personal growth opportunities, personalized employment experiences, and the groups' support will help ensure that your organization is an employer of choice and a place to stay in the future.

The workplace is changing quicker than our policies and procedures can adapt. Building foundational leadership traits will help insulate your team and your organization from the rapid fluctuations that occur with growth and change. Creating leaders who focus on learning and teaching will ensure your business keeps up, and inspiring them with a passion for adding value to others will keep your team connected.

If you are a leader at any level or are aspiring to be one, then start today. Do not worry about the person you were; take steps to become the leader you and your team want you to be. You will never have all of the right answers, and the timing will never be perfect, but by taking the first step, you are light years ahead of most people who are afraid to try. Remember, you are only as good as your team, and your influence with them should be what you do for them, not what you can do to them. Generations in the workplace come together through a synergy of respect and evolution. Create an environment that fosters growth and stimulates excellence, and you will always find success.

NOTES

BOOKS

1. Jon Gordon, (2007) The Energy Bus, John Wiley & Sons Inc., Hoboken, New Jersey

2. John Maxwell, (1998) 21 Irrefutable Laws of Leadership, Thomas Nelson Inc., Nashville, Tennessee.

3. John Maxwell; (2010) Everyone Communicates Few Connect, Thomas Nelson Inc., Nashville, Tennessee.

4. Cathleen Benko, Molly Anderson, (2010) The Corporate Lattice: Achieving high performance in the changing world of work, Deloitte Development LLC, Unites States of America.

5. Simon Sinek; (2009) Start With Why: How great leaders inspire everyone to action, Penguin Publishing, New York, New York.

ARTICLES

6. Andrew Dugan, Bailey Nelson, "3 Trends That Will Disrupt Your Workforce Forever", *Gallup*, June 8, 2017, https://www.gallup.com/workplace/235814/trends-disrupt-workplace-forever.aspx

7. Jim Harter, Annamarie Mann, "The Right Culture: Not Just About Employee Satisfaction", *Gallup*, https://www.gallup.com/workplace/231602/right-culture-not-employee-satisfaction.aspx

8. Holmes, Ryan, (Oct, 2016) Move over Millennials: 5 Things you need to know about generation C, https://www.inc.com/ryan-holmes/move-over-millennials-5-things-you-need-to-know-about-generation-c.html

9. Jim Clifton, "Are You Sure You Have a Great Workplace Culture?", *Gallup*, https://www.gallup.com/workplace/236285/sure-great-workplace-culture.aspx

10. Brandon Rigoni, Jim Asplund, "Strengths-Based Employee Development: The Business Results", *Gallup*, https://www.gallup.com/workplace/236297/strengths-based-employee-development-business-results.aspx

11. Jamie Francis, Zac Auter, "3 Ways to Realign Higher Education With Today's Workforce", *Gallup*, https://www.gallup.com/education/231740/ways-realign-higher-education-today-workforce.aspx

12. Ben Wigert, Annamarie Mann, "How Managers Can Excel by Really Coaching Their Employees", *Gallup*, https://www.gallup.com/workplace/236237/managers-excel-really-coaching-employees.aspx

SURVEYS

13. "Workforce of the Future", *PWC*, https://www.pwc.com/gx/en/issues/talent/future-of-work/download.html

14. "Millennials", *PEW Research Center*, http://www.pewresearch.org/topics/millennials/

15. "The Deloitte Millennial Survey 2017", *Deloitte*, https://www2.deloitte.com/us/en/pages/about-deloitte/articles/millennial-survey.html

16. "Millennials at Work Reshaping the Workplace", *PWC*, https://www.pwc.de/de/prozessoptimierung/assets/millennials-at-work-2011.pdf

17. "State of the American Workplace", *Gallup*, https://www.gallup.com/workplace/238085/state-american-workplace-report-2017.aspx

INTERVIEWS

18. Seth Godin, International Maxwell Conference, (March 20, 2017)

19. Simon Sinek, Millennials in the Workplace; (Inside Quest, October 2016): https://www.youtube.com/watch?v=hER0Qp6QJNU

PROGRAMS

20. "Seth Godin's altMBA", *Seth Godin*, https://altmba.com/

21. "Gallup Clifton Strengths", *Gallup*, https://www.gallup.com/cliftonstrengths/en/252137/home.aspx?utm_source=bing&utm_medium=cpc&utm_campaign=new_strengths_ecommerce_brand_search_us&utm_keyword=strengthsfinder&utm_source=bing&utm_medium=cpc&utm_campaign=New_Strengths_ECommerce_Brand_Search_US&utm_

content=strengthsfinder&msclkid=5eb10f5a8b3f
1d6cc44551b0a63b983b

22. "Meyer's-Briggs Type Indicator Assessment", *MBTI,*
https://www.mbtionline.com/

23. "Everything DISC". *Wiley Brand,* https://www.
everythingdisc.com/Home.aspx

ABOUT THE AUTHOR

For more than 20 years, Chris has been a leader or executive in the hospitality industry, learning from industry giants like Marriott, Hard Rock Hotels and Casinos, and Ritz-Carlton. Being inspired by the spirit to serve took him well past learning world-class service for guests. It showed him that world-class service has to extend to your team. He understood what it took to reach unique personalities and inspire them to greatness. He believed you do not become a leader until you learned to add value to others.

As a speaker, trainer, and executive coach, he has had the privilege of enhancing the transition experience into the workplace of many new and future leaders. Continuing to lead has provided him with a unique platform to experience what he writes about and continues to add value to others through his efforts.

Chris is also a husband and a father to two wonderful children. When he is not serving his family, he is probably running. As an avid runner, triathlete, and ultra-marathoner, he has had the pleasure of experiencing some amazing things like completing an Ironman Triathlon and running the Grand Canyon. He tries not to waste one minute of his life, and hopes to create an environment where no one else feels they are wasting a minute of theirs either.

Learn more about CHRIS CANO at ChasingHappyat Work.com